JUNKYARD SPACESHIP

JAMIE MCFARLANE

FICKLE DRAGON PUBLISHING LLC

PREFACE

FREE DOWNLOAD

Sign up for my newsletter and receive a free Jamie McFarlane starter library.

To get started, please visit:

http://www.fickledragon.com

ONE
BROTHER'S ARMS

Albert Jenkins shielded his eyes from the sun's glare and followed the smoking contrail of a failing alien vessel as it sailed across the cobalt blue of the Tucson afternoon sky. Dual explosive reports from twin F-16s hot on the ship's trail rattled the windows of his newly constructed home.

"Is that an enemy?" Diego, AJ's thirteen-year-old neighbor, asked innocently. "Is it attacking us?"

Beverly, AJ's symbiotic four-hundred-nanometer-long alien passenger and a Beltigersk, chose that moment to appear. Her current form was that of a woman from the late nineteen twenties with light brown hair of whimsical length and cut. A big fan of pop culture and history, she'd made a game of choosing a historical character to see if AJ would correctly guess who she was. Her efforts often fell flat, but she was tireless in the endeavor.

"Ratty old cotton flight suit with a leather flight jacket? Heck, you even got the hair right," he said, giving her a onceover. "Amelia Earhart. You're gonna need to up your game."

"That is a Vred shuttle, Diego." Beverly answered the boy's question while grinning at his acknowledgment. "The shuttle is in distress and has not answered repeated communication attempts."

"Looks like Air National Guard is on the job," AJ said. "Hope it's not someone we know."

Doctor Amanda Jayne slapped the back of her hand against his chest. "Don't be dumb, AJ. What are the odds of a Vred shuttle flying over Tucson in plain sight?"

"Shit, the Guard's firing." He watched a single missile detach from one of the pursuing F-16s. The sound of explosive detonation filled the air. Instinctively, he pulled her to the ground, placing his own body between her body and the far-off explosion.

"Why would they fire?" she asked, her voice muffled as she clung to AJ's shirt. "And why are we ducking? They've got to be a couple miles out."

He pulled her back to her feet. "Diego, we've got to move." Shuttling both toward the machine shop some thirty yards away, he turned to whistle loudly. "Greybeard, come!"

The three ran through the open door of the metal-clad shed, then he led them through the back door into the junkyard to a pile of old refrigerators. In the midst of the junk, a steel door was set into a column of cement.

"AJ, you're scaring me," Jayne said, as she hurried through the door and down the darkened stairs.

"That Vred ship was circling back to us. We're in the line of fire. Greybeard, get over here, you mangy mutt!"

The last comment sparked an irritated bark from the grey bulldog who'd successfully bonded with another of the symbiotic nano-meter-size aliens. When communicating with Greybeard, it was often difficult to tell where the alien stopped and the dog began. AJ, however, was just grateful that the pair responded to his call.

"Incoming!" he shouted, ducking on the third stair while holding the door open. Automatic gunfire tore through the cement structure, opening the stairwell to daylight just as Greybeard cleared the threshold and bounded down the stairs.

"We need to move, soldier!" Beverly urged, appearing in front of him now wearing dark green helmet and jungle fatigues common to the Vietnam War. The sights and sounds brought back memories of AJ's days in 'Nam. He responded instinctively, diving down the stairwell, not stopping even when the pain of ramming into the cement wall blurred his vision. Clawing over rubble, he propelled himself further into the darkness, finally clearing the heavy metal threshold of the bunker his grandfather built after WWII.

"AJ, are you okay?" Jayne slid onto her knees next to him and started running her cold hands beneath his shirt, searching for wounds.

A grin cracked his face. "Slow down there, Doc. We've got plenty of time for whatever you're thinking."

"You ass..." Her retort was cut off when an explosion tore off the roof of the stairwell, pelting them with cement fragments.

"Door!" AJ lunged for the heavy steel door and swung it closed just as a fireball illuminated the stairwell. For good measure, he rotated the ring on the back of the door, sinking steel bars into the frame to seal them in.

"What in the hell is going on out there?" she asked.

"That Vred shuttle was circling back. It was coming right for us. I figured those Guard F-16s were playing for keeps."

"The Guard can fire into a civilian population?"

"If they think the threat's high enough."

His voice was drowned out by a second, much larger explosion that shook the bunker even though it was buried ten feet beneath ground level.

"My God," Jayne gasped. "That must have been a rocket."

"That wasn't a rocket. Something crashed – and close. Come on, we can't get out this way. We'll have to go out the back."

"Where is *back*?" Diego asked, surprisingly unperturbed by the events.

AJ gestured for them to follow. "Hope neither of you is claustrophobic."

The bunker wasn't huge. He led everyone into what was currently a pantry and handed over boxes of food and other essential supplies, indicating where they should be restacked. Once the shelving unit was clear, he grabbed a prybar hidden on top and knocked down two of the shelves before prying out a panel at the back.

"Why would your grandfather cover a maintenance hatch?" Beverly asked, flipping on the bright round light in the front of an old mining helmet she now wore. Soot covered her from head to toe.

"He didn't. I did. Not much use for it and we needed the room," AJ said, working to turn the steel ring holding the small hatch closed. "Darn thing is frozen. Diego, fetch that jug of corn oil in the kitchen, would you? I don't think I have anything better down here."

"Yes, Mr. AJ," Diego agreed and ran off.

"That kid trusts you entirely too much," Jayne said. "You're nothing but a lure for danger."

"Diego and I are simpatico," he said. "We know another survivor when we see one. He's got my back and I've got his, just like in 'Nam."

"Ohhh, I see," she said, sounding a little irritated.

"Don't worry, darling, you and me are just like that except I like you having my back a whole lot more."

She slapped AJ, the sound reverberating in the small space. "Oh, I didn't mean to hit you so hard," she said, almost sounding sincere.

AJ rubbed his cheek and considered the aged surgeon. Like him, aliens had reversed her aging process until she appeared as healthy and fit as she'd been in her late twenties. It was hard to reconcile that they'd both served in 'Nam together and met at a field hospital where she saved his life. Running into each other years later after AJ's near-fatal accident, they'd had little choice but to join the fight to save the world from the Korgul menace. AJ liked to think they had formed a deep bond, even though neither had sought to put words to their relationship.

"Here is the oil, Mr. AJ," Diego said, holding the bottle out and smiling broadly at Jayne.

"Ask me, I must have struck a nerve to get you all riled up like that."

"I'm not riled," she retorted.

AJ smiled to himself and poured canola oil onto the frozen gears of the hatch. "Just keep telling yourself that," he muttered under his breath.

"I can hear you just fine, Albert Jenkins."

He set the pry bar between the rungs of the wheel and pulled. At first, he was unsuccessful. After a couple of tries the wheel grudgingly gave way.

"BB, you have any idea what's going on topside?" AJ asked, using his preferred nickname for Beverly.

"All of my connections are severed," she said. "Something caused significant damage within the junkyard. I suspect, like you, there is a downed craft. That you do not smell jet fuel suggests the craft is likely the Vred shuttle."

AJ shrugged as he looked over to Jayne. "You really need to get one of these riders back onboard," he said, pointing at Beverly. Jayne and her first alien guest's personalities had conflicted to the point that she'd risked her life to separate from it. Thomas, her second rider, worked out much better but he'd sacrificed himself to test the cure for Korgul invasion.

"Two Beltigersk symbiotes in one life seems like a nice number," she said. "Although, I dearly miss Thomas's keen intellect and gentlemanly ways."

AJ grinned at Beverly. "I believe that slight was aimed at me. Thing is girls all *say* they want a gentleman. It's a story they tell themselves."

"You're incorrigible," Jayne said. "I don't know what I see in you."

He grinned and worked the door open to the pitch black of a rusted steel pipe not much wider than a man's shoulders. "Ladies first?"

"Do we really not have a flashlight?" Jayne asked, irritated.

He handed her a D-cell battery light and flicked it on. The beam disappeared down the tight steel tunnel, not illuminating an end. She looked back at AJ, her lower lip quivering. As soon as she recognized the nervous action her jaw clamped shut.

"I remember crawling through a few tunnels like this back in the day," he said, taking the flashlight and crawling into the steeply upward-sloping pipe. "Not my best memory of the war."

Jayne crawled in behind him. "I remember some of the boys talking about the tunnels. It sounded horrific. Are you doing okay?"

"No mud, no Viet Cong. This is a walk in the park, Doc."

It took several minutes for the trio to work their way to the top of the shaft. The last several yards of the shaft widened where the tunnel went completely vertical, the only way forward a makeshift ladder of bent steel rebar. AJ paused when he reached the top of the shaft and placed the palm of his hand against the hatch.

"Cool to the touch. That's a good sign," he said, spinning the locking wheel. His first push at the hatch was unsuccessful. Pushing hard, his foot slipped and he barely missed kicking Jayne in the face.

"Careful," she said.

"Sorry, Doc. I'm having trouble moving this."

"Is it locked?"

"No. Hold the flashlight, would you?" He pulled the light from between his teeth and handed it down to her.

"AJ, I will give you a small burst of adrenaline," Beverly said. "It will increase your strength for a few moments. Be careful that you do not strain or tear your ligaments."

He grunted and his eyes widened as adrenaline hit his system. Everything seemed to go into slow motion and his mind cleared, even though his heart was racing. With a savage thrust, he pushed up into the hatch and threw it back, growling angrily as a tipped-over washing machine tumbled away.

"Quite impressive," Jayne said, chuckling. "Maybe I understand why we're together."

"I'm just a piece of meat to you, aren't I?" He reached into the hole after crawling out. With adrenaline still in his system, he lifted the lithe doctor out as if she weighed nothing and set her on the ground. When he turned back, Diego was already out.

"Not just a piece of meat," she said, grinning back at him.

He reveled for only a moment in her attention, then looked around. "Holy shit. I just finished it! How could this happen?"

Jayne followed his gaze to the burning rubble of his newly rebuilt home. Right there in the middle of the rubble was the wreckage of the Vred shuttle. The ship's fuselage looked intact, but both engines were missing. He traced a line of destruction and saw that one of the engines had plowed a furrow across the top of the bunker's entrance. The second engine had burrowed a similar track across the front of the machine shop. Both engines had missed his workshop, but the house was a complete loss.

"Oh, AJ! Your house," Jayne said. "I'm so sorry."

The sound of scraping metal drew their attention to the fuselage, still surrounded by the burning wreckage of his home. A hatch was thrown back and two human hands appeared, gripping the metal around the opening. Jayne and AJ watched in silence as a tall figure crawled out of the ship. It took a moment, but AJ realized their uninvited guest was his old friend, Army Ranger, and fellow Beltigersk host, Lefty Johnson.

"Shit, Lefty," AJ said, not sure what else to say. "Anyone hurt?"

"Sorry about the mess. Just a second." Lefty gestured to someone inside. A moment later, a reptilian humanoid followed Lefty out, purplish blood running down the side of the obviously female Vred's face. "Sharg is hurt and I think Queenie's pinned under something."

AJ looked for a safe route across that yard that would take him to the ship. "Hold on, Sharg, there's fire all around you. Diego, Jayne, get some water on this, I've got to get something."

He raced into the machine shed. This time, however, he slowed as he entered, plucked a backpack from the workbench and slung it over his shoulders. Clipping buckles into place, he sucked in a quick breath to steady himself.

"Fire is hot, AJ. The gasses rising could cause significant lung damage," Beverly warned as he fired up the rocket pack. The device didn't actually use rocket technology for propulsion but instead utilized a rare element called Fantastium known to only a few humans.

"You and Jayne will just need to patch me up then," he said. "If the ship rolls over with that hatch open, they could get roasted."

"I will do my best," Beverly said, "but if you pass into unconsciousness, I might not be able to save you."

"Aww, you ladies just can't help gushing over me today," he said, flitting over the burning structure. As promised, the heated gasses made him choke but he crossed over the flames before he was overcome.

"Sharg, you have cranial bleeding that must be attended to immediately," Beverly stated as AJ settled next to her.

"I am unwell," Sharg said in a cultured voice at odds with her decidedly reptilian features. The seven-foot-tall Vred swooned from loss of blood and fell heavily into AJ's arms.

"Can this pack hold us both?" AJ asked.

"It is beyond the functional capacity of the unit," Beverly said.

He struggled to get an arm beneath the heavy alien. "How much beyond?"

"It will not work, AJ."

The ship rocked beneath his feet, unstable atop the burning house. "Jayne, I need a path!" he shouted over the roaring flames. "Soak it down!"

"The structure is too unstable. You'll fall through," she called back while pointing the hose at the house beneath AJ. The spray was largely ineffective against the flames.

"Oh, this is gonna suck." He slid down the side of the ship onto a narrow section of fallen roof not yet burning.

"AJ, no!" Jayne called. "You'll be trapped." She doubled her efforts to soak the structure nearest his location but wasn't overly effective.

"BB, gonna need all the lift this baby can give us," He jumped onto a charred beam covered in glowing embers. "Jayne, my legs! Spray my legs!"

He ran across the beam and faltered as the structure shifted beneath him. The motors of the small rocket pack whined with urgency but failed to provide any lift. When he fell to one knee, an ember burned through his pants. He yowled in pain but managed to stand back up. A fresh wave of water struck his chest as Jayne managed to extend the stream.

"Mr. AJ, run!" Diego urged, unnecessarily.

The encouragement and his own dogged determination drove AJ forward even against the blistering pain in his feet. Cool water washed over him as he reached the new landscaping that had been planted only the day before. This time when AJ stumbled, he allowed Sharg to fall from his grasp.

"Help her," he ordered and lifted into the air. "BB, tell me I can at least carry a human."

"Yes," she said. "But, AJ, you have tissue damage to your feet. I am blocking a substantial amount of the pain. You must be careful. There is a high probability your body could simply shut down due to the shock."

"Never tell me the odds, BB," AJ said, gritting his teeth against pain that seemed almost too intense to survive. He couldn't imagine what he'd be feeling if Beverly wasn't blocking his pain receptors.

When he arrived back at the hatch, AJ was met by Lefty, holding the semiconscious McQueen. AJ lifted the lanky Ranger from Lefty's grasp. Like Sharg, Queenie was suffering from deep lacerations. Unlike Sharg, however, both Lefty and Queenie had Beltigersk symbiotes who would heal them given sufficient time and nutrition.

"Go," Lefty said.

"It is good to see you, sister." Lefty's Beltigersk rider, Rebel, appeared in her preferred outfit of Daisy Duke's and knotted jean shirt.

"What has happened?" Beverly had shifted her attire to formal black robes. AJ only saw her wearing that outfit when she was working through political issues.

"When our humans are safe," Rebel answered.

"Yes, of course."

AJ held Queenie tightly as he moved him over the moat of fire that had once been his house. Landing on the ground, pain erupted through AJ's entire body as his feet touched down.

"I'm sorry, AJ. There is so much damage, you should not go back. I am not certain you will make it," Beverly said.

"Bullshit," he said. "Lefty didn't leave me behind in 'Nam and I'm not leaving him."

This time when he crossed the ever-intensifying fire, his vision started to brown out. He put on a spurt of speed and crashed against the ship's hull, momentarily freed from the worst of the heat.

"I've got you, brother," Lefty said, pulling AJ to the hatch from where cool, clean air flowed freely. AJ struggled to grab onto his brother-in-arms and the very man who'd rescued him from captivity in the jungle so many years before. "Nah, son, this one's on old Lefty. You done your job. Just settle back."

He couldn't muster the energy to argue with the man who deftly unstrapped him from his rocket pack. It was through bleary eyes and dim consciousness that he realized Lefty was carrying him out of danger once again. He tried to say something but was incapable of even managing a grin.

AJ slipped in and out of consciousness as Lefty lifted him from the burning wreck and deposited him on the ground next to the unconscious alien Jayne was tending. Like all Vred, Sharg was humanoid but had smooth reptilian scales for skin, clawed hands, and a slightly protruding snout which boasted sharp, predatory teeth. Despite her terrifying visage, the Vred was a gentle giant and a pacifist.

"Doc, tell me my Shelia's going to be okay," Queenie implored. The six-foot-two-inch Aussie had fallen hard for Sharg, the alien woman who now lay on the ground a safe distance from the carnage.

"Don't worry about me," AJ groaned as consciousness became even more elusive. Sirens and the heavy, rhythmic thumping of helicopter blades competed with the sound of roaring flames. The war he'd fought so many years before was still a part of him and the memories came back full force to take over his pain-addled mind. "Aww, shit! Charlie's inbound! Take cover!" His exertion was soon followed by painful, wracking coughs.

"We've got you," a familiar female voice filtered through the fog as strong hands ripped his pant legs open. "That's our evac coming in. You're safe, soldier. Just let go. I've got you."

TWO

NO PATRIOT

Beeping machines and the overpowering smell of antiseptic greeted AJ as he struggled to regain consciousness. He tried to lift his arm to scratch his nose, but the tug of a shackle on his wrist and the clank of chain against metal set off warning bells.

"Ah, Mr. Jenkins, you're awake." While AJ didn't recognize the voice, he had no trouble recognizing its self-important bureaucratic tenor.

The events of the downed Vred ship flooded back as he struggled to recall how he'd ended up locked to a hospital bed. Without opening his eyes, he took stock of his physical condition, first wiggling his toes and fingers and then shifting his arms and legs.

"You're in a military hospital in Richmond, Virginia," Beverly quietly informed him. It sounded like she was sitting next to his ear, even though he knew she was attached somewhere along his optical nerve. "I've had to dismantle a significant portion of your musculature because they're only feeding you small amounts of glucose through the attached IV."

"Why am I chained to this bed? Am I a prisoner?" AJ knew his visitor would believe the questions were directed to him, but he was more interested in Beverly's take on the situation.

"It is for your own protection." The man's answer was practiced. "Your body was damaged in a fire. Tell me, do you recall the circumstances of this fire?"

AJ opened his eyes and took in the plain gray walls of the room. He wasn't in any normal hospital.

"His name is Gerald Loveit. Officially, he's a long-term staffer for the US State Department. Unofficially, he is a part of the newly formed Alien Affairs division of the CIA," Beverly said.

"It is speaking with you now?" Gerald asked. This got AJ's attention and he looked at the man seated in a chair at the end of his bed. Gerald was in his mid-fifties and was staring at a small electronic device that could pass for a phone.

"It?"

"The Beltigersk ambassador, 49231125-0-B," Gerald answered. "We know you currently harbor an illegal alien symbiote."

"You know this, do you?" AJ scoffed.

"Explain how fourth-degree burns on your feet and legs miraculously healed after only a few days."

"Who do you work for?"

"Not your concern."

"You didn't answer if I'm a prisoner."

"Why is there an alien spaceship in your junkyard, Mr. Jenkins?"

"Because Air National Guard shot it down over a highly populated area," AJ said angrily. "Nice job on that, by the way. You owe me a new house."

Loveit sighed. "Can I take it that you don't intend to cooperate?"

"Cooperate with what? You shoot something down on my house, injure me in the process and you want my cooperation? Maybe start with an apology," AJ said, struggling to sit up, but discovered the handcuffs prevented him from moving.

"You're a threat to national security," Loveit said. "You shouldn't be allowed to run around freely."

"Let's try this again. I'll take it slow, so you can keep up," AJ said. "Am. I. A. *Prisoner?*"

"For your own safety, you are not free to move about the facility."

"That's a fine distinction. Has Captain Jackie Baird been informed of my circumstances? Army researcher who sounds like she's into the same things you are, except she's not an asshole spook."

"I don't believe we've discussed my current employment. Are you confirming the presence of an illegal alien symbiote?"

"I was in 'Nam, kid," AJ said. "I can smell a spook a mile away. If I'm right, you've got no legal grounds to hold a US citizen."

"I've captured an alien, who happens to be surrounded by a US citizen, who I've placed in protective custody."

"Love the conversation: lies wrapped about misleading statements. You're a douchebag. Now, uncuff me. You have no right to hold me," AJ said, rattling the chain.

Loveit stood and gave AJ a smarmy smile. "It appears you are having difficulty. I'll request medical staff to visit and I'll return when you're in a better position to discuss matters rationally."

"Does Baird know I'm being held?"

Loveit turned his back and opened the door. "I don't know who you're talking about."

"Tell me that *after* you get her foot outta your ass," AJ called after him, chuckling.

"There is considerable electronic surveillance within this room," Beverly said, her voice still low. "For fear of discovery, I am keeping our communication at minimal levels. I sent a message to Captain Baird three hours ago. There has been no response. I will continue monitoring."

"Oh, dear! You are awake," an older woman wearing scrubs said as she entered the room before the door had a chance to close. AJ looked her over. She was in her early sixties and had a grandmotherly build. "Are you in pain, dear?" The woman hurried to the IV bottles connected to AJ's arm.

"That's morphine," Beverly said. "It's difficult to resist. Stop her."

"No pain," he said. "Slow that morphine down."

The woman removed her hands from the bottle and gave him a curious once-over. "You might still be in shock. You have considerable burns across your feet and lower legs. Trust me, you do not want to brave this out, young man."

"Army?" AJ asked.

This caught the woman's attention and she smiled as she answered, "Hooah!"

"Hooah," he answered. "Don't suppose you can release these cuffs?"

She gave her head a quick shake. "Sorry, soldier. Old Betty's job is to provide comfort and aid healing. I'll pass your request along to command, though. Are you sure you're not hurting? I saw your legs when I changed your bandages. You're in pain. No need to be a hero."

"Any chance for some grub?" he asked, ignoring her pushing.

Betty patted his shoulder as she worked her way back to the top of the bed, fiddling with the drip. A cold sensation rushed into AJ's arm and grogginess overwhelmed him.

"Too much," Beverly said as he lost consciousness.

Sometime later, his eyes slowly opened. As consciousness returned, he became aware of someone seated next to his bed. At first, he thought it was Captain Baird coming to his rescue.

"Baird?" AJ asked, groggily.

"She's not coming," Loveit answered, triumph in his voice. "You tipped your hand by contacting her."

"What do you want?" AJ asked. Loveit stood and walked around to the base of AJ's bed, lifting the sheets. "What kind of pervert are you?"

"Remarkable healing you've undergone, wouldn't you say?" Loveit asked, flicking open a pocketknife before grabbing AJ's ankle. AJ yanked his foot away, but with the help of the short shackles, Loveit easily recaptured his leg and held it tight. Pain lanced through his body as Loveit stripped the bandages, not caring if he gashed AJ's leg in the process. "I was told third- and fourth-degree burns, but your skin is fresh looking, like a baby's. Care to explain?"

"Guess you guys got it wrong."

"We have pictures, would you care to see them?"

"You're operating a black site in the US," AJ said. "I'm a US citizen. What you're doing is illegal as hell. You have no right to hold me."

"Patriot Act is a wonderful thing. The latitude I have with terroristic activities, threats to national security... the list goes on and on," Loveit said. "You can kiss the old rules goodbye. What I want is simple. I want that alien in your skull. I want to prosecute it for high crimes. I want to string you up for treason. I want that crocodile in custody and most of all I want to put you in a deep dark place."

"You're not exactly making your case," AJ said.

"I'm unable to verify that Sharg is free. It makes more sense that, just as you were captured, so were our friends," Beverly whispered. AJ smiled. It was the first time Beverly had referenced his group as *her friends*.

"You think this is funny?" Loveit asked, tipping the blade of his knife into the skin of AJ's calf.

"Shit, stop!" he growled through the pain.

"Ironic, don't you think? That alien will heal your leg and any torture I inflict will be like it never happened. I can do this all day and no one will be the wiser," Loveit stabbed the three-inch blade deep into the muscle.

AJ howled in agony. "You. Sick. Fuck."

"Good, we're finally on a first-name basis," Loveit said. "This room is air-gapped and that little message you tried to get out was intercepted. Nice try, though."

"Don't know what you're talking about."

"We've been feeding your little alien crap. It's all lies," he said. "My name is not Gerald Loveit and you're not in Richmond, Virginia. Whatever you think you know, you don't. The sooner you realize your only choice is to play ball with us, the better."

"Nice."

"Didn't catch that."

"You spooks always were good at counterintelligence. Make it seem like up is down and down is up," AJ said. "I don't believe a word you're saying."

"That works for me," Loveit said, walking up to where the IVs hung. With more force than necessary, he grabbed AJ's arm and yanked the tubes out. "Get comfortable. No more morphine naps for you. We'll see how long you last. Everyone breaks eventually, Mr. Jenkins. Maybe it'll be your doctor friend or maybe it'll be the hillbilly. Personally, I'm betting on the crocodile."

"You said you didn't have them."

"I did say that, didn't I? And now you get to wonder why I said something else. Have fun working that through."

"Fucking spook."

Loveit grinned as he turned for the door. "Bet your ass, Jenkins."

"He was able to verify that you were with Jayne, Lefty and Sharg by your statement," Beverly whispered. "He is a devious man."

"They probably had satellite imagery showing the crash," AJ attempted to sub-vocalize his answer and was only partially successful.

The door opened and a new, male nurse entered. "Time for cleanup, Mr. Jenkins," he said, too cheerfully for the suggested course of action.

"Who are you?" AJ asked.

The man quirked a smile. "You know better than that. Any name I'd give you would just be a lie. Let's keep it nice and impersonal."

"Just tell me one thing."

"Probably can't," the man answered.

"Army?"

"Civilian."

"Good," AJ said.

"Can you lift up? It smells like we've got a little boom boom to deal with."

AJ closed his eyes at the patronizing, overly cheerful tone. "Yeah, it was a real crap storm. Maybe put me in a room with a bathroom and you wouldn't need to play me like this."

"Didn't you hear? After you're cleaned up, we're moving you to new digs. Don't need all these electronics after all," the orderly said. "Now, I'm going to unlock your ankle. Don't get any ideas. Do you understand?"

"I hear you."

AJ watched as the man pulled a key that was on an extendable line from his belt. He unlatched his right ankle. "I need you to roll on your side so I can get at the good stuff."

"You should have done this when I was unconscious."

"If I have to clean shit off your backside, do you think I get to make the rules?"

"Sorry about this," AJ said, starting to roll over.

"I'd bet you don't make the rules either," the orderly said, gently pushing on AJ's leg to hold him in place.

AJ lifted his leg as if to be helpful. When the man started to work, he whipped his leg around, catching the man's neck with the back of his knee. The orderly gave a surprised squeak as his head became tightly wedged in AJ's crotch.

"Dammit," AJ grumbled, not unaware of the compromising position in which he'd placed himself.

"No," the orderly grunted as his neck was compressed by AJ's thighs. "They're watching."

"Cellphone, right jacket pocket. Just touch it, AJ," Beverly said, no longer whispering.

The door burst open and two men in business suits rushed the bed, extending telescoping batons. "Let him go, Jenkins," one of the two ordered.

The first thunk of the steel baton landed on AJ's stomach, driving the breath from his lungs and causing him to gag. Straining against the restraints, he attempted to reach the orderly's pocket. A second baton blow hit his outstretched arm and he heard the crunch of bone.

AJ instinctively pulled back but refused to release the captured orderly.

The suited men turned their attention to AJ's free leg, raining blows down on it. He lurched sideways and pushed his hand into the orderly's pocket, his fingers just brushing the case of a cellphone.

"What in the hell!" Loveit bellowed as he entered the room to join the fray. Unlike the suited guards, he attacked AJ's unguarded head, punching him violently and repeatedly in the face. The cartilage in his nose snapped as blood covered Loveit's fist and spewed down onto his chest.

He lost consciousness.

"Don't open your eyes," Beverly whispered. "It's been six hours and you've been moved to a new room. I think I sent a message to Captain Blair. I can't be sure."

"I know you're awake." The voice belonged to Loveit. "I want to thank you for giving me permission to beat your face in. I don't get a lot of freebies."

AJ shrugged as he opened his eyes. He was lying on a steel floor against a corrugated steel wall. The cell was eight feet in every direction and a plexiglass wall separated him from Loveit, seated in a folding chair. As consciousness returned, he realized the air in the cell was warm and humid.

"I'm an American citizen. You can't hold me," he insisted again, mostly because he was at a loss for what to say.

"If only that were true," Loveit said. "Nice job distracting the guards so you could send a message on that orderly's phone. You were right, too. Captain Blair has a real bitchy side to her. Fortunately, you've been *lost* in the system. Happens sometimes. We have six or seven months before she mounts enough pressure to see you released. That's more than enough time to get what we want."

"Which is?" AJ asked.

"The Beltigersk symbiote," he said. "Give her to me and we'll call it even. I'll even find money to rebuild that crap-hole you call home."

"Fuck off."

Loveit turned to the folding tray table next to him which held a plate of soggy beans and a large bottle of water.

"You're dying, Jenkins," he said. "Apparently, that healing gig 49231125-0-B does on you utilizes a lot of calories. I'll bet the six hundred calories on this plate won't even start to make up for what you've expended."

He slid part of the plexiglass panel aside after unlocking it, then pushed the plate into the cell so it landed upside down on the floor. Opening the water bottle, he tipped it upside down and allowed a third of it to drain onto the floor before tossing it in atop the plate.

AJ scrambled to catch the bottle and right it. "Asshole."

"You have no idea." Loveit walked to the only door visible outside the cell. AJ strained to see what was on the other side of the door but realized it was just more of the same corrugated steel. Just before Loveit stepped through, he half turned, a grin evident on his face. "But you'll find out soon enough."

Before AJ could answer, the door closed and he was alone.

"Drink the water, AJ. I'll do my best to filter it if it's drugged," Beverly whispered.

"Why do they want you? Blair knows you're on our side. You're a damn hero." He worked to subvocalize the conversation.

She appeared for the first time since he'd awoken in custody, now wearing a loose shirt and pants with wide black and white prison stripes. Attached firmly to her ankle was a chain and at the end of the chain was a heavy iron ball.

"It's not coincidental that Sharg's vessel was attacked," she answered.

"Aren't you worried they'll see you?"

"The electronic surveillance is minimal," Beverly said. "I am only able to detect a single camera on the other side of the plastic barrier."

AJ's stomach growled loudly. He drank a good portion of the water from the bottle and then, using his hand, scooped beans back onto the paper plate. Loveit was right. This was nowhere near enough food to fuel his body and he was left hungrier than before he'd eaten.

"Any idea how to get out of here?"

"Yes. Several, but you need more calories. You are weak, AJ. I'm not sure how best to help you," she said. "You've already lost considerable muscle mass. Your body is starting to consume your organs in its quest to remain functioning."

"That shouldn't happen so fast. How long have I been in custody?"

"AJ, it has been six months since your capture."

"I'm guessing we're not in Kansas anymore," he said, blowing out a breath.

"The available information suggests a tropical locale."

"Seems like bikini weather to me," AJ said. She switched her garb to that of a 1920's red-striped bathing suit complete with frills around the neck, sleeves and legs. He groaned, appreciating the humor. "What I wouldn't give for a shot of Scotch right now."

"We have work to do, AJ. Finish that water bottle."

"I need to conserve. We have no idea how long before the next meal comes."

Now she wore a purple, skin-tight leather body suit, complete with bat-eared leather helmet. "Not if we plan to get out of this silly cell."

"You know, flipping to the Bat Girl costume is manipulation," said he groused. "Like I'll do what you want if you show a little skin."

She turned her head and looked over her shoulder at him, smiling mischievously. "Do you really believe it doesn't work? There is no skin showing."

He chugged the remainder of the water bottle. "Okay, you've got my attention."

"Next, we'll need privacy. Scrape steel dust from the corner of the cell where it has rusted, combine it with the bean residue on the door and spread it on the paper plate."

He looked at her skeptically but followed her instructions.

"You'll need to spit a little, the beans have dried a bit too much," she said. "Now place the plate in front of the camera and move it until the paste dries sufficiently. We'll need to move quickly. I imagine they'll send in a team to remove the plate, but it will take time for them to organize."

AJ did as she said and then stepped back. "Now what?"

"I estimate we have four minutes for this next step and I apologize for the pain it is likely to cause. I would mute this pain, but we are short on resources. Your stomach will start to feel uncomfortable, but do not worry, this will be short lived."

He grabbed his stomach. "Holy cow, BB! I feel like I swallowed a porcupine." He gasped for air as the pain became more acute. His diaphragm contracted, causing him to hiccup, further intensifying the pain. After a couple of minutes, he burped and then gagged.

"I am sorry for this discomfort, AJ. It is the only option I can imagine. Fortunately, your pain is almost over."

Between gagging and unproductive retching, he said, "Just kill me already!"

"You will need to deposit the material into your water bottle," she said. "I have done what I can to protect your throat and mouth, but you will feel an intense burning sensation as you vomit. It is imperative that we capture this material."

"Garumph," was all he could manage as his stomach gurgled uncontrollably. A moment later, fire rolled up from his stomach and into his mouth. It felt as if he'd bitten into a burning ember. Struggling against his body's desire to remove the pain as quickly as possible he wrapped his lips around the bottle's opening and directed the flow inside, spilling some as he did. He yowled in pain, momentarily dropping the bottle as droplets hit his fingers.

"Pick it up! Quickly, AJ," Beverly said. "You're losing some. We can't do this again. You'll be too weak."

He fought through involuntary tears and scooped the bottle back up, surprised at how warm the sides had become. The liquid within boiled with intensity as his small meal disintegrated before his eyes.

Placing his lips on the bottle once again, he fully emptied the contents of his mouth into the bottle, overflowing it.

"On the wall!" Beverly ordered, outlining a rectangular pattern at the back of the cell.

AJ was only too happy to expel the material from his mouth and did a reasonable job of hitting his target.

"Oh, shit," he groaned, sinking to the floor, holding his stomach. Most of the pain was gone, but the strain of retching and an empty burning sensation made him feel worse than his most accomplished bender after his wife died.

A single man entered through the door Loveit had used. "Do not approach the wall," the man said, displaying a can well-marked *pepper spray*.

AJ waved helplessly at the man, barely able to even keep his head up. The man opened the sliding panel on the plexiglass wall and poked a thin, right-angled tube through. The tube was connected to a small pressure tank and a spray of water ejected from the end, quickly peeling off the paper plate.

"Don't do that again," the man said after extracting the tube.

"Or what?"

"Or you won't like it."

"Creative," AJ said, sarcastically.

"No." The man disappeared back through the door in which he'd come.

"Get the plate, AJ," Beverly instructed.

"Why?"

"We're breaking out."

THREE
WHACKIN' PATTIES

"This stuff is disgusting," AJ said, pouring a line of what had once been his stomach contents onto the metal wall at the back of his prison. When the liquid met metal, it hissed, and wafts of vapors rose along the wall.

"Use the plate to keep the liquid in position," Beverly instructed, hovering next to the wall where she projected a surprisingly jagged line.

He complied, struggling to balance holding the quickly disintegrating paper and his desire to be done with the task.

"I can't believe this is going to do anything to this wall. It's steel," he said.

"Steel in a corrosive environment," Beverly said. "I've detected significant rust along the line I've drawn. I believe you'll be able to make an opening, just like you did on Beltigersk."

He nodded. "So, you'll admit you learned something from me?"

"I've learned a lot while working with you, Albert Jenkins," Beverly said. "Some of it has even been useful."

He grunted appreciation at her sharp wit. "So, just stomach acid will break us out? How long is this going to take?"

"No. The acid is considerably more concentrated. I utilized your body's resources to protect your esophagus and mouth. Even so, you'll require further healing," she replied. "It is early evening. I propose we wait until early morning before we test the results. There will be less staff to deal with if we're successful. At worst case, we can generate more acid."

"That's a disgusting thought."

"Noted. Perhaps you should rest."

"Sure." He closed his eyes and fell asleep almost immediately.

AJ'S EYES opened to the same well-lit cell he'd fallen asleep in. It was one of the common interrogation techniques designed to keep a prisoner confused about the passage of time and isolated from social norms so they could be broken down.

"What time is it?" he whispered.

"Two a.m.," Beverly answered. She was wearing her standard blue jeans with a loose white short-sleeved blouse.

AJ glanced at the dark line caused by the powerful acid Beverly had generated. "How'd we do?"

"We were lucky. There is significant corrosion in this wall. We will need maximal pressure at this point." Beverly highlighted a point within the roughly oval burned area in the wall. "You must hurry, I hear footsteps approaching."

The ambient sounds increased in volume and he suddenly heard several pairs of running feet growing louder. "Shit."

AJ lay on his back and lined up his heels with the steel panel. Pulling knees to his chest he kicked violently. Pain shot through his heels upon impact but the steel didn't move. He pulled his legs back and struck again with the same result.

"It's not working."

The sound of the lock turning in the entry door caught his attention.

"Again, AJ!" Beverly said.

His heart raced wildly, perspiration formed on his brow, and a sour taste filled his mouth.

"Stop or I'll shoot!" A man's shout came through the plexiglass drowning out the other sounds of frantic rustling. AJ didn't look, but imagined a group of guards were working to open his cell door.

With strength driven by adrenaline and fear, AJ jammed both heels into the steel wall. The section weakened but he howled in agony at the increased damage to his feet.

Gunfire pelted the steel wall overhead as he reared back and bashed the wall again. The panel flung outward and tumbled from view.

"AJ, they're almost on us," Beverly urged.

Grabbing the almost empty bottle of acid, he swung it around behind him and squeezed, sending remaining droplets airborne. He was rewarded by screams which told him two things: the guards were close and he'd scored a hit.

Twisting onto his stomach, he pushed off the floor and directed his throbbing feet through the hole. He felt some confusion when they didn't land on the floor on the opposite side, but he pushed again.

A strong hand wrapped around his wrist, momentarily arresting his progress. AJ spread his legs out to brace his thighs against the steel opening, reared up and yanked his arm to his chest. The guard was pulled forward, off balance. Using every muscle he had left, he slammed his forehead into the guard's face. The resulting yowl and pushback, along with the immediate release of his arm were as surprising as the sudden reversal of his momentum.

Suddenly he was through the wall and blindly falling. "Shit!" He tried to gain perspective, but his surroundings were pitch black and disorienting. A gust of wind filled with a salty spray pushed at him.

"AJ, this is going to hurt. You need to reach out with your right arm and grab on," Beverly said.

He swallowed hard and focused on the only object visible to him, thanks to Beverly—a green highlighted, horizontal rope strung between two posts. Falling past, he grasped the rope and realized it was a steel cable which bit into the palm of his hand. If not for the additional strength from Beverly's adrenaline rush, he couldn't have held on for more than a moment. As it was, he held on for two counts, just enough to redirect his path back into the side of the steel building.

"Crap, BB." He grunted, lost his grip, and started to fall again.

"Don't let go!" she ordered. Somehow he managed to bring his other hand around to grasp the cable. "You're going to need to pull yourself up."

"No damn way."

"Jayne, Lefty, Sharg have all been captured," Beverly said. "They need your help. You can't give up!"

"I hate you," he complained, somehow pulling himself up enough to slide under the cable and lay flat against the hard ledge. The feel of wet steel under his back and the sounds of lapping waves drew his attention. "Are we on a ship?"

"We're on a container ship that appears to be headed to China," she said. Their conversation was interrupted by a loud *whoop whoop* and then a blaring siren. Bright spotlights illuminated the night, although ineffectively for what AJ could now see was a massive container ship. "We need to find cover."

He turned to the tall stack of containers towering over him. A small pinpoint of light showed the position of the cell he'd fallen out of. From where he lay, it seemed an impossible distance to travel and still survive. His present location was a catwalk, barely wide enough to hold him. As he swiveled his head, the only shelter seemed to be through a narrow seam between the stacks of containers. Apparently, someone else didn't think his landing spot was worth checking out because even when a floodlight passed over the orange fabric on his leg, the operator didn't stop.

An idea struck him and he tugged at the prison jumpsuit he wore, pulling it off and wadding it into a ball.

"What are you doing?" Beverly asked.

"See those spots? They're searching the water," he said, tossing the ball of cloth over the side. "Maybe they'll see that."

"They've stopped the engines."

"How do you know?"

"You can't feel the vibration?"

"Clearly I can, since you can, but no, it didn't register."

"Your body isn't in very good shape."

AJ shivered when a blast of salt spray carried by a stiff ocean breeze pelted his naked body. With equal intent to hide from the elements and his captors, he slid between the massive stacks of containers. It wasn't lost on him that any shift in their position would crush him, but the warmth of the metal and lack of breeze was initially welcome.

"I'd be dead if not for you, BB."

"Not like my prospects were looking too good if you fell overboard this far out in the Pacific," she replied.

"So, what's your take. Is this a black site ship? Seems like a lot of containers."

"Clever disguise," Beverly said. "Transiting prisoners with cargo would be quite difficult to track. Especially with a governmental agency involved."

"Do you really think they have Jayne, Sharg, Queening and Lefty?"

"It is difficult to know."

"Can't you connect to their systems?" he asked, though he knew the answer.

"I understand and share your frustration, AJ."

He nodded. "That was smart thinking about the acid. Did you know we were on a ship the whole time?"

"I suspected. There was movement I could not account for. The mass of the vessel causes it to be very stable."

"Do you have any communications?"

"Not currently."

"That's our first priority. We need to get you hooked up so we can see what we're up against."

"We should lie low. They are searching for you. It would be best for them to believe you are dead before we continue."

"Well, shit." AJ sagged against the metal box. "I can't tell if we're better off now or not."

"Out of the frying pan and into the fire?"

"Something like that. I need food and water."

"It will rain within the next hour," she said. "I would expect your captors to slow their search once it begins. We should plan so you can gather as much rainwater as possible."

"How? I'm naked."

As if to prove her wrong, the rain started in earnest at that moment and was accompanied by a heavy gust of wind.

"I suppose perhaps you could tip your head back and move to the end of this aisle. There is some possibility you will be discovered, but the reward of hydration seems worth the risk of discovery."

"That bad, huh?"

"I'm holding you together with bailing wire, AJ," Beverly tugged at a straw farmer's hat that appeared on her head. Pigtails sprouted beneath the hat and her clothing changed to overall shorts, complete with a red-check shirt beneath.

He tipped his head back. "Funny." The first taste of water was filled with salt and he spat it onto the ground.

"You're getting runoff from the containers. They've been sprayed with salt water. Keep trying."

AJ tried again, but the second mouthful was no better. He leaned against the metal container and waited as the storm intensified. Finally, as the storm seemed to reach its peak and water flowed off every surface, he ducked his head out again and was rewarded with less brackish water.

"That okay?" AJ asked, swallowing it greedily.

"Yes. Very good," she said. "More."

Over the next thirty minutes the storm did nothing but move

from bad to worse. The good news, however, was that AJ got his fill of water and immediately felt better for it.

"Looks like they've given up the search," he said, feeling a familiar rumble beneath his feet. "I feel the engines starting up."

He slid back through the containers and exited back onto the catwalk that had saved his life earlier that evening. Naked and shivering, he worked his way toward the back of the ship, cautiously looking for any sign of crew. It was slippery and dangerous, but he managed to find a wider break in the stack of containers.

"We're at the center of the ship, AJ." Beverly had donned a bright yellow raincoat and matching galoshes; a colorful umbrella was spinning behind her head.

"I'm going to peek around the corner. Can you get a snapshot of the scene?"

"Yes, I'm ready."

He poked his head out, quickly scanning the area before pulling back. Through the pouring rain, he could just make out the ship's superstructure rising from the deck. There was also a stairwell that led down to the deck, but that was all he processed in the scant seconds he'd allowed himself.

"There is a single soldier standing guard," Beverly said, projecting a small window over his vision.

She'd removed the effects of the rain and brightened the scene now presented in the virtual window. Standing at the bottom of the stairs was a soldier, armed with an AK-style rifle. He wore a heavy rain slicker with the hood pulled up far enough that it blocked his peripheral vision. A waft of smoke rose above the man's hood and a red glow was visible at the end of his cigarette.

"That's universally dumb," AJ said, his teeth chattering almost uncontrollably.

"I don't know if you will survive another adrenaline boost. Your body is in danger of shutting down."

"Just give it to me when I need it," he growled through his chattering teeth. "Now, try not to distract me."

He crouched low and crawled out from behind the containers, using the pitch blackness and sheeting rain against his back as cover. Mentally, he'd faced a lot of hardship in his life, especially in the jungles of Vietnam. The cold was new, but the disabling pain wasn't. Gritting his teeth, he pushed all the distractions away and slunk across the deck.

A massive lightning bolt crashed behind him, brightly illuminating the entire ship. Thirty feet from his position, the soldier held fast to the stair railing and turned his head. AJ froze in place.

"Shit," the man said, coughing as darkness returned to the ship.

AJ wasn't more than two car lengths from the guard. Only the discipline he'd earned through combat kept him from acting on the belief that he'd been seen. A few seconds later, AJ saw the bright glow from the end of the cigarette as the man took a final drag and flicked the butt in AJ's direction.

"Human optic nerves have difficulty adjusting to rapid, significant changes in lighting," Beverly added to explain why he hadn't been seen. "His lethargy, however, is surprising given the earlier shipwide search for a high-value escaped prisoner. He must also be immune to the nicotine stimulant."

AJ couldn't help but chuckle as he crept to where the superstructure rose out of the deck, behind the man's line of sight. He was on his own on the rolling deck of a ship in the middle of the sea, buck naked and nearly dead, facing an enemy who was loaded for bear, but Beverly was concerned for this man's health.

Carefully, he slid sideways, working himself closer and closer to the guard. A fair fight wasn't something he could win. A strategy had no more formed in his mind when his foot struck a coil of chain lying on the deck. Pain exploded as his foot contacted something flat and sharp. He grunted involuntarily and the sound caught the soldier's attention.

If not for the fact that the man had a gun, the situation might have been humorous. The soldier took in AJ's withered and naked body, a look of shock filling his face. AJ knew he had precious seconds to exploit that tiny advantage.

"What in the fucking hell!?" the soldier exclaimed, loudly enough that AJ feared he might have alerted others.

AJ lunged forward, barreling into the guard, and riding him to the deck. The man, obviously a lower-level soldier, given his middle-of-the-night assignment outside on a rain-soaked deck, struggled to gain control of his rifle. The soldier's actions bespoke a certain naivete in brawling. While AJ couldn't afford the sound of a gunshot, he also knew that fighting for the rifle was wasted energy. With all the strength he could muster, AJ slammed an elbow into the man's jaw. Unfortunately, the power behind the blow wasn't what it had once been.

"Shit! Can't you stun him or something?" AJ groused, struggling to stay atop the man who'd finally realized the gun would do him no good.

"A noble sentiment," Beverly said. "No. I don't have any stun capacity. I'm four hundred nanometers on a good day and not one of my twelve arms are even forty nanometers in length."

AJ saw stars as the man connected a blow of his own. "BB, I need help, now!"

"Your adrenal glands are depleted," she answered. "I'm working on something, but I need a couple of moments."

In a single move, the guard realized his superior strength and threw AJ off. "Shit, we're not going to have that much time." He scrambled away until his head struck the very chain that had caused him to give away his advantage.

Surprisingly, however, the guard didn't press forward. Instead, he struggled to bring the rifle to his shoulder. AJ saw the opportunity and wrapped his hands around the uncoiled length of chain. A flash of lightning lit up the deck as he curled around, ramming the thick links into the side of the soldier's knee.

A single gunshot cracked, the bullet harmlessly sailing over the ship's side and into the ocean. AJ pushed his advantage and brought the chain down on the arch of the man's foot. A yelp of pain preceded the soldier's fall to the deck. AJ grasped the slick raincoat, using it to pull himself over the thrashing body. He pulled at the chain, but it had reached its length, so he smashed the heavy metal into the man's stomach. The fight drained from the soldier who was coughing and trying to suck in air.

"Make another sound and I'll gut you like a fish," AJ growled, his face only inches from the terrified captive.

The man nodded and was subdued while AJ removed the man's walkie talkie, pistol and the knives on his waist and thigh. With weapons in hand, he directed the soldier to undress, allowing him to keep a small portion of his dignity by not taking his wet t-shirt and undies.

"I'm sorry about this, buddy," AJ said, sitting next to his prisoner. He opened the protein bar he found in the jacket pocket. "I'm a US citizen, abducted on US soil. You need to find a new line of work if you want to feel good about yourself when you're my age."

The man was nothing more than a boy and barely out of high school. He stared at the deck of the ship completely defeated.

"I now have access to the ship's communication system," Beverly said. "I've reached Seamus who says Jayne, Sharg, Queenie and Lefty were all taken at the same time we were. I've been searching the ship's computers and since there's no record of our presence here, I wouldn't expect to find any information on the others either. However, I think I know where they could be."

"Already?" AJ searched for another protein bar, disappointed when he didn't find one.

"I've looked through the ship's manifest. The CIA isn't particularly subtle about their cargo. There are seven containers from a company called Patriot Industries. If our friends are aboard this ship, they'll be in one of those containers. Also, Greybeard has informed Captain Baird of our predicament. Apparently, the message I placed on your nurse's cell phone was not sent. Most likely, this is because the cellphone I modified has not been within communications range. We must be quite far out to sea."

He liked that someone in power knew where they were, although it didn't change the fact that they were on their own. If the Army was coming, it would take longer than they had. Intercepting a cargo vessel halfway to China would stir up a hornet's nest of inter-service rivalries.

"Can you figure out how many soldiers they have on board?" AJ asked, tapping the walkie talkie he'd taken from his prisoner.

"It will take time," Beverly said. "I do not believe it is wise to stay in the open."

"Agreed. Look at the manifest. Find the closest container with something edible inside. We'll use that container to lock this one up, at least for now."

"We will need a tool to remove locks," Beverly said.

Using the enhanced low-light mode Beverly provided, a scan of the deck revealed a tool cabinet. Within the cabinet, he found a crowbar.

"The third container from the portside has a load of supplies for a U.S. fast food chain on mainland China," she said. "The sodium and nitrate balances are high and there are chemicals designed to encourage overconsumption. Overall, it will do in a pinch."

"Are we talking Big Patty Whacks?" he asked, heading toward the port side. "I love those."

"The components of, yes," she said. "And portside is the left of a ship going forward, not the right, AJ. You need to go to the other side."

"Army here," AJ grumped. "Only boats we needed in 'Nam were on the river and nobody said nothin' about ports."

Several narrow steel bands and a couple of long handled locks held the container doors closed. Missing bands would be an obvious indicator that the container had been breached, but he shrugged as he pushed the crowbar into the lock and torqued it around. The noise of the breaking lock was covered by the intensifying storm.

AJ dragged the soldier into the container which wasn't completely packed and pulled the doors closed behind him. The sounds of the storm were dimmed in the closed space and he felt comfortable lighting the flashlight he'd taken from the guard.

"It's just buns and sauce," he complained as he pawed through the first row of boxes stacked within.

"Starch and fat will provide many of the building blocks you need, AJ," Beverly said as AJ ripped open a flat of buns and stuffed several at once into his mouth.

"Who knew these would be so good," he said as the food started to hit his stomach. "I'd kill for a beer."

"There are only concentrated soda kegs in this shipment," Beverly said. "There should be packages of cured meat strips. Perhaps try further back."

"That's right! There's bacon on a Patty Whack. Seriously, they ship all this without refrigeration?"

He pulled apart the stack of plastic trays holding buns, tossing them in every direction, making a tunnel toward the back of the container. By the time he reached a package of bacon, he'd all but covered the soldier he'd captured in flats of buns.

FOUR
SPOOKS

"Unit Twelve. Check in." The captured soldier's radio crackled to life. AJ pushed on the lever to lower the volume and picked up the unit.

"This is Twelve," AJ answered, keeping his voice intentionally low.

"You're not at your post. Where are you?" the man asked.

AJ sighed as he looked around at the piles of plastic wrappings. While he was no stranger to the ridiculous consumption needed for Beverly to rebuild portions of his body, it was still surreal that he could consume tens of thousands of calories in one sitting.

"Can't a guy take a piss with you crapping down my back?" he groused. "I'm portside pissing over the rail."

"You get some balls, kid? I'd be happy to shove 'em back where they belong if you don't get your ass back here."

"Yeah, yeah," AJ answered, sneaking out of the container. He pulled out his new flashlight from his new raincoat pocket and shined it to port.

Just as he hoped, a dark figure walked toward the wrong side of the ship. The large guard turned and headed back.

"What's wrong with you? That's fucking starboard," the man shouted over the still pouring rain.

AJ brought the beam of the flashlight up and grinned as the man pushed his hand out to block the blinding effect of the beam. "Put that shit down. Where the hell do they get you guys?"

"Oh, sorry," AJ said, stepping closer and bringing the beam down. In his other hand, he had a pistol, which he swung violently across the man's jaw, dropping him to the ground. "And for the record, he's not the only dipshit on this boat."

"Ship," Beverly corrected.

"Army," AJ answered as he moved the second soldier to his temporary base of operations. Fortunately, both men carried zip ties which made securing them easier. Even better, the new guard had larger shoes, which he desperately needed.

"There's an open catwalk at the top of the superstructure that leads to a central corridor where the Patriot containers are grouped," Beverly said, lounging atop a package of smashed buns.

"Likely a lot of crew on that side, don't you think?"

"If you are feeling adventurous, you could climb the containers."

He shook his head. "They're likely to have surveillance up there."

"I've disabled their video feeds. If I hadn't you would have been discovered shortly after your first encounter."

"Can you turn the cameras back on and just black out where we're at? That way you could see if anyone is coming our way."

"Devious." She switched back to her batgirl leather. "There are three crew currently visible on video feeds. A bridge watch directly above us and two soldiers posted outside of the Patriot containers. I have not discovered the video feeds inside the containers."

"How do you know they exist?"

"We saw one in your cell, AJ," she replied.

"Oh, right."

He casually made his way up the exterior staircase, repositioning his rifle as he passed into line of sight of the bridge watch. Still dark and rainy, he was just an indistinguishable figure. There was no way the watch would be able to make out facial features, even if they knew each other well enough to make an identification. Instead of turning toward the ship and entering the upper deck, he walked around and started across the catwalk.

"What are you doing here?" He was challenged even before he made it off the partially sheltered catwalk.

The second guard started to lower his rifle, but AJ was ready for the challenge and had already raised his pistol. He aimed at the guard whose rifle was in motion.

"This can go two ways," AJ said. "Put the rifle down and live or take your chances that I can't get you both. Either way, you're gonna have a hole in you."

The man looked confused but stopped raising the gun. "Either way?"

"You know what I mean," he said, replaying what he'd said. "It's been a long night."

"You're on a ship in the middle of the Pacific," the second man said, taking half a step toward AJ. "You can't take us all. Give yourself up now or we won't be the only ones worrying about holes."

AJ glanced at the video panel behind the man showing an empty cell with a small opening at the back where water was blowing in. A good guess that cell had been his. "Put your weapons down. We'll worry about my holes later. Shit! Do you hear what you're making me say?" he asked, irritated. "Move! Now! Guns and knives on the floor."

"We can't open the cells," the man continued, carefully laying his weapons on the deck. "Only the bosses can. There are twenty men aboard. Do you think you can take us all? Think about your position."

AJ looked at the next cell over. Lefty, who lay on the floor facing the back wall, looked like he was asleep. Small shoulder movements, only visible with Beverly's enhancements to his vision, however, convinced AJ that Lefty was up to something. AJ chuckled, feeling a bit proud that he'd escaped before Lefty.

"I'd worry about yours," he said. "BB, can you open this?"

"Same encryption, I've got Seamus working on it," she said. "I think he might have it."

"Who are you talking to," the more composed of the two guards asked.

"Noneya. Get your ass over to that door and open it."

"Noneya?" the second, younger guard asked.

"Nobody ever falls for that," AJ said, smiling. "Noneya business."

"I'm telling you, they're locked and we can't open them," the first guard reiterated, clearly not amused with the conversation.

"I'm telling you to give it a try." The guard was visibly shocked when the door swung outward. AJ nodded at the door, clearly expecting them to move inside. Two walls were set up causing an S-patterned walkway that blocked the entry door from the prisoner's view. "I can see you thinking about trying something," he said. "Trust me. I'd have shot you already if I was gonna. Don't take that for weakness. I've been through shit you can't even imagine and I don't have any trouble going back there."

The first guard turned slightly. "You kill us, you'll have a price on your head you'll never run from."

"Says the guy who facilitated the illegal imprisonment of US citizens. I'm fairly sure if I shoot you, you just sink to the bottom of the sea never to be heard from again."

"AJ, we've got incoming," Beverly said. "Someone must know something's up. Six armed men are working their way toward the catwalk."

"Can you open Lefty's cell?" he asked.

"It's unlocked," Beverly answered.

AJ, still near the door, leaned out and fired two rounds at the steel superstructure. He had no expectation of hitting anything, but wanted to slow the approaching troops.

"Sorry, fellas," AJ said, swinging the butt of his pistol toward the back of the older guard's head. The man anticipated the move, but AJ caught the side of his face and he dropped just the same.

"Don't kill me," the younger guard begged, holding his hands up defensively.

"You want to live?" AJ asked. The young man nodded furiously. "Run across there and open that plexiglass."

"What in tarnation?" AJ couldn't see Lefty as much as he could hear him. The sounds of a scuffle followed.

"Friendly!" AJ called, ducking as he slid out and retrieved the remaining weapons he'd taken from the guards and dropped by the container door.

"Ugly, more like," Lefty scoffed, rounding the corner. "I might have put you down except for that good lookin' gal next to you."

AJ slid a rifle to Lefty, leaving the door ajar so he could watch for movement outside. "Lock those guys up, would you?" He knelt and tapped a couple rifle rounds through the opening.

"With pleasure."

A couple of AJ's rounds were returned but quickly cut off after some yelling.

"BB, I need visuals."

A video feed appeared in front of him. Five heavily armed soldiers were stacked up in a hallway on the ship's top deck. On split screen, none other than Gerald Loveit was running down a hallway, pulling a belt through his pants.

"Can you give me a speaker near him?"

"You're live, AJ," Beverly answered.

"That's far enough, Loveit," AJ said.

Loveit skidded to a halt, frantically looking for AJ. "Where are you, Jenkins?" he spat, pulling a knife from a thin sheaf.

"I've called the Army and we're streaming this video," AJ said, bluffing. "Your career is done. You've illegally abducted and imprisoned US citizens."

"Army isn't gonna say anything. We're in international waters. They don't want any part of this."

"Fine. News media it is," AJ shifted his voice to that of a radio announcer. "Folks, on the screen, you're looking at one of the CIA's black site operations aboard the *Bella Cruise* container ship, currently en route to Hong Kong. US citizens Albert Jenkins, Doctor Amanda Jayne, Joshua McQueen and Lefty Johnson were spirited away under the cover of darkness by a CIA bag team, led by the man shown in this video, Gerald Loveit, a longtime employee of the US State Department..."

"Stop!" Loveit roared, pounding his fist against the wall. "Don't you dare send that video! Exposing CIA agents is treason, you'll be hung!"

AJ started again, using his best announcer voice. "You heard it there, folks. Agent Loveit, CIA, threatened our intrepid group with lethal action. We'll be digging into this story more as it develops."

"Just fucking stop," Loveit said, slapping his hand against the wall, in defeat.

"Turn this ship around," AJ said. "We step out onto US soil or that video goes public. You copy?"

"You were harboring an illegal alien, who violated the sovereignty of the United States of America. What did you think was going to happen?" Loveit asked.

"Did you even talk to Captain Baird?"

"Major Baird," Loveit responded, dejection clear in his voice. "She got promoted."

"Let me guess., CIA doesn't like the Army's intelligence service?"

"They're a bunch of damn cowboys," Loveit said. "They knew about these aliens and did nothing to stop them. They raped our county, shit, they raped our entire world."

"Look man, you gotta get some counseling for that," AJ said. "Trust me, I've been there. Holding that in will just eat you from the inside."

"We can't turn the ship around."

"Figure it out," AJ said. "Anyone so much as sticks their nose down this hallway and we'll release that video. Trust me, you don't want to see what an angry Vred can do."

"Vred. Is that the reptile?"

"That's right. Vred, as in one of the most civilized, highly advanced species in the entire Galactic Empire. And your big idea was to shoot down the first one you saw," AJ said. "You're probably not making their Christmas list."

"You're an idiot, Jenkins and you're playing a game you don't understand. The stakes are the entirety of humanity and you act like you're in high school."

"You know what I did my senior year of high school?"

"Can't wait to hear," Loveit answered.

"Ten weeks of boot and then I was marching through rice patties, watching my friend die. Do you want to know why? Because you fuckers couldn't get your shit together. You thought you knew what was best for everyone. I fought for my country and the CIA got my friend killed. So, I'd save the trust-me-I-know-better speech. Heard it before. Got me a POW sticker."

"Laying it on kinda thick, don't ya think?" Lefty asked, settling into a crouch next to me. "Got anything to eat?"

AJ pulled a package of precooked bacon from his jacket and handed it over. Lefty grunted but went ahead and opened it.

"I think your speech was inspired," Rebel said, appearing on Lefty's shoulder, flashing AJ a toothy smile. Unlike Beverly, Rebel had exactly one outfit and that was a pair of Daisy Dukes and a checked shirt knotted above her belly button.

He raised his eyebrows. "Thank you, Rebel."

"What do you want, Jenkins?" Loveit asked, climbing up pitched stairs that might as well have been a ladder.

"Tell your men to stand down," AJ said. "Get me a SAT phone and turn this ship around. Oh, and we're going to need food. Anything gets in the food and I guarantee your face shows up on every social media platform pasted on top of John Holmes' body."

"Who?"

"Geeze, seriously? Just do it."

AJ watched his video as Loveit arrived at the area where the armed guards had stacked up, safe from more gunfire. It took convincing, but they slowly moved away from the door and down the hallway.

"Do you trust that guy?" Lefty asked.

"Not any further than I can throw him," AJ said. "What are we gonna do, though?"

"I say we cap the group and wait for reinforcements."

"They're US citizens."

Lefty glared at him. "They're spooks."

"I doubt those foot soldiers are. We weren't spooks. That could be you or me over there."

Lefty sighed. "This bacon is crap. Can't believe they can even call it bacon."

"Watch my back," AJ said. "By the way, we're even now."

"How do you figure?" Lefty asked.

"You saved me in 'Nam and then again a few months ago. I got you out of Sharg's ship and now today. Even."

Lefty shook his head. "I was almost out of my cell. You had maybe a two-hour jump on me."

AJ chuckled to himself. The video screen on the next cell showed it was occupied by Sharg. For the time being, he skipped that cell. In the next, he found Queenie repeatedly kicking at the bottom of the back wall. Walking through the short maze he knocked on the plexiglass before the man knew anyone had entered.

"Well, I'll be stuffed! If isn't the big man himself." Queenie's bright smile split his heavily tanned face. "Ow'd yah get back in here?"

"Good to see you, Queenie," AJ said. "We're back in the shit, so we need to double-time back to the Sergeant."

"Got some bad guys needin' a new set o' holes then?"

"Only if they come for us. I'm working on a plan to get us off this tub."

"Tub?" Queenie asked, joining AJ as he worked his way out of the makeshift cell. "What about my gator girl? They better not a done any probin' or I'll be makin' a right mess."

"One cell over. Get armed. We're barely holdin' on here."

He accepted a pistol from Lefty. "Not with ole Queenie on the loose. We get the boys back together, they better keep things nice and clean."

AJ worked his way to the next container and was surprised at who he saw on the video panel. "What in the hell?" he grumbled to himself, having expected to find Jayne.

Darnell Jackson, his best friend, looked back at him. Damn. Until then, AJ had been content knowing that at least this time Darnell hadn't been dragged into this mess.

"About time you showed up," Darnell said, shaking his head. "Lisa's gonna whoop my ass when I get home. I told her I wasn't runnin' off on any more adventures with you."

AJ slid open the plexiglass panel. "Would you believe I didn't do this?"

"Sure, I would," Darnell said, bumping fists and accepting one of AJ's two pistols. "Don't think it matters what I think, though."

"Shit," he said, remembering how angry Darnell's wife could get.

"That's right, son. You got a whole lotta explaining to do. You best start thinkin' about what you're gonna say now. Just for the record, what is goin' down?"

"I have absolutely no idea. Sharg got shot down over the junkyard and then we all got kidnapped and dumped on this ship."

"What's Sharg doin' back so soon?"

"We'll have to ask her." The video feed on the next container showed that it was empty. His heart thudded a little harder and his blood pressure started to rise. If they'd taken Jayne or if anything had happened to her, there was going to be hell to pay. His heart calmed when he looked at the final display. Curled into the corner was the figure of the woman he would recognize anywhere.

Swallowing hard, he opened the door and raced to the plexiglass separator. "Amanda?" he called. The name sounded foreign on his tongue as he normally called her by her last name. She stirred, but didn't uncurl, instead pulling her arms tighter around her body.

He slid the panel to the side and pulled his coat off as he raced to her side. "Doc, it's AJ," he said.

"AJ?" she whispered hopefully, still not moving.

He placed his coat over her thin frame, then lay on the floor next to her and wrapped his body around hers. She shivered against him, her skin cold to the touch. "I'm here, Doc. You're safe."

"They did horrible things to me," she said, her breath shuddering in her chest. "They burned me and cut me. They were angry."

He struggled to breathe. "Was it Loveit?"

"I don't know his name."

He pulled closer to her. "Doesn't matter. I've got you."

Jayne rolled over and looked into his face. She had a scar on her cheek where it looked like a propane torch had touched her skin, leaving a finger shaped burn behind. "There's more," she whispered, tears forming in her eyes but not falling. "He wouldn't believe me when I told him I didn't have an alien in me. I tried to explain, but he just didn't care."

"I'm sorry, Amanda," AJ said, smoothing her hair back.

"Where are we? I heard a storm. Are we on a ship?"

Always the curious one. He smiled. "Container ship, headed for Hong Kong."

"CIA?"

"I think so. Lefty, Queenie, Sharg, and Darnell are all here. We've taken control of these jail cell containers and acquired some of their weapons, but if these guys want us bad enough, they can probably get the job done," AJ said. "I've made some threats and some demands. We'll see if it's enough."

"Can you help me up?" she asked.

He pushed himself to a standing position and helped her up. "Of course."

She looked haggard as she gingerly accepted his help. "Tendon was strained in my knee. It'll heal eventually, but it will take a couple of months. I've got a broken toe on my left foot."

"I'll kill him."

"Not for me, you won't," she said, shaking her head.

"Doc!" Darnell exclaimed when AJ and Jayne emerged. "Oh, shit."

Darnell and AJ exchanged a look that communicated everything Darnell needed to know. He came alongside and walked with them, not pushing her for details.

"Good to see you, Darnell," Jayne said, clasping his arm.

Lefty approached and handed a SAT phone to AJ. "Sent it over in a basket. Are you sure we can't do this the hard way now?"

"No killing," She didn't look up but accepted Sharg's gentle touch as the seven-foot-tall reptilian drew her away from Darnell and AJ.

AJ flipped the antennae open and stared at the dial pad. He had no idea what Baird's phone number was and jumped when the phone rang in his hands.

"Uh, hello?" he answered.

"Are you okay, AJ?" The voice belonged to Major Jackie Baird, former assistant to General Heckard, the man who'd sacrificed himself to expose the Korgul.

"We're all up," he said. "Spooks did a number on us, though. Can you help?"

"Hang in there," she said. "You're two hundred miles from a small island off Hawaii occupied by the US Navy. Right now, a pair of Coast Guard FRBs are bearing down on your position. They will arrive in ninety-two minutes, at which point they'll take control of the *Bella Cruise* and facilitate transfer."

"What's an FRB?"

"Fast Response Boat," she said.

"You know we've got a boat load of spooks, right?"

"Trust me, POTUS got an early morning call," she said. "There might be blowback, but we'll get you home."

"Blowback?"

"Politics, AJ. This thing has taken on a life of its own," she said. "Do you know why that Vred ship crossed into US territory?"

He thought about it for a moment but had no answer. "I'll get back to you on that."

"Hope it's good. CIA wasn't wrong. We can't have aliens, friendly or otherwise, just coming and going as they want. It makes people nervous. Important people."

"Nervous enough to alienate a possible ally?"

"Depends on who you talk to."

"Shit."

FIVE
PYRRHIC VICTORY

"*Bella Cruise* is dead in the water and I've picked up a ship-to-ship transmission that indicates the Coast Guard boats are two miles out," Beverly said. "I believe I'm able to make out their engine noise."

AJ paced past Lefty. Both men were careful to stay out of the line of sight of the CIA-hired mercenaries who had lowered their weapons, but were still on guard and heavily armed.

Activating the walkie talkie, AJ leaned back against a container. "Tell your men to stand down, Loveit. Coast Guard is here and you know it."

"You're armed and have taken hostages," Loveit said. "We'll aid the Coast Guard in taking you into custody. This isn't over yet."

AJ's satellite phone rang again. "*Bella Cruise* hospitality, how may I direct your call," Beverly answered as he opened the phone. Not entirely unexpected, she was seated at a 1950s-style telephone switchboard, wearing a tight, ankle-length wool skirt and long-sleeve blouse.

"Baird, are you listening to this?" AJ asked, ignoring Beverly's antics.

"To what?"

"I'm afraid Loveit is going to make a move. They're not standing down."

"They will. Word just came down from 1600 Pennsylvania. They don't want an incident and would like to officially apologize to the Vred, Sharg."

He was watching a virtual screen that showed the CIA mercs still in position. "You need to tell Loveit."

"I'm calling to tell you to stand down once the Coast Guard are aboard," she said. "They'll take command of the ship. I need your word."

"Once those mercs are under control, we'll be unarmed," AJ said.

"Good."

A loudspeaker announcement echoed across the deck of the massive container ship. The voice demanded that all ship occupants present themselves at the starboard taffrail, which turned out to be the steel rope that acted as a last defense against falling overboard.

"Should we go?" Jayne asked, struggling to stand.

"No," AJ said. "Coast Guard knows we're up here."

Instead of moving as instructed, Loveit barked a quick order and then turned and strode away in the opposite direction, taking stairs that disappeared below the deck. Instead of following him, one by one the mercenaries stacked their weapons into a neat pile on the deck and walked down the stairwell leading starboard, their hands held up at shoulder level like it was all in a day's work.

"Weapons in the container," AJ said, placing his own rifle in an unoccupied prison container. Darnell, Lefty, and Queenie followed suit.

It was almost ten minutes later when AJ finally saw Coast Guard personnel appear on the ship's deck, having negotiated with *Bella Cruise's* crew to secure a boarding ladder.

"Albert Jenkins, Bernard Johnson, Amada Jayne, Darnell Jackson, Joshua McQueen, you are ordered to present yourselves, unarmed. This ship is secure." The man making the announcement was dressed as a Coast Guard sailor and only held a megaphone, his pistol still in its holster.

"That's us, guys," AJ said, helping Jayne walk out onto the catwalk that joined the prison containers with the ship's superstructure. The previous evening's storm had retreated into thick gray clouds that threatened to repeat the earlier drama.

"I'll need you to hold there," the man ordered once the entire group was on the catwalk. AJ could make out five Coast Guard sailors on deck and wasn't surprised when one of them was ordered up the stairs.

"Any weapons?" The bright-eyed, heavily tanned sailor wasn't even breathing hard after running up three flights of stairs to the catwalk. AJ wondered if he was a day over twenty.

"There are two CIA mercs locked in the containers behind us," AJ said. "We put all our weapons in the second container on the left side. We're not armed. Doctor Jayne needs medical attention."

Two sailors on the deck below held rifles at the ready as they watched their compatriot approach and quickly frisk each of us. "Understood. I'm a medic," the younger man said. "I just need to secure…"

AT this point the Coast Guard sailor caught sight of Sharg standing in the opening of one of the prison containers.

"Uh, lieutenant… we have an issue," the man said as calmly as he could manage.

"Looks good from down here. What's going on, petty officer?"

"I'm not exactly sure how to describe it. There's a dragon… er… woman up here," he answered.

"Not our business, petty officer. Make sure said dragon woman is unarmed and treated with respect. Do you copy? Just cuff her with the rest and assure them the cuffs are only on until we're secure on the Coast Guard vessels."

"Aye, aye. Good copy, sir," he said. "HVTs are unarmed and mobile. I have request for medical on Amanda Jayne."

"I can make it," Jayne said, hobbling forward. "I just need a little help."

"Are there any others?" the sailor asked.

"Not as far as we know," AJ said. "The main spook is hiding below decks. Not sure if you boys care or not."

"Do we need to immobilize that leg, ma'am?"

"Doctor," Jayne answered. "A foot injury prevents me from walking."

"Very good, ma'am... Doctor."

"AJ, Loveit is coming out," Beverly warned, briefly flitting in front of AJ's face.

He nodded but didn't otherwise say anything.

"This isn't over," Loveit called, emerging from a hatch about the same time the group made it onto the deck.

"Sir, you need to stand back." The Coast Guard Lieutenant turned to address Loveit. He'd been standing on the deck organizing the boarding process on the deck.

"Just need to get your name for my report," Loveit said, his voice full of menace as he passed the group.

Two Coast Guard sailors lowered their rifles and stepped forward with obvious intent. "You will cease!" the larger of the two bellowed.

Loveit stopped moving but pointed at his jacket pocket. "Do you mind if I reach for my ID? I am unarmed and work for the State Department."

"Go ahead, but understand, you're on thin ice here." Watching intently, the lieutenant waited for Loveit to extract his wallet. He accepted the credentials, looking them over carefully. "Lower your weapons, gentlemen."

"I'm afraid there's been a misunderstanding," Loveit said, his voice smooth as he smiled confidently.

"I need you to step back, Mr. Loveit," the lieutenant said. "My orders are to bring back these civilians and an unusual, reptilian humanoid. I'm to use necessary force to achieve this objective. There is no misunderstanding."

Loveit nodded. "Perhaps I could just have a quick word with Mr. Jenkins? I won't attempt to further delay your trip."

"I'm sorry, these people are under my protection..."

"It's okay. Let him have his say," AJ said, interrupting the lieutenant. Glancing over the side of the ship, he saw that the Coast Guard vessels were standing off, most likely due to choppy waters.

"Just have one thing," Loveit said, before the lieutenant could object. Closing the distance between them, he looked straight into AJ's eyes. "I've got your number, Jenkins. When you get home, look up the phrase *pyrrhic victory*."

Loveit rotated his shoulders and drove his fist into AJ's stomach. He saw the move coming, but too late to block the blow entirely with his hands cuffed in front. He did the next best thing. Shifting his arms, he trapped Loveit's elbow in a tangle of cuffs and forearms and when they fell to the deck, he dragged Loveit forward, almost breaking his arm. He then brought his knee up hard, launching the surprised CIA man through the braided metal line that announced the edge of the deck. Loveit yelped in surprise, his body tumbling over the edge of the deck, the only thing saving him, the grip AJ had on his arm.

"Oh, now someone's got their comeuppance," Rebel drawled, standing on the edge of the deck to look down at the dangling agent. "I don't think I'd want to be him."

"I can't swim," Loveit begged, struggling wildly as he attempted to throw a leg onto the deck.

AJ felt his body slipping and knew he'd overdone it. Hands grabbed for his legs, but he slipped through the railing anyway. Suddenly, he and Loveit were in freefall. AJ jerked his hands free and kicked at the side of the containership, making contact. A fall from such a height was dangerous, although the chop in the water would help. He struggled to straighten his fall but there was little time.

Water met him, as did pain. He plunged deeper and deeper into the warm water, fighting to remain conscious. He thrashed around, struggling to identify which way was up. With his hands bound, it was difficult to swim and the raincoat weighed down his movements.

"Hold on, AJ," Beverly said. "You need to calm."

His lungs begged for air.

A long arm wrapped around his body and dragged him through the water. Just as he was about to pull in a breath, his face breached the water's surface.

"Your ocean is delightful," Sharg said. "I wonder why it is so full of saline."

AJ spluttered as water splashed into his mouth. "Loveit."

"He is alive," Beverly said. "That was stupid, Albert Jenkins. You endangered both of our lives."

"Didn't exactly go like I planned," AJ said. "Sharg, how'd you free your arms?"

"The locking mechanism was easily defeated." A snick of vibration informed him that she'd just as easily released his wrists.

A life-saving ring landed in the water next to him and when he pulled himself up, he discovered that Loveit was being hauled toward a long gray Coast Guard vessel. AJ was soon brought aboard a small launch that had been deployed to recover him and Loveit.

"You're an asshole," Loveit grumbled, glaring at him from the back of the boat. One of Loveit's eyes was closed and the side of his face blackening in a long bruise that extended beneath his shirt. AJ pursed his lips and blew a kiss at the man. "Someone needs to take these cuffs off." Loveit held his hands up, but none of the sailors in the boat were willing to look at him.

Transferring from the small boat to the long Coast Guard FRB, AJ was met by the same lieutenant who had taken control of *Bella Cruise*. "Do I need to worry about you going overboard again?" he asked, staring at AJ pointedly.

"Negative, sir," AJ said. "I must have lost my footing and would not recommend that particular conveyance."

A smiled played on the lieutenant's face as he turned toward Loveit, who was just making his way onto the ship.

"I should not be in cuffs. That guy should be," Loveit groused. "He's a threat to national security..."

"Sir, you will kindly keep your remarks to yourself. You struck a man who was restrained and under my protection. I will place you in the brig if you continue speaking. Do I make myself clear?"

"I'll have your commission," Loveit said.

The lieutenant stiffened his back and stepped closer to Loveit. "Memorize the name well, then. I'll look forward to your report to my superiors. I'm sure they'll give all due attention to a State Department employee found transporting US citizens to Hong Kong against their will, Mr. Loveit. Now, do you require medical assistance? It appears you have a nasty contusion."

Loveit stared miserably back at the *Bella Cruise*, finally cutting his eyes to AJ. "You're playing a dangerous game, Jenkins, and I'm not the only one who thinks so. You have no idea how much danger you've placed humanity in by alienating the Korgul and forcing us to take sides. You think you've won, but you're a dead man."

AJ blinked as the man gave away more information than he'd intended.

"That's enough," the lieutenant said, pushing Loveit away and giving AJ a rare moment of quiet time with Sharg.

"What's this all about, Sharg?" he whispered.

"We are still being surveilled," she said. "I will speak when I can be assured otherwise."

"Sir, if the two of you would come below," a deeply tanned young woman said, her eyes nervously flitting to Sharg as the tall alien turned to regard her.

"ARE you sure you're okay to walk on that?" AJ asked Jayne as they made their way down the C-130's wide ramp to a pair of awaiting black SUVs.

"It's a small break in my toe, AJ," she said. "I'll be fine."

AJ's attention was drawn away as he slid across a leather seat and recognized the woman in the front passenger seat.

"Major, didn't expect to see you out here."

Baird sighed. "We've returned Sharg's vessel to your junkyard. I can't guarantee it wasn't picked apart, though, since it was in the custody of Homeland Security for several days. The White House has asked you all to sign confidentiality agreements. There's an official apology to Sharg and a request that future flights be pre-approved."

"What about my house?"

She lifted an eyebrow. "What about it?"

"Air National Guard shot a spaceship down on top of it. I just barely got the thing rebuilt since the last time."

"Talk to your insurance company?"

"And tell them what?"

"That an asteroid hit it, I suppose."

"That's an act of God," Darnell said, chuckling as he slid into the back row of seats. "I bet you're not covered for that."

"Are you kidding me?" AJ asked. "What about alien ships?"

"You can't tell them that," Baird said.

"Probably wouldn't help," Darnell said. "Might be considered terrorist activity. At least your shop survived and Lisa says you can live at our place for a while."

"You talked to Lisa?"

Darnell held up a cell phone and waggled it in front of his face. "Got one of these in Hawaii. Lisa was apoplectic. She was about to start her own international incident."

"Oh, that makes sense," AJ agreed.

"My condo is available," Jayne offered. The two hadn't spent much time defining their fledgling relationship and the offer piqued his attention.

"Oh?" he asked suggestively.

"Would you really take advantage of a wounded septuagenarian?" Jayne asked, raising an eyebrow.

"Gotta say, Doc, you look pretty good for your age."

"You're a hopeless flirt."

"What is Sharg doing here?" Baird asked.

"Did you ask her?" AJ responded. Sharg, Lefty and Queenie were riding in the other SUV, which was already half a mile behind them.

"She said it was not her information to share," Baird said. "POTUS wants an answer, AJ."

"I can't tell you what I don't know."

"Find out. We need to know if this impacts the US or humanity in general."

"Probably just looking to trade intellectual property or something," AJ said. "Once I know, I'll let you know. Can you work with that? Is that why you... Holy shit, look out!!"

A loud noise drew their attention and they looked out just in time to see an airplane-sized drone plow into the ground next to the SUV which held Sharg, McQueen and Lefty. A massive concussive blast blew out the windows in the SUV that AJ, Jayne, Darnell and Baird occupied, pelting them with glass and debris and overturning the vehicle.

"Get out!" AJ ordered, flicking open a pocket-knife he'd procured at their short stop in Hawaii.

"Base, this is Chicken's Roost One, we're under attack on Airport Road. Chicken's Roost Two is burning. We need fire and medical immediately," Baird called into a handheld microphone, even as she hung from her seatbelt.

AJ slashed Jayne's belt, momentarily ignoring the blood running down his face. "BB, how bad am I? I can't see."

"Blood from gashes on your head is obscuring your vision," she said. "You're good, AJ. Go!"

AJ reached over the seat only to find that Darnell had freed himself. When he looked forward, Baird was free and kicking the front window with both legs.

"Shit, Baird, don't you guys have any fucking security!?"

"There are a lot of agencies involved," she said. "We need to take cover. There could be another drone."

That got his attention. He raked his knife across the window opening to clear the glass shards and climbed on top of the turned over vehicle. In the distance, he caught sight of a small, passenger-less aircraft taking off from a nearby airfield.

"Incoming! We've gotta move," AJ said, reaching back inside the vehicle for Jayne. With her arm injured, AJ worked carefully and together they managed to get her out. "BB, can you help?"

"There's an encrypted signal controlling that drone," Beverly said. "I'm working on it."

He dumped Jayne onto the grass nearby and scrabbled over to Baird's door. "This way, Baird!"

"Corporal Hauser is stuck. I'm going to try to get him out the front window," she said, again bashing her feet against the window.

"Dammit. Darnell, get Jayne outta here," AJ said.

"Got her. We're moving," Darnell answered.

AJ assessed the situation from in front of the vehicle. "BB, give me a boost!"

He didn't have to ask when the adrenaline kicked in. The acidic taste in his mouth, accompanied by the sweat on his brow told him everything he needed to know. Using the back side of his knife, he bashed a hole in the windshield and then pulled on the mostly connected plastic sheet that held the shattered beads of glass together. The edges cut into his hands, but he had little time.

"The drone is getting closer," BB warned. "You need to get clear, AJ."

With Baird's help, they pulled the semiconscious Hauser from the vehicle. The man groaned as they all stumbled away from the vehicle and threw themselves into the drainage ditch. The drone suddenly changed direction, its engines whining with strain as it rocketed skyward.

"That can't be good," AJ said, glancing over his shoulder. "I don't think we can outrun that one."

"It is okay, AJ. With Seamus's help, I was able to take control of the device. We will disable it once it has landed," BB said.

"What in the hell is going on, Baird!?" AJ barked, racing toward the inferno that was once the SUV holding his friends. "Those were good people."

"I know," Baird said, shaking her head. "I'm sorry. I didn't think it would be this bad."

"AJ, the car is too hot, you must be careful," Beverly said, floating up in front of him. "But I can sense Rebel. There is hope."

AJ stopped and looked soberly at Beverly. "What about Queenie?"

The sound of approaching firetrucks drew their attention.

Beverly shook her head. "McQueen is alive and struggling to survive."

"What do I need to do?" AJ asked.

"Look, there. Lefty Johnson is on the pavement."

He followed her pointing arm and raced around the edge of the burning vehicle. "How is this possible?" Lefty Johnson lay on the pavement, unconscious and bleeding, with an obvious broken leg, but he was alive.

"Rebel warned him and they jumped from the vehicle in time."

"What happened to McQueen?"

"There was a struggle in the vehicle. That is all Rebel knows," Beverly said.

"What's going on, AJ?" Baird asked.

"Get your shit together, Major," he growled, spinning on her. "You're asking the wrong people. We've got CIA and who knows who else trying to take us out. Good people died today. We might as well have announced to the Galactic Congress that we're a bunch of savages, because that's what we fucking are! This is a god-damn cluster."

"You're right," she snapped back. "We have no idea what's going on right now. Rogue agents are doing whatever the hell they want. We knock one down, two more pop back in their place. There has to be some reason that Vred woman came to visit. You need to find out why."

"Sharg's dead if you hadn't noticed. I didn't have a chance to ask her when we weren't being surveilled," he answered angrily.

"Jenkins, listen to me carefully. Powerful people within our government are in league with aliens who, like Korgul, seek to take advantage of humanity's weak position. These traitors would trade our future for their own enrichment. I *can* protect you if you come in."

AJ pointed at the burning SUV. "Like you protected them? My friends died for nothing."

"It wasn't for nothing," Baird said. "We'll track down who was behind this. We'll unravel their network. We need time. We've got help from the highest levels."

The emergency vehicles had already set up and white foam was dousing the SUV's flames. "Tell that to Queenie and Sharg," AJ said angrily.

"I'm sorry, AJ," Baird said.

AJ nodded. As angry as he was, he knew Major Baird was on the right side of things. "I am too."

Small movement beneath a pile of flame suppressant foam drew AJ's attention. "Screw it," he cursed under his breath and jogged over to the wrecked SUV, ignoring shouts from the emergency workers to back off. Reaching into the foam, he braced himself for what he might find. The ends of his fingers burned as they touched the edge of heated metal. Impossibly, the foam shifted and what followed sounded like a wheeze. In one quick motion, he closed his fingers and tore at the metal, which turned out to be an SUV door. Beneath the foam, he found charred but slowly moving reptilian scales.

"Sharg, Queenie!" he exclaimed, dropping to his knees and pushing away the debris, failing as mounds of foam just pushed back in on them.

"Pain," she gurgled. A strong, clawed hand wrapped around his forearm.

SIX
SENSE OF DUTY

Jayne squeezed water from a washcloth and dipped it into the salve Beverly had instructed her to make. She lathered the cool mixture over the tender, red spot above where Sharg's thick tail protruded from her back, careful to avoid pressing too hard.

"You are a master healer," Sharg rasped quietly, waking for the first time since the incident. "I am most grateful for your attentiveness. Tell me of McQueen's disposition."

"He's recovering, Sharg," Jayne said. "We've kept you unconscious for six days as we repaired the burn damage to your lungs."

"Aww babe, you didn't think you'd be rid of me that easily," McQueen asked, appearing in the doorframe. He leaned against it with a quiet grin, looking more like a surfer than ex-special forces.

"It was you who saved me," Sharg said, struggling to roll over enough to sit. "You were valiant and sacrificed yourself for me, forcing me to eject. It was luck that I fell beneath the metal protection of the door. The joy that I feel desires to burst from me."

"Well, Queenie knows how to take care of that, he does," McQueen said, raising an eyebrow. "You say the word and we'll get right to it."

"Perhaps this is not the correct moment. We are in Albert Jenkins' bunker," Sharg observed, testing the air with several sniffs, though her eyes remained closed. "I sense no surveillance, but I would speak with 49231125-0-B – ah, Beverly."

"We're here," AJ said, walking into the light, pulling a folding chair with him. He sat so he looked across at Sharg.

Beverly appeared, wearing the formal black robes she reserved for official Beltigersk business. "I believe that invoking my Beltigerskian name indicates a matter of considerable importance," she explained. "What have you to say, Sharg, daughter of the Kingdom of Shlasan?"

Sharg dipped her head in recognition. "It is not what I have to say, but what I have brought with me."

"I understand," Beverly announced, folding her hands.

Sharg pushed against the couch modified to allow her tail to stick out behind and sat up straight. She reached across her chest to an area just beyond the scales that looked like a swirly tattoo. Using one of her long claws, she etched a deep painful-looking line across her skin. Dark-purple blood welled up along the wound and dripped down, smearing the inky pattern. Sharg pried at the scale above the cut, lifting it half an inch from her skin. With her other hand, she deftly reached into the incision to retrieve a thin sheaf about the size of a postage stamp.

"What is this that you have injured yourself to carry next to your heart?" Beverly asked.

Sharg extended the item. "Albert Jenkins, you must hold this conveyance."

The moment the object touched his skin, it disintegrated. He yelped and pulled his hand back.

"Sister?" Beverly asked, as a girl wearing the same black robes appeared next to her.

"What a strange place I find myself in," the girl said. Her high voice was wispy, matching the blonde hair curling gently against the shoulders of her black robes. She looked around with some confusion, her eyes finally settling on Beverly. "Is it really you, 49231125-0-B?"

"In the presence of humans, we do not use our Beltigersk identifiers, 64838718-0-A," Beverly said. "It is difficult for them to segregate us easily. You will adopt a moniker as I have. Sister, please refer to me as Beverly and you will be Alicia."

Alicia's wan smile was accompanied by a nod. "It would fit Mother's narrative of human intelligence. I am surprised they do not find such assessments to be offensive. I believed you to have a different opinion."

AJ raised an eyebrow, preparing to set the record straight, but Beverly spoke first. "My opinion has not changed. The names are simply a matter of convenience. Do you not like *Alicia?*"

"When mimicking human vocalization, it produces a pleasant vibration. I will keep it," Alicia said, glancing around the bunker. "What a wonderous place this is. I had expected the gasses to feel more pressing, but it is as if they do not exist at all, even though I know we are surrounded by so many."

"Princess Alicia, fourth in succession to the Beltigersk throne, I would introduce you to my hosts: Albert Jenkins and Doctor Amanda Jayne, once host to 903218876-1-J known as Jack, followed by000001366-0-0, called Thomas. I believe you already know Sharg of Halfnium-8, who transported you."

Alicia closed her eyes and bowed. "It is my greatest honor to be in the presence of humanity's heroes. May your lives be filled with bounty."

"Uh, nice to meet you too," AJ said, glancing at Beverly.

"You took quite a risk in traveling beneath Sharg's skin," Jayne said, irritated. "She was in an altercation that could have destroyed you both. Your aid could have made the difference in her survival."

"That is distressing to hear," Alicia said.

Beverly stepped in. "A princess in the line of succession is not allowed to bond with another species, which is why I was unaware of her presence before. This brings up another issue. Alicia, you should not have traveled from Beltigersk. Why is it that you have broken the laws of our people and placed yourself at such risk?"

"Dear sister, we were once such great friends. I have missed your guidance and fearlessness. Indeed, it was you who I thought of most when I made my escape. I am ever grateful that the wondrous Sharg and her brave human companions, Lefty and Queenie, were successful in bringing me to you."

"People have died," AJ said, scowling. "And we're not hosting a fucking day camp for spoiled royals."

"Anger. Shame. Sadness," Alicia said. "Human faces are so expressive. It is a beauty of its own."

"Alicia, Albert Jenkins is not wrong. The humans have suffered greatly for your presence. Tell us why you are here," Beverly pushed.

"Beltigersk has fallen, dear sister. Mother is dead as are our sisters who were on Beltigersk with her," Alicia said, her face drawn.

Beverly wrapped her virtual arms around her sister. "Alicia, are you certain?"

"A Korgul vessel visited Beltigersk three weeks ago and disrupted the volcano. While we have defenses against this, the Korgul created a channel that led the magma to our refuge. I happened to be in conference with a Vred diplomat who quite thoughtfully extracted me as he fled Beltigersk. I pressed him into silence and asked to be delivered to the ones who knew of you. I am lost, dear sister. You must come back and take your place. Beltigersk needs you, Beverly. All could be lost."

"LISA, THANK YOU FOR THE MEATLOAF," Jayne said, kissing Darnell's wife on the cheek in greeting.

"The boys seem to enjoy it now that I'm not so worried about Darnell's cholesterol," Lisa said, smiling knowingly. Unlike Darnell and AJ, Lisa was incapable of hosting a Beltigersk symbiote. Thin and in good shape, she looked a good ten to fifteen years younger than her late sixties. Even still, she and Darnell no longer acted as husband and wife in public given Darnell's much younger appearance.

"Always with the meatloaf," AJ complained, grabbing two beers from the refrigerator and offering one to Lisa.

Lisa smiled, ruefully accepting the beer. "You know, you don't have to eat it."

He gave the thin woman a one-armed hug. "What would be the fun in that?"

She slapped his shoulder lightly. "I know why you asked us to come over. You've got a fool notion to take my Darnell back into the stars for some risky adventure. I won't have it, Albert Jenkins."

"Lisa, we need to hear what they have to say," Darnell said, crossing through the bunker's kitchen to stand by his wife. Placing a hand around her waist, he pulled her to him. "I wish it was another way, but we're part of this."

"Nearly got you killed last time."

"Honestly, Lisa, I'm not sure there's anything we can do about it," AJ said, ferrying food to the table that had been set up between the bunker's living room and kitchen. "Sharg's ship was badly damaged and even if it could fly, the colony on Beltigersk-5 is gone."

"Are you planning to rebuild your home?" Lisa asked as she poured water into glasses on the table.

"Hard to think about that right now, although I did get a check from the insurance company. I've never seen them work so fast."

"You could start a bed and breakfast for expatriated aliens," Darnell quipped as he took his seat. "Maybe make it out of stone this time. Something that doesn't burn."

"Hospitality and Albert Jenkins in the same breath. Will wonders never cease?" Lisa fired back, taking a seat next to her husband. "How about it, AJ, do you want me to contact your builder?"

He pulled the insurance company's check from his pocket and handed it to her. "See if he'll give us a frequent-builder discount."

"I wouldn't hold your breath."

"Sharg, have you given any thought to how you're getting home?" Jayne asked. "You're welcome to stay with us as long as you want, of course. Is your ship repairable?"

"Heck, I'm surprised the government hasn't tried to take it," AJ said.

"Baird must be working overtime to keep the existence of that ship under wraps," Darnell said.

"Not that I don't enjoy a nice evening out, but why did you invite us to dinner, AJ?" Lisa asked.

"Actually, it was Beverly's idea," AJ said. In response, Beverly and Alicia appeared at the end of the table, both wearing formal black robes. "Uh, oh. This can't be good."

"What?" Lisa asked.

"Mark my words, black robes are bad," AJ said. "Alicia, get the hell out of the salad already!"

She looked around, slightly confused, finally finding her legs. A startled look crossed her face and she stepped away from the salad bowl. "I apologize." Greybeard barked and stood on his hind legs, spinning once in place as he stared at the two Beltigersk princesses. "Greetings, Seamus." A faint blush formed on her face.

"AJ is right. An explanation is owed," Beverly said. "Alicia, I defer to you, sister."

"Oh?" Alicia asked, confused. "It's just that there is so much to look at. This connectivity the humans have is overwhelming. So much information available over such inferior technology."

"Sometimes it's a good idea to unplug," AJ said.

"Yes. We have done this *unplugging* you suggest," Alicia said. "My sister and I have removed all information about the crash and shielded the existence of Sharg from the US and Chinese militaries. In fact, we provided disinformation as to events and locations involved. The ruse will eventually be discovered, but our efforts should provide cover for perhaps as long as three weeks."

"What do the Chinese have to do with this?" Darnell asked.

"Like other nations, they are aware that aliens have been on Earth," Alicia said. "We have only discovered the US and Chinese governments to be actively pursuing evidence to that effect."

"What happens after three weeks?" Jayne asked.

"The military units we redirected had orders to capture Sharg," Alicia said. "Their systems are unusually weak to modification of global positioning information. I fear we will need to develop alternative strategies as they will certainly discover our meddling."

"How many units are looking for us?" AJ asked.

"Two, to date," she said.

"That's not good," Darnell said. "Are they coming after Lisa and me too?"

"It appears you are a known associate but of little interest," Alicia said. "We believe the primary interest is in Sharg."

"And we have no way to get her back home," Jayne said.

"There is more," Alicia said. "Some of it is better news."

"We're all ears."

"The Tok have sent a ship and are intervening on Beltigersk-5. With their highly advanced technology they have redirected the flow of the volcano," Alicia said. "While the technology and structures of the Beltigersk colony were destroyed, the citizens were successful in fleeing to a failsafe location. Our people are alive. It is a joyous moment."

Greybeard barked enthusiastically, bouncing on his back legs.

"That is good news," Jayne said, lifting her glass of wine. Her motion was followed by everyone at the table.

"I hate to ruin the moment, but I hear a *but* coming. There's always a *but*," AJ said.

"It is Beverly's duty to go home and lead our people," Alicia said.

"And..." he prodded.

"We do not know if they will accept her," Alicia said. "She has been away for so long. Our home is in chaos and our defense against Korgul has been weakened."

"Tell the Galactic Congress to use their power to get her back."

"The Galactic Congress has scheduled a meeting to discuss the scheduling of a hearing on the matter," she said.

"You're saying they don't want to step in," he summarized.

"Correctly said. The Galactic Congress prefers to give member nations time to work out conflicts. At best, they would censure Korgul. The Galactic Congress has few methods to force a nation to do anything."

"Why would Korgul attack Beltigersk-5 and take their leader?" AJ asked.

"It is my fault. Korgul warned us to stay out of their business on Earth. This is retaliation," Beverly said.

"To what end?" Darnell asked.

"Korgul and Beltigersk have long been at odds," Alicia said. "It was inevitable given our similar interface with other sentient species. Korgul establish a parasitic relationship with their hosts, enslaving them. Beltigersk form a symbiotic relationship, and both host and Beltigersk benefit from the relationship. Our similarities have magnified our differences and Beltigersk is very quick to criticize Korgul."

"You guys don't like each other," Darnell said. "I get it. It even makes sense. What I don't understand, is what you think we can do about it."

"When Sharg escorted me to Earth, it was for the simple purpose of reuniting with my sister, Beverly, who I believed to be the last of my family," Alicia said, straightening. "As I have now learned, my people have had victory over the Beltigersk-5 volcano. I find that we are drawn back so we might serve, as our family has for centuries."

"But we're not going anywhere without Sharg's ship," Darnell said.

"Wait, what about the Tok?" AJ asked. "They came because of a bounty on Beverly. Can't you just offer them money to transport you?"

"Earth and its solar system are no longer legal destinations. No Tok captain would risk the fines that would be levied," she said. "Darnell Jackson, Amanda Jayne, Albert Jenkins, Sharg of Halfnium-8, I beg that you find it within yourselves to bring me home."

"I think we're having a *Princess Leia* moment," AJ said.

"Don't mock. The Beltigersk were there for us when we needed them," Jayne said. "You've got my help."

"You have a short memory. Momma Queen Beltigersk tried to imprison us on Beltigersk-5."

"And where would humanity be without Beverly and the other Beltigersk who sacrificed themselves?" she asked hotly.

"Look, I get your point," he said, trying to calm the conversation down. "It's just, we don't really have what it takes to get to space. Not really."

"Albert Jenkins, before you drank yourself out of your job because of your wife's death, you were one of the most talented aerospace engineers in this country," Lisa snapped.

"Oh, shit," Darnell said, sinking into his chair.

"You have a junkyard filled with spaceship debris and I've seen that manufactory thing you've been working on in your shop," Lisa continued.

"Take cover," Darnell added, earning him a glare from his wife.

"If anyone on this God-forsaken planet can build a spaceship with the resources you've been given, it's you. Do you mind telling me why you're giving these poor women the runaround?" Lisa's eyes were all but on fire.

"Uh, well..."

"That's what I thought," she said. "You're a coward. Always knew it. Sure, you talk big, but when push comes to shove..."

"Wait one damn second!" AJ said, his face red with anger. "I'm no damn coward. I have no damn idea how to build a spaceship in anything like three weeks!"

"I guess that's the end of the story. It's as far as the mighty Albert Jenkins goes," Lisa said, banging her fist on the table. "Can't be bothered to come up with another idea. If only we had an old NASA shuttle cockpit or an old test-flight space plane. Now that'd be something..."

"That cockpit is just junk," AJ said, but something in Lisa's words caused his mind to wander.

"Ahh ha! I saw that!" she said, putting a finger in his face. "What was that look?"

"Nothing."

"Bull! You had an idea."

"Well, you said *shuttle*. There was that failed Virgin Galactic hull I picked up. I mean, it's not even a ship, just a glider they dropped into the desert. It isn't big either and we'd be pretty packed in."

"You're transporting nanometer-sized cargo, how big does it need to be?" she asked.

"It's in horrible shape. The nose is beat to death. I mean, we're talking thirty feet long, so four people max, and you better all know each other well."

"Is it something I could look at?" Sharg asked. "I have an affinity for mechanical design."

"Do you know how long this kind of project takes? NASA spends years on their ships before launching," AJ said. "One damn pinprick and we lose hull integrity. We'd be goners."

Sharg straightened. "We coat a material on the inside of cargo vessels we tow into space. It is self-healing if punctured and flexible."

"Cargo, not people," he protested. "Guys, this is ludicrous. Nobody builds a spaceship in a few weeks."

"Where is this Virgin Galactic shuttle, AJ?" Lisa asked.

He shrugged. "In the yard, where else?"

"We should go look at it."

As a group, they trudged up the stairs and out into the yard. The sun wasn't far from setting. AJ walked up next to Lisa and nudged her. "I know what you're doing – pushing me like this. What I don't get is, I thought you didn't want Darnell going anywhere."

"I don't," Lisa said. "I hate to admit it, but you're right. This *is* bigger than us. How do you think my man would take it if you did this on your own and died out there without him?"

He shrugged.

"Don't play me like that." She gave him a disgusted look.

"He'd hate himself."

"That's right. And he'd hate me too, in time," she said. "I'd be a daily reminder of his biggest failure."

"Never happen," AJ said, shaking his head. "That man has worshiped the ground you walked on for as long as I've known him."

"Well, maybe *I'd* hate me then."

AJ wrapped an arm around the woman and gave her a hug. "You're a good woman, Lisa Jackson. But if you ever tell anyone I said so, I'll deny it."

"You know I've always believed that you two were better together than apart," Lisa said, chuckling. "I remember back when he wrote me from 'Nam. He told me about a skinny crazy white boy who joined his crew. Said there was something about you, like you had a purpose. Said it made him think."

"He tell you we got drunk a lot?"

Lisa shook her head, grinning. "I always assumed he'd written that letter when he'd been drinking."

"You're a shit."

"Don't forget it."

SEVEN
ROCKET MAN

Darnell slid the heavy strap of the makeshift sling over the ancient test aircraft's hull. Hanging from a line attached to the bucket truck, he had a great view of the ship's skin. None of it gave him any confidence. The thing was in terrible shape, even down to missing a myriad of heat-reflective tiles.

"You want to hang there all day or what?" AJ called over the comms provided by the Beltigersk symbiotes. Unlike Beverly, Darnell's symbiote chose to communicate infrequently and didn't show himself with a virtual human representation.

"This thing is a mess," Darnell answered.

"Tell that to Lisa," AJ groused. "According to her, it just rolled out of Virgin's laboratory."

"I hear you," Darnell said. "Virgin removed the rockets. What are you thinking for engines?"

"Still working on that. Sharg has a wonder spray to coat those missing heat tiles and the vacuum sealer should keep us in O_2 for the trip."

"We're good. Go ahead and put me down," Darnell said, holding his arm out and giving AJ a thumbs-down gesture.

AJ set his best friend onto the ground and then raised the long-armed crane, slowly lifting the untested spacecraft from the heap of junk where it had been sitting for more than a dozen years.

"That sucker's heavy," he said, working the hydraulic controls to keep from tipping the entire crane over.

"Careful, AJ." Darnell shot him an unnecessary warning. AJ had plenty of experience pushing his machines to their limit. He slowly swung the craft around, setting it on the back of an empty flatbed semi-trailer.

"You're good to roll, Lefty," AJ said.

"Movin' out," Lefty responded as he drove a short distance to place the trailer and craft next to AJ's machine shop.

"I suppose that went about as well as we could hope for," Darnell said. "I've been trying to work out a repair timeline. We're not gonna be space-worthy before the military shows up if we don't go faster."

"Seems to me a little counter intel could go a long way," Lefty said, joining the conversation.

"Not following." AJ was confused. "That's what Alicia and Beverly have been doing with all their hacking and planting of disinformation."

"Way I see it, the spooks are all spun up about a seven-foot gator woman," Lefty said. "Nothing says *gator woman* like a visit to the swamp. I figure between Sharg, Rebel, me, and Queenie, we could make quite a splash down south. It'd be on my home turf. Bet we could buy you a few more weeks that way."

"How would Sharg get home?"

"The vessel you are working on will not easily accommodate four, especially with Greybeard," Sharg said. "I am not required for this mission and would very much enjoy an extended visit to the beautiful wetlands Bernard Johnson refers to as *swamp*. I agree that it is unlikely I would be easily found in that environment."

"Sounds like you guys have been talking, Bernard," AJ said.

"If you all don't need me, I'd like to get back to the bayou," Lefty said. "And don't call me Bernard."

"Sounds like you've already decided."

"I suppose," Lefty stated matter-of-factly. "I imagine you could talk me out of it. Truth be told, I don't mind spending time with Sharg – maybe not like Queenie. You get to my age, though, and it's nice to have someone who can hold up their end of a conversation."

"I am your age," AJ pointed out.

"It wasn't that side of the equation I was concerned about with you."

"Did he just say I'm dumb?"

"No, he suggested you're not much of a conversationalist," Darnell said.

"Save a guy's life, you'd think he'd have a bit of gratitude in him. Southern hospitality must just be a rumor," AJ said. "You need any traveling funds, Lefty?"

"Negative," Lefty said. "Rebel's rather good at coverin' our tracks. Might take that old VW van you've got sitting on the north side, though. Motor seems to fire up fine. Not sure about the tranny; it hitches a bit in reverse."

"Reverse is gone," AJ said. "Should drive okay otherwise. You sure you can hide a seven-foot-tall Vred in a minibus?"

"As long as you throw in those floral curtains."

"Might be good to replace that fuel filter, change the oil and all that," AJ said.

"Rebel already ordered parts."

AJ parked his bucket truck and slid out of the seat. He didn't like splitting up, but it was for the best. He didn't have any question in his mind as to whether Lefty could take care of himself, especially in the swamps.

"AJ, there's a truck at the gate from GelGas," Darnell said. "Says he's got a delivery."

"That's more shielded wire and acetylene," AJ said. "Did he bring the A588 steel too? Should be a couple of four-by-eight sheets of three-sixteenths."

"He's got 'em."

"Diego, check the Fantastium collectors. I need to unload that steel," AJ said. At fourteen, Diego wasn't a skilled worker, but he liked to help and he liked getting paid even more. Being on soil previously unmined by Korgul, they were slowly collecting enough Fantastium to power the engines in Beverly's design.

"Yes, Mister AJ," Diego answered.

They'd successfully cleaned out the interior of the airship and coated the walls with the self-healing, puncture-resistant coating. Interior bulkheads had been fabricated with salvaged aluminum from the junkyard, but the engine cowlings required material they were confident could withstand the corrosive environment.

AJ drove his forklift across the rocky drive to the GelGas delivery truck.

"Whatcha buildin'?" the driver asked, looking at the ship which was starting to look more and more reasonable for its intended purpose. "Looks like a spaceship. You know I recently heard there've been some strange sightings around here. Is that camo cover to keep the government satellites from spying on ya?"

AJ forced a smile. "Nope. That's a sculpture for the Air and Space museum. I put the cover up because it's too damn hot to work in the sun. You know, Arizona?"

"Yeah, I can see that," the driver answered, although he didn't look convinced.

"Is the pallet on the tailgate mine?" AJ asked, interrupting.

"Yup. I can help offload if you need," the man said. "Museum wants it all painted up like that? Kind of looks a little goopy, you know? Not to be critical or nothing."

"Just a corrosion spray. We'll coat it with aluminum once we're closer to being done," AJ lied. "I got it."

He stuck the forks into the pallet. It was a little tricky lifting off the wide sheet material, but it wasn't his first time. The load represented the final materials needed for the engine mounts. He pulled up next to the deliveryman and tuned down the forklift's motor.

"We good?"

"Your buddy offloaded the wire spools and gas. Just need a signature."

AJ jumped out and signed the papers. "Thanks."

"Good luck with all that," the man called after him.

Darnell opened the large, sliding doors of the machine shed for him. "What was that all about?"

"He was just curious," AJ said. "We've been getting more and more questions."

"Museum piece?"

"He thought an aluminum skin would make it look like an Airstream."

"That's a new one," Darnell said. "Need help cutting up the metal?"

"Would you mind dealing with it? I want to keep working on the interior bulkheads. Diego and I just about have the walls to the head installed."

"I'm not thrilled to fly this thing entirely by virtual controls," Darnell said. "How are those engines coming?"

Beverly appeared between the two men wearing a rolled-up denim shirt and a red checkered handkerchief wrapped around her hair, part of her Rosie the Riveter outfit. "The manufactory is doing very well," she said. "Once you have manufactured the covers from those new sheets, I'll have several pieces for you to install."

AJ nodded. It wasn't particularly new information, as they'd been discussing and updating their plans for the last two weeks. Darnell, Jayne, AJ and even Greybeard had each taken individual tasks suited to their skills.

"I've got the two side benches ready to be installed if you're looking for something to do," Jayne said. While she didn't have a Beltigersk symbiote, she used tiny subdermal implants in her ear and on her throat that allowed her to communicate with other team members. "Did you get those mounting brackets installed?"

"Crap! Hang on," AJ said. He knew about the brackets but had pushed them off as one urgent priority stepped in front of another.

"Diego, help me carry these benches while AJ installs my brackets. We can at least get them aboard," she said.

Diego appeared around the corner of the shed, carrying the small storage device used to collect Fantastium from the specially made mining traps. "It was a good load," he said, smiling. "We collected two thousand milligrams last night."

"What is that in grams, Diego?" Jayne asked, patiently.

"Is it two?" he asked.

"You're very smart, Diego," she said encouragingly. "Could you set that down and help me with this?"

"Of course, Mrs. Jayne." She smiled. No matter how hard she tried, she couldn't get him to call her Doctor or Miss.

The two struggled to lift the long plywood bench Jayne had stapled cushions and fabric to. While they wouldn't be overly comfortable, the simple design allowed for seating and sleeping spaces. She'd even installed wide belts to strap people in while they were in zero gravity, which meant most of the initial trip.

"How are your mother and sisters?" she asked.

"Very good," he answered. "I wish you were not going away, though. It is lonely around here without you."

"You need to stay away from here once we go. You know that, right?"

"Because the bad men will come?"

"That's right," she said. "We hope they don't come too soon."

"Mr. Lefty is okay? Did the bad men follow him?"

"Yes, but Lefty, Sharg and Queenie will be okay. Lefty is particularly good at hiding."

Jayne struggled up the ladder, still carrying her end of one of the benches. Without the aid of a symbiote, she had to rely on the strength of her newly found youth. She relished the physical challenge, remembering a time not so long ago when the task would have been impossible.

"May I ask a question?" Diego asked.

"Your English is improving, Diego. I enjoy answering questions from such a well-mannered young man."

"Will you grow old and Mr. AJ will stay young? May you be special friends then?"

"*Can* you be special friends. The word *may* doesn't work there," she corrected. "And that's a good question. I'm glad we don't have to worry about that right now."

"Worry about what?" AJ asked, coming over to help them move the bench to where he was welding the bracket onto the craft's superstructure.

"Never you mind," Jayne said, wiping sweat from her brow. Without a power supply from the engines, the air inside the craft was stifling even under the camouflage canopy.

"Mind bringing back some of that hull sealant? Welder makes a mess of it," he said.

"I will get it, Mr. AJ."

"Wait before you bring that up, Diego," Jayne said. "I'll come down so we can get that other bench at the same time."

"Yes, Mrs. Jayne."

"Kind of hate leaving the little critter behind again," AJ said as Diego disappeared through the hatch and down the ladder.

"You need to convince him to stay clear of here when we're gone. CIA won't have any trouble taking an illegal into custody and questioning him."

"You don't need to tell *me*."

"I never properly thanked you for dumping Loveit off the side of that ship," Jayne said, crawling on all fours over to AJ. She kissed him on the cheek and was startled when he turned into the kiss and made it more than she'd intended. She smiled but didn't pull away when she discovered his trick.

"That's a lot of kiss for knocking one dumb ass into the drink," he said.

"I'm still healing from what he did to me," she said. "It wasn't even what he did as much as it was that I had no control. He could have done anything. I was completely at his mercy."

"I'm sorry you had to go through that."

"Made me question what I'd do to him if I saw him again. I want to hurt him, AJ, even though it's against everything I stand for as a doctor."

"Welcome to the human race, Doc. I'd suggest not tossing yourself off the side of a container ship. Believe it or not, that's not a great idea."

She chuckled. "Now, *that's* what I'd call intellectual growth."

AJ waggled his eyebrows. "I'll show you intellectual growth."

"You're a cad, Albert Jenkins."

"And don't you forget it." He reached for her, but she anticipated his move, scuttled across the uneven floor, and launched herself out of the hatch and down the ladder. "You better run!" he called after her.

TO CALL the vessel a spaceship was to insult spaceships everywhere. The interior was a veritable collection of junkyard crap repurposed into cabinets, lighting, oxygen tanks, water tanks and refrigeration units. Using parts from old RVs, they'd even fashioned makeshift black and gray water-holding tanks that could be flushed externally if the trip went too long. Perhaps the crowning conversion was an old barber's chair turned pilot's chair for Darnell by removing the swivel and installing it at the forward-most point.

"Are you sure you have enough food?" Lisa worried out loud, pushing a pan of meatloaf into AJ's hands.

"We're packed to the gills." He lifted foil from the pan and sniffed the contents. Ever since she'd gone back to cooking with lard, the dish had become his favorite.

"Is it too late to change my mind about Darnell going?"

He gave the woman a one-armed hug and kissed her on the cheek. "You can ask him. We'll get loaded up so you can say your goodbyes."

Lisa sighed as he moved to Diego. "I'll miss you, Mr. AJ."

He mussed the boy's hair and handed him an envelope. "Take care of your family, Diego."

Diego opened the thick envelope and his eyes widened at the sight of cash. "Why, Mr. AJ?"

"I won't be around. Make sure you don't come over here while we're gone. I don't want you getting mixed up in this any further."

"I understand, Mr. AJ."

AJ hoisted Greybeard through the hatch and climbed up behind the dog. He felt like he was preparing for a camping trip and was certain he was forgetting something – a feeling he always had before a long trip. To make matters worse, it inevitably turned out to be true.

A moment later, Jayne climbed in behind him. "Why does it feel like this is a poor idea of epic proportions?"

"Probably because it is. Feel like some meatloaf?" he asked, fishing a fork from one of the many totes strapped to the vessel's floor.

"You can eat?"

"Either that or nap. Flying is Big D's thing. We're just cargo now."

"Really, you're into the meatloaf already?" Darnell asked, climbing through the hatch and closing it behind him. "Did I get that closed?"

AJ set the meatloaf pan onto a tote and crawled past Jayne and Darnell. "Let me look."

Darnell grabbed the pan and winked at Jayne as he shuffled forward, landing his muscular bulk into the barber's chair. "Oh, hell, who put this kid's fairy wand on the end of my control stick?"

AJ chuckled, having checked the hatch. "Just something I found from an old circus consignment Grandpa got back in the sixties. You were saying you needed something to hold on to."

"You're an asshole. I feel like an idiot with this thing."

AJ smiled. "Want me to hold the meatloaf while you start 'er up?"

"You know this little jaunt of ours could all be over in the next five minutes," Darnell said. "Are you sure we shouldn't have warned Baird?"

"She might be good people, but if the people around her knew about Alicia, they might not be so accommodating."

"You think POTUS would get in the way?"

"There are a lot of people between her and POTUS who are balancing the good of our nation against the good of beings they can't see and probably aren't even sure exist," AJ said. "No, it's better if we keep this to ourselves."

"Our radar cover, a Boeing 737, is just departing Tucson International and will be overhead in t-minus twenty seconds." Beverly appeared in a tight gray woolen skirt that came to a couple inches above her knee, a woolen coat, white blouse and round matching hat atop her head. "Please return all food items to their approved containers and orient yourselves forward for maximum comfort during takeoff."

Darnell waved at Lisa through the forward cockpit window. She waved back and pulled at the cord holding the camouflage tarp in place. The sun had set only an hour previous and there was still ambient light on the horizon. Any satellites overhead would be at minimum clarity.

"Engines are go," Darnell said, flicking illuminated toggle switches on a panel above his knee. To anyone else, they looked like random switches that were clearly not connected to anything. To Darnell, with the help of his Beltigersk rider, generally referred to as 2F, they were clearly labeled with specific purposes. The fact that it was 2F who actually communicated with the ship's control interfaces was a secondary conversation. "Hull is holding at one atmosphere and our elevation is steady at five thousand three hundred and ninety feet."

"We're not moving, right?" Jayne asked, looking around.

"It's kind of his thing to recite useless crap before takeoff. I think it was something in his officer training," AJ said.

"I heard that," Darnell yelled back. "And it's not unnecessary. Aural prompts often trigger important responses. Now, be quiet while I do my best not to get us killed."

"The Southwest flight bound for Dallas is now in range, Mr. Jackson," Beverly announced calmly, sitting on a metal panel to Darnell's right.

"Thank you, BB. Everyone, hold on to your butts," he said and coaxed the fairy wand backward as he slowly pushed forward on a blunted pirate sword. "Seriously, these controls are embarrassing."

"Don't you need to say something about prevailing winds and altitude or something?" AJ asked, gripping the cushion on one side and Jayne's hand on the other.

"You're crushing my hand, AJ," she complained softly.

"Sorry," he grunted.

"Seven thousand feet... eight thousand... ten thousand... I've got visual on the Southwest flight. We should be effectively hidden by their radar picture," Darnell announced. "Fifteen thousand. We've got activity over at Air National Guard. Looks like they're rolling thunder. Twenty-eight thousand."

"Darnell, you need to punch it. Those boys can do sixty thousand," AJ said.

"We're not really equipped for atmospheric shenanigans," Darnell said. "Just hold on. Thirty thousand feet."

Beverly projected a virtual representation of two F-16s approaching at high speed. It was clear from their attitude and speed that the military jets would catch them.

"Beverly, call Baird. Tell them to abort that mission," AJ said. "Tell her we have diplomats aboard."

"No time. Those birds will be on us in twelve seconds," Darnell said. "Thirty-eight thousand feet. Crap those boys are comin' in hot."

"BB, see if you can raise them directly," AJ said.

"I'm transmitting," she said.

"Air Guard, this is a civilian craft with diplomatic cargo," AJ called. "We're unarmed and have no hostile intent. Contact Army Military Intelligence before you blow us up. I'm Sergeant Albert Jenkins, Fourth Infantry Division."

"Unidentified civilian craft, you are ordered to maintain level flight or you will be destroyed. Do I make myself clear?" The woman's voice was full of steel and AJ had no doubt as to her intent.

"Make the call, Lieutenant," AJ called back. "Major Baird, US Army Intelligence. We have high-level diplomats aboard. Your commander is defying orders directly from Sec Dev."

"Forty-six thousand feet," Darnell said.

The F16s were on top of them. AJ flinched as he anticipated the missiles that were no doubt streaking toward them on a mission there would be no coming back from.

The twin warbirds flared wings and passed the junkyard spaceship, one on each side. Something had stayed the hands of the pilots.

"You're ordered to return to base with us," the woman said, her steely resolve unhindered.

"Thanks for not blowing us up," AJ said.

"Just doing my job, Sergeant," she said. "Will you comply?"

"Fifty-eight thousand feet," Darnell said. "They can't have another ten thousand feet in them. Keep her talking."

"She already decided not to pull the trigger," AJ said and switched back to communication with the Air Guard pilot. "Wish us luck, Lieutenant."

"Good luck, Rocket Man."

EIGHT
REROUTED

"We might as well get comfortable," Darnell said, swiveling the barber's chair to face AJ and Jayne. "Our first jump point is sixteen days out. Boys over at NASA are no doubt tracking us, likely wondering why we're not a fine red paste on the back wall."

Beverly appeared, seated on the edge of a plastic tote, wearing a spacesuit complete with a fishbowl-style head covering. "Gravitational systems are one of the most readily available intellectual properties in all of settled space. Even though the Galactic Congress does not recognize humanity and the Earth is a forbidden destination, I suspect your scientists will experience a sudden *breakthrough* resulting in this technology being *discovered*." She enunciated the words breakthrough and discovered in a way that made it sound sarcastic.

"Are you saying not everyone in the Galactic Congress is on board with the restrictions around Earth?" Jayne asked.

"That is correct," she answered. "Just because the Korgul are no longer allowed to mine Blastorium and Fantastium does not mean other unsavory types won't find ways to separate humanity from its most valuable resource."

"People should be warned," Jayne said.

"How? It'll be chaos," Darnell said. "Half gold rush and half alien conspiracy."

"Tell me that people in the know aren't already buying up land that they think has virgin soil," AJ said. "What I don't get is why the CIA was so hell-bent on finding Alicia. How do they even know about her?"

"I do not believe your CIA has need of Alicia," Beverly said. "A powerful actor has influenced them, perhaps bribing them with advanced technology. If Alicia is returned to Beltigersk-5, the government will be restored and the Korgul attack will have been limited in its effectiveness."

"What about the Queen and your sisters?" Jayne asked.

Alicia appeared, still wearing her black robe. She managed a reasonable facsimile of Beverly, sitting inches away in the same pose. "I am part of the current administration and as an aide to Beverly will be able to resume our government's activities. She is now the rightful leader, although there is some question that she might not be accepted as such. While I am the least of my sisters, I have many who support me. If I do not return within three months, a mechanism for restoring our government after a catastrophic event will be initiated. The process is long and Beltigersk would be in chaos for years."

"Can't you tell them you're on your way?" Jayne asked. "Once we're out of our solar system, couldn't they just ask the Tok to recover you?"

"There are risks with each approach. The Tok are our allies, this is true. That they aided in the recovery of our citizens seems to suggest their fidelity," she said.

"But politics can make people do crazy things," AJ finished for her.

Alicia's laugh was airy and high pitched. "Human idioms are delightful. Yes, Albert Jenkins. Politics do indeed make people do crazy things. The fewer outsiders involved, the less complex our trip should be."

"Explain how all you aliens are more advanced than humans," he said. "You've just described humanity. I'm not seeing much enlightenment."

"This is not an unfair statement, Albert Jenkins," she said. "Many work for the enrichment of all, but even more seek their own riches without concern for the impact upon others. Does this change your mind about helping?"

"Don't get your panties in a bunch," AJ said, settling back into the cushions. "Just want to make sure we're all singing from the same hymnal."

"DO YOU SMELL THAT?" Jayne nudged at AJ, who was drifting between sleep and awareness. "We've definitely got a funky smell going."

"You're saying you expected something better after fourteen days of nothing more than baby wipes for showers?" he asked, not bothering to open his eyes.

"I'd pay a lot for a nice, long, hot shower right now," she said. "And shampoo."

"I remember being in the bush for three weeks straight. We smelled like a herd of water buffalos. This isn't that bad."

"Someone needs to stop feeding Greybeard beans. He's running a straight pipe if you know what I mean," Darnell grumbled.

Beverly hovered between the three. "Our atmospheric filter media is degrading. I suggest we manufacture a new set and replace them."

AJ and Darnell groaned simultaneously. Three of the six filters needed for the replacement were beneath a pile of plastic totes. Worse yet, all those supplies had to be moved in shifts.

"I swear, you only do this to get us off our butts," AJ complained.

Darnell slid himself into the barber's chair and reviewed the various systems. "All systems look like they're doing okay," he reported. "I'll help get things moved around. Better than smelling dog butt the entire time."

Greybeard barked defensively. Like the rest, he was tired of the confined and entirely uninteresting interior of the makeshift spaceship.

"Wait, this doesn't look right," Darnell said, stabbing a finger at the virtual display which showed their path from Earth to Mars. "What's this thing?"

"It is likely noise," Beverly said. "Our external sensor package is ineffective at that range."

"2F, show me the last four days and trace that *noise.*" Darnell watched as 2F shifted the timeline on the display. Indeed, the blip he'd seen was indistinct, blinking in and out of existence. "Something's following us. 2F, project their current acceleration with our own. We've got two days before we reach the Mars jump point."

AJ climbed over totes and banged his head on the ship's ceiling like he had so many times before. "What do you mean, following us?"

"There," Darnell said, pointing at the object. "I thought I saw it a couple of days ago, but then it was gone. I just saw it again and it was on that same line but closer."

"Maybe NASA launched something," Jayne said.

"No way," AJ answered almost immediately. "Their acceleration with chemical rockets is a twentieth of ours. Paper napkin calculation, but I think that thing is gaining on us."

"It is," Beverly answered, back in her bubble helmet and spacesuit. "Seamus has calculated that it will overtake our position only minutes before we reach the Mars jump point. The timing is too precise to be coincidental."

"Who is it? Can you get a better read on 'em?" AJ asked.

"With our current sensors, we are fortunate that Darnell noticed their approach," Beverly said. "We need to be within a few thousand kilometers before we will be able to better identify this vessel."

"Can we call someone and let them know there's an illegal ship out here?" Jayne asked.

"That is not possible," Beverly said. "Our communication devices are limited to local space. We do not have the capacity to send messages through the jump points."

"So what? We just wait for them to catch us?" AJ asked. "There's no way these guys are friendly. We need to go faster. What if we toss some of the supplies, get rid of the benches? We could probably dump eight hundred pounds of junk."

"That junk is keeping us alive," Darnell said. "We've got ten days in jumpspace and then another fifteen in the Beltigersk system. We're not even halfway done with this trip."

"I do not believe it would be helpful to reduce our mass," Beverly said. "It is true, our acceleration would improve, but I believe our pursuer is limiting their acceleration to meet us just as we enter jumpspace."

"Because?" AJ asked.

"They do not know the extent of our communication capacity," Beverly said. "They might believe we could report their activity, which, if they attempt to board our vessel, would be highly illegal, given the Galactic Congress's decree regarding human space."

"But they'd be okay to do what they want in jumpspace?" Darnell asked.

"It would be up to us to report their activities to the authority in charge of this sector of space," Beverly said. "Keep in mind, humans are not recognized as galactic citizens. You are, unfortunately, vessels for the transport of Beltigersk citizens, a nation with no current leadership."

"Back to being raccoons," AJ said.

"More offensive for me." Darnell said, chuckling darkly.

AJ rolled his eyes. "Would you prefer I said monkeys?"

"No."

"Good, because I wasn't going to."

"Didn't ask you to."

"Boys!" Jayne snapped, irritated. "Beverly, tell us how jumpspace works. Don't they have to go to the same destination as we do?"

"Yes and no. I assume you're thinking about changing our destination away from Beltigersk-5," Beverly said.

"That's right. Go somewhere else. It doesn't solve everything, but it separates us from our pursuers."

"If they enter at the same moment we do, they will be able to join with our jump envelope," Beverly said. "The physics are not difficult to understand if you'd like a more complete description."

"You mean put the cookies on a lower shelf for us raccoons," AJ said.

"Not helpful, AJ," Jayne said before Beverly could. "No, let's save the explanation for another time. How long do we have until we can identify that ship?"

"Perhaps six minutes before we enter jumpspace," Beverly said.

"Can we change our destination when we're six minutes out?" AJ asked, following Jayne's line of thinking.

"Of course, that is plenty of time," Beverly said. "I do not see why that provides advantage."

"Just a second. Can they actually attack us in jumpspace?" Darnell asked.

"Not technically. As soon as we exit, we will be physically near, although our final acceleration vectors will be re-established," Beverly said.

He frowned. "Final, as in how we entered jumpspace?"

"Yes," Beverly said.

"Talk to us about other jump points we can reach from Sol," AJ said. "For example, are there any that are specifically non-friendly to Korgul sympathizers?"

"It is not difficult to enumerate the possible destinations," Beverly said. "Please understand, I've created names as close as I can manage with English phonemes. For efficiency, the primary livable planets and their solar systems are similarly named. The planets have their orbital sequence from the primary star appended if there are multiple inhabited planets, which is less likely."

"Got it, so planet Halfnium-8 in Halfnies solar system," AJ said. "Halfnium-8 being the eighth planet from the Halfnium star."

"That is correct. Accessible by the Sol jump point are Korgul, Argon-3, Xandarj, Texnat, Pertaf and Fimil," she said. "Of course, Korgul are sympathetic to their own. Argon, which you have visited, is a neutral location. Xandarj is not a good choice. Texnat have no love for Korgul, although they have no love for Beltigersk, either. Pertaf is in the middle of a civil war and would probably not be helpful. Fimil might not be a bad choice, although their jump point is a significant distance from civilization. If our pursuers are Korgul, they could deal with us well before a Fimil ship was within range."

"That's a lot of information," AJ said. "Let's go through it more slowly. Tell us about the societies and their relationships with other people."

"And don't leave out how far their jump points are from civilization," Darnell said.

"Perhaps leave out those sympathetic to Korgul," Jayne pointed out.

Beverly started in on a longer description of each of the listed societies, ignoring Jayne's suggestion to leave any out. As she spoke, she first displayed a solar map of the systems, followed by a close-up of the inhabited planets, planetoids and moons. The next images were of typical males and females of the species in their common attire. By the end, the three friends had seen furry, reptilian, mostly human and even an avian species. Not to completely ignore Jayne's suggestion, Beverly recited high-level political information as well.

AJ sighed when she finally stopped. His mind was spinning with information overload. "I'm going to forget all of that in a couple of days," he said. "So many planets and moons and so many species. How does anyone keep it all straight?"

Beverly smiled wanly. "It is much easier to distinguish dissimilar species than those that are homogenous. I believe many would ask how it is that humans identify each other as you all are similar, at least when compared to Korgul or Pertaf."

"Pertaf, the avian species we saw last?" Darnell asked.

"Very good," she said.

"Not so hard. Sounds like parrot."

"What I think is interesting is that with the exception of Korgul and Beltigersk, every species we've seen is humanoid. Sure, there's variance in mass and dimension, but it's remarkable how similar we all are."

"Duplication is an evolutionary tool. A species with two of a certain appendage or a particularly useful organ is more likely to survive than a species without those features," Beverly said.

"I've only got one nose and one... well, you know," AJ said.

"Just goes to show how important both of those are for evolutionary advancement," Jayne said, raising an eyebrow.

"Hate to argue, but I can live without my nose. I'm not participating in evolution at all without my *business*."

Beverly shook her head. "As preoccupied as you are about this single appendage, it seems unlikely it could ever come to harm."

"Smack!" Darnell said. "Score one for the micro princess."

"I'm hurt," AJ said, holding a hand over his heart. "I thought we were friends."

"In all that info, I didn't hear about anyone who would be particularly ready to help a ship full of raccoons," Darnell said. "I'm not sure any one system is better than jumping to Argon on our way to Beltigersk. But that doesn't get us away from the bad guys."

AJ rummaged through a tote and withdrew a package of Pop Tarts. Tearing off the top, he chewed on one of the pastries, thoughtfully. "The berry flavor is really pretty good."

"They all taste the same to me," Darnell said.

AJ shrugged and took another bite. "So, no on Argon-3, which would be our direct route to Beltigersk. No on Korgul and Fimil. That leaves what? Xanadu, Texas and Parrot?"

"Do you desire that I change my translations to those names?" Beverly asked.

"No?" AJ asked. "Did I say them wrong?"

"Xandarj, Texnat and Pertaf," Jayne said, earning her a smile from Beverly.

"Fine. You didn't like Xandarj, so we throw that out. What about Texnat and Pertaf?"

"Texnat is a reasonable choice mostly because they enforce common Galactic Empire laws. A diplomatic request for assistance is likely to be answered within an hour. Pertaf, on the other hand, is likely to be slower to respond and has another set of laws that must be observed beyond Common Galactic Law."

"What is Common Galactic Law, generally speaking?" AJ asked.

"It is an adopted list of laws that virtually every member nation of the Galactic Congress agrees to enforce. Topics covered are similar to human law. For example, murder, enslavement, and rape are all considered serious crimes. Property crimes such as theft, damage, and occupation are a lower priority but enforceable. There are also lists of mind-altering substances that cannot be transported, like your narcotics," she said. "There is more, but that is a reasonable sampling. Attacking a vessel without provocation can be considered property damage and escalate to murder, depending on circumstances."

"And if they find it's just a bunch of raccoons stealing a ship?"

"If they did not find evidence of my sister or me, the act of aggression would be limited to a property crime. As this vessel is not registered and no ownership established, the crime would not be punishable."

The worthlessness of humans was a topic they'd been over a few times already. AJ found he was just as irritated with the galactic view of his race as the first time he'd talked through it with Beverly. He fumed as he considered their options. An hour alone with their pursuers might as well be infinity. "What don't you like about Xandarj again?" he finally asked.

"I do not believe I explained," she said, redisplaying the lightly furred humanoids. "The Xandarj people are a reasonably intelligent species. On average, they are between four and five feet tall and their mass distribution is similar to humans. Due to their smaller stature, therefore, they are lighter. Most are covered with a light fur that varies significantly in length from half an inch to several inches, although the longer fur is uncommon. The coloring of their hair is widely ranged and can take on blue hues in addition to the colors seen in humans. They have three fingers on each hand with an opposable digit that operates much like your own thumb."

"Nothing particularly disqualifying there," Jayne said.

"I agree," Beverly continued. "Xandarj do not regularly enforce Common Galactic Law beyond the most severe. They are highly individualistic and believe the individual bears responsibility for enforcement of laws. As a result, there are few state vessels patrolling their spaces."

"It sounds like bedlam," Jayne said. "What keeps them from falling into chaos without law enforcement?"

"There is law enforcement, but not at the level common to most civilized societies," Beverly said. "It is a difficult society in which to prosper on one's own. Successful communities band together and are suspicious of outsiders, although there is a notable exception."

"This should be good," AJ said.

"Four massive space stations orbit Xandarj. Each houses hundreds of thousands of inhabitants. The stations are under the control of powerful cartels and each acts like a separate nation. All trade with Xandarj flows through one of these stations and any unguarded cargo vessel bound for the planet's surface is intercepted."

"How far is Xandarj from the jump point?"

"I fear you will assume too much from this," she said. "The jump point is less than a hundred thousand miles from Xandarj and located at the crotch of a y-shape between the planet and its two moons."

"She said *crotch*," AJ snickered.

"Grow up," Jayne shot back.

"Do you think our pursuer would take us out before we could get to one of those stations?" he asked.

"That would be dangerous for them," Beverly said. "Once a fight is started, others will choose sides. I think it more likely that our pursuers will follow us into Xandarj, wait for us to leave, and attempt to intercept us at our next destination."

"And we could live to see another day," Darnell said.

"I haven't appropriately explained the chaos created by the lack of a peacekeeping force," Beverly said. "Our very survival on Xandarj would be in question."

"Tell me another jump point where we won't be blown up upon arrival," AJ said.

"Texnat boasts a very reasonable response time," she said.

"Help that's one hour away doesn't work for us," AJ said. "This ship is barely navigable and we can't outrun, outgun, or dodge. We might as well just paint a big welcome sign on our topside."

"Your concern is reasonable," she said. "I am afraid the choice of Xandarj is merely offsetting the inevitable and introducing us to new dangers."

"By inevitable, you mean *death*? I'm good with offsetting that," AJ said. "Darnell, tell me you're packing."

"I wasn't sure if that was cool or not," he said. "My experience is that driving around with a gun isn't such a good idea for a man of color."

AJ shook his head. "So it's cool if I drive around with a gun? Cops are just going to look past it?"

"You're so easy to bait," Darnell said. "Of course I'm packing. You need one? I've got my 1911 and brought my little shotty along too. Maybe got a hundred twelve-gauge shells and a thousand .45 ACP rounds."

"I'm good. I packed my Ruger."

"A .22 caliber? What were you thinking?"

"Lots of ammo, easy to carry, quiet," AJ said. "These Xandarj are small. A .22 ought to be enough."

"Or their hides are thick as stone," Darnell said.

Jayne was aghast. "I can't believe you brought guns on a diplomatic mission!"

"You want one? I brought one for you," he said.

"This is wrong on so many levels," Jayne said, holding out her hand. "Give me the gun."

NINE
GOING BALLISTIC

"That is a Cheell registered vessel," Beverly said, still wearing her 1960s spacesuit, complete with clear bubble over her head. "They are closing very quickly."

"Transition in three ... two ... one ..." Darnell warned. "We're in jumpspace."

"No shots fired," Beverly said.

"Remind me about Cheell," Jayne said.

"Classic aliens," AJ said. "Bug eyes, gray bodies, spindly arms."

Beverly projected the alien image that had been represented in popular culture since the 1950s. "Very impressive, AJ."

"Some stuff sticks," he said. "What's their deal? Why would they be chasing us?"

"It has long been suspected that Cheell and Korgul have a working relationship with regard to Earth," Beverly said. "Further, it is believed that Cheell have been in contact with human governmental agencies."

"For what purpose?" Jayne asked.

"To sell technology which advances humanity," Beverly said. "As we've discussed, humanity is not far from being admitted into the

Galactic Empire. Discoveries of jumpspace and Fantastium are requirements, as is a unifying planetary government."

"So that's why that jackass had his head stuffed up the UN's asshole," AJ spat.

Beverly nodded in agreement. "Your United Nations is the most likely organization to represent humanity to the Galactic Empire."

"Over my dead body."

Darnell chuckled. "With your sparkling personality, I can't imagine that'd be an impediment."

AJ glowered at his best friend. "The government already tried to kill me. Didn't go so well, did it?"

"If they'd wanted to kill us..."

"Boys!" Jayne's voice rose above the bickering men. "We're all tired of sitting in this cramped space with an unknown enemy chasing us. We can't afford to fight amongst ourselves. We have a mission. We need to use our energy to move our plans forward."

"Damn officers," AJ grumbled under his breath.

"What was that?" she challenged, glaring at him.

"Nothing."

She pulled the top off a tote and plucked out a foil-wrapped Pop Tart package, handing it to AJ. "Take one of those and give the other to Darnell." He narrowed his eyes but before he could say anything, she continued. "Look, AJ, we need each other. We're all friends here. Your blood sugar is low and it's a lot to be trapped in a small, poorly constructed ship. We need to focus. We're alive and we need to put our energy into staying that way."

He opened the foil pouch, pulled out a pastry and handed it to Darnell. He took the other one and took a bite. "Okay, BB. How do Cheell and Xandarj get along?"

Alicia, still in formal robes, appeared next to BB. "The Xandarj have standard diplomatic relations with Cheell. They have a registered trade volume of twelve billion galactic credits, or GC, as most refer to them. While they are separated by significant distances, even considering jumpspace transit, this volume is insignificant. One would be led to believe there is tension between Xandarj and Cheell."

"Twelve billion galactic credits doesn't sound like nothing," Darnell said.

"How would you classify US relations with China?" Beverly had switched to another of her favorite outfits consisting of a narrow woolen pencil skirt, white blouse, and horn-rimmed glasses. To accentuate her teacher persona, she held a pointer stick and stood in the light of a projector displaying a line chart on the bulkhead.

"Uh, it's not great," Darnell said.

"In fact, trade between US and China nears a trillion US dollars annually," Beverly said, tapping the line chart. "If I normalize the graphs for differences in population and then translate dollars to galactic credits, you will notice that trade between Xandarj and Cheell is a hundredth of that between the US and China."

"Apples and oranges," Darnell said. "US doesn't have any trading partners that'll go cheap like China. Xandarj and Cheell have multiple trading partners available."

"Missing the point, Big D," AJ said.

"Which is?"

"They're not buddies. We already know the Cheell probably won't attack when we get to Xandarj. If there's tension, maybe we use that to our advantage. I'm worried about more basic things like what we're going to breathe if we actually get to a city or station. What about atmospheric pressure and gravity? Are they compatible with human survival?"

"It is reasonable to believe humans are unique," Alicia said. "That your bodies evolved to fit the planet on which you live. While that is true, it is equally true that the parameters allowing for an explosion of life on Earth are the same parameters on other habitable planets. In fact, with relatively simple adaptations, most species are able to cohabitate."

He grinned. "Sounds dirty when you say it that way."

Jayne slapped his leg, but a smile tugged her lips. "Xandarj have furred bodies. That seems like an adaptation for a colder planet."

"A good observation. Ambient temperature for artificial Xandarj structures is fifty-eight degrees Fahrenheit," Beverly said. "I'd recommend jackets. The oxygen content is akin to life at fifteen thousand feet elevation. You would adapt over time, but I have an oxygen concentrator we could manufacture to offset the difference."

"Do we have the materials?" Darnell asked.

"We do," she said.

"How much more do we know about Xandarj?" Jayne asked, settling back into the couch. "Maybe it wouldn't hurt to get to know these guys a little better. Will our translators work?"

"Both Cheell and Xandarj communicate audibly," Beverly said. "Xandarj speech closely resembles human speech and will easily translate. Cheell have percussive expressions generated by bones within their throats. While each noise is distinct, the translation is fraught with small errors."

"Good," Jayne said. "Settle in, boys. We've got a few days. We might as well get educated."

HALFWAY THROUGH THE jumpspace leg from Earth to Xandarj, AJ leaned back to look out the sole window on the starboard side of the ship. While they couldn't make out specific stars, light from outside provided significant illumination within the vessel. He startled when an object caught his eye.

"Is it weird that I can see the other ship while we're in jumpspace? Aren't we technically in a different dimension or something?"

"You can see it?" Darnell asked, crawling over totes to join him.

"Yeah, put your head on the wall and look straight back."

"Crap. Why don't they just shoot us?"

Beverly appeared in her often used, repressed schoolteacher outfit. "It is not a technicality. We are indeed in an orthogonal dimension of space. It just so happens this dimension intersects the Sol and Xandarj systems."

"Okay, then. What Darnell said."

"If the Cheell had kinetic weapons, I believe they would have already attacked," she answered. "As it is, energy in its electromagnetic form is absorbed almost instantly by the jumpspace dimension. Simply stated, lasers and advanced blaster weaponry simply do not work."

"But kinetic do?"

"As long as propulsion is not electromagnetic."

"Like guns."

Jayne stirred. "AJ, what are you thinking?"

"How tough is it to manufacture me a spacesuit?" he asked.

"AJ..." Jayne moved onto her knees and crossed the space between them.

"You cannot exit the ship safely," Beverly said. "The Cheell ship is one kilometer from our vessel. You have no mechanism for propulsion."

"And we don't have an airlock," Jayne added.

"Airlock is simple," AJ said. "We just need a cover that seals for the hatch. Give it enough structure to hold one person. I bet we could use that hull sealer to make it. We brought an extra four gallons."

"That doesn't solve propulsion," Jayne said.

"Ballistic propulsion. Modern gunpowder is self-oxidizing," Darnell said. "My .45 has a lot of force, but it might be hard to control. That .22 of AJ's would give him some nice, fine control, assuming he doesn't run out of ammo."

"That's the thing," AJ said. "I'm only limited by atmosphere. I don't need to be in a hurry. If those Cheell had some way to knock on our door, they'd have already done it. Since electromagnetic radiation is absorbed, they'd have to be looking out their window to even see my approach. Does their spaceship have windows?"

"Most spaceships of the Galactic Empire do not have transparent material," Beverly said. "It is considered an unnecessary luxury. Sensors are more than capable of transmitting external views..."

"Except in jumpspace," AJ interrupted.

She nodded. "Except in jumpspace."

AJ cackled, "Yo, ho, ho! A piratin' we will go. What about it, BB? Can you help me make a suit and an airlock?"

"It would take a considerable amount of our manufactory's resources," she said. "What you describe is within our capacity."

"Hold on," Jayne said. "You can't actually be serious. What happens when you get to that ship? What if their hatch is locked? What if they don't have anything to attack our ship, but have a weapon that could knock you out? What if you do end up getting on that ship? I doubt they're going to lie down and let you take control. They'll fight back. I don't care who they are or what they look like, a species doesn't survive without the instinct to fight."

"Doc, stick with me," AJ said, holding her arms. "I'll take Greybeard. Seamus can open any locks I need." Greybeard barked in agreement. "We're on the ropes here. Without taking a few risks, we don't have a chance. Cheell are technologically superior to us in every possible way. This is our chance to level the playing field. My little Ruger might be stone age for these guys, but darn it, it's downright advanced for aliens holding broken ray guns."

"So many things can go wrong," she lamented. "What if you miss the ship? What if your suit gets punctured? What if you run out of oxygen?"

"How about this? We'll start off with me on a tether," AJ said. "If I can get the right kind of propulsion from my .22 or Darnell's .45, we'll adjust or call it altogether. If my O2 runs short or I have some other issue, you guys can pull me back in."

"We don't have a kilometer of line," Darnell said. "I've got a couple hundred feet of paracord, but that's about it."

AJ lifted his eyebrows at her and grinned. "It'll be enough. See, we've already got a plan, Doc. No sweat."

"What you have is an idea," Jayne grumped. "What you need is a plan. There are too many problems. I don't like it."

"We've got more of a plan than most of our actions in 'Nam," he said. "About all I ever heard was, 'Hey, grab a couple of guys and go check that out.'"

"You weren't in space being chased by technologically advanced aliens."

"Okay, Doc, just talk it through while we get ready. It's good to get all the issues on the table. We'll work through things as they come up."

She frowned. "Like you'd stop if I said so."

"That's the spirit."

"REMEMBER YOUR SIGNALS," Darnell calmly instructed, testing the knot at AJ's waist. "If you feel a tug on this end, you need to respond with a tug of your own or we're reeling you back in. Two tugs means there's trouble. One tug means everything is okay. Repeated tugs are for emergencies. We won't be able to talk to you once you're outside the ship."

"Yes, Mom," AJ said, earning him a grin. The mission brief was as much to calm AJ as instruct him and both men knew it. There was something comforting about talking through the plan in a rational manner, even though what they were about to do was beyond crazy.

"Any pinch points in your suit?" Jayne asked, tugging at material that bunched around his arms.

"Nothing bad, Doc."

"I hate this, AJ," she said, leaning close to him.

"Kiss for luck?"

For an uncomfortable moment, she looked at him, an internal war obviously raging. And then, without notice, she leaned in and gave him a quick peck on his cheek – or at least that was her plan. AJ had anticipated her move and turned so her lips landed squarely on his own. Surprised, she pulled back. After a second, she pressed back in, committing to the moment.

"Oh, man. Are things getting hot in here?" Darnell asked as they separated.

AJ smiled as the kiss lingered on his lips. He didn't think of himself as overly romantic, but he'd been affected by the show of emotion much more than he'd expected.

"Be safe, Albert Jenkins," Jayne said. "I want to see you back in one piece. You understand me?"

"Uh, wow, Doc," he said. "That's what I call a good motivational speech."

"You bet your ass it was." Darnell peeled back the self-sealing fabric that would form an airlock behind his best friend.

AJ stepped into the small chamber and pulled Greybeard onto his lap, making sure the tether between them was secure. His eyes never left Jayne's. The look she was giving him had restored the feeling of purpose he'd felt at the start of this mission. "See you later, Doc," he said.

The airlock chamber wasn't large, but there was enough room for him to turn slightly and make sure everything was working properly before he opened the hatch. Beverly had manufactured two sealed roller-guide units that Darnell integrated into the airlock, one for the paracord and one for a cable long enough to swing the hatch closed in the event AJ became incapacitated. He grabbed the lock and turned the wheel. The door swung outward with a bit of force, propelling AJ and Greybeard through the opening. Apparently, there had been a small amount of atmosphere trapped inside the makeshift airlock.

AJ allowed the paracord to stop his momentum with a small jerk. He floated back toward the ship until Greybeard reached the end of his tether. Greybeard's momentum started a jerky dance between the two.

A single tug on the line communicated the only question the crew left behind wanted to know; was he still okay? AJ replied with a tug of his own, which set off another chain of events between the rope, the ship, and Greybeard.

"You ready for this, boy?" he asked, looking at the dog. Greybeard couldn't hear him, but the dog had anticipated the question and gave a quick movement of his head.

AJ played out a length of paracord and then stopped suddenly to pull Greybeard over. He'd originally intended to let the tether keep him and Greybeard together, but it was annoying to have the dog pull him back and forth. Placing the dog between his legs, he gently applied pressure so they wouldn't be separated.

"BB, you have any thoughts on this?" he asked.

"It feels quite risky," she said, floating next to him in her white Michelin-Man-shaped spacesuit.

He chuckled. "Helpful thoughts. Like what angle to aim at to get me to that ship?"

"Oh, certainly." A pair of virtual protractors appeared in front of him, bisecting each other along the top of the pistol. A red line extended from the center of each protractor showing Beverly's preferred angle. As he adjusted his aim, the red lines approached the barrel, until one of the protractors fell below it.

"That's handy. You ready?"

"Of course, AJ," she said. "Would you like to know the newtons of force expended and the anticipated arrival time?"

"Yes and no," AJ said, squeezing off a single shot. "Might be worth showing me the O_2 we have vs. flight time, though."

The bullet's mass was insignificant compared to AJ's, but its velocity was considerable. He was surprised to discover that with just a single shot, he was moving, albeit slowly, toward the Cheell vessel. Twin countdown displays appeared in his vision. At the current rate of speed, it would take three hours to arrive at the Cheell ship, and with his current oxygen consumption, he had forty-five minutes. AJ aimed and fired until his arrival time was down to fifteen minutes, his velocity just four feet per second.

Twenty seconds into the flight, he released the cord that tethered him to the ship. It caused a pang of anxiety to know he was floating in an entirely alien dimension with nothing but a .22cal pistol by which to adjust his velocity. Jayne's questions flitted through his mind. What would happen if he missed the ship? What if he and Greybeard got to the ship but couldn't enter? What if the Cheell had weapons?

He calmed himself with mission facts. He had fifteen minutes to either gain entry or head for home. Cheell probably couldn't see him. They'd likely be surprised by his entry. A surprised enemy was a weak enemy.

Staring at the ship as he slowly approached was painful. It bristled with technology, some of which had to be weaponry. "BB, are those turrets?" AJ asked. "I didn't think Galactic Empire ships were allowed guns."

"It is up to the member nations," she said. "The weapons can likely be retracted, which is not a good sign."

"Because they're going to shoot us?" AJ asked.

"Not unless you get close to the end of one of them," she said. "No, they would not have the weapons showing if they did not intend to utilize them once we enter Xandarj space."

"I thought you said they wouldn't do that."

"It was only a guess, AJ. I thought you understood that."

"Shit."

"I'm sorry. Was I not clear?"

"No, I'm good. I thought you said their weapons wouldn't work in jumpspace. What happens if we get close?"

"It takes a moment for the energy to be absorbed," she said. "If you are too close when the weapon fires we will be vaporized."

"I'm not going to slow us down before we hit," he said. "I calculate we're doing like three miles per hour. I'll just grab something."

"That is dangerous, AJ. We could bounce off and have difficulty recovering."

"I have three bullets in the chamber and I'm wearing the equivalent of oven mitts. There's too much risk that I might drop a magazine when I try to switch it out."

"I see your dilemma," she said. "If we bounce, you will be forced into this action."

"How close to the weapon for that vaporizing thing?"

"We should stay clear of the weapon turrets. Even ten feet would be uncomfortably close."

He studied the front of the Cheell ship. "Yeah, I don't know about that," he finally said. "What are the odds they'll know where we are?"

"It is a risk I would rather not take," she said. "Although, I do not believe they are tracking us."

He pulled a length of paracord from a hook on his side and unspooled it. It was a fifty-foot piece, but he'd only need about ten. Tying off one end to Greybeard's suit and the other to his own, he cut the smaller piece holding them together.

"AJ, have you considered using your remaining rounds to slow us? It would help considerably," she said. "At a minimum, you will need to utilize one for course adjustment. Our original vector wasn't perfect."

"You get one bullet, BB. I'm saving two for boarding, so make it good."

"The calculations are not difficult. Accuracy is our only foil in this."

"A craftsman doesn't blame his tools, BB."

"You can be frustrating."

"It's an art," AJ said, holding Greybeard under one arm as he aimed the pistol. The angle Beverly projected would slow and push them into the ship that was only a few yards away. "Show me where we'll hit based on angle of fire."

Beverly projected a dot on the side of the narrow, long Cheell ship. AJ adjusted his aim, targeting just ahead of a turret on the right side of the ship.

"That is dangerous. If you would just use the remaining bullets," she pushed.

He fired and then released the weapon, which was tied to his body with a short length of cord. "Greybeard, they're gonna sing songs of your bravery." Greybeard struggled in AJ's hands, attempting to turn and look at him. The vibration of the dog's barking carried through the suit. "Dog's away."

Gently, he nudged Greybeard away from his body, causing the two of them to float apart. His angle was off, and he realized his maneuver wouldn't have the effect he'd desired and instead was causing them to spin.

"BB, get me out of this," he said, trying to keep his voice level. Without being able to feel through his gloves, he found it difficult to locate the line holding the pistol and in the process, he banged the hard steel against his helmet. Fortunately, the weapon didn't discharge and the helmet didn't crack. Spinning out of control, he and Greybeard bounced off the Cheell ship's hull and headed into space. "Dammit!"

"Calm, AJ. You can do this," Beverly soothed. "Just get the weapon into your hand."

AJ struggled as the ship rotated through his vision over and over. "I got it."

"You'll have to time this, I'll give you a countdown, get your aim," she directed. "You'll need to be steady."

"How the hell am I steady? I'm spinning like a top with a dog on the other end."

"One thing at a time. Aim, steady," she said. AJ pushed away all other thoughts and focused on his weapon. Refusing to look at the orbiting ship, he aimed. "You will fire exactly at the moment I say *zero*. Grab Greybeard if you are able."

"I got it," he said and listened as she counted back. He fired the weapon and changed his course, but not Greybeard's. The two collided and AJ struggled to hold onto the dog. Somehow, his weapon had become untied and floated away. "Oh, shit!"

TEN
MAXILLARY, PAXILLARY

"You still have Darnell's weapon, AJ," Beverly reminded as he continued to flail, although much of his *bounce* inertia had been absorbed by the Cheell spacecraft. Only a couple of yards away, AJ and Greybeard were no longer tumbling in reference to the ship, but they were slowly floating away.

"I've got this," he said, spying a couple of handholds on the outside of the ship.

"Careful, AJ, we don't have an excess of oxygen," she warned.

Knowing he had few precious moments to act, AJ pushed Greybeard in the opposite direction of the ship. The action propelled him toward the ship, an action he knew would be reversed as soon as Greybeard reached the end of his line.

Beverly quickly figured out his plan and illuminated the wide handholds on the approaching ship. Just as his glove scraped across the ship's surface, the line between him and Greybeard tightened and pulled him away.

"Ah, hell," he complained, patting down his suit in search of Darnell's .45. "Give me the angles again."

Firing Darnell's .45 was surprisingly only slightly more violent than his own .22cal, even though his acceleration was considerably more. Having had one chance at the Cheell hatch, AJ knew exactly what he needed to do. This time when he splatted against the ship, he successfully looped a hand around the metal.

"This would be comical, if not for just how fragile our situation is," Beverly said, zipping between AJ and the hatch. "I believe it is appropriate to place Greybeard next to the lock and Seamus will break its cypher."

AJ placed his hand on the long-handled latch and twisted, an effort made significantly more complex under the circumstances. When the latch turned, he was satisfied to hear a surprised chirp from Beverly. "Looks like someone forgot to lock this."

"How did you know?"

"Why would anyone lock a hatch that was their only escape from a tin can of death?" he asked. "Who's gonna break in while they're sailing?"

"We are," she said as he pulled the hatch open, exposing a well-lit airlock. Unwilling to let go, AJ pushed Greybeard in ahead of him and then found a new grip inside the vessel before releasing the hatch to swing inside. "I think it's safe to say they know we're aboard."

"One thing at a time, BB," he said as he closed the hatch. "Any idea how to pressurize this thing?"

"Atmospheric controls are standard across the Galactic Empire. You simply need to press the large green button with the universal symbol for oxygen."

"This one?" The symbol on the button was a few wavy lines with some dots over them. "If you ask me, that's a symbol for carbon dioxide."

"That is the correct button," Beverly said. "I do not understand *carbon dioxide*."

AJ pushed the button and explained. "Wavy lines are beer, bubbles are carbon dioxide."

"You're baiting me."

He leaned against the interior hatch as atmosphere filled the small chamber. "Maybe a little. Can we breathe Cheell air?" Hunching, he found a transparent panel and peered through. A pair of gray-skinned aliens stood in the short adjoining hallway, staring at the hatch, sleek weapons in their hands. And while AJ couldn't hear their conversation, he was certain they were discussing what to do with him.

"Cheell air will smell slightly of sulfur. It is not toxic to humans. I will replenish your suit's oxygen reserves. It is safe to remove your helmet and suit."

"Not likely. Those skinny little bug-eyed bastards are likely to vent this airlock if we can't get it open."

"That would be extremely difficult for them. Galactic Empire ships are all equipped with safety protocols that prevent accidental depressurization when a life is present."

"How much you want to bet on that?" He was watching one of the Cheell approach the airlock. It reached out with a three-fingered hand and started tapping furiously on the panel. His ears popped as pressure rapidly dropped inside the lock.

"That is not good," Beverly said.

"Understatement. Can you talk to Seamus?"

"If you place your hand on Greybeard's suit, I can."

"Have him unlock this door." AJ placed his hand on the dog's back. Swinging around, he was startled to see two pairs of big black eyes filling the window. The aliens stared in, their faces apparently incapable of conveying emotion. "And that's not creepy as hell."

One of the aliens tapped on the window with its weapon and then pointed a single, gray finger at the hatch.

"I believe they are requesting our departure," Beverly said.

"Can Seamus unlock the door?"

"That will not help," she said. "The door is pressurized by the ship's interior atmosphere. We do not have sufficient force to move it."

"Can he?"

"You can be irritating, Albert Jenkins," Beverly said. "Yes, the door can be unlocked. Do you wish this?"

He pressed the green button and wasn't surprised when nothing happened. The alien who'd tapped on the glass a moment before, shook its head slowly. "Unlock it," AJ said, bringing Darnell's .45 up and tapping it on the glass. "What's the chance their interior glass is bullet proof?"

"AJ, I feel I must warn you that a ricochet could be fatal as we are in a small, enclosed space," Beverly said. "I do not believe Darnell's weapon would puncture the glass in a single discharge."

"Easy enough," AJ said, turning back to the exterior hatch, swinging it open.

"What are you doing, Albert Jenkins?"

He reached around to find his previous handhold on the ship, then swung himself and Greybeard outside, taking a moment to tie them both to the ship, just to be safe.

"Testing how well Cheell ships deal with explosive decompression," he said, leaning around just enough to aim the weapon at the glass on the interior panel. "I'd start running, you bug-eyed bastards!"

"They can't hear you, AJ," Beverly said.

Translucent eyelids slid down to cover the eyes of the Cheell who'd previously requested AJ's exit. After a few seconds, the lids retracted just as quickly as they'd lowered. "Yeah, but I've got him thinking."

AJ couldn't track his first shot. The recoil slapped him to the side of the ship. After regaining his equilibrium, AJ climbed over and peered into the airlock. Spiderwebs reached out from where his bullet had struck the transparent pane. The aliens could be seen running and working furiously on the other side.

"They're trying to reinforce the seal on their airlock," Beverly said.

"Say *hi* to Captain Tom," AJ said, squeezing off two more shots.

The reaction to his gunfire was immediate. Even as he was pinwheeling from the weapon's recoil, a torrent of particles exploded from the airlock door, propelled by the pressurized environment. His suit immediately started hissing.

"AJ, duct tape at the following locations," Beverly demanded, even before he regained control.

"Hang on, BB."

A steady stream of atmosphere escaped, but the holes caused by AJ's bullet were small. He swung into the airlock, careful to avoid the plume of escaping atmosphere. He dragged Greybeard with him, releasing the line that secured them both to the ship. Finding purchase on the inside wall of the hull, he unsuccessfully tried to pull the outside hatch closed.

Suddenly, the pressure abated and the hatch jerked inward with significantly reduced resistance. He twisted the multiple handles that sealed the hatch in place. "AJ, our suit is losing pressure quickly," Beverly warned.

He pulled his k-bar knife from its sheath and turned to the interior door. As he'd expected, something had been placed over the breach. He stabbed the knife through the broken window and slashed at the material on the other side. The knife hit something hard, but the damage was done. AJ's knife rocketed across the airlock and slammed into the exterior hatch followed by a stream of atmosphere, equalizing the airlock with the ship.

"US Army taught that battles are often won by the side that takes the most aggressive action, even if they're an inferior force," he said, slamming against the interior airlock door. Pulling violently on the well-marked manual latch, he was gratified when it rotated in his hand. With the atmosphere equalized, he shouldered the door open half a foot until it met resistance.

"You surprise me, Albert Jenkins," Beverly said.

He grunted as he wedged his leg into the opening. With more leverage, he pried the airlock open even further and as he did, he became aware of a mechanical alarm as well as the squawking of inhuman voices. "What are they saying?" Grudgingly, the door slid open even further and he slid through onto the main deck of the Cheell ship.

"It's mostly chaos. They're trying to figure out who will attack you," Beverly said.

Just as she said the words, a Cheell rushed forward and placed a shiny pistol-like hand weapon against AJ's shoulder and fired. Pain like nothing he'd recently experienced exploded through his arm and he lost control of every muscle in his body. He fell to the deck as Greybeard's helmet rolled across the floor and the dog latched onto the attacking Cheell's spindly arm. The crack of bone preceded a high, keening wail of pain.

"AJ, stay with us!" Beverly exclaimed, flitting in front of his fading vision. He blinked several times. It seemed like Beverly had switched into a tightly stretched, yellow bikini. A sudden jolt of adrenaline caused him to cough and he swiveled his head, only to discover she was still wearing her spacesuit.

"That's dirty pool," he grumbled as sensation returned to his extremities. "I thought their weapons didn't work in jumpspace."

"They don't," she said. "Not at any range anyway. That Cheell made direct contact. The energy dissipated after it was expelled."

A second Cheell rushed down the short hall and AJ brought his arm up. The thin alien attempted to push the same type of weapon into AJ's body, but it was clear the Cheell were no soldiers. His block dislodged the weapon and the alien flew backward. AJ used the momentary lull to gain his feet.

Greybeard was still latched onto the first alien's arm, which seemed to be bent at an odd angle as it exited Greybeard's mouth. The muscular dog was shaking its head and dragging the unconscious alien slowly backward.

"Is it dead?" AJ asked. Not waiting for an answer, he kneeled atop the second alien as it tried to scoot away. The same keening erupted. "Can you tell him to knock that shit off?"

"Your words are being translated," Beverly said. "The Cheell are not known for physical prowess. I believe they are both alive, but terror has gripped your captive."

"Got it," AJ said, grabbing his Cheell by the back of the neck and dragging it to a standing position. He kicked the Cheell's weapon back toward the airlock. "Greybeard, I think you got him good. Probably time to let go."

"Seamus says that Greybeard is not currently listening to him," Beverly said.

"Greybeard! Knock it off!" AJ bellowed. Greybeard cocked his head toward AJ and growled, not yet willing to release his grip. "Hunt!"

"Seamus has translated," Beverly said.

Greybeard opened his jaw and started to walk away only to turn suddenly and give the downed alien a nip on its side.

"I had no idea you had such an attitude, big fella," AJ said, pushing the still keening Cheell ahead of him into the T-junction of a hallway that led forward and aft. Greybeard woofed in acknowledgment and trotted aggressively next to AJ, as only a bulldog can do. "I need you to watch our backs. Don't let any of those little creeps come up on us."

"Can Seamus get us any video?" AJ asked, looking forward at a closed door he was certain was the bridge.

"There is a terminal five feet up on the left," Beverly said. "Seamus needs to access it with physical contact."

Greybeard barked and tore off toward the back of the ship. AJ spun to follow his movements and saw three of the spindly aliens, all carrying the odd weapons that had made the entire left side of his body numb, although the numbness was dissipating. A pulse of bright light shot down the hall and fire spread across his chest. The hit wasn't as bad as the first one, but the pain was intense. If he took too many of those shots, he would be disabled.

"They're firing with maximum discharge," Beverly said. "Their weapons are overloaded, but it appears they've found a way to fight back."

AJ raised Darnell's weapon with his left arm and fired three shots in quick succession. As a right-handed shooter, his accuracy was horrible. The fact that the three aliens raced at him three abreast, making themselves easy targets, however, made up for any imprecision.

His shooting wasn't great, but one bullet clipped the rightmost Cheell in the left shoulder, spinning the alien around and spraying his compatriots with viscera. He might as well have hit all three, because the group fell into chaos as they took cover in nearby rooms, yowling in pain and fear.

"Damn, now I'm embarrassed for 'em," he said. "They should've kept firing."

"The Cheell are unlikely opponents for person-to-person combat," Beverly said. "They excel as navigators and in ship-to-ship combat. They are more likely to hire mercenaries for incursions."

"And who needs a merc to hunt down a pack of raccoons, eh?"

With a still slightly-numb left hand, AJ pushed his prisoner forward to the terminal Beverly had identified. "Greybeard! Get your butt up here."

He wasn't sure the dog heard him over the commotion in the back, but soon Greybeard came rolling into the hallway, running with his uneven gate to AJ. He woofed and pushed the side of his head against the wall beneath the terminal.

"This ship carries a crew of seven," Beverly said. "We have already interacted with five of them. Two remain on the bridge. They are watching us through a video feed just as we are observing them."

"Can they hear me?" AJ asked.

"They can."

"Look, you gray bastards," he said, stalking toward the bridge hatch. "This can go hard or it can go easy. Open the door and you all get to walk away from this, no harm. Make me come in there, I'm comin' in shooting."

He tried to open the hatch and wasn't surprised when he couldn't. He walked back to the terminal and looked at the two grey-skinned aliens who appeared to be having an argument. Finally, they stopped and turned toward the camera. "You must leave our vessel.

We will desist from our pursuit. We will otherwise remove all atmosphere from this vessel and you will perish."

AJ forced the alien he'd thought was a hostage to the ground, requiring it to sit. "You hear that? Your buddies are gonna kill you if we don't leave. You good with that?"

The Cheell just looked up at him and blinked slowly, not answering.

"Are these guys slaves, BB? What do you know about Cheell hierarchy?"

"No, they are not slaves," she said. "I do not doubt the captain's sincerity, however."

He nodded and looked back at the screen. "Are you sure that's how you want to play this? I'm not sure you're gonna be heroes when you get home."

"Yes. You must leave or you will be destroyed."

"I'll remember you said that," AJ said, nodding.

"What are we doing?" Beverly asked.

"I don't think we're gonna shoot our way onto that bridge. That door looks pretty beefy."

"It is standard to secure bridges against atmospheric decompression."

"Greybeard, watch that guy a minute. If you think they're dumping atmosphere, grab your helmet, copy?" AJ asked.

He took Greybeard's single sharp bark at his back as affirmative and went back to where the three were hiding. From video information provided by Beverly, he knew the one he'd shot was in the first door on his right. He smiled when he got to the door and found it closed and locked.

He knocked his pistol on the door. "Bubba, you need to open up. Your captain says he's gonna evacuate atmosphere from the entire ship if I don't leave. That's probably not good for you and trust me, I'm not going anywhere."

Shrugging, he walked down to the next door on his left. Two Cheell sat hunched in the corner of a galley, holding a single rifle between them that was aimed at the door. "Go away," one of them managed. "We shoot."

AJ held Darnell's pistol up and waggled it, not pointing it at them. "You shoot, I get pissed. I shoot, you die. I don't want to shoot anyone, but I'm fairly sure you guys were tailing us and I need to talk to your captain in person. Did you hear what I said about him dumping atmosphere?"

"Cabin pressure is ninety percent, AJ," Beverly warned. "You need to repair your suit."

"I bet one of you is an engineer. Look at whatever you need to. The captain is bleeding off cabin pressure. He's going to kill you. Won't be me," AJ said. "I'm just going to put my suit back on and watch you guys squirm for a bit, then I'm going to figure out a way into that bridge anyway. That's just how this works."

"You will never be successful," the Cheell who'd been quiet said, almost defiantly. "The bridge is locked down and armored against such an intrusion."

"Bet your engines aren't," AJ said. "I'll just go back and start whacking on things until I get some sparks. Maybe you guys can spend a good long while in jumpspace."

"You are a monkey. You know nothing of these things."

"Finally, someone gets it right! We're monkeys, not raccoons. Can you tell someone already? Apes would be even better, but monkey is a good start," AJ said and scanned the room. His eyes lit on an expensive-looking display and he took aim with Darnell's pistol and fired two rounds into it. The sound of ricochet made him wince, but he straightened. "Now, suppose I go back and do that a couple hundred times in the engine room. I brought a lot of ammo."

"You would cause explosion. You would die."

"Monkey, remember? I'm not that smart." AJ stepped between the two Cheell and yanked away the weapon pointed at him. "I bet this little ray gun could do some damage too. How about you come with me."

Without giving the Cheell an option, AJ grabbed one by the shoulder and dragged it out of the room. It squealed in terror.

"AJ, is this necessary?" Beverly asked. "You're breaking Galactic law."

"Pretty sure I'm not," AJ said. "I'm a raccoon, or maybe a monkey. Either way, your law doesn't cover me."

"They'll kill you, AJ."

"They're trying right now, BB. They tried to kill your entire species. At some point, you've gotta decide you just don't care." He kicked in a door and was pleased to find himself in what was obviously a highly technical area, some devices familiar, most not at all. "Holy shit. Is that a carbon scrubber?" He walked over to a broad filter that sat behind a transparent panel. On the obvious outgoing side was a wide silvery plenum. Without hesitation, he slashed his knife across the material and opened a six-inch gash, causing sweet smelling air to spill into the room.

"You'll poison the entire ship!" the Cheell erupted, hitting AJ on the back with his balled-up hand. It was a pathetic move. AJ turned and lifted his pistol, taking aim at a complex-looking device of which he had absolutely no idea what it did.

"If you're an engineer, tell me what happens when a dozen ballistic loads moving at eight hundred thirty feet per second hits that thingamajig I'm aiming at."

"You'll disable the ship, it could explode," the Cheell whined.

"Damn, got it in one." AJ gloated for a moment. "So, here's the deal again. I've already got a ship. If I bust your ship, we'll be just fine. Seems like a good deal to me. Now, if you'd like me to drop you and your buddies off at the next spaceport or whatever it's called, you get me into that bridge. And you'd better hurry, because I'm starting to feel like we're getting a bit low on air."

"Captain, you will open the bridge," the Cheell said, after touching a portion of its forearm, which caused a subdermal panel to illuminate. "This monke... human is threatening to cause irreparable damage to our primary maxillary system."

AJ whispered. "I think he just said we're attacking the ship's jaw. Is that weird?"

"It is similar sounding," Beverly said. "I will adjust future translation."

"Not jaw?"

"No."

"Good."

"The human does not have access to the bridge. It is against my directive to provide this access," the captain answered.

"The paxillary system is critical, Captain," the Cheell answered.

"Seriously, you just changed the word to start with *p* instead of *m*?" AJ asked.

Beverly shrugged her shoulders apologetically.

The Cheell engineer continued, not sure what to make of AJ's rambling. "Captain, the damage would prevent us from exiting jump-space. We will become irretrievably lost."

"The human is bluffing."

AJ aimed to the left and was about to fire when a dot appeared on a cabinet slightly further to the left. "Less chance of ricochet," Beverly said.

AJ fired. "Not bluffing, guys. Bridge open, face down on deck or I blow this sucker and head to Xandarj without you."

"You would strand us?" the engineer asked.

"Actually, you've been a good guy. I'll give you a ride in our buggy, but you gotta bring your own food. We're running a little short."

The Cheell ran over to the paxillary system and drew an X with his finger. If you hit it here, you will cause a delayed reaction that will allow us to escape," it said.

"Oh, crap, that's cold," AJ said. "Captain, you getting this? Your boy here just sold you down the river."

There was a pause until finally the captain responded. "It was unexpected," it said, resignation in its voice. "Human, we will present ourselves unarmed."

ELEVEN
ELOQUENCE

AJ got the attention of the alien engineer with a sweep of his weapon, then nodded at the forward door. "You first."

"What of our agreement?" the engineer asked.

"You mean the one where you get to live and all your buddies float around jumpspace until they run out of food or atmosphere?"

"I am not sure of the translation."

"Move." AJ discovered a new doorway was open when he and his captive worked their way forward. He could see into a large room where a pair of aliens lay on stainless steel tables with a large medical-looking apparatus hung from the ceiling. Two other aliens worked feverishly on their prone shipmates.

Greybeard stood outside the doorway and barked. He knelt and placed a hand on the dog's back to facilitate communication. "What's going on?"

BB appeared, having changed into a medium-green flight suit. "Seamus says they're providing medical assistance."

He shoved the engineer into the medical bay, drawing the attention of the small aliens within the room. "I'm closing this door. I'll shoot the first person who opens it," he said, struggling to slide the partition closed. A virtual version of the door appeared next to Beverly and she demonstrated the latch he hadn't yet seen. "Thanks, BB."

"Perhaps we could consider less violent negotiation tactics," she said.

"Seems to be working for us. Greybeard, make some noise if they open that door, would you?"

Greybeard barked once and then sat on his haunches.

"I fear the reputation you are garnering," she said.

"You want to handle negotiations then?" he asked. "I'm taking their ship, but we can drop them off in Xandarj if they don't cause too many problems."

"You want to steal their ship?"

"See, you're looking at it wrong. You need to negotiate so they feel like they're trading something valuable for their ship," he said. "Like the ability to exit jumpspace and safe passage to Xandarj."

"That's coercion, AJ."

The door to the bridge was open and Cheell aliens stood just inside but visible from the hallway. Neither wore any clothing, nor did they hold any items in their hands. Together, they slowly blinked their oversized black eyes at AJ as he approached.

"Maybe let me handle this one then. I'd hate to besmirch your reputation."

"Some days you are an exceedingly difficult man," Beverly said, disappearing with an irritated pop."

"Captain," AJ said, stepping up to the threshold of the hatch leading onto the bridge. "Before I accept your surrender, my colleague has requested that I give you the first shot at negotiations."

"I do not understand," one of them said. "You boarded my vessel, assaulted my crew, and threatened to strand us in jumpspace. What is there to negotiate?"

"I'm sorry, but I gotta ask," AJ said. "Have you guys been nabbing humans from Earth? It's kind of a big thing down there. People make movies about it."

The two Cheell erupted in quiet gibberish with each other. After a couple of moments, they quieted and turned back. "Is this why you attacked our vessel?"

"No. It's just ... I saw the operating room and your guys working on the crewmember I shot. It looked like a scene from every alien abduction movie ever," AJ said. "I attacked your vessel because you tailgated us into jumpspace and I believe you're looking to do us in once we get to Xandarj."

The gibberish started again and then ended just as quickly.

"You would like to know if Cheell visited Earth and participated in the creation of fictionalized accounts of those visits?" the alien asked.

"Oh, for Pete's sake! Forget about the damn operating room. I'm sorry I brought it up."

"You're asking us to modify our memories that our shipmates were injured?"

"BB?" AJ called, his face starting to turn red.

She appeared, wearing her black robes. "Captain Snerif, your vessel was found operating illegally in the Sol system. I am prepared to report this infraction through diplomatic channels of Beltigersk, along with my observations."

"Madame 49231125-0-B, we are honored by your presence," Snerif said, blinking a couple times. "As you know, humans do not fall within the protections of Galactic Empire treaty. It is not illegal to detain humans who wander beyond their assigned territory."

"Was it your intent to detain the human vessel you are currently pursuing?" she asked.

"It may or may not have been our intent," Snerif said. "But as I have stated, if that had been our purpose, it would not have been illegal."

"You would have detained several Beltigersk if you had pursued that course of action," Beverly said.

"That would have been a grievous error on our part. We were not knowledgeable of your presence aboard the unexpectedly advanced vessel. With this knowledge, we will cease all actions that might be considered inappropriate. In a show of good faith, I would offer to escort this human vessel through Xandarj space to a port of your choosing."

"There is a matter of how my host came to enter your ship. Damage was caused. Crew were injured."

Snerif raised his hands. "My crew was not damaged beyond our ability to repair. The ship received only scratches. I would agree that these infractions could be overlooked. No actual damage was done and the mission to bring to my attention your own presence was both noble in purpose and diplomatically executed."

"It would seem we only have the remaining issue of your presence in a restricted system," she said.

"I'm afraid my crew has been under sail for many cycles and we were not properly up-to-date on these matters. I am quite grateful that you have brought this error to my attention," he said. "Since humans are not used to operating in civilized society, a gift to local representation would help to overlook this small breech of protocol."

"It is a difficult topic as my human host struggles to restrain the impulses of a violent evolution. Is there something you have specifically in mind?"

"Seriously? I'm the one with impulse control problems? This asshat was gonna pop us once we got to Xandarj," AJ growled. "I have half a mind to do the same right now."

"Just a moment, dear," Beverly said, condescendingly. "Let's see what the noble captain Snerif has in mind. Perhaps he will find a solution that is amenable to all parties."

Snerif looked from AJ to Beverly, his eyes blinking every few seconds, which was a feat given how large they were. "Perhaps a transfer of galactic credits," he said, his voice pinched.

"I was thinking something more immediate," Beverly said. "Something that is often used to limit the electronic tracing of funds transferred."

Snerif blinked and then uncharacteristically brought his three fingered hand to the back of his head, extracting a pair of narrow wires that were only an inch long. "Ten thousand?" he asked.

"A hundred," AJ said.

Beverly's eyebrows shot up and she looked back at AJ.

"No captain carries a hundred thousand credit in chits," Snerif said plainly.

"Then take up a collection," AJ said. "Look, I agreed to let BB take a run at you guys, but I'm tired of the BS. Maybe I'll ask the rest of my crew to join me and we all ride in to Xandarj together. We'll have a press conference. Talk about how you guys were part of the crew who tried to take out Beltigersk-5. I bet it'd get a helluva lot of coverage, what with a single raccoon taking down your entire crew."

"What is raccoon?" Snerif asked.

"My host does not favor how humans are viewed by the Galactic Empire. He finds it insulting, exploitive even. I'll be quite honest with you. I agree with his assessment," she said. "Our offer is one hundred thousand in Galactic Credit chits. For this, we will never speak of this incident unless it is first exposed by you or your crew."

Snerif turned to his copilot and the gibberish began again, only this time with more guttural tones and animation. It finally ended when the copilot withdrew a handful of thin wires from two separate locations on his body. Snerif collected the wires and offered them to AJ with an extended hand.

"BB, is that a hundred?" AJ asked.

"In actuality it is one hundred two thousand. It appears they did not have appropriate denominations to reach your number."

"Three fingers, I get it."

"That is actually correct," she said. "You intuited that a three-fingered species uses a trinary numbering system?"

"I count with my fingers all the time. Doesn't take a genius," he said. "How exactly am I supposed to hold these? Oh, I've got it." AJ peeled off a small piece of duct tape and pressed the wires into the glue. He then pulled back the neck of his suit and pressed the duct tape to his skin. "That's gonna hurt like a bitch coming off but at least they won't get lost."

"You will leave our vessel now?" Snerif asked.

"Get them to manufacture a fire extinguisher or something," AJ said. "I'm not doing the whole navigate-by-bullet thing again. And I want one of their ray guns."

"Have you not negotiated in good faith already?" Snerif asked.

"I forgot you could hear me," AJ said. "No problem. I'll just hang out here until we get to Xandarj. I appreciate your hospitality."

"What is this fire extinguisher device that you speak of?"

"AND THEN, AJ says, 'No, we'll need one hundred thousand credits,'" Beverly said, looking across the virtual campfire she'd projected between where Darnell, Jayne, AJ, and Greybeard were resting. "I thought Snerif was going to lose his mind right there and then."

The group laughed as much in relief at having AJ and Greybeard back as they did at Beverly's insistence at telling her side of the story over a pretend campfire.

"Did they give you an answer about the exam room?" Darnell asked. "Because I knew a guy whose buddy was taken by aliens. They totally did a number on him."

"Probes in the you-know-what?" AJ asked.

"The works."

"That's gross."

"What's the chance they'll keep their word and not blow us up as soon as we reach Xandarj?" Darnell asked.

"There is still some chance of this," Beverly said.

"What? You didn't tell me that," AJ said. "I could have tied 'em up for the rest of the trip and guaranteed one hundred percent survival."

"A necessary risk," Beverly said. "To be branded as criminals would call attention to our location. I imagine there will be a reward for our return and possibly even a bounty on Alicia's head. That we have recorded the Cheell captain admitting to crimes, he will not be quick to expose us."

"So, there is a price on our heads?" Jayne asked.

"Not so much yours," Beverly said. "There are those who would keep Alicia from arriving on Beltigersk-5 by illegal means, hence the bounty. The collection of harmless, unrecognized sentients is a low priority and would not merit special attention. If we can manage to stay out of custody of Galactic Police, our movements should not be restricted."

"But we need to fear the assassins we'll probably never see, who want to take out Alicia," Darnell said.

"At least we got this fancy little ray gun," AJ said, twirling the gun on his finger.

"Careful with that!" Darnell said. "What happened to your .22?"

"I had gloves on. You know you can't feel a gun with gloves," AJ said.

"I, for one, am very glad you three made it back in one piece," Jayne said, wrapping a hand around AJ's arm to pull him closer. "Just how much is a hundred thousand galactic credits?"

"Value of currency is difficult to communicate without reasonable exchange rates," Beverly said. "We could speak in terms of rare minerals, but gold, which trades for eighteen hundred dollars an ounce on Earth at this time, is not nearly so rare amongst space-faring nations."

"Well, how much would a decent spaceship cost?" Darnell asked. "Say, like the one those Cheell jackwagons are chasing us with?"

"Sixty million would be that vessel's basic configuration," Beverly said. "The weapons were added later as they are generally not available to non-governmental entities."

"Or pirates," Darnell said, chuckling darkly.

"And all we got was a measly hundred thousand? Wait, why do we need money? You and Alicia should be loaded with credits. She's the Beltigersk high fluffity-fluff," AJ said. "Can't you guys just buy us a new ship?"

Alicia appeared sitting atop Jayne's knee, still in her formal black robes. "Until I am recognized by the people of Beltigersk, I do not have access to national funds. My sister, Beverly as you call her, has been disassociated with financial resources, primarily because she chose to occupy an unrecognized sentient."

"You could have just said you're broke," AJ said.

"We're broke," Alicia said, humorously and disappeared.

"Wow, what's got her panties all twisted up?" Darnell asked.

"Alicia did not appreciate the level of coercion utilized with the Cheell crew. She felt the entire exercise was an unnecessary risk and beneath the diplomatic standards of the Beltigersk people," Beverly said.

"Got that when we were in 'Nam, too," AJ said. "Put a gun in a guy's hand and then act surprised when someone gets shot."

"It is a sensitive topic for Alicia. She is trying to adjust to the expectations placed on her upon her arrival."

"So, scratch off buying a ship," AJ said. "You know, if she was just going to be pissed anyway, we should have taken that Cheell ship."

"The Cheell captain would have identified it as stolen and it would have been seized at the first port of entry controlled by a member of the Galactic Empire," BB said.

"Fine," AJ said. "Wake me up when we're out of jumpspace. I'm so damn bored."

"I'M NOT sure I like the way that guy's looking at us," Darnell said, moments after transitioning from jumpspace into the Xandarj system.

Beverly projected a hologram of our small Virgin Galactic vessel in front of the much larger Cheell vessel. Instead of sailing off with its significantly more powerful engines, the Cheell ship sat in space, pointed directly at them, matching their pathetic rate of acceleration.

"Think they'd pick up on UHF?" AJ asked.

"What would you say? Sorry about the money. Please don't shoot us?" Darnell asked.

"I was thinking something like that."

Without warning, the Cheell ship peeled off, accelerating out of the virtual space Beverly provided.

"Uh oh," Darnell said as a trio of even larger vessels slid into view. The vessels lacked much in the way of aesthetics and resembled large shoeboxes with short, broad round engines strapped to the back third.

"BB, can you transmit for me?" AJ asked.

"Certainly. I suggest a certain level of diplomacy," Beverly said, switching visually to her best example of a mid-century phone operator. "Xandarj people are not known for patience. Connecting you now." She made a show of inserting a thick, silvery plug into a panel full of orifices.

"This is Earth One hailing the big three ships that just showed up outside our door," AJ said. "We're requesting safe passage to one of your fair-trade hubs or space ports. This is our first trip to Galactic Empire space, so we're not really sure what the right protocol is for this sort of thing."

"Earth One, this is Xandarj patrol." The voice was gravelly and higher pitched, like a teenage human male's might be. "Do you have any weapons to declare? Our scans can't quite make out your vessel's manufacturer of origin."

"You'll need to add Virgin Galactic to your database," AJ said. "Are you asking about personal weapons or ship weapons?"

"Weapons capable of exerting in excess of one-hundred-ninety-two thousand joules of energy."

"BB?" AJ asked. While he knew that joules was a good measure of work or energy, he had no practical reference.

"No. Darnell's firearm exerts three thousand joules. The Cheell energy weapon is capable of twenty-three thousand," she said.

"No weapons to declare," AJ said. "This old girl is pretty much held together by glue and luck at this point."

AJ's answer drew a quick expulsion of air that sounded like a laugh from the Xandarj. "Are you truly from Earth as you have identified? I feel I must inform you that Sol is a restricted zone and you could face harsh penalties for travel to and from."

"That would suck for me and a few billion of my fellow humans."

The same chuff he'd heard before was repeated, only this time louder and with repeats. The Xandarj was absolutely laughing. "Truly? This is humanity's best space faring vessel?"

"Everybody's a critic," AJ said. "We just learned about Fantastium and we're a few centuries behind. Everybody's got to start somewhere."

"Oh, don't get your nose bent," the Xandarj said. "You have to agree, it's not much to look at."

AJ muted the conversation. "Does this guy sound like any sort of official?"

"Xandarj are individualistic and temperamental. They gather in loose groups called associations," Beverly said. "You should be careful not to incite him. These appear to be patrol craft owned by Dralli Associates. They could fire upon us with few repercussions."

AJ released his finger from the mute button. "You're right. Our ship got hit by an ugly stick a few times. It's been a long trip getting here and I'm tired of smelling myself. Tell me you guys aren't some sort of nutty religious culture that doesn't like humans and don't drink beer."

"What do you know? Humans figured out jumpspace. They came here first and their first question was if we had beer. Are you sure you are not Illaden, trying to sneak into our space? I am not fooled by this low power broadcast thing so we're gonna have to board," the Xandarj answered.

"Hope you don't get claustrophobic," AJ said. "We're packed in to about forty cubic feet and not one of us has showered in nearly a month."

"I hope you're fibbing on that one," the Xandarj said. "I've had some ugly refugee pickups in the past. Hard on the olfactory."

"We don't have much of an airlock, either. Been using anti-puncture gel blankets and then we cut our way out," AJ said.

"This is a jest."

"How about this," AJ said. "Run us back to Dralli headquarters and help us crack this egg open. I'll buy every one of your crew a beer if I'm not shooting you straight."

"If you are lying and are Illaden, you'll be in much trouble," the Xandarj said. "And then I would not get my beer in the only case in which I could earn it."

"Okay, I see how you're rolling," AJ said. "Take us home, help us find accommodations where we can get cleaned up and stash our ugly ship, then we'll all go out for drinks and dinner. Assuming humans aren't on the menu, we'll buy the first round."

More laughing preceded the Xandarj's answer. "You swagger like a Xandarj. You are aware that humans have sharp teeth and lack fur on their bodies. Dralli will not fool us with elaborate costumes and grooming."

"I've got hair on my head and a bit more on my chest," AJ said. "Once you smell us you won't believe for a minute we stopped to groom. I'm telling you, I'm willing to risk it. Don't board, I'm not sure how well our makeshift airlock will handle it. If you still think we're Illaden when we get there, you can lock us in whatever hole you think makes sense."

"Your proposal is accepted," the Xandarj said and paused for a moment before continuing. "Are all humans so eloquent?"

"Oh, they only wish," AJ said.

TWELVE
HAIRLESS APES

AJ smiled broadly as communication with the large, boxy ship's captain ended. "Tell me again why we're afraid of Xandarj?"

"We are in grave danger," Alicia said, hovering unnaturally in the space between AJ, Darnell, and Jayne. "The Xandarj are a tempestuous and unstable people. Placing ourselves in their hands will certainly lead to the ruin of this mission. We should have immediately returned to jumpspace to travel to Beltigersk-5."

"Noted, your highness." AJ's voice dripped with sarcasm. "Maybe you didn't notice, but we're surrounded. Our choices are limited."

"It was you who chose, against all counsel, to come to Xandarj," Alicia snapped. "Had we chosen another direction, we would now be free to choose our destination."

Beverly appeared next to Alicia along with a small floating platform beneath their feet, complete with lifters that periodically exhausted tiny smoke rings. Unlike her sister, Beverly wore a shiny purple spacesuit that looked like it belonged in a Jetson's cartoon.

"What my sister means," Beverly said, holding out her hand to keep AJ from boiling over, "is that we will need to be careful with the Xandarj. All accounts of this species detail how they highly value individual freedoms and can be mercurial in their decision making. We will need to be careful in any negotiations. I believe we can all agree that what has transpired to this point is not reversable, so a further review is not productive."

Alicia's face turned red as she looked at her sister. "How can you? This is outrageous. I am here to rescue you. The entirety of Beltigersk society relies on our success and you're deferring to *humans*. Just look at the trouble we now find ourselves in. We're already in the custody of Xandarj. *He*," Alicia stabbed a long finger at AJ, "even offered to have us placed into custody if those unreliable apes decide we deceived them. *Which* we have!"

"Apes?" AJ asked, finding the reference ironic. "Did you just profile the entirety of Xandarj as dumb primates? Here's a news flash for you. If you keep judging people who don't meet your standards, you're not going to have any friends. Now, sit down and shut up you daffy broad."

"AJ!" Jayne snapped. "You apologize right now."

AJ glanced at Jayne and saw the fire in her eyes. Irritation coursed through his veins and he wanted nothing more than to pop Alicia off her floating platform with a finger flick.

"What? She called Xandarj apes. Why are you jumping down *my* back?"

"Because you're better than that. We don't need to resort to name calling. And that goes for you, too, Alicia," Jayne said. "If we're going to work together, we can't devolve into petty bickering."

With raised eyebrows, Alicia looked from Jayne to AJ and then back to Beverly before she simply disappeared.

"On behalf of my sister," Beverly said. "I apologize for her misspoken slight to the Xandarj. The Beltigersk people only wish peace and prosperity to the Xandarj people."

"Damn, BB, is that really how she feels about Xandarj? What about humans, then? Do you feel like that too?" AJ asked.

Beverly's platform floated closer to AJ and lowered so that they were at eye level. Her voice was soft when she asked, "AJ, do you really question how I feel about you? Do you not know that I hold you in the highest esteem? I cannot pretend to always understand your actions or even your words, but I value you both on a personal level as well as an equal member of our team."

"I know. It's just she can be infuriating," he said, sighing as his blood pressure returned to normal. "Wait, are you pumping me with dopamine right now? That's manipulation."

"Only a little and doesn't it feel good?" Beverly asked. "AJ, you're in control. I trust your instincts just as I trust Doctor Jayne's compassion and Darnell Jackson's loyalty."

"You should not use AJ's body chemistry to control him," Jayne said.

"No, Doc, it's okay. I'm calm now," he said. "You're right, I shouldn't have called Alicia names, even if she was acting like a butt."

"You do understand that is not an apology," Jayne said and then fixed her eyes on Beverly. "I need you to stop manipulating AJ. Use conversation to achieve your objectives. Humans are easily addicted and if I think that's happening, I will find a way to remove you. Are we clear?"

"Yes, Doctor Jayne. I understand your concern," Beverly answered. "The essence of Alicia's concerns remain. Xandarj are well documented as an unpredictable species."

"But you've never met one in person?" Darnell asked.

"No."

"And you're judging a couple billion Xandarj from a few reports you accessed on your special Galactic Empire database," Darnell said.

"There are more than a few reports of unpredictable behavior from Xandarj."

"Man, so much for advanced civilizations," Darnell said. "You all are as screwed up as we are."

Jayne pointed at the small window at the front of the craft. "Would you look at that."

Through the window, a huge round, white tire-shaped station appeared above the horizon of a primarily green planet that had a multitude of blue and red splotches randomly strewn across it. On AJ's HUD, Jayne projected data about both the station and planet. Xandarj-3 held the same solar position as Earth. While it was fifteen percent smaller, it had an atmosphere that closely resembled that of Earth, only with more argon and less nitrogen.

"That station is huge," Darnell said, his voice full of awe. "Am I the only one? Does that look like a big, white Michelin tire sitting on its side?"

"The Dralli faction of the Xandarj inhabit a space station of the same name. The station is home to eighty thousand souls, most of whom are native Xandarj, although there are minority populations of Rosengul, Pertaf, and even some Cheell. Overall, Xandarj are not known for speciest behavior, which should work to our benefit. I believe we have discussed the disadvantages at some length," Beverly said.

"Appreciate you recognizing that," AJ said, all traces of his earlier grumpiness having evaporated.

"Hold on," Darnell said, spinning his barber's chair so he was looking forward. "We've got an update on navigation." Straightening in his chair, he answered a communication only he could hear. "That's a good copy, Dralli Patrol captain," he said. "Will comply."

He tipped the child's fairy wand that served as a flight controller to the right and slowly rolled the makeshift spaceship to an alignment only he could see. With a sure hand, he tapped the top of the wand, causing another strand of colorful foil to fall off as he nudged the ship into compliance.

"The first thing I'm doing when we get a chance is, I'm gonna replace this flight stick," Darnell said. "It's embarrassing."

"I noticed you didn't pull off the sparkles and streamers," Jayne said. "Why is that?"

"Are you kidding? If you think I'm gonna mess with this old girl's magic fu-fu you're nuts. At least not until I can get a proper replacement," he said.

IT HAD TAKEN ALMOST three hours to negotiate the steadily increasing traffic around the massive station and Darnell's shirt was drenched with sweat as he fought the poorly tuned vessel.

"Their technology is fantastic," AJ marveled as they slowly sailed into a giant hangar inside the massive station. "I'm seeing antigrav components everywhere. Transparent bubbles of some material that can't be glass. It's got to be some sort of metal or alloy. There are a million tiny drones going everywhere at a million miles an hour. I can't fathom how they're not running into each other. And look at that tube filled with water. What happens if this place gets hit with debris? It's incredible."

His external view of the space station was cut off as Darnell guided the ship past the threshold of the hangar. "Hold onto your butts, this is gonna be a rough one," Darnell said.

A moment later, the ship slammed into the station's deck hard enough that it bounced against the artificial gravity trying to arrest its momentum. "Oh, hell," AJ complained as he was dumped from his seat and a pile of plastic tubs careened into and over him. The ship impacted the hanger deck again and a loud metal-on-metal screech ingloriously announced their arrival.

"We're full stop," Darnell sighed as he hung his head. "What were we thinking? This ship is suicidal."

"Hey, human, did you survive that?" AJ recognized the voice as belonging to the patrol ship's captain. "Hope you have some funds to repair that deck. Hangar master is already storming his way down. He's gonna want a piece of your fur."

"We're gonna try to exit. It's not gonna look pretty. We'll be unarmed," AJ said. "We're reading that our atmospheres are close enough that we'll be comfortable."

"Unarmed?" the captain asked. "That does not sound comfortable."

"No weapons," AJ quickly clarified.

"Ah, odd saying. You are not required to remove your weapons and I recommend reading about the restrictions for their legal use. Probably best if you don't shoot anyone to start with."

AJ couldn't figure if the Xandarj captain was joking or serious but decided to strap the Cheell weapon he'd commandeered on his side. It might require an explanation, but if the Xandarj searched their ship, it would be more difficult to explain later.

"We'll be right out. Close communications," AJ said. "BB, we're going to keep you guys to ourselves. If you see me doing otherwise, stop me."

"That is a wise course of action," Beverly said.

He pulled out the K-Bar knife he'd strapped to his belt and started working on the vacuum sealed exterior hatch. As before, the material attempted to flow in around the knife as he sliced it open and he had to struggle to keep the sheet separated by wrapping thin strips of tarp material around the opening.

It was anything but an elegant maneuver that saw AJ squeeze through and drop to the hangar deck. Fortunately, the ship wasn't tall and he was able to help Greybeard, Darnell, and finally Jayne through the same, tight opening.

The entire process was disorienting. Still befuddled, AJ turned to discover a small band of burly men and women who maxed out at five feet tall. Each wore a sort of uniform which was nothing more than faded olive drab coveralls with sleeves removed. More interesting, however, was the fact that their arms were covered by different lengths and colors of fur ranging from half an inch long and dirty blonde to almost an inch and a half and cobalt blue.

To an individual, the Xandarj were muscularly built but not out of proportion for humans. Their faces were human in appearance, with the exception of the matching fur taking the place of hair. In some cases, their faces were ruddy flesh tones with no fur and in others, there was a light covering.

"Well, pigs and pickled flat bugs! If you're not just a bunch of hairless apes." The male who stepped forward wasn't the tallest of the three males, nor was he the burliest. He had fine bright blue, tightly packed fur on his head and arms. His face was tanned, devoid of fur and had brilliant gray eyes that flashed in the bright light of the hangar bay.

Greybeard barked but didn't advance other than to bump into AJ's right leg, letting him know that he was all in for a confrontation if required.

"Albert Jenkins," AJ said, stepping forward and extending his hand. The move was misunderstood and four of the five Xandarj raised weapons threateningly, causing Greybeard to lunge forward, snapping but not actually attacking.

The blue Xandarj gave AJ's outstretched hand a quizzical look. "Settle down, you pack of monkeys," the Xandarj said. "That hand is as clean as a baby's ass. What's he gonna do, wipe it on me? Tell me, human, what is the meaning of this gesture?"

"It's how humans introduce themselves," AJ said. "I hold out my hand to signify that I'm unarmed and don't intend harm. I announce my name so we know what to call each other. Your response is to grab my hand gently, tell me your name and then we shake, letting people know nobody's gonna get rowdy."

"So, you're Albert Jenkins, then," the Xandarj said, carefully gripping AJ's hand. The Xandarj's skin temperature was significantly warmer than his own. "They call me Blue Tork on account of when I was born, I bit my momma when she was feeding me and got a bit of fur wrapped up around my teeth."

"So, what's it gonna be?" AJ asked. "Are you tossing us into a hole or are we getting snockered?"

"Well, you need to deal with the Hanger Master. My crew just came off shift and we'll be grabbing our pay chits for the day, which almost always leads to drinking."

"What in the blazing butt crack of Xandarj orange hind end kind of crap-toed pilot drags the bottom of their ship across my pristine flight deck?" a woman's voice bellowed from over forty yards away. "If you can't fly better than... What kind of pasted-together piece of ass-ended refuse is rusting... I can't believe I let that..."

"That's Hangar Master Mads Bazer," Blue Tork said. "She's within her rights to dress you down, so don't be drawing on her if you want to live through the storm."

It was almost more than Greybeard could take and he barked furiously at the heavyset, older Xandarj woman's approach. When she was eight feet from AJ's position, she stopped and looked the group up and down. "What in the saggy, scrubbed hind end are you?" she asked, glancing down at Greybeard and back up, only to look down again, growing more confused each time she looked. "What is that thing?"

AJ held his hands up defensively. "I'm Albert Jenkins and these are my friends, Amanda Jayne and Darnell Jackson. The short barking one is my companion, a dog, named Greybeard. We're humans. He's a canine and I apologize for the rough landing. Our ship's a little rough around the edges."

"Blazing phosphor, but that's the angriest canine I've ever seen."

It was at this point that the unexpected happened and Mads Bazer knelt on one knee and held her arms out to Greybeard. Even more remarkable was the fact that Greybeard scrabbled against the slippery deck with his claws and raced at her.

"Greybeard, no!" Jayne called after him, expecting the worst. "AJ, stop him."

"Oh, hell," AJ was already too late. He stopped a moment later when Greybeard jumped into the thickset Xandarj's open arms and half licked, half nibbled at the light grey fur on her pronounced chin.

"Hehehe," Mads Bazer cackled. "Oh, you're not so mean as you sound. Mads Bazer knows her way around an angry little monster or two."

"What in the hell, Greybeard?" AJ said, pulling up short.

Mads Bazer, stood, holding the thickly muscled bulldog in her arms. AJ looked at her with surprise as the dog was quite heavy.

"Blue Tork, explain these hairless apes," she said. "How did this *thing* even make it off planet."

"They're not apes," Blue Tork said and turned to his crew. "If you kids want to get rolling, I'll catch up to you after I let Red Fairs know we're back."

"They look like apes. No tail. No hair. Kinda skinny, maybe," Mads Bazer said.

"They're humans. Came from the restricted zone, Sol," Blue Tork said. "Not sure how they got through jumpspace, though."

"That right?" Mads Bazer asked. "You humans come from Sol?"

"Third planet, we call it Earth," AJ said. Greybeard wiggled, throwing back his head so Mads Bazer had to release him. With newfound freedom, Greybeard ran over to the broken strut that held their makeshift vessel from resting on its belly and had damaged Mads Bazer's deck. Before AJ or Jayne could stop him, he lifted his leg and relieved himself.

"Crap, sorry," AJ said. "He does that sometime. We'll get it cleaned up."

Before he'd even stopped talking, a shoebox-size contraption zipped out from a panel in the nearby wall and ran over to the spreading circle of pee.

"That's right, angry little Greybeard. That's that damn thing that scratched up my hangar," Mads Bazer said. "Eighteen hundred GC plus four hundred GC fine for not letting me know you needed assistance landing that pile of carnival dropping."

"Mads Bazer, they just came from another world that's not part of Galactic space. They might not have Galactic Credits," Blue Tork said.

"They got here, didn't they," the woman said. "I'll impound that ship until they've got the credits. No exceptions, not even for hairless apes with a sassy hound."

"Any chance you've got a place to park it for a couple of days?" AJ asked. "I'm not really sure what the protocol is for requesting that sort of thing."

She looked at the ship and appeared to be doing some calculations. "Two hundred credits a night, eight hundred credits for a full week. Add five hundred and we'll get that strut repaired. Impound adds another thousand."

Beverly appeared, sitting on Mads Bazer's shoulder, wearing a sleeveless tan jumpsuit identical to Blue Tork's. "Ask if she has a chit splitter. She should be able to extract the balance from one of your five thousand value chits. Don't let her see the twenty-five thousand value chits."

"Do you have a chit splitter handy?" he asked.

Mads Bazer's nose twitched. "Awful smart for a human who's never seen our technology."

"Never said we hadn't seen your technology," AJ said. "Look close, you see we've got Vred engines in that bird we flew in on."

"Well now, that is a mystery. Say you come from Earth, though."

"I do say that," AJ said.

"Good story in that, I'd bet. Where'd you say you were drinking tonight Tork?"

"Didn't, Bazer."

"You're a snobby blue hair. Never liked your kind. How about you? Where you drinking?" Mads Bazer asked, looking at AJ.

"We just got here. Told Blue Tork I'd buy him a drink. I figured it was only polite to let him choose where," AJ said. "Tell you what, though. If you want to get drinks another night, I'm sure we'll be open."

Mads Bazer pulled a thin device out from a strap around her wrist. "See that you do that. That'll be thirty-five hundred for the lot of it."

"Couldn't we make that more like twenty-five hundred? I'm sure your autonomous robots will fix that scratch in no time. Probably be good to let 'em run once in a while," AJ said. "I'll even throw in dinner."

"She'll never negotiate," Blue Tork said, only to be interrupted.

"Well, aren't you just an all-knowing blue fur. Maybe you could learn something from these fine hairless apes. At least they know how to treat a gray fur," Mads Bazer said. "Twenty-eight hundred, not a credit less."

AJ pulled out a five thousand credit chit and held it out to the angry grey-furred Xandarj. Without hesitation, she slipped the thin chit into a device on her wrist and then extracted it, handing it back. Virtual numbers appeared over top of the chit, showing its new value of twenty-two hundred Galactic Credits.

"Nice doing business with you, Mads Bazer," he said, nodding to her.

"I'll send a message about dinner. Be sure to bring that delightful canine along."

"Wouldn't have it any other way."

"You know you didn't need to mention the Vred engines," Blue Tork said after Mads Bazer was out of earshot. "You're wearing a Cheell blaster on your side. We already know you've got a story in you. How you came to have those things isn't anyone's business but your own. Xandarj are big on privacy."

"Is that why you didn't identify yourself when you approached our ship?"

"That is right. Now, tell me, Albert Jenkins, do humans drink fermented grains like Xandarj? Some species seem to like that, others not so much. I'm thinking that since you're basically apes, you probably do."

"Is it necessary to call us apes?" AJ asked. "Most humans don't love that reference."

"Really? Apes on Xandarj were the first sentients to evolve. They don't reproduce as fast as we do, so they kind of got pushed to the back. Highly respected amongst Xandarj."

"Maybe I need to work on my translator, then. Apes back home aren't sentient."

"So, which one of you is Amanda Jayne and which is Darnell Jackson?" Blue Tork asked.

"Call me Darnell," Darnell said, offering his hand which Blue Tork accepted and shook.

"You must be Amanda Jayne."

"Friends call me Jayne most of the time," she said, accepting Blue Tork's hand.

"Then call me Tork, since everyone else does," Blue Tork said. "Crew has a table at Bare Hiney. Remember, it is impolite to shoot someone if they haven't at least fired one over your shoulder. We'll do our best to back you, but it can get a little wild this time of night."

Jayne sighed. "Why would we expect anything different?"

THIRTEEN
LANGUAGE OF BEER

"AJ, you can't seriously be considering entering a drinking establishment with Blue Tork?" Beverly was putt-putting along in front of him with her rocket pack on as the group followed Tork through the hangar. He was having difficulty hearing her words because of the sheer amount of new technology on display and how it was utilized as if such tech was nothing special.

"Wait," he said, stopping suddenly. He turned back toward their ship.

"Did you forget something?" Tork asked.

AJ pointed over their vessel's aft at the football-field-size opening in the side of the Xandarj space station. "How is that possible? This bay is open to space. How is there pressure?" He patted down his chest as if trying to determine if he had donned a spacesuit and not noticed.

"Photonic pressure barrier," Tork said. "You don't have those?"

"No. Shit, we barely have a space station, if you could even call it that. Holy crap, how much energy does that thing use?"

"Quite a bit, but how else are we going to land ships? It's not like anyone wants to build an airlock big enough to process a whole ship. That'd take forever."

"Did you guys invent the photonic barrier or is that a Vred design?" AJ asked.

"Yup, that one is all Xandarj," Tork said. "As far as I know, it's not real complex. Like you say, though, it burns through a bunch of energy. Completely worthwhile if you ask me."

AJ shook his head in amazement. "I have so many questions."

Tork's laugh sounded like something between a growl and a choking cat. At first, AJ thought he might have caused offense and trouble was incoming, but when Tork spoke, he was a jovial as ever. "Better get 'em in quick. Big bonus for bringing in humans, we will get gonked."

"Gonked?" Jayne asked.

"Drunk," AJ filled in. Beverly's translation had so far been perfect as she substituted common phrases and speech patterns to make Tork sound as human as possible. That she missed the translation for *gonked* didn't surprise him, given her lack of experience with the subject matter.

Not far from their position, transparent twenty-foot-high doors stood open, marking the transition from the hangar bay to station. They watched with interest as Tork stuck two of his four fingers into a slot on the wall and waited patiently as a foam-like material closed over them. Just as quickly as the device had closed, it released.

"That's crap," Tork complained, turning back to them. "It says we weren't the first to bring a human vessel in."

"No bonus?" AJ asked.

"Bad bonus," Tork said. "Only five-hundred GC which includes a small commission for hangar work. Good for a shift, but bad for bonus. No complaints."

"Commission for the damage we did?" AJ asked.

"That's right, about forty-five GC."

"You get paid each shift?" Darnell asked.

"Let's walk and talk," Tork said, turning toward the open doors.

"Daily pay is pretty common around here. No sense in leaving money in the boss's hands. Isn't theirs. We earned it. And really, it's up to me to transfer it. Best to keep after it, that way if I get blasted into dust, Tonka is only out that shift."

"Tonka is your mate?" Jayne asked.

"Mate's brother."

"I don't follow," Jayne said. "Why would your mate's brother get the money you earn?"

"He's our domestic. Takes care of the little monkeys and keeps the domicile clean and full of bananas."

AJ glanced at Beverly. "I'm not sure my translator did that right. Did you say bananas?"

"That's a little specific. Our diet includes a good portion of fruit, though."

The passageway was as wide as it was tall. Instead of the solid bright white that was the paint scheme of the hangar, the walls were covered with colorful geometric patterns on a neutral beige background.

"Reminds me of an airport," Darnell quipped as they loped along behind Tork.

"You keep saying monkeys," Jayne interjected, stepping up even with Tork. "My translator could just be off, but on Earth, apes don't have tails and monkeys do."

"Good reminder," Tork said, deftly flipping a tail out from his pants. AJ tried to resist looking to see how it was attached, but failed, noticing that Tork's clothing perfectly covered the tail's exit.

"Do all Xandarj have tails?" Jayne asked, unabashedly inspecting his blue-furred tail.

"There are exceptions," Tork said. "They're all different sizes though."

"Why didn't Mads Bazer have her tail out? Or anyone else we saw in the hangar," AJ asked.

"Safety protocol," Tork said. "We're not lizards, so if you lose it, it's gone."

"Do you have good control of it?" Jayne asked. "Is it strong enough to support your body weight?"

Tork looked at Jayne and then back to AJ. "This one needs a drink," Tork said. "Amanda Jayne, I will find you a Xandarj encyclopedia and you can learn everything you want about us."

"You would do that?" Jayne asked. "Please. That would be amazing!"

"Sorry, Tork, she's just really curious," AJ said. "We're not trying to be nosey."

Foot traffic steadily increased as they walked further into the space station and the group gained more and more attention with some Xandarj simply stopping and staring at the unlikely group.

"My God," Darnell said, pulling to an abrupt stop.

At the passage's end, it joined with another hallway along the extreme outside of the station. Floor-to-ceiling transparent panels comprised the outside wall, giving the occupants a great view of the inky blackness of space crowded with bright stars. Myriad busy vessels of all sizes buzzed around, going about their duties.

"Inspiring view, Darnell Jackson. It does you credit to be inspired by the Creator's work," Tork said. "And to answer your question, Amanda Jayne, Xandarj live only for freedom," Tork said. "We believe a person should follow their passion. If learning facts about Xandarj is Amanda Jayne's passion, I would like to take part in fulfilling that path. Now, personally, I have no such interest, but I am a free Xandarj. You will get no judgement from me."

"What does that mean?" Jayne asked. "Are there Xandarj who aren't free?"

"Freedom is nobody telling me what to do. Fair pay for good work. The right to defend myself and my family from anyone who wants to do me wrong," Tork said, his hand gestures turning sharp and his tail twitching back and forth. "Basic ideas that most of the Galactic Empire understands but can't bring themselves to support. Bunch of farg-assed, loose-bowled politicians looking to make GC for selling out the people they represent. Shist, now I really need a drink."

"I didn't mean any harm," she said, nervously glancing at AJ, who had stepped between them. "I was just curious if Xandarj and humans define personal freedoms the same way."

"Damn good question too, Doc," AJ said, placing a hand on Tork's shoulder. "Sounds like Tork here is a brother-in-arms. We've got the same problems on Earth. The damn corporate types and lawyers try to hem us in and tell us what's what. Once in a while we just gotta put 'em back on their heels and by force if necessary."

Tork looked at AJ's hand on his shoulder and then up into AJ's face. "You talk like a soldier."

"All three of us were," AJ said. "Big D and I flew combat missions in a shitty little war sixty years ago. Did our country proud even though our country shit on us for it. Doc kept me and the boys alive with those magical hands of hers. She might sound like a scientist, but she's good when crap hits the fan."

"That's a good one, crap and fan." Tork's laugh sounded like a gagging heron, but it made AJ laugh all the same.

They'd been making their way around the gentle curve of the station's outer wall, which created a sort of horizon on the inside wall. As they continued down the hallway, the number of Xandarj passing them increased, just as did the ambient noise. At the end of their visual range, a small brown Xandarj suddenly came flying across the hallway, impacted the glass wall and slid to the floor. For a moment, loud music rolled down the hallway like a wave until it was momentarily lowered.

"Just what kind of bar are we talking about?" Darnell asked.

"The best kind," Tork said. "Where the drinks are cheap and the music is loud!"

"What happened to that guy?" AJ asked.

Before Tork could answer, the hallway was again filled with music and two more Xandarj, one big and the other small, were rolled out into the passageway by two large bouncers.

"Looks like they're being told to go home," Tork said. "We're getting here at just the right time. Brothers Fesk work a salvage store down in the Trailer. They're always getting into trouble. Sorry I missed it."

"Tork!" One of the two bouncers turned and looked down the hallway. Tork picked up the pace, his jog more of a skip. When he reached the very thick and almost five and a half foot tall Xandarj, they bumped forearms.

"Pankee. I can't believe I missed Brothers Fesk getting tossed," he said as AJ and the rest of the group caught up with him.

"What in Mape's hairy ass are you dragging along? Chok said you ran into some humans," Pankee said, eyeballing AJ, Darnell and Jayne, although mostly Jayne. "Are these humans?"

"Damn straight we are." AJ placed his shoulder between Pankee and Jayne and reached his hand out to the much heavier, albeit shorter Xandarj.

Pankee looked at AJ's hand and then back to Tork. "You shake it, like he's handing you a chit and trying to be secret about it. It's a human greeting." With a shrug, Pankee accepted the gesture but gave AJ a good squeeze as he did.

"Most of the time we don't try to crush the other guy's hand, though," AJ said, wiggling his fingers.

"Kind of wanted to see if you'd cry." Pankee turned his attention to Jayne. "Nobody said human women were so nice to look at. You could make some real credits dancing tonight. Want me to talk to the bosses for you?"

"No," AJ answered before Jayne managed.

"Human women do not speak?" Pankee asked, innocently.

"We do except when interrupted by over-protective human men. I do not wish to dance, Mr. Pankee," Jayne said. "And if it is of any consequence, I am rather plain looking as far as human women are concerned."

"That is not the case on Dralli station. If you change your mind, just talk to one of the beer tenders," Pankee said. "Tork, you better get her in a booth or I'll be tossing out more than Brothers Fesk tonight."

"Chok said they got a table," Tork said. "Don't suppose they got a booth."

"I didn't see," Pankee said. "Follow. I'll rearrange."

Tork gave the group a winning smile and held his hand up, with three fingers extended. "I told Chok this was gonna be a big night. Pankee's gonna get us set up."

"You should not go in this bar," BB said, appearing in front of AJ. "Xandarj are unpredictable. This is extremely dangerous, especially for Jayne."

AJ looked through BB. "I wouldn't miss it for anything! Tell me, Tork, what kind of beer do you have?"

The interior of Bare Hiney was loud and dark, with colored lights flashing randomly throughout the interior. A wave of humidity that smelled of barbeque and cinnamon met them at the door. Darnell coughed uncontrollably for a moment but stopped himself, glancing at AJ with big eyes.

"This is a lot to take in," AJ said, loudly covering for his friend. "That music is almost familiar."

"AJ! You need to listen to me," Beverly said, waving at him. "Xandarj are unpredictable. You are in danger."

"You were just kidding about needing to shoot someone, weren't you, Tork?" AJ asked.

Tork waved over his shoulder, clearly not hearing AJ's question. "Don't fall behind!" His yell was barely audible.

AJ took advantage of the noise to cover his conversation with Beverly. "Look. We need help from these guys," he said. "Tork seems like a good sort of fella and we're really hitting it off. What do you think is going to happen?"

"Thank Beltigersk!" Beverly said. "I thought I'd lost contact with you entirely. Xandarj are an unstable species. Tork could turn on you at any moment. From my analysis, their smaller bodies and warmer body temperature will be a problem with alcohol. AJ, I'm not trying to cause trouble, I'm genuinely concerned, especially for Jayne. All primates are known to make unwarranted advances on females of related species."

"Well, stay alert then," AJ said. "I'm not above staking my territory."

"Doctor Jayne is not a possession," Beverly said.

AJ felt Jayne's hand snake around his elbow as she pulled close to him. "Still feels nice to have the consideration," she said.

Pankee plowed a path through the crowded throng of dancing Xandarj. Between the speed of his movement and the poor lighting, only a few Xandarj even recognized that there was something different about the group. Arriving at a large booth, Pankee was surprisingly gentle as he offered the occupants over a hundred GC to vacate their seats.

"Remember, if you wish to dance, we will accommodate," Pankee said, pointing up at an elevated platform that was only a yard in diameter. "You would not be touched, on my honor."

"Thank you, Pankee," Jayne said, sliding into the booth.

"If not for all the Xandarj, I'd believe we were back home," Darnell shouted. Greybeard scrambled onto the narrow-cushioned chair and set his paws on the table. "Except for the no dog policy."

Two more Xandarj approached the table. AJ felt like he recognized both of them as they exchanged a few words with Tork.

"Chok wants to know what you're buying for the first round of drinks," Tork said.

Over Tork's shoulder, a narrow Xandarj looked demurely at the group and managed a smile. She had short white hair with red highlights making it almost appear pink. As she came to the front of the booth, he saw that the same fur covered her body, including most of her face.

"Why don't you pick, Chok?" AJ said. "I don't suppose we could get something to eat, too? We haven't had anything fresh for a few days."

Chok spoke quietly to Tork and he relayed the message. "She says you are pretty like a female. She says you probably can't take a strong drink. That is not supposed to be an insult, if it would be to humans."

"He's taken," Jayne responded, pulling AJ closer. "Is your hair naturally white, Chok? It looks pink with those red tips."

A loud whistle emanated from between Chok's lips as she turned to look across the floor. A harried male Xandarj nodded and pushed through the crowd toward the table.

"It is only white," Chok said, sliding into the booth. "I use a special applicator to color the tips. Are you fully mated to the pretty man or is he available to make choices?"

AJ raised an eyebrow and waited to see what her answer would be. She didn't disappoint. "Well you see, we haven't exactly gotten that far," Jayne said. "I suppose he is available to make choices."

"Whoa there, girls," AJ said, only to be interrupted by the server, which caused Tork and the other yet unnamed crewman to slide into the booth. There were now seven seated around the table and they still didn't fill the entire booth.

"Seven Marfon Ale, four jiggs, the others twicers. We'll take a platter of starch flats and veg paste and another platter of fruit. We've got important guests, so make it super fresh." Chok turned to AJ. "Do you like a protein?"

"The more proteinier the better," he said, nodding his head. "I'm a meat eater."

Something he said caused Chok to giggle and her eyelids dropped, showing pink to match her fur. "Four carobener slabs with fermented stock. That seem like enough, Tork?"

"You buying, Chok?" the server asked.

"Nope. Human treat tonight," she said and giggled again.

The server held out his wrist toward AJ.

"I don't know what to do," he confessed.

"Put your chit on the blue stripe," Tork said.

"How do I know how much it is?"

"No wrist display?" Tork asked, holding his left arm over the server's. "We'll need to fix that. One hundred twelve GC."

AJ nodded, withdrew his semi-depleted chit and placed it onto the server's wrist. The server must not have noticed until that moment the fact that AJ had five fingers and was completely hairless. "Ohh," he said, drawing a surprised gasp.

"Hey, keep it to yourself, eh?" Tork said. "We're trying to have a nice, quiet night."

"Of course, Tork Tork. I'll get your food out right away, Chok," the server said and disappeared into the crowd.

"You guys been patrolling together for long?" AJ asked, turning to Tork.

"Seven point three years," Tork answered. "Nagon just joined one point four years ago. He's the baby."

The third member of the crew looked sheepishly across the table and waved but didn't say anything.

"Seven years is a long time to serve together," Darnell said. "I've been with this jackass for almost fifty. We're not in the service anymore, but I let him come around once in a while."

"You're such a jerk," AJ said. "Big D and I met during a big war. I was his door gunner and part-time mechanic. He just flew the ship."

"Flew? Ground-based flight?" Chok asked.

"Rotors," AJ answered. "We don't have antigrav, so we have to use airfoils. Big D's bird had big old rotors that spun around and caused downdraft."

She frowned. "That is not wise. That vessel would be very unstable."

"Oh, sweetheart, those birds flew like silk over a beautiful woman's butt," Darnell said. "They had a perpendicular blade that offset the rotor's torque. Humans are good at refining technology. In the beginning, things were a little dicey, but by 'Nam we were dialed in and dangerous. Kings of the jungle."

"Your space vessel looked dangerous to operate. I would not take that into the dark of space. You were outside of specifications for that puncture lining. Is that how your *bird* looked also? Are all human vessels so dangerous?" Chok asked.

Darnell chuckled. "No, little one. That spaceship was an AJ special. We had the devil himself chasing us and were lucky to get moving when we did."

"How is it you came by a Cheell blaster?" Tork accepted the drinks from the returning server. He set four-inch-tall translucent glasses in front of AJ, Jayne, Darnell, and Greybeard.

"Probably not the best place for that conversation," AJ said. "Suffice it to say a Cheell was looking to limit my personal freedom and I offered him an alternative perspective." Tork guffawed loudly and had to set his own drink down, which was almost four times the size of AJs.

"Yes. I would very much like to hear this story, Albert Jenkins," Tork said.

"Humans have a tradition where we toast important moments. Everyone at the table should lift their drink and hold it in front of them," AJ said and was gratified when everyone did. "I dedicate this drink to the coolest cats ever to sail a Dralli patrol ship. To new friends!" He clinked his glass with Darnell and Jayne, following suit with the confused but amiable Xandarj. With the toast complete, he tipped back the liquid which was sweet and had only the smallest alcoholic burn. Figuring it was going to be a long night, he drained his glass and set it down, to the gasps of the Xandarj.

"You should be careful, Albert Jenkins," Chok said. "Marfon Ale is strong. You must build a tolerance that your body might process it. Rest your head, I will order water to offset this."

"Three percent alcohol," Beverly said, leaning against a bottle of something unknown in the middle of the table. "The fruit of the Marfon tree resembles a light blue giant grape. The drink is one of the largest exports of Xandarj. There's not much else in it."

"Three percent, Doc," AJ said, noticing that Jayne was looking suspiciously at her own drink.

"We could mix with water," Chok said. "Sometimes that is wise."

"Humans have a stronger tolerance," Jayne said, tasting the ale. "It's delicious. How unexpected. It is like a light sparkling wine."

Three large platters were set on the table with food almost overflowing the sides.

"Is this a Marfon fruit?" AJ asked, picking up a large, light-blue berry.

"Yes, bite it," Chok said. "They are delicious."

"This is a lot of food," Darnell said, accepting a plate that had long, pinkish-brown strips in the center. The serving size seemed small as most of the plate was filled with piles of leafy green vegetables and strong-smelling fermented pale leaves. "Is this the meat?"

"Yes, but I don't like it," Chok said, wrinkling her nose. "It is supposed to be good for you."

Darnell stabbed one of the strips and tasted it, grimacing as he chewed the undercooked, stringy meat. "I think I know why you don't like it," he said. "You're cooking it wrong."

"Tell me why three humans and their companion are in Dralli station," Tork said, ignoring the comment while plucking a large piece of fruit from the platter.

"Would you believe tourism?" AJ asked.

As he answered, a narrow Xandarj male approached the group, swaying dangerously and clearly drunk. He flopped his arms onto the table, burped and fixed his eyes on Jayne. "Pankee says you won't dance. I'll pay you a hundred credits right now if you just wiggle on my lap."

Unexpectedly fast, the Xandarj reached across the table, spilling drinks and plowing through the plates of food. He grabbed the lapels of Jayne's flight suit and yanked her to him, bringing his face to the side of her neck.

"Awww, shit," Darnell was heard to say.

FOURTEEN
FIGHT TO SURVIVE

With adrenaline-boosted speed, AJ's open hand shot out and caught the side of the Xandarj, knocking him back. Anger clouded his thoughts and he scrabbled onto the bench to follow through with the strike, tackling the Xandarj back into the crowd of dancers, who miraculously cleared a spot.

"Keep your hands off her!" AJ bellowed, surprised as the Xandarj rolled with him and managed to kick him over to the floor.

"AJ, we need to leave!" Beverly said, flitting in front of his face. "We're all in danger."

Gaining his feet, AJ swatted at Beverly's image.

"Hairless ape is tall but I see no muscles," the drunken Xandarj chided.

"Tork, do something," Jayne urged.

"There is nothing I can do," Tork said. "Albert Jenkins accepted Snortex's invitation to fight. I see Pankee coming. He will not allow a lethal end."

Snortex bent and did a sort of half-flip as he raced into AJ. By time he struck AJ, the only move AJ had was to lean over and wrap his arms around the Xandarj's back. AJ howled in pain as teeth bit into the side of his upper leg.

"You bastard!" he cried out as Snortex struggled in his grasp. His adversary was strong for his size and clearly dexterous. Grappling was probably AJ's best bet to end things quickly. An idea flitted through his mind and he pushed Snortex downward, bringing the Xandarj's head between his legs. The move earned him another painful bite on his inner thigh. AJ jumped back, lifting them both, and then kicked his legs out so they were perpendicular with the floor.

He recognized the danger of his maneuvers and loosened his grip on Snortex's body just before the Xandarj's head hit the bar floor. The slap of their bodies striking the sticky floor was audible enough that the crowd around them quieted. Snortex slumped in his arms and AJ let go, pushing the Xandarj's limp form away from him.

"Aw, shit," he managed, getting onto his knees, before rolling the Xandarj onto his back.

"He is unconscious, Albert Jenkins," Tork spoke into AJ's ear. "There is no honor in attacking a fallen man."

"I'm not attacking him. Jayne, help, I heard something break when we hit the floor."

"You are concerned for Snortex?" Tork asked.

"I didn't want to kill him. I just needed to back him down. Then he bit my damn leg. It pissed me off, so I might have overdone the slam."

Jayne knelt next to him. She ran her fingers along Snortex's throat, pushing against various locations as she looked back to his chest. "Got it," she said, her fingers freezing just under his chin. "He's breathing. we should get him a back board. You could have broken a vertebra."

"As amusing as it is to watch the pretty humans care for this drunk," Pankee said, dropping his massive hand onto Snortex's chest. "This one needs some fresh air."

"No!" Jayne objected, grabbing Pankee's arm. That drew an

audible gasp from the crowd. She gripped even harder. "You could kill him if he's got spinal damage."

Pankee looked at his arm where Jayne's hand rested and then at her face. "You would challenge Pankee?"

She shook her head. "I don't know what you mean. I just don't want this man hurt."

"Amanda Jayne, you should not touch Pankee," Tork said solemnly. "You have issued a challenge. Release his arm and beg that he does not accept."

"I will not!" Jayne said defiantly. "His actions could cause lifelong damage to this unconscious man. I can't let that happen. It's unconscionable."

Pankee's upper lip curled as he backhanded her, flinging her to the ground. Red rage clouded AJ's vision as he launched himself at the shorter, but considerably heavier Xandarj. Unbalanced, he twisted to gain momentum and smashed his fist into the side of Pankee's face. The pain in AJ's hand caused him to yelp even as Pankee reeled away from where he'd stood over Snortex.

"You dare!" Pankee roared.

AJ just managed to get to his feet when Pankee's two hundred ninety pounds of flailing furred arms descended on him, raining punches onto AJ's body. He tried to cover himself, but the damaging blows were furious and nonstop, driving him back into the crowd. Through blurred eyes, AJ searched for an opening, but the massive beast's attack was relentless.

"Need a boost!" AJ cried out.

"AJ, this is reckless!" Beverly argued, but the dry taste in his mouth told him that she'd complied.

With clarity that would last only moments, AJ managed to slip a few of the blows. He couldn't figure if the brute was slowing or if it was only a matter of the adrenaline surge. It didn't matter. He had to act. After a particularly brutal barrage, AJ found an opening and brought a fist into the side of Pankee's head. The blow snapped Pankee's head to the side a second time. AJ grabbed Pankee's shoulders as he brought his knee into the Xandarj's stomach and was rewarded with his opponent's cough.

He followed up his successful blows with a left roundhouse. His fist connected with Pankee's forehead and stunned the massive bouncer, causing him to stumble backward, completely unprotected. AJ bounced away on his heels, unwilling to take advantage of the boggled fighter. It was a mistake. Pankee shook his head and cleared the confusion that had rocked him.

Rage twisted every facet of the Xandarj's face as he re-entered the fight. This time when he approached AJ, he lifted AJ from his feet, tossing him to the ground with a great clatter. Quiet filled the bar. Even the music stopped playing.

"You dare come into my house and challenge the great Pankee!?" Pankee slapped his own chest and turned to the crowd, walking around with his back to AJ, who wasn't moving. "No one challenges me and lives!"

Pankee grabbed a heavy metal chair and lifted it over his head as he turned around and roared, standing over AJ. "Human weak! Pankee mighty!"

Just as the chair started its swing at AJ's unmoving form, two loud gunshots rang out and the chair toppled to the ground. "There is no honor in beating an unarmed woman or striking an unconscious man. You insult us by asking Jayne to dance for you like a whore and care nothing for the drunk who was injured. Are all Xandarj this careless with life?" Darnell asked.

"This is not about you," Pankee growled, starting toward Darnell.

"You attack my crew, you attack me," Darnell growled back. "My next shot adds a hole to that thick skull of yours, Pankee."

"What is this ruckus that has stopped the beer from flowing!?" The crowed separated as a short, fat Xandarj female waddled toward them.

"I am doing my job, Sandke," Pankee said, glowering at her.

Sandke pointed at the ceiling. "I watch everything, Pankee," she said. "I *see* everything. I *hear* everything. What is my only rule?"

"Keep the beer flowing," he answered.

"Is this *your* house, Pankee?"

"No. It is Sandke's house."

"If these pretty humans come to my house, will people come to see them?" Sandke asked.

"Yes. The hairless woman was asked to dance. She did not like it." Pankee sounded like a teenager who'd been caught out after curfew. "She attacked me. I could not allow patrons to feel Pankee was weak."

Sandke made a show of dragging her eyes across Jayne, who was now bent over AJ as he regained consciousness. "That little slip of a thing challenged the great Pankee? That is odd. From my view, this alluring vixen was tending to the slovenly Snortex. A princess caring for the ugly serf. The dreams she must have inspired, but you only felt her challenge and savaged her. You certainly won that fight, Pankee."

"Pankee is strong. I do not lose. She was weak, like the pretty male."

"The pretty male knocked you senseless and stopped. Everyone saw it, Pankee," Sandke said.

"He did not hurt Pankee."

"Your shift is ended for tonight, Pankee," Sandke said. "You will drink beer with the pretty man or you will not have a shift tomorrow. You should buy beer for the other pretty man. He did not add a new hole to your face. Perhaps you should ask him why he did not."

With Jayne's help, AJ struggled to his feet. "What in the hell happened?" he asked.

"We need to get out of here, AJ," Jayne said, trying to keep it quiet.

"Trust me on this," AJ said with a wince. Jayne held his attention for a few uncomfortable moments until they were interrupted.

"Pankee pounded you," Pankee said.

AJ wobbled and used Jayne for support. "That sounds right to me. I thought you said you were going to keep us from getting into trouble tonight."

"Pankee has a temper," the bouncer said.

"I think your name should be pancake, because that's what I feel like," AJ groaned, holding his side gingerly.

"Is pretty human not angry?" Sandke asked.

"Seems like we were just getting to know each other." AJ reached into his shirt and extracted an already depleted credit chit. "I swear I heard someone say something about drinks. How about you hand out beers until this runs out?"

"AJ, what are you doing?" Beverly asked, floating in front him. "Alcohol caused this."

Sandke plucked the chit from AJ's fingers and with sleight of hand, it disappeared. "Let the ale flow!" she shouted gleefully. Her cheer was echoed by the rest of the bar's patrons.

"WHERE WILL YOU SLEEP TONIGHT?" Tork asked almost three hours later as the group worked their way through the considerably thinned crowd.

"Come back, pretty humans," a voice called from behind them.

Another voice joined in. "We love you, pretty humans."

"I was thinking we could sleep on the ship." While he still hurt, Beverly had done wonders in repairing much of the damage to his body. The bruising across Jayne's chest and face, on the other hand, was getting worse.

"No, Tonka insists you stay with us this night. He has arranged guest pads and wishes to look after Amanda Jayne's injuries," Tork said, pushing through the bar's doors into the main hallway. Surprisingly, there was no sign of Pankee, who'd joined them for almost an hour, drinking and making conversation as if nothing at all had happened.

"That was a savage attack," Jayne said. "I had no idea he would be so quick to violence."

"Pankee is dangerous," Tork said. "I am sorry that he struck you,

Amanda Jayne. My family apologizes for the insult to your body. Albert Jenkins, you are lucky to be alive. You should have killed Pankee when you had him stunned."

"Have I made an enemy?"

"No. It was brilliant of Sandke to require him to drink with you. It was even more brilliant that you made little of the fight and purchased so much beer. Pankee would not dare cross someone who would spend so much on Sandke's beer. "How is it you no longer seem to feel pain from this fight?"

"Oh, I'm hurting," AJ said. "Pride is the only thing keeping me up right now."

"Your weapon was most impressive, Darnell Jackson," Chok said, looking at him with unabashed desire. "I have room for one more in my crash pad if you would like to discuss diplomacy of species."

Darnell chuckled. "Little Chok, you are a beautiful woman and your bed sounds like it would be warm and inviting. I, however, am married to a jealous woman who would sooner see me crippled or dead than in the arms of another. I will save us both a great deal of pain by politely declining."

"Your smooth tongue only makes me want you more, beautiful human."

"If I keep talking to you like this, there's some possibility that Lisa will send that tongue to you in the mail," Darnell said.

This seemed to get Chok's attention. "She sounds vile and vicious. Why would you burden yourself so?"

"Because I can't imagine loving anyone else as much as I love her," Darnell said, looking off wistfully.

"Aww," Chok said. "Now I would bring her to my pad also."

AJ barked a short laugh but cut himself off.

"Something you want to say about that, AJ? Remember, I'm sending video back to Lisa. I'll be sure to pass along your comments if you'd like," Darnell said.

"No, " AJ laughed. "I was just hoping I could be there when you asked Lisa if she wanted to join you and Chok."

"I never said," Darnell spluttered. "I'd never. It would never..."

"Think about it," Chok said over her shoulder as she turned down a passageway. "Tork can give you directions."

"Okay," Darnell answered, weakly waving at the petite Xandarj.

"You're so dead," AJ chuckled.

"You will *not* say anything to Lisa about that."

"Do not worry, Darnell Jackson. Chok will respect your Lisa's wishes," Tork said, leading them down the next passageway. "She is quite taken by your appearance, as were many at the Bare Hiney. Fortunately, you have shown that you are capable of defending yourselves. Word of your run-in with Pankee will spread and become something of legend."

"We'd rather be known as peaceful," Jayne said.

"We are here," Tork said. "Be prepared. Tonka has allowed my children to await our arrival, they will be quite interested to meet you. You will need to say something if you feel overwhelmed."

"How many children do you have?" AJ asked.

Tork placed his hand on a relatively nondescript door in the hallway and pushed it open. "Twelve," he said as a mass of excited, tiny Xandarj boiled out of the doorway and enveloped the group.

"Oh, my," Jayne exclaimed. "Please, my face is damaged."

"Back, you beasts," a male voice cut through the throng of excited children.

"Tonka, save the one named Jayne. She was hurt this evening," Tork called.

"Yes, you said." Tonka was roughly Tork's height but considerably thinner. He, however, took no prisoners as he peeled off the intensely curious children who had few inhibitions in meeting the new humans.

A series of loud barks and a couple of snaps of his jaw created a small amount of distance around Greybeard as one of the larger children quickly let go of the dog's tail. "Sted, behave," Tork ordered.

Wedging himself in next to Jayne, Tonka guided her inside and batted off curious fingers until the excitement died down.

"Husband, you have returned." The female Xandarj was only four feet two, shorter than Tork, and she was narrow like her brother Tonka. Like Tonka, her face was furless, but the color of her light fur was a strawberry blonde. She could pass for human except for the light blue of her eyes.

"Tork said her name is Red Fairs," Beverly said, hovering next to the pleasant looking Xandarj woman.

"Is this the Red Fairs you've told us all so much about?" AJ asked, grinning. "She is every bit as beautiful as you said, Tork. Thank you for inviting us into your home."

"Call me Fairs," she said. "Flattery is an acceptable trade for bringing my rogue home in one piece. Is it true that Pankee struck this woman who stands next to you? While tall, she is but a tiny thing. What would possess that brute to do such a thing?"

"Amanda Jayne," Jayne said, stepping around Tonka who was still fending off curious children for her. "Are you sure we aren't imposing?"

"The house is Tonka's domain. And you are most welcome," Fairs said. "He has arranged bedding for all, except perhaps the small animal that accompanies you. Is that some sort of companion? Would you be interested in receiving offers of trade?"

Greybeard, who'd already endeared himself to a trio of small female children throated a low growl, causing squeaks of concern. Recognizing his error, he quickly rubbed the side of his head against the closest child and all was forgiven.

"Does he speak?" Fairs asked, even more curious.

"Greybeard understands more than most give him credit for," AJ said. "As a crewmate, he is more than a companion."

"I did not intend to offend, small grey beast whose fur is so beautiful," Fairs said. "I would gladly brush out your coat to demonstrate my sincerity."

Greybeard snuck a long tongue out and plastered the side of one of the girl's faces in response, which sent the pile of children into a giggling fit.

"I have a salve that will help with swelling," Tonka said, holding out a short bottle with a white cream in it. "I do not understand why you are so damaged and Albert Jenkins, who battled the monster himself appears relatively uninjured."

"You should distract him, Doctor Jayne," Beverly said. "The cream will help as he has suggested and is not toxic."

"What is in this salve?" Jayne asked, turning her attention to Tonka.

"Why is it that you and your crew are here, Albert Jenkins?" Fairs asked. "Who would come through a Galactic Empire quarantine to visit Xandarj. We are hardly a preferred destination."

"Why is that, Fairs? Why are the Xandarj avoided by Galactic Empire?"

"An answer for an answer, Albert Jenkins."

"I can only tell you a small amount," AJ said. "The rest is information that endangers others."

"It is not a story you are required to tell," Fairs said. "But without information, I cannot help you. I assume that you and Tork have become friends out of necessity and opportunity."

"Careful of this one, AJ," Darnell said. "She's got a thinker on top of those shoulders."

"Truth has been spoken," Tork said. "My spouse is as direct as she is shrewd and as shrewd as she is beautiful. It is no lie that I see opportunity in your visit. Perhaps you could start with how you came into possession of a Cheell blaster and how a Cheell vessel that occupied your jumpspace left without hostile exchange."

Beverly popped up in front between AJ and Fairs. "Careful, AJ, Beltigersk has little standing with Xandarj. It is dangerous to expose our presence."

"I see," AJ said, answering them both. "Before we speak, I need to know with whom you'll share the tale?"

"Tonka, take the children to bed," Fairs said coolly.

There were complaints, but Tonka was apparently practiced at herding the energetic crowd. AJ cracked a smile as he watched

Greybeard trot after the group, his shoulder pushing into the smallest.

"Albert Jenkins, only a threat to our family or Dralli faction would prompt us share information you request to keep private. Tork brought you to my home because he believes you might have a trade that interests me. I find it best to place intent in the open so the future is not tainted by misunderstanding."

"Darnell, show them your 1911," AJ said.

Darnell pulled his gun out and dropped the magazine and cycled the chamber a couple of times, ejecting the bullet. He set the items onto a table near where Fairs stood.

"It's unarmed," Darnell said. "You can pick it up without hurting anyone."

Fairs plucked the bullet from the table, held it between her fingers and then sniffed it. "Chemical propellant?"

"Sort of," he said. "Contained explosive. We call it gunpowder. Not sure if you have the same thing."

"It is an ancient technology," Fairs said and looked to AJ. "How does this explain the Cheell?"

"Well, it started out when they hopped into our jumpspace..."

FIFTEEN
A WAY OUT

When AJ completed his story, Tork and Fairs stared at them, unable to speak. While he left out the presence of the Beltigersk, he'd spared few other details.

"You used a projectile weapon to navigate jumpspace?" Tork finally asked. "What if you had calculated wrong? You would have been lost forever."

"Would you have stopped the Cheell from firing on us in Xandarj space?" AJ asked.

"We wouldn't have been in position to do so. We would have also believed the conflict to be between the two vessels and awaited a victor."

"And then what?"

"The secondary objective of every Xandarj patrol is salvage," Tork said. "As long as you and Cheell had not attacked Dralli, we would allow the fight to conclude before stepping in."

"Okay. Now ask your question about our motives in jumpspace," AJ said.

"Desperation was your motivation," Fairs said. "It is a good story, Albert Jenkins. I believe most of what you have said. You are holding back information which is a right every Xandarj respects. Your motivations are your own. I would seek to understand what you would accomplish now that you have found safety on Xandarj. Do you plan to continue your journey with the vessel in which you arrived? Do you seek to immigrate to Xandarj?"

"Xandarj is just a waypoint. We've got places to go, people to see," AJ said. "None of us want to spend any more time in that death trap we arrived in, though."

"Ahh, you do seek trade," Fairs said.

"I think we're looking for a ship to buy or borrow."

"That is a good place to leave this evening," Fairs said, noticing that her brother had reappeared. "Tonka, can they sleep in the canopy room?"

"Yes, sister. It is prepared as you requested," he said. "Some of the children are quite excited, but sleep will find them all very soon."

"Is six hours a reasonable sleep cycle for humans?" Fairs asked.

"Yes, but I have a very personal request," Jayne said. "I noticed in your sanitary facility it looks like you have a shower. Would it be too much to request access? We have not been able to clean ourselves thoroughly for many days."

"What an interesting way to use this word *shower*," Fairs said. "You are welcome to use our bathing. Please use haste as there is a fee associated with water usage. It is reasonable, but there is no reason for waste."

"We'll be quick," Jayne said. "And I'd pay just about anything to rid myself of this stench."

"We should have tended to that first. I did not wish to insult you. As beautiful as humans are, you have developed a powerful odor. I feared it was permanent."

"I hope not," Jayne said.

Thirty minutes later, Jayne, Darnell and AJ had all cycled through the bathing unit, which was little more than a wand and powerful jets. The available soap was fairly caustic and smelled lightly of cinnamon. As each finished, Fairs' brother led them to a small room, eight feet square with a low seven-foot ceiling. Stretched between heavy hooks were two wide woven hammocks.

"Want me to bunk with Darnell, Doc?" AJ asked.

Jayne climbed into the top hammock. "If you can behave, I'd share your company," she said, surprising both AJ and Darnell.

Darnell and AJ exchanged raised eyebrows and Darnell found he couldn't let it go. "Behave. We're talking about Albert Jenkins here," he chuckled.

"Shut up," AJ said, unlacing his boots and setting them next to the entry door. Hooking his feet onto the rope ladder, he climbed up after Jayne, his body complaining with every turn. "No hanky-panky, Doc," he reassured, carefully sliding onto the surprisingly stable surface.

"Say the word, Doc, and I'll give him a swift kick down to the ground," Darnell said.

"Thank you, Darnell," she said, turning toward AJ and pulling her knees up, creating space between them. "I'm sure he'll be a perfect gentleman."

AJ sighed as he looked at the purpling bruises on her face and neck. Twice, abusive men had taken out their aggression on her while he'd failed to protect her. Anger bubbled in his stomach as he gently traced the line of the bruise on her face.

"I'm sorry this happened to you," he said, quietly.

"Why did you stay and drink with that monster?" Jayne asked. "I was terrified he was going to explode again. It was the worst night of my life."

AJ swallowed hard. She had been the perfect picture of someone who had pushed aside the large Xandarj's assault while she'd been under scrutiny. He understood that her willingness to share her feelings with him was important, but he wasn't sure how to make things right. More importantly, he wasn't sure it would ever be right. Violence happened quickly but effects were often felt for a lifetime.

"In the war, I was around people like Pankee a lot," AJ said. "They don't think like you and me. Everything is a test of machismo, a threat to who they see themselves as. If we'd run from him, we'd have sent a message that we are weak. That humans are weak."

"Message to who? That was about Pankee, not the others," she said.

"Do we really know that? How many other Xandarj think like him? If they think we're weak, they'll try to take advantage of us," he said. "I had no idea that he would respond like he did, though."

"He almost killed you, AJ," she said, tears running out on her cheeks.

"Darnell would have shot him before it came to that."

"Darnell did shoot him," Darnell's voice floated up from beneath them.

"Thanks, buddy," AJ said.

"We're in over our heads. We all know it," Darnell said. "You're one tough broad, Doc. You've really taken a beating. I'm sorry we haven't been able to protect you better."

"I'm not some weak woman," Jayne said. "We all know the risks of our mission. I just needed to understand why I had to sit and look at that monster. I wanted to scream the entire time. I've never felt so powerless in my entire life."

AJ felt a bump on the back of his leg and recognized the shape of what Darnell was pushing at him. He reached beneath the hammock and gripped Darnell's .45 caliber pistol. He checked the chamber and handed it to Jayne. "It's chambered, so don't put your finger on that trigger unless you mean it. We all saw the chunk of Pankee's shoulder that thing took off. It might take a couple of shots center mass, but he'd go down, all the same.

Jayne handed AJ her .22 and he passed it back to Darnell. "Thank you, Darnell. I'll try to give it back when I feel more in control." She turned over and spooned into AJ, going so far as to drag his arm over the top of her. AJ hugged her to his body and relaxed against the bed. It was only a few moments later that the only sounds in the room were the light snores of sleep.

WHEN AJ AWOKE, he found Jayne staring at his face, otherwise unmoving.

"Morning," he said quietly, shielding his bad breath from her.

"Darnell is already up," she said. "Tonka has breakfast for us. You won't like it. The menu is completely vegetarian, but you're not going to complain."

He grinned. "How did you sleep?" She strained forward and kissed him lightly on the forehead. He looked at her incredulously. "What was that for?"

"For being you," she said. "I slept about as well as a woman who has a damaged orbital socket can, but I felt safe."

"I wish you hadn't taken that Korgul antidote," AJ said. "I wish BB or one of her friends could help you."

"AJ, we know why we're here. I should have taken more precautions with Pankee. It was hubris that made me think he would react like a human. While I'm not sure I wouldn't have protected that fallen Xandarj, I also don't know much about their physiology. I put us at risk last night. I'll be fine after a few weeks. Pain is a tremendous instructor."

"Are *we* okay? You've been kind of distant lately."

Her smile was small. "We've both got a lifetime of baggage, AJ. Some days I want to run into your arms and have you hold me until I can't breathe."

"And the other days?"

She chuckled ironically. "I just want to be an old war buddy."

"Not likely."

"What's that supposed to mean?" she asked, irritated. "I didn't serve in the right way to be one of your buddies?"

"Whoa, hold on there, Doc. That's not it at all. Well, it is, but not like you think."

"Inform me."

"I never thought about any of my buddies from 'Nam like I do you."

"It's like that, is it?"

"What am I saying wrong? I'm trying to pay you a compliment and you're getting all huffy."

"Could you be any more dense?" she asked and climbed down from the bed.

"Probably," AJ called after her as she slammed the door behind her.

Beverly chose that moment to appear. She wore a sparkling silver spacesuit with rocket packs strapped to her back and a transparent fishbowl-styled helmet over her head. "Have you ever watched the Jetsons? I can't believe I haven't found those videos before now."

"Go away, BB," he growled as he climbed out of bed and lowered himself to the ground. He could still feel the injuries caused by the previous night's fight, but the soreness was significantly better than when he'd gone to sleep.

"Big day ahead," she said. "Darnell has been talking with Tork about going down to the Trailer, which is where Fairs works. She has a trading stand. Apparently, she's kind of a big deal."

"What are we trading?" AJ asked, opening the door Jayne had slammed. "And do you know why Jayne is pissed at me?"

"I do," Beverly said. "I believe it is best if you discover it for yourself, though."

"You girls form a club or something?"

"Something like that."

"Ah, Agee, you are awake," Tork said as AJ entered the room where they'd sat and talked the evening before.

"A. J.," AJ corrected. "And I slept like a rock. So much better than sleeping on totes and trash."

Tonka set a bowl of mushed grain covered in brilliant orange fruit in front of AJ. Next to the bowl, he set a slightly indented wooden utensil which AJ had already seen Jayne use to scoop up food.

"Tell me, A.J.," Tork said, enunciating each letter as AJ had just demonstrated. "What is this mission you have spoken about? How can Fairs' family help you become successful?"

"We need a ship," AJ said. "Either one that's fast or one that can shoot. I'd take both, but I don't think we have enough credits."

"Where will you go?" Tork asked.

"Three trips through jumpspace," AJ said. "I can't say more."

"A ship such as this is very expensive."

"How expensive?" AJ asked.

"Seven million Galactic Credits, give or take."

"Right. We don't have seven million credits."

"I suspected this would be true. Tork has a solution."

"Oh?"

"Hire Tork and Chok. We will steal a vessel from Goras."

"Who are Goras?"

"Like Dralli, they have a space station. We hate them. They steal from us all the time."

"They take your people?"

"That would create war. No, they steal our shipments. Goras are strong, Dralli are sneaky. If we take ship, a journey we would need. It is perfect."

"That's a bad idea," Jayne said. "We're not trying to attract more attention."

"Hard to disagree with that," AJ said.

"Tork and Chok are very good at this," Tonka said. "They have stolen many ships. The Goras eventually take them back, but Tork is wily and he provides much for Fairs to trade. He is good spouse."

"What happens when Goras catch you?" AJ asked.

"Goras do not catch Tork," Tork said. "That would be very bad. Tork would be taken to Goras home and put into jail. I would not like that."

"You've never been caught?" AJ asked.

"Sometimes very close," Tork said. "If we leave system it would be easy. Just need Fantastium."

"How much Fantastium could we buy?" AJ asked.

"How much credits A. J. have?"

"Twenty thousand, give or take."

"Need twice that. Maybe trade parts of ship with Fairs. Make credits and buy Fantastium," Tork said. "We should look at ship."

"Hold on, so we're doing this?" Jayne asked. "We're stealing a ship?"

"We're not doing anything right now," AJ said. "But if we can raise money by selling stuff, that might be nice to know. Maybe we could hire a ship outright instead of, you know, Tork's plan."

"That's the first sensible thing I've heard," she said.

"Keep an open mind, Doc," Darnell said. "Sometimes when you're in-country, you have to make decisions that aren't ideal."

"You too, Darnell?"

"Are we at least in agreement that we're not taking our ship anywhere?" AJ asked.

She huffed out a laugh. "There's no way I'm getting back in that thing."

"I say we take a trip down to Fairs' trailer," AJ said.

"The Trailer," Tork said. "Fairs does not own it. It is the lowest level of Dralli Station. If you have weapons, it would be best to bring them, but make sure they are not easily taken."

"Where's Greybeard?" AJ asked, only to be answered by a bark. The thickly muscled bulldog came bounding out of another room, a tiny Xandarj child riding him, wrapped around his torso.

"You want to stay here or check out the trading place, Trailer?" AJ asked. Greybeard barked twice and AJ didn't need Beverly to translate that he wanted to come along. "Looks like we're all going."

The trip through the station was much like the night before. Passageways were clean and traffic was light. Most Xandarj were curious to see the humans, but they largely gave the group a wide berth. A few stared and a periodic "pretty" or "gorgeous" comment filtered through the background noise.

"Are we really that pretty, Tork?" AJ finally asked when they stepped into an elevator.

"Pretty good looking," Tork said. "I've seen plenty of aliens. There's a bias amongst Xandarj for thinner fur and clear faces. Humans seem to take this to a considerable degree."

"Most of us anyway," AJ agreed.

"Darnell Jackson's dark skin is a very unusual trait," Tork continued. "He will need to be careful. There are many Xandarj females who could be quite aggressive for his attention."

"I'm married," Darnell said. "And she's the jealous type."

"Your wife would receive even more attention, much like Amanda Jayne did in the Bare Hiney last night. It would not be safe," Tork said as the doors opened.

A wave of humidity and warmth rolled into the elevator car, accompanied by the din of thousands of voices. For as far as the eye could see, there were booths in loosely arranged aisles. Some establishments were more substantial with wide rows of shelves full of large items and others were quite small, only a few yards in width.

"Fairs is this way," Tork said. "Stay together and don't let anyone pull you into a booth. They'll talk your ear off and you'll want to buy something just to leave."

He set off, moving into one of several wide corridors where the walkway was uninterrupted from one end of the station to the other. Unlike the other floors, there were no floor-to-ceiling walls except for a ring of station service rooms in the middle.

"How big is this place?" AJ shouted, pushing off a pair of questing hands that attempted to pull him from his group.

"The station is four point two miles in diameter," Tork said. "Fairs is only a mile from here. It is an easy walk."

The smell of roasted meat caught AJ's attention and he was almost drawn to a vendor who had several unidentifiable animals turning slowing on a spit. "What is that?"

"Buddin from the Xandarj. They are a domestic animal," he said. "The meat is not sweet, so not very tasty."

"Do they have any near Fairs' booth?" AJ asked.

"There are many vendors," Tork said. "Keep up. Many eyes."

As the group rounded the corner into another wide aisle, AJ looked over the heads of the generally shorter Xandarj packing the area. He realized they were at the front edge of a much larger group. "Now I know how it feels to be the only pretty girl in a bar." He said as something touched his butt. "Knock it off!"

"Almost there," Tork said, pointing at one of the largest booths they'd seen so far. "Fairs' staff will deal with this crowd. She sees us. Keep moving."

The sound of an electric zap preceded a yelp and pandemonium broke out. The zaps and yelps grew louder as the crowd parted, showing a group of burly Xandarj making their way toward Tork and their group.

"Shove off," urged one of Fairs' staff. "Move along," from another. The crowd thinned and the zaps and yelps slowed.

"How glorious your arrival!" Fairs said effusively, to AJ's surprise. He had expected her to be irritated at the chaos and distraction their group was causing, but she was anything but. "Our shop will be filled with the curious for many days, all hoping for eyes on humans. You bring good fortune. I thank you."

"Thanks for saving our bacon," Jayne said, putting her back to one of the many short walls in Fairs' shop.

"They grope you too?" AJ asked.

"Like a fourteen-year-old boy on his first date."

He chuckled. "Hadn't thought about it that way."

"Perhaps wear a robe. Hide pretties. You're small for Vred, but keep the hood up. Fewer pinches," Fairs said, holding out a brown robe to Jayne, who quickly pulled it around herself.

"That's nice. It's warm too," she said.

"Tork says you will trade components of your ugly ship," Fairs said. "Raise credits for Fantastium for long journey."

"We don't exactly have a replacement ship," Jayne said. "We were hoping to hire someone to take us."

"Tork and Chok take you. I will make their price not matched," Fairs said, confidently.

"But they don't have a vessel and there's no way we're taking ours. I didn't think we were going to make it to Xandarj, much less three more jumps," Jayne said.

"Fairs will think on problem," Fairs said. "Donner, robes for humans, quicks. Humans sell Earth weapons? Price good."

"Then we wouldn't have any weapons," Darnell said.

"Earth weapons loud, not strong. Collectors drool, though," she said. "Human weapons rare. Fairs take cut, four of ten."

"You mean twenty percent," AJ said. "You're not doing anything but selling."

Fairs teeth showed in a sort of grin, but no one particularly believed she was smiling. "Three and half is fair. Fairs knows market. Human lose much credits."

"And since you're willing to be honest and admit that forty wasn't fair, I'd be willing to take twenty-five percent," AJ said.

"Hold on," Darnell said. "I didn't say I wanted to sell my weapon."

"Fairs, what are we looking at for his weapon and twenty-five rounds of ammo?" AJ asked.

"Fourteen thousand credits," she said. "Perhaps more."

"What if I said we had two thousand rounds of ammunition?"

Fairs chuckled. "Human have more. Most credits is for weapon. Maybe fifteen hundred."

"Which is why twenty-five percent commission is reasonable."

"No ..., Fairs desperate. I will bend to three stones and a small piece," she said.

AJ stuck out his hand. "Thirty percent," he said. "Shake and it is done."

"Tricky, Albert Jenkins. Yes. Thirty percent."

"Hand her the gun, Big D," AJ said. Jayne pulled the gun from beneath her cloak and handed it to Fairs. "Rest of the ammo is in our ship."

"This shoot Pankee?" she asked.

"The very one."

"It has a reputation. Good for market," she said. "What other goodies for Fairs?"

"A pair of Vred engines and a manufactory?" AJ said, hopefully.

"Manufactory good. Vred engines are meh. Someone always buy, though."

"Maybe we should visit the ship," he said. "You could tell us what is valuable and not."

"Give Fairs vessel. Let Fairs sell all," she said. "My team strip and clean all. Much credits."

"Okay, but we have a few things we'd need to get first," AJ said, thinking of the hidden container of Fantastium. "We also have a smaller weapon that you might find interesting."

Darnell extracted the third .22 caliber pistol they'd brought along. "We have, what? Twenty thousand rounds for this thing?"

"I'm thinking about that."

"What about the shotgun?" Darnell asked.

AJ sighed. He hated the idea of handing it over, but they needed the money more than they needed a weapon that would weigh them down. "In the ship," he said.

"AJ, look," Jayne said, grabbing his shirtsleeve and pointing surreptitiously across the marketplace.

"Are you kidding me?" AJ asked, ducking down. "Big D, take cover."

"What is fear, Albert Jenkins?" Tork asked.

"Remember when you said you hadn't seen other humans?"

"Of course. You are the first I have met."

"Look over there, tell me what you see," AJ said.

Tork stood on a stool and scanned the crowed for a few moments. He was about to give up when he froze in place. "Three humans and six Cheell. Pankee is leading them through the Trailer. There is no concern. Aliens come to Trailer often."

"That might be, but that human has a name," AJ said. "It's Loveit. I guarantee he's looking for us. I'm gonna end this now, once and for all." AJ picked the .45 caliber 1911 from the counter and racked the slide, ejecting a bullet from the chamber.

"No, Albert Jenkins," Tork said. "Much trouble."

"That human hurt Jayne and killed one of my friends," AJ said. "I'm gonna put him down."

SIXTEEN
TRUTH AND CONSEQUENCE

"Many Cheell, they kill Albert Jenkins and friends," Tork said. "Albert Jenkins not live."

Darnell and AJ quickly donned the robes Fairs pushed at them.

"We stand out in this crowd. They won't have any more trouble seeing us than we do them," AJ said.

"Are you sure it was Loveit?" Darnell asked.

"I'm sure."

Jayne pulled on AJ's arm. "We need to get out of here."

"Not fears," Fairs said. "I have sent two to create a noises. The one called Loveit will look at noises. Pankee is good for Albert Jenkins. Pankee likes credits. Give two thousand credits and Fairs will have Pankee be poor guide."

"How can you be sure he'll honor your deal?" AJ asked, pulling out a new credit chit, this time a ten thousand denomination.

"Your Loveit will leave one day," Fairs said. "Pankee must live with Fairs each day. Pankee understands which tree drops the best fruit."

"You were talking about stealing a ship, Tork," AJ said. "Why not the Cheell ship?"

"It is under Mads Bazer's protection," Tork said. "Mads Bazer earned her name. No cross Mads Bazer."

"Is that a rule or a guideline?" AJ asked, huddling so his height wasn't so obvious.

"What are you proposing, Albert Jenkins?" Tork asked.

"Would she look the other way for Galactic Credits?"

"Oh, yes! Now, Tork understands. Not know answer, Albert Jenkins. Mads Bazer will talk if you wish."

"We need weapons," AJ said, setting the 1911 back on the counter. "Ideally, a few less lethal items and something that will put down a big ape like Pankee."

"Your Cheell weapon is very good," Fairs said. "It can change with dial. Better with HUD. Fingers slow. Make mistakes."

"Do you have two more of these?" AJ asked, unholstering the unfamiliar weapon. "What does it use for energy? Let me guess, Blastorium."

"No Cheell weapons. Not hard to find Tok weapons. Let Fairs help. You want two? Greybeard no weapon?" Fairs asked.

"Let's go with no for the moment," AJ said, eliciting a woof from the dog. "Do you have access to a vacuum suit that would fit us? Ours were makeshift."

"Please, stand talls," she said, pulling a palm-sized device from a basket that sat on a nearby shelf. With it in hand, she traced it around each of them, including Greybeard. "Fairs have measures. Fairs find suits?"

"Sure. Did I give you enough credits? How close are we getting on that chit I gave you?" he asked.

"Fairs thinks," she said, fidgeting with virtual controls that only she could visualize. "Bribe, weapons and travel suits between fourteen and eighteen thousand. Better weapons, more credits. Better suits, more credits."

"We can't afford to skimp on suits or weapons."

"Fairs use credits from Earth weapons."

"That sounds fair."

Fairs held her thumb to AJ and on a whim, he mimicked her movement, touching her thumb with his own. A small electric shock passed between them. "What was that?"

"Sealed our deal," she said, glancing at another of her staff. "My boys approach Pankee with Albert Jenkins bribe right now. Pankee will say yes."

AJ looked at Tork. "Can you get us out of here and up to see Mads Bazer? I would stop by our ship first to offload a few essential items."

"Fairs get travel suits and guns soon," Fairs said. "How big of journey Albert Jenkins take?"

"Thirty-two days."

"How soon to leave if Fairs find ships?"

"Today?" AJ asked. He looked at Blue Tork. "Do you and Chok want to come along? I'm not sure what I can pay right now, but I believe it will be worth your while."

"Tork cost two hundred credits each day. Chok cost one hundred twenty-five credits each day. Foods for seven adds sixty-five hundred. Yes. Fairs must see ship to know if Albert Jenkins has credits enough to sail the darkness," Fairs said before Tork could answer. "Take Fairs to see Earth vessel."

"With Loveit around, I'd feel better if we had weapons," Darnell said, eyeing his pistol now sitting next to Jayne's .22 caliber on a shelf.

"Fairs' girls very fast with credits," Fairs said, gesturing with her hand for one of her many workers to approach. A younger looking female came forward and set a translucent bag on a table in front of Fairs. Fairs extracted two identical weapons similar in design to the Cheell pistol, but more compact. She handed one each to Jayne and Darnell. "Weapons easy. Dial on back sets power. First notch is best. Shock no kill. Highest is for bad. Shoots far. Uses much power. Cannot use much."

"Sounds simple enough," Darnell said, eyeing the back end of the pistol and ratcheting the dial up a single notch. What Fairs didn't know was that 2F, Darnell's Beltigersk symbiote had already linked to the weapon and was displaying its status on a HUD. "You good with that, Doc?"

"I'm leaving mine on the lowest setting," she said. "I don't like the idea of hurting someone, but Pankee taught me that I cannot afford to be naive."

"Travel suits transmitted to textile manufactory. Choose pigments," she said, plucking a thick electronic pad from a nearby shelf and setting in front of AJ.

AJ pushed the tablet between Darnell and Jayne. "Just don't make me look stupid."

Darnell swiped through a number of screens. "I don't suppose you'd go for olive drab, Doc?"

"Perhaps something more like a navy blue," Jayne said. "Fairs, how tight are these suits? Are they loose like my clothing is now?"

"Travel suits are thick. Like four times fine woven cloth the pretty woman wears," Fairs said, pulling on Jayne's linen blouse. "The fit is tighter. Xandarj are easily distracted by pretties. Best for females to wear more clothes. Fairs' robes are good choice. Common in all Galactic Empire ports."

"The evolutionary similarities between human and Xandarj are remarkable," Jayne said. "Darnell, if you prefer the olive drab, that works for me."

Darnell pushed the tablet back to Fairs.

"Olive drab?" Beverly asked, facepalming as she appeared on the edge of a shelf in her silvery space suit. "You get to choose one color and you go with something that literally translates to *boring?*"

"Everyone's a critic. Can we go now? Is there anything you can do about the translation? We're getting caveman talk," AJ said, impatient to be moving after losing track of Loveit.

"Caveman?" Fairs asked.

"Sorry, I'm adjusting my translator. It's not doing a great job," AJ said.

"I thought it was cute," Beverly said, pouting.

"Unusual that you're able to modify with vocal command," Fairs said. "You're right. We should get going. I'm anxious to explore this vessel that has traveled from Earth to Xandarj."

"Much better. Trust me, Fairs, it's not much," AJ said. "I don't suppose you could bring some air freshener. We were getting pretty ripe by the end of the trip."

"Am I to understand you would have run out of supplies if you had not stopped at Xandarj?" Fairs asked, leading them through her large booth and out the back.

"No, just all the fresh stuff," Darnell said. "We're loaded with MREs. The problem is, when eating is the only thing you can look forward to every day, an MRE is hard on morale."

"M R E is a travel ration?" Fairs asked, quickly dodging behind a knot of Xandarj. "Move quickly now. The Cheell seem to have located us."

The group tightened up and struggled to keep up with the small, quick-footed Xandarj woman. On more than a few occasions, AJ found himself apologizing as he ran into the smaller Xandarjians, only to catch them by their shoulders to keep them from falling. Surprisingly, each time they looked into his face, they quickly accepted his apology and allowed him to keep moving.

"They will not follow us in here, even if they have seen us enter," Fairs said, pushing open a plain metal door at the end of one of the elevator complexes. "A vendor key is required to access the lifts utilized for heavy equipment. Step quickly now or our ruse will be for naught."

Instead of the silent, smooth operation of the elevator they'd utilized to come down to The Trailer, the equipment lift was clunky and loud.

"Fairs, tell us why your marketplace is called The Trailer," Jayne said. "In our world, a trailer is either a mobile home or an open vehicle in which items can be transported."

"It is really both," Fairs said. "When we all lived on Xandarj, traveling merchants moved between settlements with their goods inside moveable homes. These were called trailers."

"That's interesting, we had the same thing on Earth at one point," she said. "It isn't common anymore."

"It is perhaps not that unusual. What society does not require items made by others? An economy based on the value of labor creates specialization. Specialization leads to efficiency. These are basic market principles common amongst many civilizations. That it is efficient to travel with sought-after items is also common," Fairs said. "It is clear you have not been exposed to many other species. You will soon be more impressed with the differences between species more than our similarities."

"Like what?"

"Small things, Xandarj have four digits on our hands, humans have five. Our numbering systems are adapted to this. I noticed this when you spoke. Somehow your references are always ten-based. It took me a few adjustments to identify your base number, but the number of digits at your extremities was a giveaway that I should not have ignored," Fairs said. "Do you know what else I learned?"

"I have no idea," Jayne said.

"You all have translator units that are flawless," she said. "Where would humans who cannot afford a spaceship come up with something so valuable?"

"It's simple Vred tech," AJ said. "We have a manufactory. It didn't cost anything. Jayne, show her your implant."

"That is not necessary," Fairs said. "I have already guessed you are carrying Beltigersk symbiotes. It was not a difficult chain of information, mind you. The most interesting, recent news about humanity was that Korgul were found on your planet, exploiting resources. This was followed by a quarantine and then a couple of months after that, you show up in Xandarj space. It's well known that Beltigersk is at war with Korgul for their part in exposing them."

"What do you want, Fairs?" AJ asked.

"She is just showing off," Tork said. "She is the brightest merchant who always comes out on top because she knows more than her competitors."

"It is dangerous to send Tork with you," Fairs said. "You are taking him into a war zone. The Cheell have taken sides with Korgul. Now there is a human searching for you, no doubt one who is paid by enemies of your planet. While this makes me angry, I cannot help but think that you should have let us know of the dangers. I allowed you to sleep under the same canopy as my children."

"We're not trying to put you in danger," Jayne said. "We're very sorry."

"My measure of you is that you are indeed sorry," Fairs said. "It has not changed this fact."

AJ leaned over and flipped a lever that stopped the lift from moving. "I asked you what you want, Fairs," he growled. "Are you going to expose us? Sell us out?"

"Do not speak to my mate in this way, Albert Jenkins," Tork said. "I will not have her threatened."

"I'm not the one doing the threatening here."

"See, Amanda Jayne," Fairs said. "Anger and misunderstanding are common for all species."

"So is greed," Darnell said, his voice low and irritated.

"I understand the three of you participated in war on your planet," Fairs said. "Were you compensated?"

"Not very much," AJ scoffed.

"But you were paid. Why did you not provide this service for free?"

"What's your point?" AJ asked.

"I wish to speak to the Beltigersk who is of highest rank," Fairs said. "I have no quarrel with humans who I believe have noble intent. I would quarrel with Beltigersk who have not communicated what all in the Galactic community know to be true."

Alicia popped into existence, wearing her black robe. By the expression on Fairs' face, AJ knew she could see the Beltigersk's virtual avatar. "What is it you wish to discuss, Xandarj," Alicia's voice dripped with disgust.

"Did your Beltigersk tell you how they treated Xandarj only a few centuries ago? Is that why they have remained hidden or did they give you another reason?" Fairs asked.

"I'm not following," Jayne said.

"Is this necessary?" Alicia asked.

"Beltigersk once freely enslaved Xandarj because we were identified as limited sentients, much like humans are today. When the Beltigersk symbiote decided to part with their Xandarj host, it was often done in a way that left the Xandarj mentally crippled," Fairs said. "We know the Beltigersk people very well. We do not forget."

"You'll be paid handsomely," Alicia said. "Return me to Beltigersk and you will be wealthy beyond any of your peers."

"What I cannot understand is why Beltigersk aided humans when they so recently did exactly what Korgul did to my people," Fairs said. "Do you really believe your money can buy anything on Xandarj?"

"Hold on, Fairs," AJ said. "Alicia wasn't involved in what happened on Earth. It was her sister, Beverly, and a group of other Beltigersk who helped us develop a vaccine against Korgul and Beltigersk alike."

"Why would they do that? Such a vaccine would cripple their power," Fairs said.

Beverly popped in next to Alicia, also wearing her black robe. "Because there is no such thing as limited sentients," Beverly said. "It is a label, created by bureaucrats so certain populations can be taken advantage of. Not all Beltigersk embrace our legacy. Personally, I am sickened by our behavior. I brought war to my own people by my actions, but I am unapologetic. Humanity is a young species, with beautiful minds and creativity the likes not seen in the Galactic Empire for centuries. We should be uplifting them so they can embrace their potential."

"Shut up, sister," Alicia said. "The war you brought to Beltigersk has killed tens of thousands. You will be dealt with in time, but you will get me home so that I can bring peace."

"Yeah, that's pretty much a third-rail conversation," AJ said, holding up his hand. "Fairs, this is messed up, but we're just trying to get Alicia home. Beltigersk might have done some terrible things but right now, they need help. Do you really want Korgul and Cheell to eradicate them? Because that's what's on the table and without the Tok, that's exactly what would have happened. Like her or not, Beltigersk needs a leader."

"This shit sure got deep fast," Darnell said. "You do know that we've got Loveit on our tail, right?"

"No, that is not the case," Fairs said. "They are still at The Trailer, searching for you. Pankee was successful at redirecting them." She rounded on AJ. "Why was this vaccine not made public?"

"As far as I know, it was," he said. "There was an announcement made through Vred channels."

"I would know. It was not. No Xandarj would ever overlook this information. If what you say is true, this cure will be the biggest news of our generation."

"My blood!" Jayne said. "I helped develop the vaccine. I was the first test case. Find a researcher. Use my blood to develop it."

"You would submit to this?" Fairs asked.

"I'll do more than that. I remember most of the steps. Beverly, will you help recall the formula?"

"Of course."

"You. Will. Not!" Alicia said. "Have you not caused enough strife for our people? Can you not once think about something other than your petty agenda?"

"Alicia, we have no right to withhold this information from the Xandarj. Ahhhhh!" Beverly screamed as if in pain and then blinked out. A moment later, Darnell also screamed and sagged forward, but he did not fall.

Before AJ could react to the swiftly changing circumstances, Darnell drew his weapon and pointed it at the group, backing up so he could cover them all. "Weapons on the ground, now," he said.

"Big D, what's going on in there, buddy?" AJ asked, holding his hands up defensively.

"There is no Big D, there is only Alicia." Darnell's voice was strangled as he spoke.

"BB, we're going to need some help here." AJ said.

"Beverly has been deactivated, so to speak," Darnell said. "It is unfortunate that I had to eliminate 2F to take over this host, but things have gotten out of control."

Fairs glanced at AJ. "Beltigersk cannot be trusted, Albert Jenkins. Your secrets were indeed dangerous."

"You will be quiet, Red Fairs," Darnell said. "I believe I have required that you place your weapons on the ground."

"Big D, are you sure you can't hear me?"

Darnell turned to AJ and grimaced, his voice once again strangulated. "Which word in limited sentient did you find difficult to understand?"

"Damnit, Darnell! I'm so sorry," Jayne said, firing her weapon.

Chaos erupted within the lift.

SEVENTEEN
FAMILIA

"Ow!" AJ complained as a reflected bolt of energy bounced off the elevator wall and nicked his arm. Fighting Darnell had always been one of his concerns. The man was naturally strong and with a Beltigersk driving his adrenaline, it was like riding a bull to bring him down.

Fortunately, the energy bolts from Jayne's weapon sufficiently stunned Darnell so AJ was able to wrap him up. It was an age-old problem of pinning a tiger to the ground. Just exactly how did you let one up without getting mauled? As AJ struggled, Beverly appeared, hovering just above the floor of the lift, concern on her face.

"Did you fucking shoot me?" Darnell yowled, struggling against AJ and Tork.

"Who are we talking to? Angry princess or the big guy?" AJ asked.

Darnell's voice was strangled as he answered. "You cannot hold me!"

"BB, I thought Beltigersk riders couldn't take control like that," AJ said, grateful for the leverage he had on his big friend.

"It is the difference between can't and won't." Beverly had reappeared at the same time Darnell went down. "It is against everything our family holds dear to take away the free will of a sentient."

"Only huuumaaan," Darnell panted.

"Princess Alicia, you know that Mother would see you ostracized for this," Beverly said, standing next to Darnell's face, wearing her black robes.

"Why do you think I was not allowed to attend court?" Darnell asked, his voice still pinched. "I was already an outcast."

"I think the more important question is if she had anything to do with the attack on Beltigersk," AJ said.

"I will not answer to a human," Darnell spat. "That the Galactic Empire recognized Xandarj only shows they will do the same with humanity in time. Is it not offense enough that the furry monkeys of Xandarj are given trading status? Will we afford the wretched, violent humans the same rights just because they have a planet filled with riches? No! We will not stand by for this atrocity. I have sent a signal to the Cheell who lead your human traitor, Loveit, around by his leash. You will be stopped."

"We need to get him up to the ship," Jayne said. "I have vaccine shots in one of my totes."

"You have samples of the vaccine that would stop Korgul and Beltigersk alike?" Fairs asked, turning sharply toward Jayne.

"Let me speak to Fairs," Beverly addressed AJ.

"I've got this," AJ said. "Fairs, get us to our ship. We'll give you vaccine and the recipe under one condition."

"I will not hide this information from my people," Fairs said. "If you ask. I will strike you down where you stand."

For a moment, AJ wrestled with Darnell, who was attempting to make a last-ditch effort to be free. The pause gave Jayne a moment and she jumped on it. "There's no dealing to be made with the vaccine," Jayne said. "I took an oath to do no harm. If Beverly can't share the entire manufactory process, I will stay with the Dralli people and devote my life to reproducing the cure. I will only do this with the condition that the formula becomes public information to all Xandarj when it is complete."

"You would do that?" Fairs asked. "You do not seek pay?"

"Our planet was recently enslaved, Red Fairs," Jayne said, keeping her pistol aimed at Darnell. "I can't think of a more noble pursuit."

"Or maybe we give BB a chance to share the recipe," AJ grunted, still struggling with Darnell.

"I was unaware that the Vred were unsuccessful in sharing the formula," Beverly said. "I am quite willing to provide this information."

"Seriously, BB. You're doing that *thing* again," AJ complained.

"What thing?"

"Just say you're in or you're out."

"I'm in," she said. "And you can be frustrating."

"I'm not the one who didn't want to 'fess up about not being welcome on Xandarj," he said. "You might have wanted to come clean about that."

"Is he arguing with his parasite?" Fairs asked.

"We consider the Beltigersk to be symbiotes," Jayne said. "And yes, they're arguing. She says she'll provide the formulation freely."

"How will we know if it works?" Fairs asked.

"Do I have to solve every problem?" AJ asked. "You inject Darnell with it. It'll be pretty obvious if the angry princess gets ejected."

"There is a medical manufactory at the back of Mads Bazer's landing bay. It will not be difficult to test if your formula works, Beltigersk," Fairs said, distrust evident in her voice.

"What about Loveit and the Cheell?" Jayne asked. "They'll know we're coming."

"Fairs, we need to get moving now," AJ said. "We need Big D on our side, not fighting us."

"It'd be faster if we got the drugs from our ship," Jayne said.

"That is not our bargain," Fairs said. "We will know if this vaccine is real. This is how you will have our help."

"We better get moving, whatever we're doing," AJ said.

Fairs reached out and flipped a lever that caused the heavy lift to move. "I have notified Chok that we will need her help in the landing bay."

The next few minutes were filled with tension as the lift slowly climbed through the center of the Dralli space station. Finally, with a disquieting lurch, the lift stopped.

"Jayne, you need to get eyes on the bay," AJ said as Fairs opened the heavy doors. "See if you can find the Cheell."

Jayne dialed the power of her weapon up a single notch and nodded. Keeping her back to the side of the lift's walls she turned into the massive opening and scanned across the dozens if not hundreds of Xandarj peacefully going about their business.

"I don't see them," she said, then, "Shit, they just came in from the side."

"Where?" Fairs asked.

Jayne ducked and pointed at an entrance that was a hundred yards away. "There. Shit! They saw me," she whispered, harshly. "Where's that manufactory?"

"This way," Fairs said, leading them off the lift. Unfortunately, they were headed in the direction of the Cheell.

"Alicia has given our position away," Beverly said, having shifted into her silvery flight suit.

"Never trust the in-laws. She's a real piece of work," AJ said, struggling with Tork to push Darnell along.

"Transfer the formulation," Fairs said. "I have the manufactory interface up."

"BB, do it," AJ said.

"Of course I will," Beverly said, pointing her finger at Fairs and causing a virtual blue bolt of lightning to streak across and land on the woman.

"Jayne, they're getting too close," AJ said. "You need to buy us some time. Shoot Loveit!"

"They're too far away. I might hit someone else," Jayne said.

The four Cheell escorting the three humans were all fast-walking in a direct line with the medical manufactory's position. The two groups would arrive almost at the same time.

"Give up, Jenkins," Loveit shouted across the bay. "You're in over your head. Your actions are treason. If you ever loved your country, you'll stop right now!"

Jayne squeezed off a pair of shots that went high and scorched the wall ten yards over the heads of their pursuers. The action didn't slow the Cheell, but the blaster fire caused the three humans to draw and aim their own weapons.

"We're not going to make it," AJ said, shoving Darnell hard, but finding that his friend was able to resist him enough to slow them all down. "Tork, take Fairs and get out of here. You've got the formulation. Go!"

"There is no honor in that," Tork said, also struggling with Darnell.

The Cheell were generally difficult to distinguish from each other, but AJ wasn't surprised when he recognized one of them as being the traitorous engineer aboard the Cheell ship in jumpspace.

"Well, this shit's about to go south."

"You have brought much excitement. I hope you and Fairs come to an agreement. This is an exciting start to a partnership," Tork said.

"We're going to get our asses kicked," AJ said. The two groups were both within ten yards of the medical manufactory and a firefight was imminent.

"The Cheell are hesitant to fire," Tork said. "They know that Xandarj have little respect for Cheell. It would be best if Jayne did not fire again."

Fairs closed the final yards to the medical manufactory and turned her back to the approaching Cheell, even though Loveit and his thugs had their weapons drawn.

"Surrender, Jenkins," Loveit said. "No reason for this to get ugly."

"I will reward you!" Darnell squeaked.

"That's not creepy," AJ said, glancing nervously between Fairs, Loveit and the expressionless Cheell.

"We have been fired upon," the Cheell engineer said, raising a weapon similar to AJ's. "Xandarj recognize our right to respond in kind. Do you wish to receive harm?"

"Albert Jenkins, Amanda Jayne, trust Tork. Put your weapons in your belt as I have," Tork said.

"Shoot them," Darnell gurgled.

Loveit aimed and shot AJ in the abdomen. With one less person to hold him, Darnell ripped free from Tork's grasp and barreled his way through Jayne, heading toward Fairs.

"Damn," AJ groaned, grabbing his side, his weapon falling to the ground.

"I do not believe this weapon is yours," the traitor Cheell engineer said, watching AJ writhe as he scooped the weapon from the deck.

Half a dozen energy bolts impacted the ground between AJ and the Cheell, barely missing both.

"We've got company. Fall back!" Loveit called out. "This isn't over, Jenkins."

Jayne took advantage of the distraction and launched herself onto Darnell's back, wrapping an arm around his neck and her legs around his waist. The large man stumbled as he ineffectively reached for Fairs. Within seconds, he was tackled at the knees by Tork, bringing the three to the ground in a writhing pile.

Ding

The sound came from the medical manufactory and in a deft maneuver, Fairs pulled a loaded hypo medical device from the machine's delivery port. With dexterity born of small fingers, she guided what was nothing more than an advanced hypodermic needle into Darnell's side.

Darnell thrashed as Chok and a group of Xandarj, wearing Fairs' company uniforms descended on the failing expedition.

"What's wrong with my beautiful dark-colored human?" Chok asked, kneeling next to Darnell who was foaming at the mouth.

"Does this not work? Have you given me a false recipe?" Fairs asked, leaning over AJ who was starting to lose consciousness.

"Move aside, Fairs," Jayne said, coming to AJ's side. "Oh, AJ, this is bad. Loveit must have nicked your intestine."

"Good formula," AJ gurgled. "Need time. Old not permanent."

"We need a hospital, Fairs," Jayne growled, turning angrily toward the Xandarj.

"Beltigersk will heal him or Beltigersk will die," Fairs said, seemingly just as angry. "They cannot be trusted. Do not expect sympathy from Red Fairs. Beltigersk killed much family."

"Beverly, tell me what you need," Jayne said, tearing open AJ's shirt.

"Fairs needs to get a wound wrap from the manufactory," Beverly said.

"Well, hell." Darnell's low voice, while concerned was no longer strangled. "How did I get here and why does my mouth taste like chalk? Did you shoot me, Doc?" His voice rose as he seemed to recall the traumatic event.

"No time, Darnell. AJ got shot," Jayne said. "He's bleeding badly. It was Loveit."

"I hate that guy," Darnell said, moving but not trying too hard to escape Tork's grip.

Chok pulled a package from the medical manufactory and handed it to Jayne. "I do not know why Fairs is refusing to help," she said, turning back to Darnell. She stroked the side of his face with the fine white fur on her small hand. "Tell Chok why you are confused, my beautiful human."

"Speak English and don't do that," Darnell said, ineffectively pushing her hand away. "I'm serious. Lisa will kill us both."

"So you have said," Chok said. "Fairs, Darnell Jackson is of clear mind. I do not believe he is influenced by Beltigersk."

While Fairs spoke, Jayne spread the prepackaged bandage across AJ's skin, wrapping it so both the entry and exit holes were covered.

"Jayne, you must be careful," Beverly said. "Alicia could physically transfer to any being."

"What happened to 2F?" Jayne asked. "The vaccine would dislodge him also."

"Do not physically contact Darnell Jackson until Alicia is located," Beverly said, not answering but also not looking at Jayne.

"Is it true?" Fairs asked. "Has the Beltigersk been removed from Darnell Jackson?"

Jayne turned to Darnell. "Darnell, are you listening? Fairs asked you a question."

"If that's what you call it," Darnell said. "They sound like a bunch of chimps at the zoo to me."

"I definitely won't pass that along," Jayne said. "I am afraid for 2F, Darnell. Alicia took over your body. We had to hit you with the Korgul vaccine."

"He is dead, Doctor Jayne," Beverly said suddenly. "Alicia would have had to destroy him to take over Darnell Jackson the way that she did. The implications are that she might have had something to do with my mother and sisters' deaths."

"The knowledge that you have freely given this vaccine will be spread amongst the Xandarj people," Fairs said. "I cannot see you, one called Beverly, but you are welcome in my nest. Albert Jenkins, Darnell Jackson, Amanda Jayne and even Greybeard have a place beneath my canopy for as long as I draw breath."

"Can someone make me a damn translator thingamabob?" Darnell growled. "That sounded important."

"Not missing anything, buddy," AJ said. "She was just asking what kind of pizza we wanted."

"AJ!" Jayne said, scandalized. "Don't listen to him, Darnell. Fairs made an impassioned speech about how because of Beverly's gift, we're basically considered family. Did I get that right, Fairs?"

"That is correct, Amanda Jayne," Fairs said. "Chok, I will pay for Darnell Jackson's translation device."

"You can understand him?" Jayne asked.

"Yes. It is the receiver who must translate," Fairs said. "I am not so easily offended when called a chimp. They do not have tails and are not sentient, but they are overall very enjoyable creatures."

"Good. As long as this situation isn't getting any weirder," AJ said, pushing against the floor and trying to sit up. "Am I the only one who's hungry?"

"How are you recovering so quickly? Is it your symbiote?" Fairs asked.

"Thank you," Beverly said, startling Fairs. For the first time, Beverly appeared so the nearby Xandarj could see her.

"Thank you for what?" Darnell asked.

"She recognized that Beltigersk can establish symbiotic relationships with our hosts," Beverly said.

"Do you always look like a little human?" Tork asked. "You are quite enjoyable to look at."

"Man, you guys gotta put down the rose-colored, all-humans-are-pretty glasses," AJ said. "She looks like a 60's television actress in a tin foil suit. Save those compliments for a bikini."

"What is bikini?" Tork asked.

"You'll know it when you see it," AJ said. "Any idea where Loveit and his boys went?"

"Alicia is still dangerous," Jayne warned. "If she's like Thomas, it'll take her a couple of days to physically exit Darnell's body. What will stop her from jumping into a Xandarj?"

"Did we not just produce a vaccine?" Fairs asked. "Why would we not utilize it?"

"You should," Jayne said.

"You know this is all messed up, right?" Darnell asked, accepting a translator earpiece from Chok. He seemed perturbed that he had to push her hands away, but finally allowed her to push it onto the side of his ear, where it embedded itself.

"How's that, D?" AJ asked.

"Our mission was to take Alicia home. Uh, I don't know about you guys, but my thinking on that has recently changed," he said.

"Perhaps we could discuss this in a more private location," Beverly said.

"Are we still going to bribe Mads Bazer?" AJ asked.

"Seriously, which part of private are you missing?" Jayne asked.

He shrugged. "I was just wondering."

"I would like to see this vessel you arrived in," Fairs said. "I assume our previous negotiation is still valid."

"We're not sailing in that junkyard spaceship again," Jayne said. "We risked everything once. We don't need to do it again."

AJ raised his eyebrows and looked at Jayne. "Looks like that's a strong no-confidence vote."

"Tork, would you take us to this human vessel?" Fairs asked.

"Of course, but you need to send Mads Bazer a hundred credits for the blaster scorching," he said. "We don't need her to be aggravated with us."

Fairs glanced at one of her employees, who nodded knowingly.

"Don't we need to be worried about those Cheell?" AJ asked. "I mean, I know we've got them outnumbered right now, but Loveit isn't the type to let things go."

"I have closed my shop in The Trailer and twenty staff are watching us right now. This is the correct moment for that human to retreat," Fairs said.

"You never told me your girl was such a badass," AJ said, holding Tork's shoulder for support.

"That idiom does not translate well," Tork said. "At least I do not believe you desire to describe difficulty with elimination."

"It means people don't mess with her," AJ said, chuckling. "And not because of stuff sticking to her backside."

"Oh, yes. A merchant has to be strong," Tork said. "It is up to every Xandarj to protect what is theirs. Red Fairs has much to protect."

"I protect my family first of all," Fairs said. "Beverly of Beltigersk has shown herself to be my family."

"You can see his vessel over there," Tork said, as they rounded the corner of a boxy patrol ship. "Mads Bazer placed it where it would be secured."

"It is very small," Fairs said. "You traveled a great distance in this vessel?"

"It wasn't nice," Jayne said. "You smelled us. That was even after we wiped ourselves down. I don't know if I can bring myself to climb back in there. I would like my medical bag, though."

"I can get it for you, Doc," AJ said.

"Blue Tork's description of your bravery was not exaggerated," Fairs said, chuckling. "This vessel is pure madness. I question if you are in fact human or if perhaps your parents were Xandarj. No other species would risk so much to such a vessel."

"Come on, now," AJ said, defensively. "We had goo that sealed us in and those Vred engines were great. Now, the spacewalk in jump-space was a bit nutty, but the ship is solid."

"I am afraid to even consider taking pieces from it," Fairs said. "I think a collector of the unusual might pay a great sum for this historical vessel."

"I've got a couple of things I need to grab," AJ said. "And that ammunition we promised."

"Albert Jenkins we are family now," Fairs said. "I will not think badly of you nor will I change my mind as to our negotiation. What is it that you are protecting aboard this vessel? You do not need to tell me, but my curiosity burns deeply."

"Like BB said, maybe this isn't the right place for that conversation," AJ said, ducking through the opening in the side of the ship.

EIGHTEEN
TROJANS

"Fluffy angry dog," Mads Bazer said, opening up her arms and kneeling as Greybeard ran to her and alternated between barking and lapping at her face. "Why do humans visit Mads Bazer? Your fines are promptly paid. Humans are good customers."

Jayne and Darnell had gone home with Tork, Chok, and a number of Fairs' staff while AJ, Fairs, and Greybeard had gone to meet with Mads Bazer.

"Mads Bazer, greetings," Fairs said. "Albert Jenkins wishes to make private conversation."

"Mads Bazer is intrigued, but Mads Bazer has good spouse."

"BB, fix the audio, please," AJ growled under his breath.

He held his hands up defensively. "No, not that kind of deal," he said. "Could we talk somewhere quiet?"

"Yes. Mads Bazer like this group of humans. Good money. Easy dealing. Other humans angry. Like needled moths."

AJ tried to picture a moth with porcupine needles but failed. "The conversation is kind of about those other humans," he said.

"Yes. Does human drink Marfon?" Mads Bazer asked.

"That is not fair, Mads Bazer. Getting a trader drunk before a deal is an unfair advantage," Fairs said.

"Maybe you don't know much about humans," AJ said, grinning as he pulled a flask out from his robe. "Your Marfon is like water. If you ladies are looking to drink, we should do it up right."

Mads Bazer barked out a laugh. "Albert Jenkins, you had better be able to follow your words with actions. Drinking is serious business for Mads Bazer."

AJ and Fairs followed her up a long flight of stairs. At the top, they entered a wide but shallow room along the back wall of Bazer's landing bay and boasted a large window overlooking the same.

"What would Albert Jenkins say to Mads Bazer?" Bazer asked.

"Drink first?" AJ asked. "That way if you don't like what I say, you'll still have experienced an Earth drink you'd like not to miss."

Mads Bazer nodded. "Polite human," she said, opening a cupboard hanging from the back wall. Inside were plates and glasses similar those used at Tork and Fairs' home for dinner. Bazer pulled out three tall glasses. "I accept this proposal."

"Do you have anything smaller? This is not something you drink quickly. It's meant to be savored a few sips at a time."

"Very unusual," Mads Bazer said. "I am delighted by the very idea of this mystery drink."

"Humans drink several types of alcoholic beverage," AJ said. "Your Marfon Ale is closest to our beer. It's sweeter than human beer, but if I understand the fermentation process, the drink is definitely beer. I'm surprised you don't have trouble with excess carbonation."

"That is a brewer's secret," Bazer said, finding smaller glasses. She set them on a table that had no chairs near it.

AJ unstoppered his flask and poured roughly a shot into each glass. "This is called Scotch," he instructed. "It's a form of whiskey. The best Scotch is old, fifteen years or better, but that age makes it expensive. This is a five-year Scotch. It's a compromise between cost and taste."

AJ pushed the glasses to Fairs and Mads Bazer, keeping one for himself. Mads Bazer picked hers up and sniffed deeply. "Is this straight alcohol?" she asked, her eyes blinking as they watered. "But no, only now do I smell things beyond that. You humans drink this?"

"If the drink is sufficiently refined." AJ picked up his glass and gave the amber liquid a quick spin in the glass. "Some people like to have ice with their Scotch which waters down the bite a little and leaves an amazing taste behind on the ice – sort of like getting a double treat. I'm more of a neat guy, which means no ice."

He tipped back his glass and allowed the Scotch to tumble over his lips onto his tongue. The familiar burn warmed his throat as he swallowed and relished the taste.

Mads Bazer squinted her eyes and followed suit, taking the entire shot into her mouth. She clamped her hand over her mouth and her eyes shot open as she swallowed and then howled. "It's like drinking fire!" she exclaimed. "How can any civilized being drink that?"

AJ pointed to his glass. "Remember when I said sip?"

"It burns!"

"That'll go away," AJ said. "Try to enjoy the flavor. Don't focus on the pain."

Fairs looked skeptically at the drink and then tasted a small amount, smacking her lips uncomfortably. "That is very strong."

"I feel as if I've been drinking ale all evening," Bazer said. "With such a small drink, how is this possible?"

"Maybe you should eat something," AJ said. "Clear your head."

"Why would I do that? It is like Greybeard. Angry and loving at the same moment. Are you here to sell this to Mads Bazer? Tell me what you must have," she said.

AJ looked at his pint-sized flask and pursed his lips. He'd intended to just break the ice with the alcohol. He sighed, knowing what needed to be done. He slid the flask across the table to Mads Bazer.

"For agreeing to talk to me and hear me out, I'm giving you this flask of Scotch," AJ said. "Regardless of how things go, the Scotch is yours."

"I will not make a bad deal because of your Scotch," Mads Bazer said, looking at the flask wantonly. He wasn't sure her words were completely accurate.

"I want to steal the ship the humans arrived in," AJ said. "Their leader, Loveit, attacked us on Earth and now he's attacked us here in Dralli. I want his ship."

"It is under Mads Bazer's protection," she said.

"I understand," AJ said. "And that's why I've approached you with respect. If you can't help, I'll leave and you can enjoy my Scotch."

Fairs coughed as she took a second sip of her drink. AJ looked at her and tried unsuccessfully to read her facial expression. He continued to watch in case she was trying to get his attention, but it appeared her cough was tied only to the effects of the alcohol.

"This human, Loveit, is not respectful," Bazer said, eyeing the flask. "You must tell me. Do humans often drink this?"

"Scotch," AJ filled in. "I wish I'd known a stronger drink was going to be a hit. I'd have brought some other stuff. Something tells me you might be a schnapps kind of gal."

"You tease me."

He grinned. Mads Bazer was anything but mad and seemed to be flirting with him in her own, crotchety way.

"I feel like you'd be good at a party," AJ said.

"Drink one more?" she asked.

"If you let me pour," he said.

The grin on her face was wide and her yellowed canine teeth showed proudly as the dark hair on her face compressed. He had no trouble understanding why people were afraid of her.

"Yes. Pour."

"You haven't answered my question," he said, pouring another couple of fingers for both of them. One look at Fairs told AJ that she had no interest in more.

"You did not ask a question," Mads Bazer said. "Drink it at once?"

It was AJ's turn to grin. Bazer was trying to get him drunk. Two

Scotches wouldn't do it. "I got shot this morning. I need to take it easy," he said. "Aw, what the hell?"

He held his glass up in front of Bazer. When she lifted hers, AJ swallowed his drink quickly, sighing as the burn worked its way down his throat.

Mads Bazer coughed uncontrollably for a moment and hooted like a train whistle. She finally gained control of herself and slapped the table between them, knocking Fairs' half-empty glass off the edge. AJ intercepted it, managing to save most of the contents. Greybeard, seeing the chaos in the room, jumped up and barked, pushing his paws against Bazer's legs.

"I would never have believed a skinny, hairless ape could out-drink old Bazer," Bazer said. "Ask me your question, Albert Jenkins. I am in a mood to listen."

"I want to pay you to look the other way when I steal Loveit's ship," AJ said. "I'm prepared to pay handsomely for this service."

"It is my honor to protect those vessels in my charge. The payment would need to be considerable. So much so that you might as well contract with another vessel's captain," she said. "There is no economy in this."

"Loveit is going to keep chasing us," AJ said. "If I take his ship, I kill two birds with one stone. It's like I've both shot him down and bought a ship."

"Killing birds," Bazer laughed. "I like this. If I could use a single stone and kill two birds, would I do this in a single throw?"

"It's an idiom and yes, the idea is that a single throw kills two birds. It's efficient," he explained.

"It would be," she agreed.

"Perhaps we should take our leave," Fairs said. "I do not believe Albert Jenkins has sufficient funds to meet your needs, Mads Bazer. We are grateful for the time you have allotted us."

"If you bring Scotch, you will forever be welcome, Red Fairs and Albert Jenkins," Mads Bazer said. "I feel that a nap is perhaps the correct action."

AJ reached into his cloak and wrapped his hand around a palm-sized container. He hadn't intended to blow his advantage, but he saw no other way. He dropped the containment device onto the table and depressed the button that illuminated the display gauge.

"Two hundred grams of pure Fantastium," he said. "I give you this. You and your crew look the other way for two hours and you give us access to your video feeds for the ten hours leading up to that."

Bazer sobered as she realized what she was looking at. She placed her hand over the device. "How is it that you have this much wealth?" she asked. "You could buy your own ship with this. I have two ships I would sell you myself."

"I'm hunting birds, Bazer," he said, dramatically.

"Thirty minutes," Bazer responded, equally dramatic. "You can have as much video as you can consume. I'll make it available now. Your Loveit arrived in that vessel." Bazer pointed across the landing bay to a bright white spaceship with an American flag painted across its side. The vessel was rounded at the front and squared off toward the back where engine ports similar to most Vred vessels were located.

"Yeah, that's it, all right," AJ said. "How many crew do they have?"

"They declared six," Mads Bazer said. "Only three leave at any time. The adjacent vessel is Cheell. They have a larger crew, perhaps twelve. Cheell do not like to fight, though."

AJ recognized the design of the Cheell ship as similar to the one he'd boarded in jumpspace.

"What's the scoop on the human ship?" AJ asked. "Weapons?"

"I do not believe so. The technology is unfamiliar to Xandarj aside from the Vred engines," Mads Bazer said.

"They'll have cypher locks and motion monitoring. Probably stuff I haven't thought about."

"It would not be difficult to have several of my associates regularly walk past this vessel," Fairs said. "It is unusual and has probably attracted attention."

"Pisses me off that he has Old Glory on the side," AJ said.

"What is *old glory?*" Bazer asked.

"That flag represents my country," AJ said. "Like Dralli for Xandarj. I fought a war for what that flag represents. Big D, Doc, and I bled for that flag. Hundreds of thousands of my people died defending that flag. I'm so damn angry, I can't believe he'd have the nuts to... I bet that bastard took the ship from our Space Force. Probably made up some stupid story."

"AJ, you need to calm," Beverly said, not appearing. "Make your plans but do not give in to this anger."

"Albert Jenkins wishes to fight right now," Mads Bazer said. "It is not a good time, but if this is your half hour, I will accept your offer."

"No. No. No," AJ said, trying to calm himself. "It just caught me by surprise. Fairs, how soon could we get supplies? I'd like to take you up on bringing Tork and Chok along."

"I thought your mission had changed."

"It did, but it didn't. I need a ship, no matter what," AJ said. "Tell me, Mads Bazer, if I come back with this ship, will you return it to Loveit if he's still here?"

"It is not mine to give. I only secure vessels and keep this landing bay clean and well repaired," she said. "If Loveit produces a similar fortune, I cannot say I would not do the same to you as I will do to him. It would depend on the Scotch that he brings, I suppose."

AJ looked at the scraggly Xandarj and saw she wasn't joking. He had no doubt Bazer would sell him down the river to Loveit just as quickly as she was betraying Loveit now. It concerned him that Loveit probably had access to even greater reserves of Fantastium than he did.

"But you wouldn't act against me."

"I will not act against Loveit unless he threatens my protectorate."

AJ held his hand out to Mads Bazer and she looked at him with confusion. "Humans shake hands to signify a deal has been struck." She shrugged and limply responded, allowing AJ to shake their clasped hands.

"I DON'T LIKE THIS," Jayne whispered into the darkness. Only a dim glow of light enabled her to see AJ's face directly across from her own.

"Kind of creative if you ask me," he whispered back. "They'll never know we're here and with BB giving us an outside view, we're perfectly positioned."

The position he was talking about was directly across from the main loading ramp that led into Loveit's vessel. AJ and Jayne were hidden at the center of a large pallet full of crates that had been carefully stacked to conceal them and to mimic all the other supplies waiting to be transferred in and out of the busy Dralli landing bay. Greybeard and Darnell were similarly situated in another stack nearby.

At some point during the busy morning, the two stacks of crates had been delivered to a vessel opposite the human ship. A third stack nearby held real supplies gathered by AJ and his new crew for their journey.

The plan was not without its flaws. The primary problem was the need for the stowaways to stay immobilized until the right opportunity presented itself. For several days, from the safety of Fairs' and Tork's home, they'd monitored the comings and goings of Loveit and his crew. Like clockwork, they exited and entered the ship, sometimes meeting Cheell and sometimes not. In most cases, three crew left at 1100 and returned by 1200 and then three crew left at 1400 and returned by 1600. Loveit was always one of the crew that departed.

"How are you doing? Looks like the Xandarj medical kits are working. Your eye isn't nearly so puffy," AJ said.

"The orbital bone around my left eye was crushed," Jayne said. "I'm not sure how it's possible, but the injury is slowly healing. This type of medicine would ease untold suffering on Earth."

"Probably something we should push," he said.

A light appeared next to them, drawing their attention. A small video screen showed three figures exiting the spaceship.

"You seeing this, AJ?" Darnell whispered.

"Copy," AJ answered. "Can you make out if one of them is Loveit? They're wearing those damn robes again."

"Negative. Guy on the left is about the right height. We've never seen him *not* in the group. Does it matter?"

"No. Chok, you see these guys yet? They're coming your way," AJ said. Chok and Tork were stationed on opposite sides of the landing bay.

"They're meeting with Cheell," Chok said. "It looks like a normal breakfast run."

"We're on, people. Fairs, confirm with Bazer that we're starting our thirty minutes now," AJ said.

"Bazer has acknowledged," Fairs answered.

AJ shuffled and pulled out his Cheell pistol. "Set phasers to stun," he said, grinning madly.

"That's so stupid. I knew you were going to say that at some point," Darnell said.

"BB, give us a ten second timer," AJ said.

On every HUD a timer started counting down. When the numbers got to four seconds, Chok's voice came back, panicked. "They're coming back," she said. "Abort!"

"Are you fucking serious?" AJ asked.

"They're moving quickly; they'll be on your position in forty seconds."

"AJ, we've started Mads Bazer's timer," Fairs said. "You'll lose your investment if you stop now."

"They might have just forgotten something," Darnell said. "We should wait it out."

"Everyone, hold," AJ said. "We're going to do this the hard way."

"What do you mean?" Jayne asked.

"I mean, we'll skip the part where Greybeard breaks their cypher. We'll tailgate in on these guys," AJ said.

"That'll be six on three. We'll be outnumbered," she whispered.

"I can see them coming," Darnell said. "We need a decision."

"What about the Cheell?" AJ asked.

"Negative Cheell," Darnell said.

"Chok? Did Cheell come back too?"

"No Cheell, AJ."

"Chok, Tork, crash the ship. We're going in," AJ said, watching the group of humans rush back to the ship. Something was off. Loveit wasn't in the group and the three human crew members were looking around wildly, like they were expecting an attack. "Shit, someone gave us away."

"Are we going?" Darnell asked.

"Wait one," AJ said, watching the lead crew member race up the ship's ramp and punch in a code on the door. The crewman's hands were shaking so much that he failed to punch in the correct code and had to try a second time. "Almost..."

AJ saw the light turn green.

"GO!"

The Trojan crates were designed to blow apart with minimal explosive force but enough to keep from tripping up the inhabitants. The female crew member from the ship let out a whoop of surprise and spun abruptly as a panel tumbled against her leg.

"He's going to escape," Darnell called as the lead crew member pulled the hatch open and lunged inside.

"Shit, so much for surprise," AJ grumbled, firing several quick shots at the man. Having participated in plenty of combat, he wasn't particularly surprised that his first shots went wild. Fortunately, Beverly traced the shots, projecting each impact with large virtual green splotches, allowing him to see his error in real time. It was his fourth, fifth and sixth shots that impacted the man and caused him to slump halfway into the hatch.

Gunfire erupted in front of him, but it was cut off as Greybeard tackled the woman who'd reacted more quickly than either of her peers. Unfortunately for her, she wasn't prepared to defend against a determined, super-intelligent canine.

An object flew from the open hatch and bounced into the aisle between the ships. AJ's eyes flew wide open as he recognized the object.

"GRENADE!"

NINETEEN
FRIEND OF MY ENEMY

In a blur of motion, Chok flew past, swatting the still bouncing grenade back into the US vessel. AJ, who was already in the process of diving away from the explosive, turned his momentum into a shoulder roll for which he had a bit too much speed. Coming up on his feet, he impacted the bottom side of the ship's hull.

A muffled explosion was followed by the ejection of smoke from the ship's open hatch. "Big D, breech!" he ordered, placing a hand on the sloped ramp. Bunching his powerful leg muscles, AJ vaulted onto the ramp and raced to the ship. They'd already disabled three of the six people who should be onboard. The grenade, which must be a variant of a flashbang, should have had considerable impact on the rest of the ship's inhabitants.

Stepping over the prone body of the crewman partially blocking the entry hatch, AJ charged through the smoke with Darnell close behind. Rotating quickly, he scanned the smoke-filled space, grateful that Beverly was able to enhance his ability to identify shapes. The green wire frame of a human, stumbling and holding their head with their hands wasn't unexpected. AJ fired a pair of stun-level shots, dropping the man to the ship's deck.

"Clear, aft!" he cried out, having felt a tap from Darnell on his right shoulder, indicating that his buddy was covering forward.

"Clear, forward," Darnell responded.

"Shit, that's four. Where are the other two?" AJ asked Darnell.

"Seventeen minutes before Mads Bazer causes more trouble than we'll want," Tork said, jumping in behind them. Without being told, the small Xandarj rolled the prone human out of the hatch and helped the body fall off the ship's ramp. "We must load supplies and depart."

"What about the woman Greybeard attacked?" AJ asked.

"Amanda Jayne used plastic straps to bind her," Chok said, appearing in the hatch. "Are we ready to load supplies? All must help except pilot." She looked at Tork expectantly.

"I am not familiar with a human vessel," Tork said. "This might be a problem."

"Big D's a pilot and ran an aerospace company. If anyone can figure out US tech, he can," AJ said. "You boys grab a seat. We'll get loaded. BB, can you do anything about the smoke already?"

Following Chok's example, AJ lugged the unconscious crewman from the vessel and dumped him off the ramp. Scanning the area, he found Jayne tending to the woman who'd been bitten by Greybeard and talking quietly with her.

"Jayne, we gotta go!" AJ said. "Mads Bazer will do all the medical stuff once we're gone."

"Greybeard really got her arm," Jayne said. "She needs stiches."

"Not your rodeo, Doc. We've got nine minutes to get our asses outta here." He raced to the stack of crates atop a deactivated gravity repulsing sled.

"Press green button. It will keep cases level," Chok said, coming up behind him. "No, let me do this. You must move debris from my path."

"Big D, you making any progress?" AJ called.

"No. Looks like there's some sort of lock on this damn thing,"

Darnell answered. "I've got Seamus working on it. Would someone clear the damn smoke out of the cockpit!?"

AJ pulled on the front of the stack of supply crates and was surprised at how easily the heavy items moved across the landing bay's deck. With Chok pushing and AJ pulling, the hovering stack sped up and immediately plowed into the debris caused by AJ, Jayne and Darnell's explosive exit from their hiding spots.

"Stop!" AJ called, pushing back on the crates as they started dragging debris.

"Move that out of the way," Chok demanded unhelpfully. "Stop pulling."

Fortunately, Jayne recognized the problem and joined AJ in the struggle to free the junk.

The sound of gunfire and the ping of a round ricocheting off the ship's hull caused the three to flinch. A blinking red arrow in AJ's vision warned him to move just seconds before another round struck inches from his face. With limited options, he viciously kicked at a piece of metal that had become lodged against the deck and was impeding their progress. Chok had momentarily stopped pushing against him and AJ managed to free the load even though it hurt his foot.

Only a couple of seconds had elapsed since they'd been fired on. Beverly's visual locator blinked a red outline as she identified Loveit thirty yards away firing at them with his pistol. "Jayne, return fire!"

He ducked around the crates as Loveit fired three more times. The sizzle of Jayne's high-energy rounds leaving her weapon and the flash of blaster energy instantly bridged the gap between her and her target. A shout of surprise from Loveit followed and he ducked behind a Xandarj vessel.

"Chok, go!"

The small, white-furred Xandarj slammed the supply stack onto the pitched ramp. While the stack had no issues with tipping, Chok didn't have sufficient inertia to push it up the ramp.

AJ joined her, throwing his weight into the back of the stack. For a moment, they were barely able to move until AJ felt another body slam into his own. "Get this crap moving!" Jayne urged, shouldering the load as she exchanged fire with Loveit.

The crates zoomed up the ramp. AJ raised his head to look around the corner of the stack and knew they would be too late to stop the disaster ahead. Their crates were piled higher than the hatch would allow and before AJ could do anything, the arched opening caught the top of the containers, jarring everything and everyone with the force of the ricochet. Considering the circumstances, he knew they couldn't afford to be picky about the condition of their supplies. Digging in, he jammed his body into the stack, spilling the center two crates through the opening. The bottom containers stayed put and AJ fell forward on top of them. The smaller crates on top of the pile tilted back and fell away from the ship, barely missing him. One ended up hitting Jayne and knocking her from the ramp, the crate hanging precariously above her, teetering on the edge.

Loveit seized on the shift in circumstance and rushed toward them, firing wildly, managing to send bullets ricocheting into the ship.

"What the hell?" Darnell exploded on comms. "Take care of your shit, Jenkins!"

AJ struggled to free himself from the crates, which wasn't easy to do given how he'd wound up twisted and wedged inside the gap between the heavy boxes. That they were taking fire, however, was critical and he didn't need Beverly to boost his adrenaline levels to respond with a strength he normally couldn't manage.

Just as he freed himself, one of the crates moved sharply, rammed against his thighs, and bent his knees backward. He yelped and threw himself to the side, barely escaping the unexpected push as Chok burst out from under the pile.

"Oh, I am sorry, Albert Jenkins," Chok said, recognizing that she'd almost plowed him over.

"Jayne, report!" AJ called, ignoring Chok.

"About to put that jackass on his butt," Jayne said, uncharacteristic anger in her voice.

"Ninety seconds, Albert Jenkins," Tork said. "We are not yet running. This could result in poor consequences."

As a group, they'd all discussed in length what Mads Bazer's offer of temporary protection had entailed. She would look the other way for thirty minutes. In that thirty minutes, they needed to move the US vessel from its current spot to outside the Dralli space station. Xandarj, as it turned out, didn't recognize ownership beyond possession on a governmental level. That is to say, if someone took control of some property, there were few repercussions from anyone but the original owners as long as you weren't breaking a contract like the protection contract Mads Bazer offered to ships that landed here.

"Dammit!" AJ scrabbled and pulled at the crate next to him, finally freeing himself from the mess. As he exited, bullets pinged off the ship's hull not far from his position.

"Nice!" Jayne shouted, after letting loose a pair of blaster rounds that elicited a surprised cry from Loveit's position.

She popped up from where she'd been lying prone on the deck and held her free hand up to AJ, who grabbed it and hoisted her around onto the loading ramp. Together they sprinted back into the ship.

"Close the hatch, AJ," Beverly instructed, appearing next to the entry, wearing her sparkling silver spacesuit and being held up by her jetpack. "I believe it is controlled by the levers I'm highlighting."

He smiled. One of the systems his old firm, Pacific Aerodyne, had manufactured for the US space industry had been electro-mechanical locking systems for high-pressure differential egress ports. The mechanism was familiar and he locked the hatch, which in turn caused the ramp to start retracting.

"Big D, tell me you've got something," he said.

"We do, but it's gonna suck," Darnell said. "Grab a chair, fellas, it's about to get rough."

AJ grabbed the back of Jayne's ship suit and pulled her to one of the back-facing, plush white chairs. "Strap in, Doc," he ordered, cinching the seat's five-point belts. These particular belts, while manufactured by one of his old competitors, was also familiar due to Pacific Aerodyne's attempt to reverse engineer them.

Seeing her struggle, AJ leaned over and tugged on her straps, tightening them to her body. He left her to finish the bottom buckles before trying to buckle himself in.

"Hold on!" Darnell called.

With no further warning, the ship moved violently backward and AJ slammed into Jayne. Neither had managed to completely secure their harnesses, but Jayne was able to keep her seat and grab AJ's suit. He looped his elbow through two of her straps so he wouldn't be jerked away. "Sorry, Doc. If I'm right, this is about to get worse."

"What's happening?" she asked, as inertia reversed and she doubled over atop AJ. The crates, which had been pinned against a forward bulkhead, were tossed violently into the curved back wall, only to bounce out of view.

"Somebody can't figure out how to turn the inertial dampening field on," AJ grunted. "Assuming this thing has one."

"I know how to turn it on," Darnell growled over the comms. "It isn't freaking working."

"We're clear of Dralli Station," Tork said. "I am not certain that we were within Mads Bazer's deadline. Without an inertial system, we will not be able to outrun the Dralli patrols. It will become clear very soon if we have created enough of an infraction for Mads Bazer to initiate a contract to return or destroy this vessel."

"She could do that?" AJ asked as acceleration suddenly ceased and he was no longer being pulled away from Jayne.

"Red Fairs reviewed the contract. Mads Bazer will honor it," Tork said.

"Are you okay, Chok?" AJ had just noticed the small white Xandarj who'd managed to wrap herself around another chair. Her limbs, including her tail, were holding on for everything she was worth.

"No!" she answered. "I believe I have watered this chair because of my great fright and I find I am angry and embarrassed."

"Are we done for a minute, Darnell?" Jayne asked.

"Done until a Dralli patrol comes for us or we decide to move on our own," Darnell said. "If we don't get that inertial system going, we'll never get anywhere. We can't survive the g-forces required to get out of Dodge, if you know what I mean."

"AJ, turn to the side while I help Chok get cleaned up," Jayne said, pushing herself free from AJ, who hadn't quite let her go yet. As he pushed away from Jayne, he took one final glance back at the terrified Xandarj, whose hair was puffed out like a cat who'd been hit by a blow dryer.

"Fine, Big D. You have anything up there that looks like a manual?"

"Negative."

"US made, so gotta have manuals somewhere," AJ said, pushing out of his chair and walking aft to inspect the hull around them. As far as he could tell, he and Jayne were in the main passenger space where there was little room for storage. "See if you can find a hardcopy."

"We're looking," Darnell said. "Got a few cabinets up here. Looks mostly like electronics, though."

"AJ, there appear to be trap doors in the deck," Beverly said, floating aft from the oval seating arrangement. While there had once been six chairs in the oval, now there were five and a half as one of the once pristine, leather-covered chairs had been split in two and blackened where a flashbang had landed.

"Trap doors?" He found her hovering over a glowing four-foot-square panel on the floor. At one side of the panel was a pull-ring styled lock that was not particularly high tech but effective in keeping out of the way so as to not trip the ship's occupants.

"Careful, AJ," Jayne said, from where she was helping extricate Chok from the chair.

He raised an eyebrow. He hadn't considered there might be a

stowaway. "A little backup?" he asked, reaching for the pull ring. Greybeard nudged his knee, making his presence known. "Atta boy. You smell something?"

Greybeard whined, which meant he didn't smell anything concerning. All the same, AJ had his weapon ready. Anticlimactic, all they discovered was a half-empty hold. Bright LED lights illuminated the hold which was nine feet by twelve feet and roughly five feet in depth. Wide cargo straps held a dozen crates to the Tween deck's floor. If someone *had* been hiding, there was no other place for them to go but inside one of the crates, something Greybeard wasn't indicating.

"Cargo hold has crates, no people," he said. "One of those crates might have manuals. I'll check 'em out once I clear the rest of the ship."

"You think we've got a stowaway?" Darnell asked.

"No idea," AJ said. "Probably be a good thing to figure out, though. Chok, do you think you could work on getting our crates stored in here while I search the ship?"

"Yes," she said simply.

"AJ, I think Chok could use a break," Jayne said.

"I'm fine with that," AJ said. "Nothing like a little work to take your mind off things, though."

"I will store the crates," Chok said. "Albert Jenkins will show Chok how to use irritating restraints."

"That'd be a good lesson for everyone," he said, chuckling.

"There is another trap door, AJ," Beverly said, flitting over to the opposite side of the ship, where she highlighted another panel on the deck.

"Greybeard, you want to give that a quick sniff?" he asked unnecessarily as Greybeard trotted to the hatch embedded in the starboard-side decking. Greybeard pawed at the pull ring and gave two deep woofs.

"Seamus says Greybeard believes there is a human beneath the panel. The human is quietly moving away from the hatch," Beverly said.

"Jayne, a little backup over here?" he asked.

She pulled her pistol from her belt. "Okay,"

"For the record, you've been shooting a lot of people today. I thought doctors took an oath about that sort of thing," he said.

"My weapon causes a mostly harmless electrical discharge," she said. "In each case, I believe the person I've shot is in less danger for my actions."

"Bullshit."

She grinned as she approached. "Fine, you got me. It's so darn satisfying to shoot these jerks. It's not like the stun rounds are harmful, not really."

"Wait 'till you get hit with one."

She shrugged. "You're saying you'd like me not to defend you when you open the door?"

"No, forget I said anything."

"Listen up, down there." AJ cupped his hand next to his mouth and shouted at the trap door. "I'm going to open this hatch. If you've got a weapon pointed anywhere near us, you'll be shot. Really, if you make any trouble at all, you'll be shot. If you hide, we'll send the dog down. He likes to bite and if you hurt him, you'll be shot. If you'd like to avoid all the preceding ways of being shot, just put your weapon down and raise your hands. Knock on the hatch to let me know you understand."

A far-off voice said something. Even with Beverly's enhancement, AJ couldn't understand the words.

"Can't hear you," AJ called. A week knock on the floor beneath his knees startled him. "I'm opening up. Don't get cute."

AJ looked to Jayne, who nodded at him to proceed as she aimed her weapon at the floor. He twisted the ring and gently pulled open the hatch, fully prepared to slam it closed if things got out of control.

"Don't shoot. I'm injured," came a man's voice. "My weapon is on the floor by my feet."

"What are you doing in there?" AJ assessed the man and the position of his weapon, which was just out of reach. He noticed a bend in the man's leg. "Is your leg broken?"

The man was muscular, with sandy brown hair and a ruddy, outdoor complexion. AJ immediately recognized the look in the man's blue eyes. He was not only a soldier, but he had special forces training of some sort. He'd be a handful if things got out of control.

"I got tossed around down here a bit," he said.

"What's your name, son?"

"Master Sergeant Crawford Reed," Reed said. "Can I assume you've taken command of the *USSF Cardinal?*"

"Cardinal? Spooks get a spaceship and they call it *Cardinal?*"

"I'm active duty in the Space Force, Sergeant."

"Loveit's a spook and I dumped your friends out on Dralli Station. They're gonna need to find their own ride home," AJ said. "We'll provide aid to you, but don't get any stupid ideas. As long as you're in cahoots with Loveit, you're an enemy of the U. S. of A. I bled for my country and I'll bleed anyone who looks to do her harm. You read me?"

"Good copy, Sergeant. I'm not your enemy."

"Last time I saw Loveit, he was torturing my crew on a prison ship," AJ said. "I'll treat you a fair bit better, but don't be playing games with me. I've been around the block too many times for that. Now, I'm gonna help you up outta there. You try anything and the good doctor is gonna blast you with a couple hundred thousand volts."

"I didn't have any part of Loveit's rendition plan," Reed said.

"But you knew about it."

"After the fact." Reed accepted AJ's hand and help getting out from the Tween deck.

"What'd you do to the ship?" AJ asked.

"Don't know what you're talking about."

"That broken leg of yours suggests otherwise," AJ said. "You know we'll figure it out, right?"

"My team. Are they dead?"

"You mean the team that was shooting live rounds at US citizens?" AJ asked.

"No, Mr. Reed," Jayne interrupted, keeping her distance and her weapon leveled on the injured man. "Unlike you, we were shooting stun rounds."

"I imagine he's hoping his Cheell friends will come and rescue him," Darnell said, coming around a forward bulkhead into the open passenger space. "Because using enemies of the state to chase down citizens is the mark of a good soldier. Right, Mr. Reed?"

"Cheell aren't our enemies."

"Sounds like a confession to me," Darnell said.

"I didn't say that," Reed argued back.

"Your buddies, the Cheell, were looking to shoot us down. Your boss, Loveit, tortured us," AJ said. "You want to explain just how we're gonna get along?"

TWENTY
CHECK THE TAPES

"Can we take it as a good sign that Dralli station hasn't sent a patrol after us?" AJ asked, cinching chair restraints around Reed's chest.

The design of the straps was twofold. Primarily, they were made to keep a body pinned to the chair, regardless of the state of consciousness. A secondary and less public function was to restrain a team member who'd become irrational for any number of reasons. While not common, *losing it* while on a space mission wasn't unheard of and keeping crew in their chair forcibly was more desirable than building brigs.

"Mr. Reed, I'm going to have to set your leg bones. It's going to hurt," Jayne explained, having cut most of the leg material off Reed's suit. Reed was struggling to maintain consciousness from blood loss, even though Jayne had stabilized his condition. One of the many benefits of being on a human-built vessel was the familiar medical supplies.

"Take me back to the Dralli Station. They have better medical technology," he mumbled.

"I'm going to ask you one more time," AJ said. "What'd you do to the ship?"

Reed closed his eyes and shook his head. "Nothing."

"Way to convince us we're on the same team, hero," AJ said, shaking his head. Irritated, he walked back to a room-height freestanding cabinet in the middle of the space. It was the same cabinet where they'd found medical supplies for Reed.

"I will catalog the cabinet's contents," Beverly said. "I'll highlight items I need a better view of."

"Copy," AJ said. He moved quickly through the cabinets, uncovering more medical supplies, blankets and various repair kits.

"Bingo," Beverly said, her rocket pack streaming little o-shaped smoke rings behind her as she jetted to the top of the starboard cabinet.

AJ grinned despite his foul mood. "Sure enough," he agreed, his eyes lighting on the row of gray manuals she highlighted. The spines of the manuals proudly displayed the US Space Force logo along with overly complex titles.

"This one," she said, highlighting a three-inch-wide, nine-inch-tall volume. He pulled the manual from the shelf and plopped onto the deck, cross-legged, flipping it open to the index. "Page 247," she instructed. He sighed and flipped to the page. "Turn. Turn. Turn," she urged impatiently.

"You're reading all this?" he asked.

"Pertinent details. Turn. They're using a Cheell system. Turn. I'm not familiar with it. Turn."

"Is that bad?"

"Turn faster. Don't pause to talk."

"Bossy much?" AJ asked, flattening each page for only a second before turning to the next.

"Missed one, go back."

He complied. "I guess that's a *yes* on the bossy?"

"Cute," she said. "We need another manual, the one that was two to the right of this one."

AJ grabbed the requested volume, opened to the index, and started paging, waiting for her to stop him. He struggled to understand what he was looking at. With a career as a top-level engineer for an Aerospace company, he was familiar with this style of manual. The problem was, he was having difficulty focusing quickly enough on any part of the page to decipher what he was looking at. As far as he could tell, they'd moved from the inertial system content to a general layout of the electrical system paths.

"Any thoughts yet?"

"One more," she said, highlighting another book. "I can simulate everything Reed has done to sabotage three different systems on the ship. I'm hoping he didn't intend permanent damage because reproducing some of the systems will be beyond the ship's capacity. You can stop paging. We need to get into the hold where Reed was found."

"Can you multitask?" AJ asked, keeping the manual open while he jumped into the hatch.

"Of course. Go forward and follow the blue arrow I'm projecting."

He was all too familiar with Beverly's virtual arrows, glowing outlines, and other various methods she used to draw his attention. That she seemed confident in finding a solution to their current predicament was good.

"Uh, guys," Darnell prompted. "We've got company."

"It's that Cheell patrol ship," Tork said. "This could be bad. Dralli Station won't help, especially since they know we swiped this ship."

"You're getting distracted. Turn back two pages and stay focused, AJ," Beverly said. "You're not the best multitasker."

"Big D, you need to handle it," he said.

"You better get locked into a seat then," Darnell said. "I've got exactly one move and I'm pretty sure you'll turn into a pink cloud at the back of the ship if I use it."

"Give me a minute, already," AJ said, arriving at Beverly's marker. The space in the Tween deck had narrowed and he'd been forced to crawl the last few yards.

"This isn't good," Beverly said. "You need a special tool to remove that panel."

"You didn't say we were going to need tools."

The loud clank of metal caught AJ's attention as a tool bag flopped onto the floor next to him. "There's an old joke," Chok said, climbing over AJ's hip. "A human, a Beltigersk, and a brilliant Xandarj engineer walk into a bar..."

"You do bar jokes?" AJ asked.

She withdrew an odd-looking tool and with a quick flick of her small wrist, the panel popped open. Beverly gave her instructions and Chok's hands moved in a blur as she withdrew tools from the bag with both hands. She even used her small, white-furred tail to hold a crush of wires away from where she was working.

"The bartender asks, 'How many human/Beltigersk combinations does it take to fix a spaceship?'" Chok continued. "And the Xandarj says, 'None, because neither thought far enough ahead to ask the brilliant engineer if she knew how to fix Cheell inertial systems.'"

"AJ, they're going to try to board. There's a boarding party coming our way. They're saying they'll shoot if we move," Darnell called out.

With a final twist, a green LED illuminated the inside of the panel Chok held open with her tail.

"Inertial systems are good, Blue Tork," Chok said. "And of course, we have bar jokes. Do we look like uncivilized monkeys to you?"

Chok's face was only inches from AJ's. It wasn't lost on AJ how her delicate features were very feminine. She must have followed his train of thought because suddenly she pushed her lips onto his and nipped his top lip as she kissed him.

"Whoa, there," he said, pulling back, his face flushed.

"Chok needed a reward for saving ship," Chok said, caressing his cheek with the end of her tail. "Next reward will be more expensive."

"Hold onto your butts," Darnell said.

AJ wrapped his hands around two structural girders. Chok seemed to agree with AJ's assessment of Darnell's warning and wrapped her legs around his waist while locking her hands and tail onto nearby structural components.

"Darnell should let Tork sail vessel. Tork is good pilot," Chok said.

"Tork *is* sailing," Darnell grunted as the ship veered and the inertial system strained to adjust.

"BB, can you project video of what's going on?" AJ asked.

"Of course," she said. "The battle is one-sided. The Cheell vessel is slower than *USSF Cardinal* but has weapons that will easily destroy us if its captain so desires."

A video screen appeared against the bottom side of the deck above AJ's head. Dralli station was slowly moving away from a ship twice the size of the *USSF Cardinal*. They were clearly outpacing the vastly larger vessel.

"That patrol ship didn't appear from nowhere," AJ said. "I've been wondering why Loveit was sticking around Dralli Station. He couldn't figure out how to take us on the station, so he called in reinforcements. Loveit, the Cheell, people trying to kill us... none of this shit happened until Alicia showed up. I can't help but feel you're holding out on me, BB."

"I would never," she said.

"You already have," AJ said. "I had to learn from Red Fairs that Beltigersk are as bad as Korgul."

"That is not a fair assessment," Beverly said. "The majority of Beltigersk have always recognized the immorality of forcing ourselves on *any* sentient. I did not know Alicia was of the Master Voice. If my mother had known, Alicia would have been removed from succession. Our trespasses against Xandarj and other species remains a dark part of our history and a great embarrassment for my family. I have spent the entirety of my life working against the so-called *ascendant species* taking advantage of those who have few defenses against them."

"Fine," AJ said, somewhat mollified. "We're not done with that conversation. It still doesn't change the fact that Cheell are hard on our asses and we have no idea why."

"You believe I know something about this," she stated.

"Yes! Exactly my point!" he said, emphatically.

"I don't possess proof, but I feel it must have something to do with

Alicia."

"Now we're getting somewhere."

"This is great, guys," Darnell cut in. "Glad you're hugging and making up and all, but we're about to get our butts handed to us by some very angry aliens."

"In politics, there are few coincidences," Beverly said, ignoring Darnell. "This must be related to the attack on Beltigersk."

"You said Cheell and Korgul are generally enemies of Beltigersk, right?"

"That is correct. Korgul does not like that many Beltigersk stand against their co-opting of lesser sentient species," Beverly said. "But Korgul would have much in common with those who support Master Voice."

"Seems like the timing is convenient. Beltigersk is attacked, the queen is dead, and Alicia shows up on Earth," AJ said. "What if that Cheell captain was actually right? What if he had no intention of blowing us up when we got to Xandarj?"

"You dismissed that possibility before. What has changed?" Beverly asked.

"When the captain said he wasn't planning to destroy our ship, he thought I was going to shoot him and his crew," AJ said. "I figured he was just lying. People tend to do that when they think they're about to get shot."

"But now you think he was telling the truth."

"What if he was trying to grab Alicia? What if Cheell wanted to get her back to Beltigersk?"

"Not sure this is helping," Darnell said. "They're demanding we heave-to and they're warming up their weapons. What's the word, AJ? They've got us dead to rights."

"Bubba, I need you to trust me on this," AJ said. "Cheell aren't going to attack. We need to keep going."

"Where to?"

"Not here," AJ said. "Either way we need to get to jump-space."

"Last time I let you plan things...," Darnell grumbled. "I can't believe we didn't think past stealing the fricking ship."

"Well, shit's changed," AJ growled back. "I'm not even sure how we get out of this mess."

"We start by going to Beltigersk and find out what happened to my mother. Beltigersk will be in chaos but I cannot lead," Beverly said.

"Why not? You're in the line of succession, aren't you?" Jayne said.

"Yes, under normal circumstances. I fear there will be a struggle for power. I am not well-known and have little support amongst those who would need to fall in line behind a leader. Only one of my eldest sisters would have been successful at uniting Beltigersk, but they are dead," Beverly said.

"Maybe we should have a talk with Alicia," AJ said. "We need to find her."

"I fear she murdered 2F when she took over Darnell Jackson," Beverly said.

"There were a couple of seconds, right before she grabbed me, where everything got real still like. I got this strong feeling like everything was going to be okay, but then all hell broke loose. I thought it was 2F saying goodbye, but now I'm not sure. Just how do you find a Beltigersk who doesn't want to be found?" Darnell asked.

"It is not information I desire to share," Beverly said, "but I can manufacture a scanner that only I can control."

"Is there any chance of returning 2F, you know... if he's still alive?"

"2F said that you'd grown close," Beverly said. "Your loyalty honors his memory."

"He was a quiet sort," Darnell said, "but he's got a good sense of humor. It makes me sad to think he could be dead."

"I did not know 2F well," Beverly said. "I too have mourned his passing. I retain little hope that he has survived Alicia's attack."

"What do you think that Cheell ship's weapons range is?" Darnell asked.

"I do not understand why they have not fired," Tork said. "Albert Jenkins is brave beyond reason. I did not believe we would survive."

"Maybe you'd like to get off me now?" AJ locked eyes with Chok, who was still draped over him.

"I am quite comfortable," Chok said. "Am I correct that you and Amanda Jayne have not announced intent to live as mates?"

"That's kind of a personal question," he said, gently pushing the small Xandarj woman back. It wasn't at all lost on him that with his eyes closed, he would not know that Chok was an alien.

"Is it not relevant? Or are you opposed to cross-species relationships?"

"Are you propositioning me?"

"Yes, was I not clear? Darnell Jackson would have been my first choice, but it appears that his mate, Lisa, is quite jealous and would not entertain a third. For some reason, I believed his Lisa was like Red Fairs' brother, who is only interested in keeping their household organized."

AJ chuckled at the thought of Lisa hearing the conversation and what her reaction would be. "Jayne and I have not made any decisions. We've been mostly just trying to stay alive."

Fortunately for AJ, Chok had extricated herself and moved away toward the hatch. AJ followed her and they both emerged into the main passenger area of the ship where Jayne stood waiting, staring pointedly at him.

"Cozy down there?" she asked, her lips pressed into thin lines and her eyebrows raised.

"A little closer than I would have liked," AJ said. "Chok's quite a mechanic, though. I suppose you heard that whole conversation?"

"I did," Jayne said, flatly.

"No idea what the big flap is," AJ said. "Did I misspeak?"

"I don't know, did you?"

"Hell, Doc, you tell me. One day you're all warm and fuzzy, the next day I might as well be a giant bag of piss for all the interest you have in me," AJ said.

"Kids, seriously, can we do this another time?" Darnell asked. "We're still being chased by Cheell in an alien solar system. There's got to be a better time for the star-crossed love routine."

Jayne wasn't ready to be finished. "Is that how you see it? That I think you're a giant bag of urine? When have I ever said anything remotely like that?"

"Oh, boy," Darnell sighed. "Here we go."

"Try every day on this trip, except for like ten minutes at Tork's house."

"You're so aggravating," Jayne said. "What do you want from me?"

"I do not mean to interrupt," Beverly said. "But I have instructed *Cardinal's* manufactory to generate a sensor that will allow us to scan Darnell for the presence of Beltigersk."

"Let's say we find Alicia, then what?" AJ asked.

"It is difficult for a Beltigersk to move between hosts. We will find a way to restrain her if it comes to that."

AJ turned back to Jayne. "You want to know what I want? It's real simple, Doc. I want there to be an *us* and you don't seem at all interested."

He stalked toward the rear of the vessel, picking up on details he hadn't paid attention to before. The outside walls of the ship curved inward steeply, forcing him into a narrow center aisle, roughly six feet across. Along the curved hall, four circular hatches about three feet in diameter were inset into the wall. Etched above each hatch were the designations Berth 1 through Berth 4. Irritated as he was, curiosity got the better part of him and he opened one of the hatches. Inside was a mattress, pillow and a few personal effects. A pang of guilt hit him as he realized he'd left the previous occupant of the berth behind on Xandarj.

"The manufactory is built into a starboard bulkhead just aft of the berthing bunks," Beverly added helpfully.

He ran his hand along the smooth, curved wall as he followed it around. The ship hadn't been built only with function in mind and had a pleasing, modern aesthetic. He wondered which of the many private space companies had built the ship as it was clearly not built by a company with the lowest bid.

Working his way around the curved berths, he recognized a microwave-like manufactory – or at least he did once Beverly highlighted it. Punching open the door release, he extracted a small, palm-sized device with grooved finger grips on both sides. Squeezing the handle caused the device to activate and a virtual display window jumped front and center on AJ's HUD. AJ fingered the window's virtual grab handle, dragging it down and to the right so it didn't obscure his vision, figuring that Beverly would monitor the scanner.

Running it over his arms, AJ wasn't particularly surprised to find that he was still carrying four Beltigersk riders. Their designations showed on his HUD as he ran across them. He felt a little weird about carrying them, but he'd mostly put it to the back of his mind.

"Looks like it's working," he said, turning around and moving forward. "Jayne, you okay if I give you a quick scan? Not trying to be a jerk or anything."

She met him halfway. "Do you really think I see you as a bag of pee?"

AJ chuckled. "Maybe that was a little overstated."

"But you think I'm aloof."

"Yeah, if that means what I think it does."

"I get worried, AJ," she said, holding her arms out so he could run the scanner over her body. "Getting tortured, then the bar. I just don't know how to feel safe. It ties me up inside and it's hard to think of starting a relationship. I'm getting weird vibes from you, too, you know."

"I imagine. And you'll be pleased to know you have zero Beltigersk aboard," AJ said, after running the scanner up her backside.

"Talk to me, AJ."

"I'm not sure what to say," he said. "I feel like a failure for letting first Loveit and then Pankee hurt you. I've failed you a lot but I don't want to stop trying. I haven't felt this way since Pam."

"That must be confusing."

"Understatement of the year. I feel guilty and I know Pam would yell at me for that. I'm pretty messed up about it, so yeah, I know I'm the problem," AJ said. Reed groaned and moved against his restraints. "Of course, you'd wake up right now."

"I need the head," Reed grumbled, almost incoherently.

"Yeah, I'll get right to that," AJ said. "Doc, if you go back, those hatches in the curved wall are berths. Why don't you grab one and catch some shuteye? I think we're out of the shit for a while."

"I think I will," she said, placing a hand on his arm. "AJ, you need to know that I feel the same way you do. Work with me, okay? Don't give up."

"Same here, okay?"

She nodded in response and then walked over to enter one of the berths.

AJ worked his way to the cockpit and rolled his eyes when Darnell gave him a shit-eating grin, eyebrows raised to his hairline.

"Shut up, you," he said, running the scanner over his body.

"Scan his back," Beverly said as AJ ran the scanner over Darnell's left eye. AJ did as she bade. The window showed that he'd found 2F.

"Is he alive?" Darnell asked.

"He is not," Beverly said. "There is very little of him left."

"Dammit," Darnell swore quietly. "Are you sure you didn't find Alicia?"

AJ was frustrated when Alicia didn't show. "Crap, let me run it again." He did, but with identical results.

"Did the vaccine kill her?" Darnell asked.

"Nah, she's trickier than that. I've got this," AJ said. "Maybe we're not the only ones capable of playing Trojan horse."

"I do not understand," Beverly said.

AJ walked back to where Reed sat and pushed the scanner to the back of the man's head where the spinal cord entered the skull.

Suddenly, Reed was alive and animated as he thrashed back and forth, attempting to free himself from the chair's restraints.

"Check the tapes, ump," AJ said, triumphantly. "Reed wasn't an accidental stowaway. I bet you run back the instant replay of Darnell entering the ship and you'll find Reed here making contact with him. This old boy is packin' a Belti rider. He's not here by accident. He was a failsafe for Alicia."

"Please explain," Beverly said.

"You're not looking at it right," AJ said. "What if Alicia is working with the Cheell and Korgul? Suddenly, this all makes sense. Let's say she wants to go back to the good old days when Beltigersk had their way with us *lesser* sentients."

"She'd never! The Korgul attack could have wiped out all of Beltigersk."

"Convenient that it didn't," AJ said. "I wonder if the Beltis who were killed all had a particular leaning? For instance, were they all opposed to the good old days? Someone needs to check that out, but I bet you'll find some very convenient losses. Alicia didn't come all this way to get your help, BB. She came to make sure you got put down. They can't afford to have any royals running around sticking their noses where they don't belong."

"You'll never stop us," Reed growled.

AJ rolled his eyes. "Says the guy in restraints."

TWENTY-ONE

HUNTING PRINCESSES

"We're approaching jump-space and we'll need a decision on our destination," Darnell said.

"Beltigersk," AJ said. "Nothing changes except we're not turning Alicia loose."

"You will turn me loose," Reed spat. "I am the rightful leader of Beltigersk!"

"You're a prisoner of war," AJ said. "Be quiet."

"Well, we've made it to jump-space," Darnell announced, stress draining from his body as he sagged into the highly engineered pilot's chair.

Tork glanced at AJ and smiled. "The Cheell patrol did not join us. It appears they do not wish to share jump-space with you again."

"Good. Seems they can learn a lesson," AJ said.

"I imagine Cheell will follow along shortly," Darnell said.

Tork's head quivered for a moment, a gesture AJ recognized as equivalent to a human shrug. "Maybe. If Cheell wanted to destroy this vessel, they would have done so in Xandarj space as it would have been without diplomatic risk. There is someone on this vessel they wish to keep alive, and therefore, their actions support your theory."

"Geez, I hate to ask, BB," Darnell said. "Do you think your sisters could still be alive?"

Beverly appeared, seated on the edge of the forward bulkhead, her black-robed legs hanging in front of one of several displays. "Thank you for your sensitivity, Darnell Jackson. I will not give up hope for my family, but I am having difficulty coming up with another reason for Alicia's actions."

"Damn," AJ said, under his breath. "That's cold. So, you think she came to Earth with the sole purpose of taking out her competition? That being you, BB?"

"It fits what we know," Darnell said when Beverly hung her head and didn't respond.

"Well, crap. What a cluster," AJ said. "Any chance we could get word back to Lefty? There's no reason for those three to stay in hiding. Sharg will want to work on getting a ride home if she can get around the blackout."

"It will take a few days, but I will send a message with what we currently surmise," Beverly said. "Would you like me to also inform Major Baird? The implications for humanity are significant and potentially dire."

"Do we know enough – for sure?" Darnell asked.

"Let me work on a message," AJ said. "You're right, Darnell. We're guessing about a lot of this. Baird would probably like to know that Loveit is working with the Cheell, though. I suppose we could tell her that we swiped *Cardinal* too."

"That will go over well," Darnell said. "Stealing a top secret, billion-dollar Space Force vessel could raise some eyebrows."

"Do you really think a billion dollars?" AJ asked.

Darnell patted the wall next to him. "Oh, yeah. This girl is a work of art. So, what, we go to Beltigersk and just look around? I'm hardly a detective."

"We need a line on what happened to BB's sisters, so we can figure out if the invasion happened as we've been told. We'll probably irritate folks along the way," AJ said. "Which begs the question, does this ship have any offensive capacity?"

Darnell shrugged. "No idea. Might be worth taking time to read through that stack of manuals. Tork and I have been struggling just to keep from running into anything. We'll get it figured out, but it's hard without any training."

"We'll need to put that on hold," AJ said. "We'll be in jump-space for several days and then it'll be a long trip to Beltigersk. We have plenty of time and right now, we're all pretty beat up. First order of business is for everyone to rest. We'll need at least one person awake to watch the prisoner."

"I am reasonably rested," Tork said. "I will watch this prisoner."

"Are you sure?" AJ asked.

"Oh, yes. I will happily be awake for five hours thirty minutes, which is enough rest for Chok. We have much experience with shifts of this length and can maintain them indefinitely, assuming our biological needs are taken care of."

Chok slid in next to AJ and rubbed her jaw against his arm. "I have biological needs, Albert Jenkins."

There was a tiny part of him that wanted to agree, but he'd ruin any chance he had with Jayne. "I've got some things to figure out first, Chok," he said, sighing. "As much as it hurts me to say."

She did her best to look disappointed. "Are all human men so chaste?"

"I'm gonna grab a shower and catch some shuteye," he said with a grin. "I'll be up in five hours to take a shift."

"I will create a schedule," Tork said. "It will be more beneficial for you to spend your time learning of this vessel's capacities. Your Beltigersk will be able to translate that information so Chok and I are capable of sailing and performing repairs."

AJ worked to contain a yawn and walked aft. "See you in five," he said, waving over his shoulder. "So, BB, tell me they've got a shower in this thing."

"There is good news, AJ," she said. "As the USSF *Cardinal* is equipped with gravity fields which generate .7g while in ordinary flight, showers were not difficult to facilitate. The head is fully wet and will almost perfectly recycle all gray water used for this purpose."

"I'd kiss you right now if I could."

"I thought you were not interested in alien girls," she said, switching to an ivory, sleeveless dress. She bent forward and the back of her dress blew up as she struck a famous Marilyn Monroe pose.

"Sure, *now* you want to get risqué."

Beverly smiled mischievously as she smoothed the dress, which still showed a considerable amount of skin. "It's only fun when two can play."

He shook his head as he removed his suit and stepped into the shower. A blast of cold water made him jump and he frantically twisted valves until the water finally warmed enough to stop his shivering. He was impressed when he read directions for the utilization of heated air to dry both his body and the shower.

"Your blood pressure is reduced," Beverly mentioned after he'd clothed himself.

"I'm not sure why a shower is so cathartic," he said, padding to the bunk rooms. Only one of the doors had an occupied flag on it and he almost avoided it. He had a better thought, however, and knocked softly. "Doc, you awake?"

The occupied flag disappeared with an audible thunk and the door opened. "What's up?" she asked, rolling in her personal bunk space so she could look out at him.

"I figured out the shower," he said. "Wondered if you wanted to give it a try."

"We have a shower?"

"Gravity does great things for plumbing," AJ said, grinning. "Now, if I just had a razor."

"Show me," she said, grabbing a handle on the inside of her bunk area and swinging her legs around and out, shimmying at the last moment. The bunks weren't perfectly suited to getting in and out easily and AJ guided her, gently grabbing her waist.

"There's a screen," he said, pulling it in front of the head and holding it for her to enter. "You probably need to doff out here. The shower recycles, so you can use as much water as you want. The valves act like a shower back home and there's an air-dry unit. I'm not sure how much soap they have loaded, but I imagine it's plenty."

"You smell nice," she said. "I want to smell nice again."

AJ grinned. "I'm not sure you stopped."

She chuckled and pulled the screen to separate them. "I'm pretty sure I did. You know this whole space flight thing might not be so bad if we don't have to smell like a pack of rats."

"Won't get an argument from me. I'm gonna turn in. Call out if you need help."

He returned to the bunks and chose the one next to Jayne's. The previous occupant had her personal items neatly stowed in a single, small rucksack. The only other evidence of her occupation was a picture of a young woman sitting next to a young girl, looking out over a forested canyon. AJ swallowed a guilty feeling as suddenly humanity was assigned to a person he'd left behind on Dralli Station. Sliding the picture into the rucksack, he lowered both to the floor and tried to ignore the light smell of perfume that pervaded the space.

Punching up the pillow, AJ pulled the hatch closed and slid the occupied flag into place. The bunk had enough room for him to sit up and he noticed a light breeze moving around the cabin. Controls and a video screen were built into the bulkhead next to the hatch. AJ located the control to douse the lights until there was just a faint glow illuminating the inside.

"I'll wake you in four hours, forty-two minutes," Beverly said, lying prone on his chest with her hands beneath her chin.

"You're all right BB, you know that?"

"Thank you, AJ," Beverly said. "Do you really believe Alicia was part of the attack on Beltigersk? That she endangered both our species?"

"I don't know. She's said some pretty damning things."

"She has. I've known her a long time and always counted her as a friend. I guess I knew she was in favor of limiting our interaction with…"

"Raccoons," AJ filled in for her, bringing a grin to Beverly's face.

"Yeah, raccoons. I wish she could know what I know. I wish she could have experienced the joy I've experienced, the sorrow, and how Darnell Jackson morns 2F's loss. That was never the case for those who were part of Master Voice. Subjects weren't allowed to express feelings or interact with their Beltigersk masters. How empty that must have felt."

"Master Voice, is that a cult?"

"Really not much different from any fascist organization that would seek to prevent a being's free expression," she said. "Master Voice is both a belief in Beltigersk superiority and a group that was once out in the open but has become clandestine."

"Why would Cheell be involved?" AJ asked. "I get Korgul. They just got spanked by a Beltigersk scientist who obviously wasn't Master Voice. But why Cheell?"

"We believe Cheell aided Korgul in their activities on Earth. Cheell are technologically advanced but had limited capacity to mine resources," Beverly said. "I think it was likely a Cheell plan to plunder Earth and they utilized Korgul to perform the deed."

"That's crazy," AJ said. "You're saying it wasn't all Korgul?"

"Cheell involvement would be very subtle. Removing Korgul stopped their plans for harvesting Fantastium, but Cheell might have other objectives," Beverly said. "That they are involved with your Central Intelligence Service is concerning. Cheell will manipulate humans for their own purposes."

"Like what?"

"The reasons will always be monetary in the end," Beverly said.

"Cheell are amoralistic and value no life beyond their own. Korgul are little better. I am disturbed to discover they are involved in an attempt to overthrow the Beltigerskian government, but I don't find surprise in this discovery."

"Attempt? If you ask me, they were successful," AJ said. "Who's running the show now?"

"AJ, in lieu of current events, that duty falls to me," Beverly said. "I could not have anticipated a series of events that would bring me back to Beltigersk, but that has happened. When we return, I will ask that you take the Korgul vaccine and allow me to fulfill my duty."

He blew out a breath. "Wow, BB, that's heavy. Have you considered how your people are going to respond when they figure out Alicia was in on the whole volcano thing? Maybe you guys are just that enlightened, but if we were talking humans, there'd be a revolt and the whole lot of people with your last name would be out on their ears."

"We have neither last names nor ears, but I understand your point. If events transpired as you fear, I will not be welcomed back as royalty," she said. "The damage to our people's standing within the Galactic Congress will also be severe. It is possible that without our support of humans, Korgul will be allowed to return to Earth."

"You've gotta be kidding," AJ said. "Cat's outta the bag on that one, don't you think? Everyone knows that Korgul were sneaking around."

"You are correct. They would not come back in stealth but rather with force," she said. "If the Galactic Congress lifts the quarantine on Sol, Korgul could make a claim of sovereignty. It would be an extreme measure, but Korgul could potentially utilize advanced weaponry to tame the lesser sentients... humans."

"We'd... they'd... it'd be war," he sputtered.

"You've seen the technology of Xandarj."

"It's pretty great."

"It is not advanced with respect to Cheell. The Cheell have weapons that can neutralize entire cities," Beverly said.

"We've got the A-bomb, too," AJ said, irritation in his voice.

"Not kill, neutralize. They can cause all inhabitants to enter a sort of stunned state where they cannot move for hours," she said. "There's little defense against such an attack."

AJ shook his head. "And the Galactic Congress allows that?"

"There is little that can be done," Beverly said. "The Galactic Congress relies on member nations to enforce laws. It is a fine balance that must be maintained. Preventing atrocities is not a stated objective."

"You've got to be kidding. If that's not a goal, what in the hell is?"

"To create a forum for discussion. To allow member nations to attempt diplomacy before war. To appeal to the most common ideals amongst the broadest coalition. To facilitate trade."

"If Beltigersk has to form a new government, Korgul and Cheell get to take Earth?" AJ asked.

"At worse, Alicia's plan did not lack ambition," Beverly said. "Perhaps she would gain the crown by removing Beltigersk's support for humanity."

"Why wouldn't Cheell just shoot us down then? They would get rid of Alicia and you so there's nobody to take the crown. Korgul and Cheell get what they want."

"I have also wondered this."

"A couple of missing princesses would be a pretty big fly in their ointment," he said. "What if you were just low hanging fruit, but Alicia was somehow still important to their plans? She came out to make sure you got taken care of, but things didn't work out. Since she landed on this ship with us, that would explain why Cheell can't squish us. As explanations go, it doesn't solve the whole mystery, but I think there is hope for your family."

"Your mind is quite devious to explore so many twists and turns," Beverly said. "You have given me hope."

"Good, so I don't suppose you'd let me get some sleep now, would you?"

"I'll do better than that." Beverly held her hand in front of AJ's face and snapped her fingers, sending him instantly to sleep.

A WARM BODY pressed into AJ's midsection and groggily he adjusted, making room, pulling the small figure close with his arm. Consciousness slowly returned and a feeling of dissonance pervaded his waking. He wasn't at home in the junkyard. The warm body wasn't Pam's. He was on a spaceship and his fingers were interlaced in soft fur.

"Chok, is that you?" he asked, holding very still.

"No talk. Chok tired," she answered, moving under his arm.

AJ chuckled. After Pam's death, he'd felt cut off and entertained fantasies about scantily clad women with loose morals. With Jayne, everything had changed. The idea of sex was compelling, but he'd never be fulfilled without a relationship to accompany it.

"Chok, you're very sweet," he said. "Most humans aren't okay sharing a bed unless there is a relationship."

"Chok and Albert Jenkins are friends," she argued.

"More of a relationship," AJ said. "I like you and you're definitely very pretty. I just, well, I'm interested in Amanda Jayne."

"You have said. Chok change Albert Jenkin's mind."

"Chok, you know that's not fair," he said. "I've been truthful with you and you're pushing things. I want to be friends with you, so don't make this hard."

"Chok is good in bed."

He groaned as his mind invented the beginning of an inappropriate clip. "Aww, crap. No, Chok. Not that I'm not tempted, but I just can't."

She turned toward AJ and stroked his chest. That was enough to spur him to action. He reached up and opened the hatch.

"Albert Jenkins angry?" she asked, surprised.

"I don't feel like you're getting the message," he said, pulling on the handle above the hatch opening.

"Don't go," Chok said. "Chok be better. Just sleep."

Cool air pervaded the sleeping bunk and again he was tempted, but then he felt Chok's hands on his waist, stroking his skin. "I'm not sure either of us would be sleeping, Chok." Careful not to kick the small alien, AJ swung inelegantly out of the bunk. Standing on the deck, he leaned into the chest height opening. "Get some sleep, Chok. We'll talk next shift."

"Albert Jenkins no fun."

"I won't disagree," he said, closing the hatch behind him while breathing a sigh of relief.

The sound of a hatch unlocking drew his attention to Jayne's bunk. "Great," he muttered, wondering how much of the interaction she had caught on the video panel within her own capsule, which had the capacity to view any part of the ship, except inside bunks and the head.

Surprisingly, however, she smiled at him. She lay sideways in her bunk with her head resting on her hand. "Trouble in paradise?"

"I think I finally get how you pretty girls feel around guys who don't get the message," AJ said. "She's relentless."

"In this story, you're the pretty girl? Never thought I'd hear that. Give me a minute to adjust."

"Brutal."

"I was a young female doctor in Vietnam," she said dryly. "Please explain to me how it feels to have unwanted passes."

AJ grinned. "But you gave so many of our boys hope, Doc."

"You're incorrigible. And now you go from hunted to the hunt."

"Only with you, Doc. I'm gonna see if I can rig my next bunk to keep out a Xandarj engineer. I don't like my chances."

"You could crawl in with me. I'll keep you safe," she said. "That is, *if* it doesn't give you whiplash."

"Called that right. Are you serious?"

"I'm being selfish, AJ," Jayne said. "I can't sleep. My anxiety is through the roof, but I feel safe when you're near. I'd be using you."

"But you like me, right? More than just someone you've stitched up a few times?"

"I was hoping someone could make this conversation more awkward."

He chuckled. "Awkward is kind of my specialty."

"Get in here."

AJ wasn't about to wait for a third invitation and climbed carefully into the bunk next to Jayne. It was a little close, but there was room for two of them, especially if he kept his back pinned against the wall.

"I'm not sure we could have done this without showers," he said, wadding a blanket under his head for a pillow.

"I want to make this work, AJ," Jayne said, apparently still not done with the conversation. "I'm just not good at the touchy-feely stuff. I kind of get stuck in my head."

"I'm going to hold you, Doc," he said. "Are you okay with that?"

"Yes," She crossed her arms and held her wrists in front of her chest.

AJ scooted over so they faced each other, their knees touching but nothing else. He swept Jayne's hair from her face so it hung behind her ear. "Still okay?"

"This is nice," she said, her eyes searching his face.

He used his free arm to pull them closer together. He stroked her hair, smoothing it back. He ran his hand along her arm, gently grabbing her wrist and laying it on his side. "Doesn't need to be anything more. You don't have to be so closed. Maybe you'd be more comfortable if you rolled over."

She nodded and rolled in place, finding comfort in the fact that their clothed bodies fit so easily together. AJ straightened her hair once again and removed a few strands that had stuck in his beard. Without thinking, he gently kissed her neck as he draped his arm over her and pulled her tight.

"Not too fast," she whispered.

"Shh," he said, allowing his head to sag onto her pillow, his face barely an inch from the back of her head. "Go to sleep, Doc. I've got you."

Jayne's next breath shuddered in her chest but when she released it, much of her tension had dissipated and she drifted off to sleep, her fitful dreams warded off by the grizzled old warrior who gently held her.

TWENTY-TWO
RE-UPPED

"It's about time you two got your heads outta your asses," Darnell greeted AJ as he climbed from the bunk he'd shared with Jayne. "Coffee?"

"Nothing happened," AJ said, keeping his voice low.

Darnell handed over coffee, fruit, and a protein bar. "Looked like something to me."

"I should have stopped Pankee. She's pretty messed up about what both he and Loveit did."

"And you're not?" Darnell asked. "I don't know about you, but I've never been tortured. I can't say I was a big fan."

AJ nodded. "No, I get it. Makes you question things you never thought about before. I let her down."

"And climbing into bed made that better?" Darnell said, grinning. "That's kind of the definition of a *letdown*, isn't it?"

"You're an asshole."

"You couldn't have stopped either of 'em. Doc's a big girl. She's making her own decisions. Pankee taught her an important lesson: we're not in Kansas anymore. It's good to be scared of giant ape-men who have anger issues. AJ, like it or not, she's one of us now and she's gonna get handed a beating once in a while. What you need to do is show her that she can recover; that there's life after an ass-whooping. Give her something more important to think about."

"Loveit got after you pretty good too," he said. "You doing okay?"

"If, by okay, you mean the next time I see him I'm going to reach down his throat and tear out his heart, then sure, I'm doing great," Darnell said without a hint of humor.

AJ chuckled darkly. "If I don't get there first."

"What I don't get is what Loveit's role is," Darnell said. "I get Alicia selling out her family for power. I don't like it, but that's not exactly a new idea. I get Cheell and Korgul playing tag team on the unprotected, unsophisticated humans and trying to steal all our shit. Those three concepts make sense. It's messed up nine ways 'til Sunday, but it's basic greed. But Loveit? How the hell do you sell out your own fricking species? I just don't get it."

AJ shook his head. "I've got nothing. And Reed? That guy reads Air Force Academy all day long. I don't like those chair force boys any more than you do, but he smelled red, white and blue to me."

"It's those damn spooks like Loveit. Saw it a million times in 'Nam," Darnell growled. "They get those kid's heads twisted so bad they don't know which way is up."

"BB, can Reed see what's going on while Alicia's got him on brain lockdown?" AJ asked.

Beverly appeared, wearing her sparkly silver spacesuit and hovering with the aid of a Jetsons-style rocket pack. "That is up to the Beltigersk. It would take considerable effort to completely replace the sensory input. She'd have to be careful. Complete block will drive the host mad."

"Should we get her out of him? I know Jayne has plenty of vaccine left. She never leaves home without it."

"You may think less of me for saying this, but Alicia is trapped in Reed's body. If she is released with the vaccine, we will have difficulty holding her."

"And so we hope she doesn't drive Reed or whatever his name is, mad?" AJ said. "It's crap, but I get it. Keeping Alicia on lockdown is critical. It's not like it wasn't his choice."

"I'll second that," Darnell said. "When she had me, I saw everything going on around me. I just couldn't talk."

"You know I can hear you?" Reed said.

"Sure do, bean curd," AJ said, not looking at him. He followed up by setting his coffee on an oval table. He picked up one of the manuals he'd been breezing through and started flipping pages.

"You getting this, BB?" AJ asked.

"Yes, you can go faster if you want," Beverly said. "Hopefully, we won't need to repair the septic systems."

That made him laugh out loud. "Oh, I wouldn't count on that."

Tork stuck his head around the bulkhead. "Darnell Jackson, if you would take a shift, I will rest. Please wake me if our status changes – which I do not believe it will for a few days. I have located an entertainment package. When we are next together, you will explain to me how a man with a hammer chasing barrels being thrown by an ape is related to donkeys."

Darnell blinked and then understanding dawned. "If you figure it out, you'll have to let me know."

The sound of someone opening a bunk drew their attention aft. A flutter of angst hit AJ as Chok swung out of the bunk she'd run him out of earlier. Darnell stopped in his tracks, clearly interested in the exchange that was about to occur.

"Good morning, Chok," AJ said, trying to keep his voice level.

"An interesting phrase," she said, stretching her narrow frame and smiling as she realized she had Darnell and AJ's full attention. "It is a good morning. Are you reading manuals? I've been dying to get my hands on this beautiful vessel's components, but I cannot translate the manuals by myself. I'm most interested in her power coupling."

"Ah, sure," he said, grateful that she seemed disinterested in discussing the events of the previous night. "I'm hoping to get through most of the manuals this morning."

"Since we are conversing about coupling, was I successful in finally getting Albert Jenkins and the elusive Amanda Jayne to explore coupling of their own?" she asked, causing Darnell to cough on a poorly timed sip of coffee.

"Off limits!" AJ said, more loudly than he needed. "I'm not talking about this with you or anyone."

"That does sound like you had good success then," Chok needled. "You know I would be willing to complete a third if you and Amanda Jayne were so interested. I would bring a lot to our family."

"Chok, no," he said. "Just, no. That's not how we do things."

"I understand," Chok said. "You need to claim your mate before you entertain a third. That is completely understandable. Don't wait too long though. I do not have unlimited patience and I will be highly sought after once I visit Earth."

Darnell chuckled and disappeared behind the bulkhead.

"Not another word, Darnell Jackson," AJ growled. "Not another word."

"I'M NOT a big fan of jump-space, but this is pretty. It seems like there are a million more stars in the sky than around Earth," Jayne said, snaking her hand into AJ's as the two looked forward through the pilot's windows at a quickly growing planet. It had been two jumps and nearly twenty days of sailing, but they'd finally arrived in the Beltigersk solar system.

"Doesn't get old, does it?"

The two had grown closer during the trip but still there was distance, an unease that AJ couldn't find his way around. He'd decided his best course of action was to be patient. The slow pace of space travel had been a nice reprieve, but there was no doubt things would soon get exciting.

"Big D, how's the sensor package working? Are you picking up on any ships?" he asked.

"Dozens," Darnell said.

"I will show them." Beverly projected a top-down view of the solar system and a cluster of vessels around the planet.

"Shit, is that an enemy fleet?" AJ asked.

"No," Beverly said. "Those are mostly Vred with a few Tok and Cheell vessels. They are all sailing under a flag of peace, with a stated mission to provide aid to the Beltigersk people."

Relief flooded his face. "That's good news, right?"

"If you are asking if Cheell will harass *USSF Cardinal*, they will not. It does bring up a new issue. The Cheell might know of Alicia's presence. She has rank beyond my own. It is possible we will be required to turn her over to the Beltigersk High Council that formed to review the events of the attack on my home."

"How do you know about this High Council?" AJ asked.

"Because she's got access to communications, you big dumb oaf," Reed said.

AJ shook his head with irritation.

"You have three days until we get to Beltigersk-5. Probably good to get things figured out before we arrive," Darnell said.

"What if things get dicey?" AJ asked. "How are you feeling about *Cardinal's* handling?"

"Generally good. I wish 2F was still around, but Seamus has been doing a really nice job catching problems and letting me work through them. As long as Greybeard doesn't mind hanging out, I think we can put this youngster through her paces. I like our chances." Darnell patted Greybeard's back and the dog preened at the attention.

"Don't get too comfortable, because I'm pretty sure you don't want Greybeard wearing a Marilyn Monroe dress," Jayne said.

"Hey! That was a private conversation," AJ shot back.

"Like there's any privacy on a ship this small," Darnell said. "I think Greybeard would look pretty good in an ivory dress."

Greybeard barked excitedly, although it was tough to tell if he was for or against the idea.

"Are all humans this pathetic?" Alicia asked through Reed. "It's annoying that you allow your hormones to drive you all over this vessel like animals in rut. I cannot understand why you would resist our rule. You are barely more sentient than the fish that swim in your seas or the worms that crawl through your substrata. If it were possible for Beltigersk to become ill, I would be in a constant state of vomiting."

"If you don't mind, Alicia, this is a private conversation that you are not required to listen to," Jayne said. "You are being rude by interjecting your vitriol. Please do not require us to mute the human you've enslaved against his will."

"It wasn't against his will," she said. "This human was a volunteer."

"Not for this," AJ said. "I guarantee it. And double what Jayne said. Keep talking and I'll introduce a new term... a gag."

"You would be wise to treat me with more respect. You have come to believe that you have more power than you actually do," she said.

"Last chance," he warned.

Alicia clamped Reed's lips shut and grunted with dissatisfaction, although her negativity had effectively shut down the conversation.

A muffled whump announced the closing of the trap door hatch that led to the Tween deck.

"That is a fantastically overdone mechanical system," Chok said, grinning broadly, the white fur on her forearms covered in black grease. "I've never seen a ship where every system has at least one backup. Some of them have multiple."

"We don't have much of a choice," AJ said. "Humans don't have experience designing or manufacturing systems for long-range space travel. Most of what you're looking at inside this ship was manufactured or at least significantly modified specifically for *Cardinal* with little real testing."

"That is not efficient, but I will say that the craftsmanship is quite amazing. There is even a cast aluminum manifold. Such extravagance."

"The overdesign is mostly because we don't have the luxury of knowing what we've messed up. We make up for the unknown problems by tripling any stress we can imagine, which are often already tripled."

"It is like working in a museum," she said. "But that was not why I was below. I was looking into the gravity systems. They are of Cheell manufacture, not just design," Chok said. "They appear to have taken heed of your design objectives and are quite powerful. Much more than a small vessel like this needs even for atmospheric navigation. Now that Blue Tork and Darnell Jackson know how to navigate this vessel, it will be a fast ship while in ordinary space."

"Ordinary?"

"No atmosphere," Chok filled in. "Acceleration is almost never limited by the vessel's engines but rather the quality of the gravity system. Both Cheell and Vred have excellent gravitational systems. The Cheell system is quite expensive. It is nice to work as engineer on such a good ship."

AJ nodded. While he was glad that Chok thought the ship was well built, the presence of so many ships weighed heavily on his mind. Before he could change subjects, however, Beverly appeared before him wearing her sparkly silver spacesuit. In the corner of his field of vision, he noticed something odd. There were half-dollar sized avatars of Greybeard, Jayne and Darnell. It occurred to him that Beverly was showing him who she was letting in on the conversation.

"I've received a response to the message you sent to Major Baird of Army Intelligence," she said.

"What'd you say to her?" Jayne asked, before AJ could ask. "Oh, thank you, Beverly."

AJ glanced at Jayne and grinned as he noticed a virtual sheet of paper floating in front of her. He had no doubt that it was the message he'd sent to Baird almost three weeks previous.

"How'd she send a message back?" AJ asked.

"I appended your message with instructions on how to respond.

She must have expended significant resources to have built the communication device I specified."

"Well, I think her resident nerd, I can't remember his name, was pretty sharp," AJ said. "She probably had him do it."

"Alan McAlistair," Beverly filled in. "Perhaps. I provided an engineering diagram using components available on Earth."

"She probably had an entire NASA team working on it," Darnell said. "Those kids don't mess around."

"Yes. An achievement in such short time without access to a manufactory," Beverly said. "The message is audio. Would you like me to play it?"

"Doc, you caught up enough?" AJ asked.

"Certainly," she said. "Although, I'm not sure why you didn't share this earlier."

"Honestly didn't think we'd get a response. Figured it was more of a last will and testament type of thing."

"Still could be," Darnell said. "Go ahead, BB."

To Albert Jenkins, et. al.

Your message was received and to say that its contents are surprising is somewhat understated. We are not aware of the Xandarj species or their solar system. Our scientists would appreciate detailed location information so we could study their portion of space in more detail. Your departure from Earth was both highly unconventional and unexpected. While I am grateful that you survived the encounter with US Air Defense, it is only by the grace of God that our pilots used unwarranted discretion. You should know that this discretion ended a highly decorated warrior's career. I tell you this so that you know your actions are not without consequences.

In the past weeks, we have not been idle. An investigation into Gerald Loveit's illegal capture and interrogation of you and your companions is underway. Your accusation of Loveit's coordination with potential hostile alien forces - Cheell and Korgul are being reviewed at the highest levels. The Secretary of Defense has called you, Darnell Jackson, and Doctor Amanda Jayne back to service in the

Army, attached to US Military Intelligence and under my command. This is for the single purpose of taking custody of Gerald Loveit and returning him to US custody. It is highly preferred that this be accomplished in the most humane way possible.

You are congratulated on your retrieval of USSF Cardinal. It is requested that this be returned in good working order as quickly as possible, given your current orders. If you still have Sergeant Reed in custody, it is requested that he be returned for questioning.

A word of warning. I implore you to understand that your actions will have long-lasting effects on humanity's diplomatic interface with the Galactic Empire. You are advised to proceed with utmost caution. Please take great care in every interaction. Your words and actions will and have already had long lasting impacts on our world. Please do not overlook this most fearsome responsibility.

Finally, I find it of great surprise that the entirety of US intelligence is unable to locate Marion "Lefty" Johnson, Joshua McQueen or the Vred alien only known as Sharg. If you have the capacity to communicate with same, please inform them I need to speak with them urgently and that their safety is ensured at the highest possible levels.

Respectfully, Major Jacqueline Baird

"Well doesn't that beat all," AJ grunted.

"They can't call us back," Darnell grumbled.

"I don't think that's the point," Jayne said. "They're trying to provide us cover. Imagine when this gets out to the public and people figure out how ineffective the US Government has been. At least this way, they can say that military intelligence was involved."

"Or hang us with it," AJ said.

"Do you really think that wasn't happening already?" she asked. "It's one thing for the CIA to illegally capture and torture civilians. I'd hope it's another thing entirely to grab service members. I think she's trying to provide protection for us."

"I don't want to work for Sec Def Baird or anyone else," AJ said.

"Right there with you, AJ," Darnell said.

"Didn't sound optional to me," Jayne added.

"Do we want to tell Lefty they're looking for him?" Darnell asked.

"Is it even possible?" AJ asked.

"Yes," Beverly said, putt-putting up in front of him, her rocket pack spewing out little round smoke rings. "Sharg has a receiver that should not be difficult to reach. It will take several days for the communication to arrive, but it is reliable."

"Why would I even question it?" AJ said.

"They need to be up to date so they don't walk into something unexpected," Jayne said. "We should send your initial letter to Baird and her response. Let them decide what to do with it."

"That's actually not a bad idea," AJ said.

She grinned. "It hurts that you're surprised."

TWENTY-THREE
ONE WAY FORWARD

Darnell pulled a pouch of coffee from a small opening in the side of the manufactory and walked up to the bunk AJ and Jayne had been sharing. He knocked. "Wake up, lovebirds. Beltigersk-5 is visible. You're not going to want to miss the next couple of hours."

"Go away," AJ grumbled.

The sound of the latch sliding preceded the opening of the hatch. "Everybody has clothing on," Jayne said. She'd been awake for some time and was seated cross-legged next to the hatch, reading on a tablet.

Darnell's smile was kind. "You go as slow as you need, Amanda. That boy isn't going anywhere."

"Except maybe the head. How long before we make orbit?" AJ asked, rolling onto his back and looking upside down at Darnell.

"Close to three hours, give or take," Darnell said. "You can't believe how fast we're slowing down. Chok wasn't kidding about these gravity systems."

"Sounds like a lot of techno babble to me."

"Whatcha reading, Doc?" Darnell asked.

"Beverly gave me a medical primer," Jayne said. "Alien physiology is remarkable. Did you know that Vred are almost one hundred percent efficient in their consumption of oxygen? Well, closer to eighty-five. More importantly, they exhaust carbon dioxide through a fine network of scales around their neck and on their backsides."

"Yup, exactly what I need to do," AJ chuckled, grabbing a handle and pulling himself from the shared bunk.

"More like methane, if I know my gasses," Darnell said. "Not sure why that's impressive, Doc. Chok figured out how to lower the bulkhead between the cockpit and passenger spaces. You might want to relocate so you can watch our approach."

"Do you know why people suffocate if they try to hold their breath too long?" Jayne asked.

"I always figured they'd pass out first," Darnell said.

"They do," Jayne said. "But imagine they're under water. They suffocate because they can't expel carbon dioxide. They have access to oxygen in what they breathed in. This adaptation allows Vred to hold their breath for a long time."

"And people find them because their butts are bubbling," AJ called, just before he closed the door to the head.

"It's not too late to run, Doc," Darnell said. "I'll hold him down next time we get to civilization."

Jayne grinned. "Actually, he's right. They would bubble."

"Don't say stuff like that. It just encourages him."

"It's cute, in a kind of juvenile way," Jayne said, handing her tablet to Darnell before sliding out. "My world used to be filled with pretense. Not so much anymore."

"No, the big man has plenty of faults, but pretense isn't one of them," Darnell said, handing back the tablet and leading Jayne forward.

"I wish we'd known about lowering the bulkhead before," Jayne said. "That's a spectacular view."

"Enjoy it," Alicia said through Reed. "You'll be in a cage once we reach Beltigersk-5."

"It speaks," Darnell said. "And it probably shouldn't if it'd like to continue to have unobstructed breathing."

"I will enjoy it when our roles are reversed, Darnell Jackson. Remember, I was in your head. I know what you fear."

"Last warning," Darnell said.

To this point, the trip with Alicia controlling Reed hadn't been difficult. She had no need to move the sergeant's body and generally kept to herself. Every few days, short conversational barbs were exchanged, but the encounters fell well below any threshold that would cause the crew to further restrain her.

"Did you have a morning meal, Darnell? Blue Tork?" Jayne asked. "I believe we still have a considerable portion of the sweet orange breadfruits."

Blue Tork lazily turned and blinked. "No," he answered, shaking his head like a sloth might.

"That whole thing just freaks me out," Darnell said, raising eyebrows at Tork.

"I read about that," Jayne said. "Xandarj are able to enter a semi-conscious state where the stimulus around them is muted. Under the right circumstances, they can push themselves further awake if necessary. I probably shouldn't have asked about breakfast because in that state, he burns a lot less calories and limited atmosphere. For him, time passes really fast. It's an amazing adaptation for a space-faring species."

"Kind of twists how I think of evolution taking a long time," Darnell said.

"I'm not sure the adaptation was for space travel. It's just convenient," she said. "So, breakfast? I know AJ will want some when he gets out of the shower."

"I'll tell you that's a nice change," Darnell said. "He's much more interested in keeping clean now that he's sharing that bunk with you."

"Benefits of endorphins."

AJ flopped into a chair next to Jayne and handed her a fist-sized orange fruit resembling a potato. "You guys just can't help talking about me."

"Feel like playing chess?" she asked, setting her tablet on the table in front of them with a chess board displayed on its surface.

"Your move, Doc," he said, lifting an eyebrow as he stared at her.

"Patience," Jayne said, not missing a beat, moving the pawn from in front of her king.

The two periodically paused the game to take stock of the growing orange and brown disc that was Beltigersk-5. Finally, a warning alarm sounded and Blue Tork sat up, stretching his arms and legs to draw blood out to his extremities.

"Did I miss anything?" he asked, checking the various gauges.

"I was just about to wake you," Darnell said. "We've been given orbital instructions. I've got them entered and I'm about to take us in."

Blue Tork focused on the display in front of him as Xandarj words and symbols scrolled past. "I do not see error in your navigation. Please execute when it is suitable to you."

"Chok, please report to your seat. We're going to get strapped in for final approach to Beltigersk-5," Darnell called over ship comms.

"I will not miss you," Alicia said. "You are a trivial species with petty, uninteresting concerns. I have never been in the presence of those who show such a lack of nobility. I no longer wonder why humanity was enslaved by Korgul with none to care."

"I wondered when you'd get started," AJ said, picking up a black cloth he'd brought forward with him after his shower.

"Yes. Please show human temperament to the Beltigersk Council and the peaceful coalition of Galactic Empire citizens who have arrived to provide aid."

"AJ, don't," Jayne said. "She's right. She has a right to express her opinion. I'm sure Beverly is recording her words for posterity."

"My words could not be truer," Alicia said. "Humanity needs a strong hand to help it grow to ascendance. It is a surprise that Earth has not already destroyed itself. Oh, that's right. If not for intervention by Cheell, humanity would have used weapons of mass destruction many years ago."

"That's bullshit," AJ said, angrily.

"Ask my sister," Alicia said. "The Cheell intervened with the aid of your own Central Intelligence Agency to remove critical components from not one but two nations who were planning on utilizing them. Such is the inbred hatred on your planet."

"BB?" AJ asked.

"There was a report about this," Beverly said. "It was not verified."

"I've had about enough of this shit," AJ growled, standing up and lunging at Reed.

"No!" Jayne ordered, stopping AJ a moment before he made contact. "No," she said more softly. "I believe finesse is required. Beverly, are you not concerned that Alicia would find footing with those who seek to undermine your people?"

"What are you asking, Doctor Jayne?" Beverly asked, having switched to her black robe.

"Wouldn't it be better if Alicia were to speak second, not first, to your council?"

"That is not my decision to make," Beverly said.

Jayne smiled craftily as she produced a syringe. "No. I don't suppose it is." And before Beverly could argue further, Jayne plunged the syringe into Reed's arm and delivered the contents.

"Was that..." AJ asked, looking at Jayne like she might have come unglued.

"Korgul, Beltigersk vaccine?" Jayne asked sweetly, extracting the emptied needle from Reed's arm. "Yes. Yes, it was. If previous timeframes hold, we'll have a nice, quiet couple of days while Alicia puts on her swimsuit and figures out a way out of Reed."

"We could lock him in a cabinet," AJ said.

"That was not wise," Beverly said.

"Why?"

"We can't lock Master Sergeant Reed up, even though Alicia is currently working to expel herself from his body. We will report this interaction to the council and they can respond however they see fit," Beverly said.

"You know we were within our rights to do this," AJ said. "As agents of the United States of America, we are tasked with returning Mr. Reed home so he can be interrogated. I imagine Doctor Jayne recognized this particular wrinkle and came up with what looked like a win-win. Beltigersk can have their angry little princess back and we get our man back."

"I had no choice," Reed groaned. "It was my mission to provide a failsafe. I had no idea that bug would infect me like that. I never signed up for this crap!" He started slapping his legs and torso, like ants were crawling over his skin.

"Hey, slow down there, buddy," AJ said. "What are you doing?"

"If she's on me, I'm gonna crush her!" He was on the verge of hysteria.

"He has an implant. I'll talk to him," Beverly said. "Crawford, stop! Talk to me!"

"You're one of them!" he said, trying to get away from her, which was impossible given the restraints.

"I am, but I'm one of the good guys," she said. "Alicia will make her way to your dermis between forty and fifty hours from now. The vaccine Doctor Jayne applied makes it impossible for her to ever take control of you again. Your slapping has no effect because she is not a bug that you can squash. All Beltigersk are in the nanometer range, so you cannot physically affect her. You are only hurting yourself."

He calmed and looked at Beverly. "How can I trust you? You're one of them."

"I know you're part of a special operatives team," Beverly said. "You have certainly been informed on the interaction between Albert Jenkins and me. I have no more intent to harm you than I do him. Beltigersk and human can live in harmony, as symbiotes. Together we're more than we are apart."

"How old are you, son?" AJ asked, crouching in front of the man and pulling on the restraints that held his arms.

"Twenty-four."

"That's what I'd first thought," AJ said, successfully releasing the man's arms. "What's with all the gray hairs?"

"Brown."

AJ nodded. "Now, Sergeant, I'm going to release your legs. You'll be free to walk around the cabin, but if you cause trouble, we'll lock you up. Do you understand what I'm saying?"

"Why are you being nice to me? We hunted you down."

"I feel like you might have seen the light about Mr. Loveit's plan," AJ said. "You'd be a strong asset if you got on the right side of this. You know, undo some of the damage you've caused."

"I wasn't even part of it. Not really. They told us about you guys. Said you were selling out."

"You still believe that?" AJ asked.

"I don't know what to believe."

"That's reasonable," AJ said. "So here are the rules. You don't make trouble. You don't leave the ship. Screw that up and you'll be in leg irons for the rest of our trip. It's a long way back home. Good copy?"

"Good copy."

"Perfect."

"Hate to break up your little love fest, but there's a big damn ship approaching from below and it's moving fast," Darnell said and then picked up a microphone. "This is Darnell Jackson of the *USSF Cardinal*. We're here on a diplomatic mission, with Beltigersk passengers. Please modify current heading to avoid collision."

"Darnell?" AJ asked. Suddenly, a ship half the length of a football field, completely blotted out their forward view.

"I have initiated communication, Darnell Jackson," Beverly said. "The Tok ship has no hostile intention, although the captain is amused by your response."

"Would you get a look at that thing?" AJ said in awe.

What they could see of the Tok ship was all gentle curves and highly polished metallic surfaces. There were no obvious breaks in the ship's skin, including engine ports, antennae, weapons, viewing glass or even seams where the metal skin had been joined.

Suddenly and without warning, the Tok ship jumped away from the *Cardinal*, becoming a small dot thousands of miles away in moments.

"How is that even possible?" AJ asked.

"Only the Tok know," Blue Tork answered.

"And they don't share with Xandarj," Chok said, sliding into one of the open chairs.

"My presence is requested on the surface," Beverly said, wearing her black dress robes. "Would you make your way to these coordinates, Darnell Jackson? I believe you will recognize the location once you have arrived."

"I'm not getting locked up again," AJ said.

"I communicated this," Beverly said. "The habitation will have a readily accessible door and the *USSF Cardinal* will not be threatened even if you decide to leave. I beg that you do not, however. Discussions will be sensitive. If I were to disappear in the middle of a negotiation, the impact would be negative."

"We've come this far. Might as well see it through."

"If you're not already strapped in, this will be a bit bumpy. Hold onto your butts," Darnell said. "We'll be planetside in thirty-five minutes."

USSF Cardinal tipped nose forward toward the planet and accelerated, encountering the first bumps of planetary atmosphere within a few minutes.

"This whole gravity thing makes it hard to tell when you're accelerating and decelerating," AJ said.

"We're decelerating," Darnell said. "Even with the heat shielding this baby has, we've gotta keep things down to a dull roar. Good news is, the gravity systems are even more efficient this close to the planet. We can use them..."

"Just looking for faster or slower, Big D," AJ said, cutting him off.

"What? Jayne gets to talk about carbon dioxide farts, but I can't talk about gravity systems?"

"Farts are funny, Big D."

"I suppose that's hard to argue," he agreed.

Twenty minutes later, they were sailing over the top of red sand dunes.

"Good Lord! Is that what's left of the volcano?" AJ asked. For their benefit, Beverly provided a wireframe of the original mountain. A third of the mass had been lost from the top. "I bet the explosion cleared out the valley where we stayed last time."

"You can see the force waves along the ground," Jayne said. "Amazing how it pushed all that sand to the side. It must have been an incredible explosion."

"Crap, that's fast," AJ said, pointing at a cluster of buildings that sat on the edge of a still-cooling lava flow. "Is that area safe for us to set down?"

"Temperature is roughly the boiling point of water," Beverly said. "Your vessel will not have difficulty, though you should not venture outside without your ship suits."

"Good advice."

"Darnell, the highlighted habitat has been modified for human and Xandarj. You should set down where I am indicating," Beverly said.

"Got it," Darnell said, adjusting their flight. "What do you think, Tork? Am I doing okay with this?"

"You are very quick to learn these skills," Tork said. "You would not have difficulty finding work at Dralli Station. There is a shortage of good pilots."

After setting down, a low-slung, spidery robot emerged from a panel in the side of one of the habitats. In two of its eight articulated legs, it held a thick roll of material that it set down next to the dome, slowly extending a walking path between the two ships. As soon as the material was fully stretched out, a thin transparent membrane popped up, one side sealing to the habitat and the other to the ship, creating a tunnel.

"Didn't get that before," AJ said.

"I am surprised," Beverly said. "They are more prepared for visitors than I had expected."

"Okay, kids," AJ said. "I want everyone packing, except for Sergeant Reed."

"You cannot do that," Beverly said. "We are here for diplomacy."

"Just raccoons, BB," AJ said. "It's not optional. We've had a lot of shit come our way and I'm not going to be unprepared."

"I understand, but I wish you would listen to me."

"We don't exactly have a good track record with people treating us like equals," he said. "We'll keep our type of persuaders."

"It would be best if Crawford Reed accompanied us," Beverly said. "The council will want to extract Alicia once I inform them of her presence."

"Tork, Chok, and I will get things shut down here and be along shortly. I doubt we'll get lost," Darnell said.

AJ nodded and made his way to the airlock which showed green. Beverly assured him that meant both proper pressure and atmospheric content had been achieved.

"How bad is this going to get?" he asked, trooping down the stairs, keeping Reed in front of him.

"This will depend on the composition of the council," Beverly said. "When I was last here, there were few who would admit to the ideals Alicia now espouses. I fear that might have changed. I will not know until I stand with the council."

"Is there any danger you'll be attacked?"

"Not physically," she said. "Censure is a severe form of punishment. For a society that lives primarily for the purpose of communicating with each other, becoming cut off is considerable punishment. Enough to keep our citizens to reasonable standards of conduct."

"When will you talk about Reed's visitor?" he asked, not sure if they could be overheard.

"I will broach the topic immediately, only waiting for the proper introductions and a description of the council's purpose. It is possible they will offer to elevate me to queen. I hope to inform them of Alicia before that occurs."

"I feel like you're missing an opportunity," AJ said. "What if Alicia couldn't be found."

"Then we would be no different from her and my mission to elevate Beltigersk society would become a lie. My desire to undo the wrongs of our people would be similarly undermined." Beverly abruptly changed the subject. "The manufactory is well stocked with raw materials suitable to create most things you might enjoy. I've even taken the liberty to upload a few attempts at recreating your homemade beer recipes. You'll have to let me know if I was successful."

"And you'll let me know if I need to get you out of here, right?" AJ asked, suddenly concerned for his friend.

"I will, Albert Jenkins. I have no doubt of your loyalty and bravery. I thank you for this reassurance."

"Be safe, BB."

"The only way forward is through, Albert Jenkins. I believe it was from you that I first heard this saying."

TWENTY-FOUR
TWIST

"Well, if this doesn't feel like a full circle," Darnell said, tapping on the manufactory's touch screen. A moment later, he opened a panel and withdrew two tumblers filled with amber liquid.

"Feels more like we're sitting at the kids' table," AJ grumbled.

Reed eyed the drink jealously. "Could I get one of those?"

"Sure, you've been a decent sport," Darnell said. "Just know that this is home brew, or at least Beverly's rendition of it anyway. Doc Jayne, you need anything while I'm up?"

She looked up from her reading and smiled. "I'd take tea."

"How long will they leave this thing in me?" Reed asked, nervously flicking dust from his arms.

"You need to take it down a notch. You've got the vaccine so it's not like she can actually do something to you if she wanted." AJ accepted the beer from Darnell and gave it an experimental sip.

"You know, I think I'll run food out to Tork and Chok," Jayne said, changing her mind on the tea. "Anything you need from the ship?" So ingrained was their fear of the Beltigersk people that the two Xandarj refused to exit the ship even though Beverly had given her word they would be safe inside the habitat.

"Can't think of anything," AJ said.

She tapped on the manufactory and made her way out through the umbilicus to the ship.

"Glad you guys are working through things," Darnell said after she disappeared through the habitat's exterior hatch.

"Easy to be patient when you're old," AJ said, grinning.

Suddenly, Beverly appeared on the coffee table in front of them, wearing her formal black robes.

"Heya, BB," AJ said. "We were just talking about you."

"I apologize for the extended delay," Beverly said. "The diplomatic situation is considerably worse than I had anticipated."

"What kind of worse?" he asked.

"Many of the details are considered state secrets," Beverly said. "Much is as we feared, many of mother's most powerful supporters were killed when the volcano's lava flow was diverted by Korgul. The Master Voice cult has gained significant power. Crawford Reed is requested to place his left arm into the port next to the manufactory so Alicia is able to return to our gathering."

"She's on my arm?" Reed asked, the panic in his voice rising.

"She will depart as soon as you comply with the request from the Beltigersk Council," Beverly explained patiently.

"How bad are things, BB?" AJ asked.

The fuzzy image of a haggard old man appeared.

"77-A, why are you here? We are not allowed to meet outside of council. This is a violation," Beverly warned, stepping back, her face full of concern.

As she talked, Reed walked over to the manufactory and placed his left arm against a plate that throbbed with a dim blue light. Upon contact, wide bands wrapped around his forearm and bicep, lashing him to the counter. "AAAAAHHHH!" he exclaimed, startled by the unexpected appearance of the restraints. "Help me!"

"Shit!" AJ said, jumping up.

"Listen, quickly!" The haggard old man's voice filled the room, distracting AJ.

"They've got Reed!"

"Your man is a loss," the old Beltigersk said. "You must leave now. The queen is alive. You must travel to Fimil-2 planet and talk to..."

He disappeared. Reed's anxious pleas turned into screams of pain as metallic tendrils emerged from the thick bands holding his arm, piercing him, and snaking into his body. AJ started to move toward Reed when pain like he'd never experienced before coursed through his body. Every nerve seemed alight with fire and all thoughts were forced from his mind. A single image appeared before him. Alicia was free and she was pissed.

"I told you there would come a time when our fortunes would be reversed," she said. "You should have released me from the airlock when you had your chance. I could kill you quickly as I have the soldier, Reed, but there will be no mercy for you."

"AJ, you must leave." Beverly's voice was a whisper, barely audible over Alicia and the pain.

He struggled to gain control of his body, but was awash in a sea of fire and pain, his nerve receptors overriding any commands his mind was trying to give. Dimly, he became aware of Darnell's screams next to him and hope of salvation ebbed.

Something roughly jerked his arm up, nearly dislocating his shoulder. He shrank from the violence and managed to break free, only to feel his chest hit the floor.

"AJ, crawl!" Jayne's voice was a shout, but the sound was barely audible over the rushing in his ears. He had no idea how to crawl, as he had no feedback from his arms and legs, but he did his best.

A sharp pain tore through his side, momentarily overriding everything else. Something had pierced his skin and his body was being ripped in half. AJ was certain the end was near and a part of him was hoping death would come quickly.

"Crawl, AJ!"

He tried again to mimic crawling, but every motion seemed to focus intense pain from his side. "Leave me," he rasped.

He was jerked off his knees and his face hit the floor. Frankly, it was surprising he could even tell he'd been on his knees. Perhaps he'd been crawling after all. He reached out with his hands and dragged himself forward and all of a sudden, the searing pain was gone – well, most of it anyway.

A line grew taut in front of his face and the painful tugging began again on his torso. Wildly, he looked around, finding himself lying halfway through the umbilicus to the *Cardinal*. A thin cable protruded from his side and blood gushed from around the wound.

"What the hell!?" He reached for the line just as someone gave it a pull causing him to slide about a foot forward. "Stop!"

"AJ?" Tork's voice carried through the umbilicus. "Are you, *you*?"

"Stop pulling on that line!" He cried out, nearly passing out.

"Darnell. We couldn't get him," Jayne called down the walkway. AJ looked back through the hatch of the dome and saw Darnell lying on the floor inside. "I don't think we hit anything critical, but don't pull the prongs out. You could cause more bleeding."

AJ looked down at what he soon discovered to be some sort of mini harpoon. Chubby, round spring-loaded arms extruded from his back and wrapped around the wound. His friends had dragged him from the habitat like he'd been the prize catch of a twisted spearfishing tournament.

Inspecting the front side of the harpoon device, AJ saw where the head could easily be detached, something he proceeded to do. Ignoring Jayne's instructions, he reached behind and pulled the head through his body, screaming in agony as he did. Fortunately, the pain passed almost as soon as the metal was gone.

Reattaching the head, AJ looped the cable around his waist and tied it off.

"Give me slack!" he ordered.

"No, you've got to come back," Jayne called. "Beverly was clear. They control the umbilicus. We can't come down there."

"Tough shit. I'm not leaving Big D!"

The cable loosened, allowing him to spool several yards at his feet.

"What are you doing, AJ?" she called worriedly.

"Reel it back in when I start screaming again," he said, shaking his head ruefully, considering his next move.

"No, AJ," Jayne pleaded.

He ignored her and dove into the room. Darnell lay too far in for AJ to reach him in one leap and when his feet landed on the habitat's floor, excruciating pain exploded across his body.

"Nobility is for the weak," Alicia growled in satisfaction. "You should not have come back."

He leaned forward and extended his arms, holding his lips together, trying not to scream. He still held a mental picture of where his best friend lay, so he inched forward until he bumped against something. Not able to feel much of anything, AJ grabbed tightly, wrapping his whole body around what he hoped was Darnell. He opened his mouth and screamed in agony.

Time seemed to disappear as AJs entire universe dissolved into pain. He concentrated on nothing else except keeping his arms tightly clenched. For all he knew, he was hugging himself, but he hoped he'd been successful at grabbing his thickly muscled friend.

At some point, he must have lost consciousness and then slowly awoke to what felt like peace. Pain, yes, but not the agony he feared. He heard Darnell's complaint. "You're bleeding on me."

"What?" AJ asked, too far out of it to piece things together.

"You've a hole in you," Darnell said. "You're losing a lot of blood."

AJ felt a heavy hand around his back and pressure under his shoulder. His knees were dragging across the ground, but he couldn't seem to do anything about it. He shook his head groggily and tried to open his eyes but found he could not.

"Reed?" AJ croaked.

"He's down," Darnell said, hefting AJ through *Cardinal's* hatch to the waiting arms of Jayne and Tork.

"You dumb, brave man," Jayne cried, slicing through AJ's shirt with scissors already in hand as Tork unwound the cable from around his waist. "You could have bled out."

"Beverly," he said, still unable to form more than a single word.

"We don't know," Jayne said, working on the large wound in his abdomen. "You're bleeding a lot. I'm going to have to open you up."

"Marska," AJ grunted. "Alicia knows."

"Marska?" Jayne asked, pushing him on his side to work on the exit wound.

"It is a city on Fimil-2," Blue Tork said, fiddling with his HUD. "It is two jumps. We will need more information. Marska is quite large."

"Go," AJ urged.

HARSH WHITE LIGHT filtered into AJ's eyes and he became aware of something on his face. Trying to breathe, he choked around a foreign object in the back of his throat. He reached for his face, but his arms felt like they were made of lead.

Cool fingers wrapped around his hand and gently redirected it away from his face. "AJ, you're safe." Jayne's voice was soft. "This will feel a little weird. We had to intubate you and I'm going to pull the tube out."

Weird was a poor description of the tube leaving his body and without Jayne's reassurance, his panic might have overtaken him. "What happened?" he rasped.

"You were attacked on Beltigersk," she said. "My best guess was by some type of neurological disruptor. I don't know about Beverly."

He tried to sit up, even though he couldn't yet fully open his eyes. Pain in his abdomen was intense and he reached for his side. "Not neurological."

"Don't get up." She pushed him back onto the cushions. "No, that is on me and I feel awful. We shot you with Xandarj fishing equipment. It was the only way we could drag your body out of the habitat."

"Darnell?"

"I'm here, buddy," Darnell said. "They hit me with some sort of darts. Knocked me right out."

"No pain?"

"Not even a little," he said. "Just put me down like a side of beef."

"Reed?"

"He didn't make it," Darnell said. "Alicia did something bad to him – *Dante's Inferno* bad. They would have done the same to me, but I wasn't within range of the device Reed was attached to. I owe you one."

"More than one," AJ managed between pained breaths. "Beverly?" he asked, trying to rouse his constant companion for the last year.

"She might be hurt too," Jayne said. "She hasn't been helping with your recovery. I had to operate to stop your bleeding. We're lucky there was a full surgical kit on board."

"Did you shoot me with the fishing thing?" AJ asked Jayne.

"That was me," Tork said as AJ blinked, wincing in the bright light. "Amanda Jayne told me where the safest shot would be. I am sorry. It was actually your symbiote's idea."

"Beverly told you to shoot me?"

"She sent instructions with me when I left the habitat. She knew an attack was coming but didn't want to spook Alicia before I could get to the ship," Jayne said. "I think she was expecting to patch you back up herself, though."

"BB?" he called, looking for the familiar HUD or the sparkling reflection of her Jetsons-era spacesuit. Instead, he only heard the thrum of *Cardinal's* systems and the beeping of a medical push pump next to him.

"I was afraid of that," Jayne said. "The neurological attack was an attack on her. Otherwise, they wouldn't have had to attack Darnell with darts."

AJ swallowed hard, his mind flitting back to his first moments with Beverly lying crushed beneath a pile of space junk. He still remembered their conversation, when Beverly delicately convinced him to allow her to take up residence in his body. He'd had no choice then and while there had been growing pains as they learned to live together, he couldn't imagine what life without her would be like.

"You think she's dead?" he asked, a single tear forming in the crusty old soldier's eyes. Grief washed over him and he thought about his wife, Pam. Feelings long buried threatened to overwhelm him.

Jayne shook her head. "We don't know, AJ," she said, holding his hand and stroking the tear from his cheek.

He closed his eyes and allowed sleep to take him.

THE SOUNDS of daily life aboard USSF *Cardinal* slowly filtered into AJ's subconscious. Opening his eyes, he was glad to discover he wasn't intubated again. He was lying in a lower berth and if his body was any indicator, he'd been out for a while. Attempting to sit up, he felt the familiar pang of staples pulling against flesh but overall, the pain was down to a dull roar.

"Beverly?" he asked. He kept his voice quiet, not wanting to share his grief with anyone else if she failed to answer. Instinctively, he knew she wasn't there. If she'd thought sacrificing herself for him and his crew was the only option, she would have done it without hesitation. He didn't feel he was worthy of that sacrifice.

A certain urgency drove him out of the berth and he was grateful to have been placed at the lowest level. He ended up spilling out onto the deck with far better results than if he'd had to try to lower himself from the top.

"Albert Jenkins, you should not be up," Chok said, crouching down beside him. "Why have you fallen out of your nest?"

"How long?"

"Perhaps six feet," she answered. "I do not believe you were made taller."

"No. How long was I out?"

Her head quivered in a way that let AJ know she found the

exchange humorous. "Eight cycles." As AJ worked to stand, she helped him. "I am glad that we no longer need change your diaper."

AJ looked down and discovered he was indeed wearing what looked like a diaper. "Oh, gawd," he complained as he stumbled with her help to the head.

"It is much better than requiring your shipmates to clean you."

He stepped into the head and closed the hatch behind him, stripping off clothing that felt like it needed to be burned. A knock on the hatch caught his attention as he sat naked on the toilet.

"It's busy."

"AJ, I'm coming in," Jayne said.

"Doc, I'm naked."

"Good warning," she said, opening the door and slipping inside. He struggled to pluck his shirt from the ground to lay across his lap.

"No privacy?" he complained weakly.

"You know I'm the one who put that shirt on you and have been changing your dressings," Jayne said. "Besides, I'm a doctor."

"You saved my ass again, Doc. Thank you."

"That's more like it," she said, crouching next to him.

The head was cramped and Jayne had no issues getting closer than AJ felt comfortable with. Paying little attention to his emotional discomfort, however, she poked at his wound and pulled at his shoulder.

"We good?" he asked.

"I guess I don't have to ask if Beverly showed up," she said, opening an alcohol wipe and cleaning his skin.

"I can't believe she's gone," AJ said. "I didn't even know she was so important to me. I feel lost, like when I lost Pam. I can't even believe I just said that. How could I grow so attached?"

She looked into his face and pulled him into a hug. "I'm sorry, AJ."

He returned her hug. "This is kind of weird, though, right? Hugging on the toilet?"

"It's a little weird," she agreed. "I think the shirt on your lap makes it okay though."

"I need a shower. Can I take one?"

"That's why I came in. Let me put something on your lacerations." He sat back and allowed her to place bandages over his wound. "I'm going to help you into the shower, AJ. I don't care about your man parts. I don't want you falling and reinjuring yourself."

"That has to be the most depressing thing I've ever heard."

"Okay, I care a little. I'm compartmentalizing, which is a skill surgeons develop because we see people under extreme circumstances," she said. "Change the setting and I'll care plenty about all your parts."

"I can't tell if you're hitting on me or trying to bust my nuts. If you're not messing with me, we've got to work on your pillow talk."

She smiled and held her hands out to help him stand. "We'll see what you think after a good soap cycle."

"Shit, don't talk like that either!"

Jayne turned on the water which soaked them both. "You're as fickle as a long-tailed cat in a room full of rockers."

"That's not a saying," AJ said, reveling in the rush of warm water over his skin.

"I thought I was going to lose you, Albert Jenkins."

He shook his head. "You shot me with a spearfishing arrow. What'd you think was going to happen?"

"Actually, Blue Tork did. He's a really good shot, too. You should thank him,"

"I'm not going to thank him for shooting me."

"If I'd taken the shot, I would probably have hit your intestines," she said. "That's a bad way to go."

"Is Darnell okay?"

"Minor injuries," Jayne said, moving around so she stood directly in front of AJ, her clothing completely saturated. "I'm serious, AJ. I've had a lot of time to think about this. I know I was protecting myself by keeping distance between us, but my plans didn't change anything. I'd never felt so alone when I thought you'd died."

"I know the feeling," AJ said, his mind going back to Pam and then Beverly.

"But you also knew intimacy," she said. "You had a partner, two partners really. I've never had that. I've always been able to look past death because it was just me. I didn't really know how else to be. I've been terrified of you, of what a relationship with you could mean."

"What's changed?"

"Nothing and everything," she said and leaned into him, kissing him without reservation. When she pulled back it was only a few inches. "I'm all in, Albert Jenkins."

"Are you saying you want to go steady?" he asked, his lips curling into a smile.

"You're such a dork."

TWENTY-FIVE
MAD SCIENCE

"Who knew space travel took so long?" AJ asked, impatient for the final transition from jump-space which would drop them in the Fimil system.

"We've sailed further than any human in history and you're complaining about a few days?" Darnell asked, eyeing the countdown.

"Please focus, Darnell Jackson," Tork interrupted. "The space around Fimil will be quite busy. It will be imperative that we quickly locate and occupy our assigned approach vector.

"I thought I read that we'd be at least four days travel from Fimil-2," Darnell said.

"That is true. The population of the Fimil system exceeds six hundred billion souls. The amount of trade is considerable and discipline is necessary for safe travel," Tork answered. "There will be repercussions if we are not able to sufficiently control our vessel."

"Great," Darnell said. "No pressure."

Greybeard barked, bumping his head against Darnell's thigh. AJ imagined Seamus was communicating his willingness to help, although the conversation was not broadcast in any way he could hear it.

"AJ, would you mind sitting with me a minute?" Jayne asked. He looked out at the opaque sheath of jump-space that surround them. They had several minutes before Fimil, although he really didn't want to miss their arrival. She seemed to understand his hesitance. "It'll only take a minute, I promise."

He shrugged and took a seat next to her. Distracted by a million thoughts, she drew his attention by holding his hand and stroking the back of it with her thumb. AJ smiled as he searched her face. "What's up, Doc?"

"You know that's a line from the Bugs Bunny cartoons, right?"

AJ grunted a laugh. "I guess so." He sighed as he pushed away thoughts that were invading his consciousness to focus on her.

"You're worried about finding Beverly's family," she said.

"That's an understatement and I'm afraid it's an impossible task. Six hundred billion people is a big damn haystack and we're looking for the smallest needle ever."

"I don't think Alicia killed Beverly."

"She's been gone for almost eighteen days," AJ said. "She'd have shown up by now if she was around."

"Didn't you ever wonder why they knocked Darnell out instead of doing to him what they were doing to you?"

"Aside from Alicia wanting to peel back my skin?" he asked. "She hates me, Doc."

"I'll give you that. But there might be another, simpler reason."

"Hate is a pretty simple motivator."

"What if Alicia couldn't do to Darnell what she did to you?" Jayne said. "What if she had to knock Darnell out because he could have saved you?"

"Seemed like she had plenty of tricks up her sleeve."

"But with all those tricks, she had to lock Reed down with arm cuffs and she had to use sleeping darts on Darnell," Jayne said. "No.

The reason she didn't light up Darnell's nervous systems is because she couldn't."

"You have any proof of that?"

"Proof might be too strong," Jayne said. "I've got precedent, though."

"Where? How?"

She held up her reading pad. "Beverly loaded a huge amount of information onto this reader before we made it to Beltigersk."

"You read about what Alicia did to me?"

"Synaptic Displeasure is the translation in my text," Jayne said. "It's something the Beltigersk rulers did to punish rogue Beltigersk symbiotes and their hosts."

"I've heard of that," Tork called back. "Not the displeasure thing, but the rogue Beltigersk. Some of them got along too well with the Xandarj they'd taken over and couldn't order them around anymore. Such disloyalty was a big deal. Beltigersk rulers would order both killed if they found a pair like that."

"That's what I read too, Tork," she said.

"Why would they need that synaptic displeasure thing, then?" AJ asked.

"Beltigersk aren't good at manipulating the physical world. They would use the disruptive technique until the host died," she said. "Sometimes it took weeks."

"That's horrible."

"It was the only way they could disable the host and keep the symbiote from healing it."

"But you stopped Alicia before I was dead," he said. "So where's Beverly?"

"According to what I'm reading, she's been short-circuited or placed in a state where she can't connect," Jayne said. "More accurately, your body has been changed in a way that makes it incompatible with your connection."

"I don't like where this is headed," he said.

"No, you really don't," she agreed.

"You want to experiment on me."

"I do."

"And it's gonna hurt."

"It is."

"And you have no idea if it's gonna work."

"I don't."

"Then what the hell are you smirking about?"

"I feel a little like a mad scientist."

"Is it dangerous?"

Jayne tipped her head to the side as she considered the question. "Yes and no. The voltage we're talking about is high. Like a hundred fifty thousand volts."

"That's three times that of a Taser. How many milliamps?"

"Two-thirds, but I'll need to find Beverly first. We need to use the Beltigersk locater," Jayne said.

"Beverly was the only one who could use it. She didn't want the technology getting into the wrong hands." AJ was interrupted by Greybeard announcing his presence, barking and jumping up to bump AJ with his front paws. "Seriously, Seamus? I thought you said you couldn't use it when I asked before."

Greybeard barked again and wagged his tail.

"I think he's saying he'll give it a try," Jayne pulled the locator from behind her back. "What do you say, AJ? Do you want to at least try?"

"To locate BB? Of course I do. If we don't find her, there's no reason to be zapping me, is there?"

"True."

"What aren't you telling me?" he asked as she ran the sensor over his body.

"I don't know if it'll be enough."

"What won't?"

"Point six milliamps," she said. "At one hundred fifty thousand volts, it's the equivalent of a high-powered Taser."

"Have you ever seen someone get hit by one of those?"

"I have."

"Tell me the odds, Doc," he said. "Give me some hope, here."

"Honestly, I'd say maybe twenty percent." The sensor beeped as Jayne passed it over the inside of AJ's right thigh. "Now that's an unusual location. What would she be doing in your femoral artery?"

"Is she moving?"

Jayne nodded her head as she ran the sensor back and forth. "Yes and no. It's like she moves and then somehow moves back. Like she's fighting for position, but how is that possible? She's tiny."

Greybeard barked excitedly.

"Guys, we're getting close to dropping out of jump-space," Darnell called back. "You're going to need to hurry things along back there."

"Maybe we should deal with this after we get our travel into Fimil space figured out," AJ said.

"Maybe," Jayne agreed. "But the process shouldn't take long if it's going to work."

"Let me get this right," AJ said. "You're going to shock me in the crotch with a Taser. If I didn't know you better, I'd say this was some kind of sick joke. Do you know how bad this is going to hurt?"

Jayne pulled a pencil sized device from behind her and held it in front of him. "We don't need to do it if you have any hesitation."

"You said the experiment might need more power," AJ said. "Bump it up. I'm not doing this twice if I can avoid it."

"You do want to proceed?"

"Beverly is alive. She's obviously in trouble or she'd have made contact at least with Seamus."

Jayne twisted the top of the pen-shaped object. "I'm putting it up to a full milliamp. I'm afraid any more could cause permanent damage."

"What does that book of yours say we need?"

"It's not exactly clear," she said, chewing on her lip nervously.

"What does it say?" AJ asked.

"Two milliamps."

"Do it."

"You've got three minutes," Darnell said. "You need to crap or get off the pot."

"Pull your pants down," Jayne said.

AJ smirked. "So that's what this is all about. You saw something in that shower you liked and now you're going in for a second look."

Jayne raised her eyebrows and her eyes twinkled. "You might keep the sass down to a minimum given what I'm holding in my hands."

AJ slid his butt off the chair and pushed his pants down to his knees. As he was wearing underwear, his promised exposure was somewhat oversold. "Give me a second," he said, taking deep breaths.

"I'll count you down. Three..." Without finishing the countdown, she activated the electrical shock device and pushed it into his thigh. AJ's response was immediate and violent as his feet shot forward and his back arched up into a plank, a ghostly howl of pain barely escaping his lips. Jayne counted to ten as she held the device firmly to him, finally releasing it.

"Seamus, we need you up here," Darnell said. "We're exiting jump-space in forty seconds."

Groggily, AJ looked at Jayne, drool running down his chin. "Did it work?"

Jayne ran the sensor across AJ's leg only to find that Beverly was no longer in place. "I don't know," she admitted. "I was kind of hoping she'd talk to you."

Greybeard barked and ran forward, taking his place on a shelf next to Darnell which gave the K-9 a good view through the cockpit glass.

"Welcome to Fimil," Darnell announced. Suddenly, their view of local space was filled with ships of all sizes, some within only a few hundred yards. The line of ships stretched as far as they could see. "Holy crap! Okay, I've got it," he said, talking to Seamus. A moment later, he banked *USSF Cardinal* away from their position and onto a nearly perpendicular heading from the line of vessels streaming away from them.

"I was hoping to avoid this," Blue Tork said. "It is to be expected, though, with your limited navigation equipment."

"What's that?" Darnell asked.

"We've been pushed out into a safety lane. We didn't respond quickly enough to the system controller's AI," he said. "It's fine. It'll just take us a little longer to get where we're going."

"How much longer."

"Maybe a day. It really depends on how your boarding interview goes," Tork said.

"Does a boarding interview have anything to do with that big white ship with the twin forward-mounted lasers approaching us?" Darnell asked.

"Those are particle cannons," Chok said.

"FTA," Tork said. "Fimil Tax Authority. *Cardinal* doesn't have a tax id and I'd bet the three of you don't either. There'll be a fee for registration."

AJ was suddenly worried. He had only a fraction of the credits left that he'd had when arriving at Xandarj.

"Ship is five thousand. I'd guess you'll get a special rate for humans. Maybe another thousand apiece," Tork said. "It's standardized, but just be careful about getting assigned extra fees."

"Fimil tax authority?" Darnell asked.

"Tok Primacy is the actual authority. You'll be scanned and your registration will transfer between both Thamhut and Holai sectors. I assume you'll pay to renew Chok and me."

"We're in Tok space?"

"Kind of. Tok space is huge, like a tenth of the entire Galactic Empire. Tok settled it a long time ago and they brought their entire Primacy into the Galactic Empire all at once. It was a big deal maybe three hundred years ago," Tork said.

Darnell held up his hands. "Sorry I asked. I assume we need to let these FTA boys boss us around."

"Those particle cannons aren't toys," Chok said, "but they won't chase us if we run. Thing is, if you don't get an ID, you can't trade anywhere legit in this entire sector. You'd probably starve or get blown up by pirates if you were stupid enough to go looking for them."

"This is Darnell Jackson, *USSF Cardinal*. We will comply," Darnell answered over comms and then muted. "Kids, put your Sunday best on, we're about to have visitors."

"AJ?" Jayne asked with concern. He was barely conscious and needed assistance just to sit back in his seat. "Are you okay?"

He attempted to speak, but his first several attempts ended up in a mishmash of syllables that didn't add up to any recognizable words.

"Is he going to be okay?" Darnell asked, hustling past the passenger compartment before extending the flexible airlock.

"The effects should wear off," she said, still watching AJ with concern.

"Gooed, skay," he managed, the right side of his face not responding as quickly as the left.

A loud knock on the outside of the ship caused Darnell to jump, but he set to evacuating the atmosphere from the lock. After a minute, the exterior hatch cycled and a single humanoid figure appeared inside.

"You need to close the hatch behind you," Darnell said, pointing behind the five-and-a-half-foot alien wearing a stark-white spacesuit molded tightly to its body.

"Very well." The alien nodded, its voice nasally. The reflective polarized film which covered the face shield of its suit made it impossible to even guess at any facial features. With little effort, the alien figured out the simple latch and closed the exterior hatch. "Please, the number of sentient occupants." The alien got right down to business as Darnell directed the ship to refill the airlock with atmosphere.

"Two who are already registered, three unregistered," Blue Tork said, coming to stand next to Darnell.

"Curious. Human is a species we have seen few of," the FTA

agent said, touching a button beneath his chin. The polarized plate disappeared behind his head, exposing a light blue colored, bald figure with his facial features in the expected places. Most shocking was his nose which looked like a short elephant trunk that hung almost to his chin and waggled as his head moved.

"Things look to be in order," the man said and his eyes fell on AJ. "Does this human require medical assistance?"

"No. I'm a doctor," Jayne said.

"Do you seek to practice your skills while in the Tok Primacy?" the FTA agent asked.

"No. Just taking care of my friend here."

"Very well. Tax IDs will be assigned for the humans: Darnell Jackson, Albert Jenkins, Amanda Jayne. They will be renewed for Blue Tork and Carista Chok. Also, the vessel *USSF Cardinal* is recorded and requires a registration fee. Will this be paid for individually or as an aggregate?"

"Owfh Mush?" AJ asked.

"I'll assume that was an inquiry to cost. The total is four thousand twenty-two credits. I can provide a breakdown if requested."

"Shith," AJ said, his fingers fumbling as he struggled to extract a credit chit.

"Sir, are you being held against your will? Do you request assistance?" the Fimil FTA agent asked.

AJ shook his head and held Jayne's arm for support as he held out the chit with a shaky hand. "Naah, friend."

The agent swiped the chit and gave a friendly smile as he pressed a button on his wrist. A hologram of a Fimil woman hovered above his arm. She wore a dark gray, wide-lapeled suit, white dress shirt, and an intricately crafted orange flower centered between the lapels. The female Fimil's voice was higher, although just as nasal. "Hello. I'm Bersten Brightbend, mayor of upper Marska. I am pleased to welcome you all to Tok Primacy. Please take time to read all appropriate regulations and I wish you a prosperous venture."

The FTA agent closed his helmet and stepped into the airlock, giving Darnell an expectant look. Darnell wasted no time and closed the flexible portion of the airlock behind him.

"Safe travels," the agent said as he opened the hatch and launched himself at the patrol craft alongside the *USSF Cardinal*.

"They don't waste time, do they?" Darnell said. "Collect their fees and they're on their way."

"We'll spend the next day sweeping all the tracking bugs he deposited," Chok said. "I'll find my scanner."

"Why would they track us?" Darnell asked.

"It's not personal," Tork explained. "They have systems that track the movements of their citizens and look for issues."

"Kindath like that moofey," AJ said. "Wath did you thoo to my thung?"

"I think you bit it," Jayne said, sympathetically wiping drool and a small spot of blood from his chin.

"Duh," he said, reaching into his mouth to gingerly poke his tongue.

"There are jump lanes available for twelve thousand credits," Blue Tork said. "It would save us the three-day approach but we need to know where we are going so we can adjust our path."

"Jump lane? Like jump-space?" Darnell asked.

"It is a Tok technology," Tork said.

"Thspend it," AJ said.

"I can front you the credits," Tork said, "but I'll need a transfer from your credit chit when we get on station."

"*Lower Marska. Growler District.*" The words were a whisper in the back of AJ's mind.

"Betherly?" he asked but received no response.

"Are you talking to Beverly?" Jayne asked, suddenly interested.

"I don't know. What is Growler District? It's supposed to be on Lower Marska."

"That's a universally bad sign." Chok worried out loud. "Nobody goes to Growler District."

"Are you sure that's where you want to go?" Tork asked.

"Dumb idea," Chok cautioned again.

"Stop, Chok," Tork said.

"What's wrong with Growler District?" Darnell asked.

"Marska is a city of extremes," Tork said. "It might as well be two entirely different places, really. There's the part of Marska that's called Upper Marska. It's a space station kind of like Dralli, but on a massive scale."

"How massive?" Darnell asked. "Dralli is huge."

"Not really," Tork said. "Marska is so big and so oddly shaped that they don't measure it in area but in volume. I don't recall how many cubic feet but we're talking like six hundred thousand cubic miles. I hope the translation worked on that because it is a really big number."

AJ blinked as he tried to wrap his brain around the idea of cubic miles. It didn't initially work for him. "Big," he finally agreed.

"Right. Big," Tork agreed. "But that's just the Upper Marska. There's a whole other part of Marska on the planet surface. It's called Lower Marska, which is where the Growler District is located. Just about all of Fimil-2 is covered in city, so it's hard to say where Lower Marska ends and another city starts, but Growler is on the northern edge near one of the north elevators, so it doesn't get as much attention from law enforcement."

"Elevator? Like space elevator?" Darnell asked.

"That's a reasonable description. You'd have to see one to understand," Tork said. "We need to make a decision soon about the jump lane. If we're going to Growler District, there's a place I know where we could dock. It's a little seedy, but not as bad as Growler."

"*Hurry.*"

"Take the jump lane," AJ said, a smile breaking out on his face.

"Why are you smiling? You like seedy," Jayne stated with a smirk. "You've got a thing for the cute little elephant noses?"

"Nah," AJ said and then reconsidered. "Well, I guess you never know."

TWENTY-SIX

FIRST CLASS

Tork adjusted the communication channel and spat out a nonsensical stream of requests. The response from the ship's computer was immediate and the previously straight navigation route changed, directing *USSF Cardinal* on a twisting path.

"Now this is more like it." Darnell tipped the flight controller, following the curving route. "Holy crap! Hold on, we're gonna dump a lot of acceleration in a hurry."

"What's going on, Big D?" AJ strained to look around the bulkhead that separated passenger space from cockpit.

"Uh, you might want to come up and see this, it's getting a little freaky," Darnell said.

AJ unclipped his seat belt and stood, the ache in his side a constant reminder of the wound he'd taken on Beltigersk and the fact that Beverly was out of action. With Jayne right behind him, he leaned against the wall to look over Darnell's shoulder into space. At first, his eye was distracted by the spaceships sailing both overhead and in front of *Cardinal*.

Then he discovered what Darnell had already seen: a silvery, egg shaped object, twice the size of *USSF Cardinal*, sliding quietly through space on a collision course. "Shit Big D, get out of the way!" AJ spat, grabbing Darnell's shoulder.

"That's not what our instructions are," Darnell said.

"That vessel is expected," Tork said. "Do not be concerned."

"You gotta be kidding me," AJ said, nervously.

The massive silver egg accelerated, seeming to jump so it landed only yards from the front of their vessel. And then the most unexpected thing occurred. The egg split apart, opening like a massive alligator's maw. The silver ship swallowed *USSF Cardinal* whole.

"That is freaky," Darnell said as the Fimil starfield was snuffed out.

Blinding light poured through a crack in the alien ship that surrounded them and *Cardinal's* windows darkened in response. Moments later, the crack expanded and the surrounding alien vessel opened completely and slid effortlessly away from *Cardinal*.

"What in the hell?" AJ asked as thousands of ships filled the viewport, all zipping about at breakneck speeds. In the background, a massive white wall of steel, glass, vents, ports, and everything that makes up a space station stretched in all directions for as far as his eye could see.

"Welcome to Upper Marska," Tork said, clearly enjoying the spectacle.

"What? How is this possible? That's millions of miles almost instantly," Darnell said.

"Don't worry, you don't really ever get over that feeling. That's my third time on a jump lane and it never gets old," Chok said. "Ask me, I think it's the Tok's way of showing everyone they better not mess with Tok."

"Well, message received," Darnell said. "I can't even imagine the technology involved in what just happened."

"Do we have time for a beer?" Tork asked, punching coordinates into *Cardinal's* navigation computer. "I know we're in a hurry, but there's this place..."

"I don't know how long we're going to be here," AJ said.

"No Xandarj. Hurry."

AJ was concerned about how much recovery Beverly would be capable of; she didn't seem to be growing stronger as he'd expected.

"I think we'll be headed to Growler on our own," he said. "I need you and Chok to stay with the ship. I'm sure there will be enough time for you guys to grab a beer."

"You should take us," Tork said. "There will be dangers. You'll need all the help you can get."

AJ shook his head.

"You're the boss, but I don't like it," Tork responded.

"AJ, are you sure?" Jayne asked.

He tapped his head. "Not my call."

Jayne's eyes lit up and she smiled. "Really?"

He nodded, which caused her to hug him in celebration. AJ grimaced as his wound pulled against the sudden movement.

"What about weapons?" he asked.

"There aren't that many places where weapons are disallowed in the Galactic Empire," Tork said. "If you end up using one, though, especially in Upper Marska, you'll probably run into trouble. They've got video everywhere and if you break their laws, you'll get a huge fine. If you can't pay, they lock you up. Best not to push anyone into a fight because there's no running from Marska law enforcement."

"What about Lower Marska?"

"Depends on where you are," Tork said. "Near the space elevators, it's the same as Upper Marska. The further out you get, the video capture gets spotty and the law enforcement has a different focus."

"Sounds familiar," Darnell said.

"Are we really getting into this?" AJ asked.

"Just sayin'." Darnell swore under his breath as a small craft veered away, narrowly missing *Cardinal*. "This is just damn nuts. These guys are suicidal!"

"Don't move," Tork said suddenly as Darnell adjusted to miss another small vessel. "If they hit you, it's their fault. If you move out of your lane, it's ours. Trust me, these pilots know what they're doing.

The fines are high if they hit us and we'll get a repair judgment that's punitive."

"It's like when I need a new paint job," AJ said. "I make sure to hit that intersection on Twentieth and Lake."

"You're so full of crap," Darnell said, carefully threading *Cardinal* along the provided approach vector.

"That's not new," AJ said. "Jayne, let's get loaded up."

"Have you checked your credit balance?" Tork called back as AJ and Jayne started grabbing the supplies they'd set out for the venture into Marska.

"I have a credit balance?"

"Red Fairs has most likely sold the items you left behind with her and given you credit," Tork said. "You should be able to get a balance update."

"How do I check?"

"Use the terminal by the manufactory," Tork said. "Request a credit inquiry."

"That terminal was built by my people," AJ said. "There's no way it interfaces with Galactic Empire banking."

"Do not be so sure," Tork said. "Communications and navigation in this ship are interfacing correctly with Fimil Space Authority. Perhaps you should try."

AJ finished strapping a holster around his waist and pushed his Cheell pistol into place. With a *why not* shrug aimed at Jayne, he made his way to the terminal Tork suggested only to have Chok sidle up to him as he did.

"Chok will help you," she said, bumping him out of the way in an overly familiar manner. If AJ had any idea how to do what Tork had suggested, he'd have rejected Chok's help on principle alone, but time was limited. She grabbed his hand and before he could object, she pressed his finger against a pad he hadn't realized contained any sensors. The screen shifted and his name appeared at the top. "Now, tell it you want a credit balance."

"How? I want a credit balance," AJ said.

AVAILABLE: 142,931. PENDING: 81,044

"Holy cow," AJ whistled. "What's pending?"

"Stupid," Chok said. "That means Dralli Station is holding money. Probably because there's an investigation into damage caused by our departure."

"They think we did that much damage?"

"No," Chok said. "That is why it is stupid. Mads Bazer will not treat you wrong. Dralli Station will hold ten times the amount of estimated damage for two months. It is a scam."

"How much?" Jayne asked.

He frowned. "Can't you read the screen?"

"No. It is blank as far as I can tell," she said.

"Interesting."

"Not very interesting," Chok said. "It is simple technology to encrypt the data on a video screen. Everyone has this technology. Why do you think the advertisements are different for you than for me?"

"Advertisements?"

"On the walls of Dralli Station and the sides of vessels," Chok said.

"I don't see advertisements," he said. "Never mind, I'm getting distracted."

"That is something we must talk about when you are back," Chok said.

AJ nodded, donning the cloak Red Fairs had supplied when they were on Dralli Station. He cast an appreciative eye at Jayne as she did the same. "Do you have good access to your pistol?" he asked.

"Inside pocket on my cloak," Jayne said. "I don't like having it on my body, just in case I want to take my cloak off."

"You guys might want to see this," Darnell called.

Together they walked forward and were greeted with the sight of the station growing larger and larger in front of them. While at a distance, the size of the station had been easier to underestimate. As they came closer, however, what they saw was almost impossible to fathom.

"It's like we're dust particles next to a battleship," Darnell said. "I've never felt so small in my life."

"There are one point five billion souls who call Marska home," Tork said. "I have not been here often, but this docking bay places us on the edge of Barrel Five division. It is only two miles to the entry port for the Growler District elevator. There is a bar nearby that is frequented by Xandarj. Once the vessel is secured, Chok and I will likely make our way over to it."

"What's the name of the bar?" Jayne asked, watching carefully as *Cardinal* floated through a soaring opening in the side of the station.

"Monkey Butt," Chok said, smiling broadly. "The owner is Xandarj. He was being ironic when he named it but I think it is funny. There are few Xandarj on Marska, so the place is not popular. The station is an expensive place to live."

"What are those floating balls with the blinking lights?" Jayne asked, pointing at one that *Cardinal* was directly heading toward.

"Mooring balls," Darnell answered. "My question is, how are they held in place?"

"It is another Tok technology," Chok said. "I believe it is with focused gravitational fields but that is only a theory. Tok do not share how they make their inventions."

Darnell slowed *Cardinal* to a halt, nudging into the ball. The ship slid forward, but was pushed back into place after the floating device locked onto the hull with wide-fingered clamps.

"I know there's going to be a smart answer to this, but how do we get over there?" Jayne asked, pointing at the station side of the docking bay. Several levels were visible from where they'd moored, although they were directly in line with one numbered 1405.

"Look," AJ said, pointing out the window at a semi-opaque, golden bridge that extended from 1407 to the side of a vessel. Three small aliens of unknown species had already exited their vessel and were walking toward the station. As they made forward progress, the bridge disappeared behind them. "Let me guess, Tok technology."

"If it seems wondrous and impossible, it is likely developed by Tok," Chok said. "And they're about as fun to talk to as a Xandarjian butthole after beer has been consumed."

AJ grinned as he caught Jayne's eye. She was doing her best not to crack a smile at the Xandarj's choice of words.

"Greybeard, come on back. Let me get you suited up," AJ called.

"He only needs the atmospheric adjuster. None of you should even need a bottle of O2. If you do, they're not hard to find. Just check a kiosk terminal," Tork said. "All of Marska is pressurized and with all that fur, I bet Greybeard won't get cold on Lower Marska."

"Well, that's easier," AJ said, pulling out the small formfitting mask they'd manufactured for Greybeard and slipping it over his snout.

"Belsik. Exotic Imports. Growler District."

"I'm ready," Darnell said, shrugging his robe into place after attaching his holster.

Tentatively, AJ cycled the exterior hatch without first stretching back the flexible airlock. Cool air poured in through the opening and with a sudden brilliant flash, a golden walkway appeared on the outside of the ship.

"It is safe, Albert Jenkins," Chok said. "Make sure you pay the slip fee or you will not be allowed to return to *Cardinal*."

A faint, smoky blue outline appeared above the walkway. AJ smiled, recognizing Beverly's touch. She was present enough to notice his hesitancy to step out onto the translucent walkway with no ground in sight below. Boldly, he stepped through the hatch, his foot sinking into the walkway as if it were made of soft rubber. Turning, he held his hand out to Jayne who was looking at the surface just as tenuously as he had.

"There's good traction," he said as she stepped out next to him.

"This place is beyond my imagination," her eyes wide as she

slowly scanned the docking bay, taking in the hundreds of ships of different sizes that were nearby.

"I guess those little Tok pricks deserve to be cocky," Darnell said, stepping out next, followed by Greybeard. "You know where we're going?"

AJ nodded and pulled Jayne's hand, following the glowing golden sidewalk that disappeared behind them. The promise of solid ground, or at least steel decking, kept the group moving at a quick pace.

"This place is more crowded than Dralli Station," Jayne said, stepping off the floating walk. "Feels like Times Square."

AJ pointed at a kiosk and led the group over. The terminal recognized his presence and offered a few suggestions for meals, lodging and different types of shopping. At the top were options for paying their slip fees. His jaw fell open when he saw the prices for Fantastium. Each milligram was valued at ten thousand credits with a suggested refill of five milligrams. He declined, although he wondered if leaving *Cardinal* unguarded was a good idea, given the veritable treasure trove of Fantastium Space Force had left aboard.

"How much time did you give us on the slip?" Darnell asked.

"Two days with an automatic renewal," AJ said. "I have no idea what we're into here, but it's not expensive. Fantastium, on the other hand is ridiculously expensive. They're getting ten grand a milligram."

"No wonder they're trying to sack Earth."

"We need to go that way." AJ pointed across the jetway that was at least a hundred yards wide. "The elevator is about a twenty-minute walk. Let's try to stay together as much as possible."

"Lead the way," Darnell said.

The jetway soared above them, giving the area the feeling of a grand space. Floating passenger vehicles and unoccupied craft holding boxy packages sailed overhead as vessels unloaded their cargo bays and sent items along to their destinations. As they moved forward, the crowds in the jetway thinned, most pedestrians reaching their destinations. Even though they tried not to gawk at every new wonder, the team struggled to take in the sights without attracting too much attention.

"It's hard to believe a society is this advanced," Jayne said. "I understand why Tok might look at humans as uncivilized barbarians."

"They consider us little more than pets," AJ said, recalling an encounter he'd had with the captain of a Tok vessel.

"Imagine how we'd treat Neanderthals if they showed up in our timeline," Jayne said. "We'd give them a pat on the head and ask them to learn how to make their fire somewhere else. They'd be a novelty and I doubt we'd take them seriously."

"You think?" AJ pointed at a sign that showed they were getting closer to the elevator that would take them planetside.

"I have to wonder if the technology gap is larger between Tok and human than between human and Neanderthal," Jayne said.

"Really know how to give a guy a complex," he said, pulling Jayne closer as people crowded in.

A chime sounded and a loud announcement began. An alien voice, sounding very much like the Fimil FTA agent, started speaking. *Surface descent in four minutes, thirty seconds. Please board immediately.*

"Crap," AJ said, pulling Jayne and breaking into a jog as he made for the doors indicated by Beverly's smoke trail. "We're gonna need to hurry."

Pushing through the doors, they were surprised to find subway-type turnstiles without the spinning metal bar that allowed entry. Unlike most subways, the turnstiles were sparkling clean. Sprinkled throughout the boarding area, Fimil aliens wearing matching red uniforms trimmed out with gold piping stood with friendly looks on their faces as they directed people through.

AJ made a beeline for the closest agent. "Through the gate. You'll want to hurry, there are only two minutes before departure."

"Do we need tickets?" he asked.

"Ah, yes," the agent said, looking at a small, wrist mounted device. "You should have purchased already, but afternoon drop is rarely full. Let me see here. Yes. Standard tickets for two hundred fifty credits. First class are five hundred. I'm afraid only first class remains. But I can see you are visitors. I will sell them to you at our standard rate."

"Four please," AJ said. "I'd like to pay."

"We'd best be quick about it," the agent said, tapping onto his wrist as his little elephant nose rose up and expelled a short blast of air. "There are four tickets. I just need your acknowledgement."

"Good. Acknowledged."

"No, sir, please any part of your finger will suffice," the Fimil ticket agent said, holding out his wrist, a small toot expelling from his raised snout.

AJ tapped his finger onto the Fimil's wrist just as a chime sounded. *Thirty seconds for final boarding.*

"Please make good haste through the gates and enjoy your visit."

Greybeard barked excitedly as the group gave up any pretense of calm and sprinted for the turnstiles that were now flashing red.

"Where are we going?" Jayne asked, turning her head but not slowing as she passed through. "I don't see an elevator."

AJ scanned the crowd, trying to identify movement that might lead them to their destination but couldn't find anything. A tug on his robe nearly pulled him off his feet and he spun quickly, only to find Greybeard latched on.

"Hey, we've got to hurry," AJ pushed, trying to free the hem of his robe from the dog's clamped jaws.

Instead of following, Greybeard dug in his legs and shook his head, like he was playing tug-of-war.

"Bubba, I think he's saying we're in the right spot," Darnell said, jogging back to AJ.

"What and we get teleported to the surface?" AJ asked skeptically.

The deck beneath them lurched and the three companions froze in place, warily assessing the situation. Without further warning, the floor simply started dropping, slowly at first but accelerating.

"Holy crap," Darnell said. "This entire area is the elevator. Look, it goes all the way back to the turnstiles."

"A technological marvel that many of us take for granted," a Fimil woman said, approaching. She was heavyset and the base of her trunk was wide and soft, jiggling as she spoke. Aside from her trunk, however, she had an open, friendly face. "Are you new to Marska?"

"First time," AJ said, holding his hands up.

"Then indeed, you are welcome to our beautiful city," she said. "I wish you safe travels and prosperous trading."

"Uh, thank you," he said, not sure exactly how to respond.

"She was nice," Jayne said, when the Fimil woman bowed slightly and walked off, joining a small knot of Fimil who had heavy bags set at their feet.

"Would you look at that," Darnell said.

The Fimil sun was just breaking over the horizon and flooded the globe with light. From their position hundreds of miles above the ground, they were afforded a breath-taking view of morning breaking across the planet.

"Everywhere you look, it's all city," Jayne said. "How can they survive like this? Where do they produce food?"

AJ shook his head and soaked in the cityscape below. "No idea," he said, awe filling his voice. "Every time I think I've seen it all, we see something like this. My idea of the universe has changed so much, I'm just trying to keep my head from exploding."

TWENTY-SEVEN

SUMMIT

The elevator slowed as it approached the planet's surface. The entire journey had taken about twenty minutes. Studying the city's layout, AJ felt mostly confusion. Unlike Earth, the cityscape was continuous with no breaks for rivers, forest, lakes or any other natural phenomena. Architectural styles varied wildly, however, just as the heights of the buildings did. Slowly, patterns became evident like groupings where all the buildings were built of the same materials and had the same color of roof. Some areas stood out because of the general repair or disrepair of an entire several-block section.

"I think we might have been taken by that ticket guy," Jayne said, interrupting AJ's thoughts.

"Really?" he asked.

"Look around," she said. "There's no first-class or economy, we're just on a big disc with everyone else."

AJ estimated the platform held two hundred people. To Jayne's point, there seemed to be no organization. Some people stood and many others sat comfortably on stools they seemed to have brought with them.

"I think she's right," Darnell said. "I was hoping we'd at least get some peanuts."

"You're hungry?" AJ asked. "We ate before we left."

"*Peanuts*... get it?" Darnell said, giving AJ the impression he was missing something. "Airline food... elephant food... It's funny."

"Funny," AJ dismissed the topic. "We need to find this Exotic Imports shop."

"Don't move," Darnell said, pulling on his hoodie, covering his head.

The elevator was just forty feet above a wide landing pad surrounded by glowing red turnstiles. It had slowed significantly and continued to decelerate as the ground rushed up to greet them.

"Why am I not moving?" AJ asked.

"Behind you at two o'clock. There's a roadway opposite the ticket booths," Darnell said.

"Okay..." AJ said, and started to turn.

"Don't turn," Darnell said, reaching up and stopping AJ and then acted like he was brushing off lint. "There's a Cheell and another guy looking at the elevator. They've got some kind of scope. I can't get a great look, but I think Loveit is the other guy."

"What the hell is he doing here?"

Jayne pulled up her hood and kept her back to the area Darnell had indicated. "We need to leave," she said, pointing to the opposite side of the platform. "Dammit, there are two more Cheell. They're looking right at us."

"Take it easy," AJ said. "Maybe they haven't spotted us. Don't stare at them."

"I noticed something that I think might be an open-air market to my right," AJ said. "It's only half a mile away. Just follow me and try to act natural. The turnstiles should open soon, people are moving. Let's start walking."

AJ struggled to walk with purpose but not overdo it. As predicted, once the platform settled into place, the turnstiles' glow switched from red to green and the crowd started moving off, passing those who'd been waiting for their ride to Upper Marska.

"I can't tell if they're following," Jayne said, stepping quickly to keep up with AJ.

"There weren't that many people on the platform," AJ said. "It depends on how long they've been waiting."

"How would they know to wait here?" Darnell asked. "How would they know we're here now?"

"I think the secret's out," AJ said. "Alicia knows the queen is alive. I just hope we got here soon enough."

The street they were on ran by boxy buildings that were ten to fifteen stories tall, their facades made of aging materials stained black along the edges from weather. Looking up, AJ saw short and tall figures moving behind windows that were seamlessly integrated into the building's face. He imagined families waking up and starting their mornings.

"What direction?" Darnell called as they neared an intersection. The street they were approaching was larger and a curb separated it from the pedestrian walkway they'd been on since exiting the elevator. In the street ahead, small vehicles hovered inches off the ground and whizzed about their business, careening wildly with no sort of obvious organization.

"Kind of diagonal." He pointed across the busy street, not yet willing to jump the curb and enter the thoroughfare, instead leading the group left, staying with the pedestrian traffic.

A shout caught their attention. AJ knew better than to look, but he couldn't help himself. Sixty yards ahead, Loveit stood in the middle of the street, calm as a cucumber where vehicles narrowly missed him. He didn't seem to care as he raised his arm to aim a weapon directly at AJ. A flash of light and the *buzz-zap!* of an energy weapon impacting the building next to him told AJ everything he needed to know.

"Move!" AJ demanded, jumping into the street with abandon, pulling Jayne along behind him.

Greybeard barked furiously as they raced across the street, dodging pedestrians, and expecting to be struck at any minute by the random traffic flow. Loveit's second shot hit a Fimil man who screeched in surprise and spun, falling to the ground. Chaos erupted as people, primarily Fimil, hooted warnings, ran in all directions and generally acted just like a human crowd would when shots were fired unexpectedly.

"We have to help him!" Jayne tried to pull AJ back, but he wasn't having it.

"Their medicine is better," AJ demanded, pulling her along.

The group gained a temporary reprieve by ducking behind a narrow building once they crossed to the other side of the street, blocking Loveit's line of sight.

"Where are their police?" Darnell asked.

"Not helping," AJ said, pulling Jayne around the end of the building and launching out onto another busy street.

"How are they missing us?" Jayne asked, whipping her head around wildly.

"No idea," AJ said.

They continued to run, racing blindly away.

"*Get in.*" Beverly's voice was quiet but firm.

"What?"

"Look out!" Darnell said, just as AJ became aware of a vessel dropping down from overhead. Unlike the scooters and carts at street level, the vessel was roughly the shape of a passenger van, albeit without wheels.

"Please, you will ride with me," a Fimil man called from within as a wide door slid open on the side. The man's accent, like many of the Fimil they'd talked to, sounded Indian.

Greybeard leapt in. Beverly's prompt and Greybeard's action were all AJ needed. "Get in, Jayne!" he said.

An energy round sizzled into the side of the vessel, blackening the van's faded green pigment beneath the transparent windows. AJ jumped into the van and pulled his own weapon, searching for the shooter. Loveit stood sixty yards away, steadying himself into a shooter's stance with a pistol, his cloak billowing out behind him as Fimil citizens screamed and ran away from him. AJ wanted to return fire, but Loveit was backdropped by dozens of innocents.

"Get down," Darnell ordered, plowing into AJ with his shoulder, knocking them both to the floor of the vehicle. Twin energy rounds struck the interior of the van, one ricocheting and glancing painfully off AJ's arm.

"Oh, hell," he complained, kicking at the door that hadn't closed. "Get out of here."

"Are there no more? I was told six including the canine," the Fimil driver said.

"Four," AJ said. "We're all on."

"That is very good." The van lurched forward and then tipped sideways, depositing AJ atop Darnell and Jayne. "You should attempt to close the hatch. I am receiving an error."

AJ struggled to move off Darnell and ended up being thrown onto his face as the driver adjusted the van's orientation.

"How am I supposed to do that with you flying like a cabbie at rush hour?" AJ growled, grabbing onto a chair bolted to the van's floor.

"I do not know who Cabbie is," the driver said. "I am Belisk. I hope you are Albert Jenkins. If that is not the case, then please accept my very humble apologies."

"Belisk, we were supposed to find your shop," AJ said. "How'd you know we were in trouble?"

"I was contacted by one called Seamus," he said. "Considerable urgency was communicated."

Wind continued whipping through the vessel as it sailed along, several hundred yards above ground level. "Can you just hold straight for a minute? I'm going to try to close the door and I don't want to fall out."

"Yes. Of course. I am aware of the dangers of an open vessel."

AJ grunted, biting off a response that would have contradicted the Fimil. Pulling himself to the door, he discovered the problem. A good portion of the track had been slagged by the energy bolt that had barely missed his head. Wires and cable were exposed and AJ imagined there was no immediate fix available.

"Big D, Jayne, Greybeard, move to the back," AJ said. "Look for some way to strap in. That door isn't closing anytime soon."

"There is little need. We have arrived," Belisk said.

AJ's stomach felt like it jumped into his mouth as the bottom dropped out of the van. In the space of seconds, the vehicle plunged from the traffic lane and through a narrow, rectangular opening barely large enough for the van to fit through. Having become momentarily weightless, AJ hit the ceiling and then slammed back down, ricocheting off the bench seat nearest the broken door. Only hitting half of the bench, he fell to the floor, his face inches from a wall the van was sliding past with virtually zero clearance.

All at once, the wall disappeared and they were in a large room, jerking to a halt and landing hard on the floor, smashing AJ against the van floor. Everything went still.

"Everyone up?" he grunted, peeling himself from the floor.

"What the hell was that about?" Darnell asked.

Without warning, Greybeard barked wildly, stepping on AJ's back as he leapt from the van. "Man's best friend, my ass," AJ grumbled, trying to get up on all fours again. "Jayne?"

"I'm here," she said. "These seats are remarkably soft. I saw you hit the ceiling, are you okay?"

"Definitely not my experience," AJ said, looking into the warehouse space Belisk had landed them in. "What in the heck?"

"See now, Queenie, that's how you make an entrance." The voice belonged to none other than Lefty Johnson.

"I don't know, Lefty." Rebel, still dressed in her Daisy Dukes and now wearing a straw cowboy hat, stood on the edge of the bench seat, her eyes level with AJ's as he attempted to sit back on his haunches. "It looks like that really hurt. Are you okay, AJ?"

"Okay is a relative term at the moment," AJ grunted as Belisk snuck around him and jumped out into the warehouse.

"Albert Jenkins, Darnell Jackson, Amanda Jayne, I am very pleased to see you all in such grand condition," Sharg said, stepping up to the van and offering her green scaled hand to him. Ordinarily, AJ would have rejected an offer of help, but he'd had the wind knocked out of him and he wanted to know for certain that the seven-foot-tall reptilian Vred wasn't some sort of apparition. The warmth of her soft hand was enough to reassure him that she was indeed real.

"I think that boy's had his bell rung," Queenie said. "Good thing we brought along some barley pops. Fix you right up, they will."

"How'd you guys get here?" Jayne asked, beelining for Sharg, whom she embraced companionably.

"You didn't think the *USSF Cardinal* was the only ship in our fleet, did you?" Major Jackie Baird asked, stepping from behind a stack of crates. Over her shoulder, AJ noticed a group of men wearing modern fatigues. Baird extended her hand in greeting and AJ shook it.

"Is this where you arrest me for taking your ship?" he asked.

"Not at all," Baird said. "The US Government is quite pleased that you've retrieved our shiny little *Cardinal*."

"Who are those guys?" he asked, nodding at the men who were obviously special forces. Even more interesting was that they were carrying weapons the likes of which he'd never seen before. "Those boys belong to Lefty or you?"

"They're the Major's. Sorry AJ, didn't have any more riders to hand out," Lefty said. "But those boys are plenty squared away. Most of 'em have at least two tours under their belts."

"They're kids," AJ grumbled.

Lefty grinned. "How old were you when I dug you out of that mud shack back in 'Nam?"

"Shit, I dunno. Twenty-one, maybe twenty-two."

"I was twenty-four and had been in country for three years," Lefty said. "Different war but the bullets haven't changed that much."

"Got that right. They know everything?" AJ asked, looking at Baird.

"As much as they need," she said.

"You guys run into Loveit yet?"

"Loveit's here?"

"Guess you haven't," AJ said. "Yeah, he tossed a couple of shots our way when we got off that elevator. If not for Belisk, we could have been in trouble. He was traveling with a group of Cheell. I hope we lost 'em, but I wouldn't count on it."

AJ's words drew the attention of the dangerous looking team Baird had brought along. With efficiency borne of practice, they picked up their weapons and disappeared into the aisles of the warehouse.

"What happened to Reed?" Baird asked.

"Didn't make it," AJ said. "Loveit had him all twisted around. Alicia killed him about the same time she tried to do the same to me."

"On Beltigersk?" Baird asked.

"Yeah. Beverly said she needed to get home and help restore order," AJ said. "Alicia went all Carrie on us and tried to take us out. Nearly had us too if Jayne hadn't shot me with a speargun."

"That's not exactly what happened," Jayne said.

He lifted an eyebrow. "Pretty sure that's what happened."

"Well, right, but there was more to it. You can be a jerk, you know that?"

He grinned and turned back to Major Baird. "That doesn't explain why you're on Fimil with a special forces team."

"I'm here on official US business," Jackie said. "They're advisors."

AJ chuckled. "I'll bet. What kind of business?"

"Beltigersk has requested the assistance of the United States of America in the matter of escorting two high ranking government officials to Beltigersk," Baird said.

"What envoy?" AJ asked.

"Rebel is Beverly's sister," Jayne said. "She'd have some sort of rank."

"Quite a reasonable deduction," Rebel said, popping into existence on Lefty's shoulder.

"You're the envoy?" AJ asked.

"Yes, like all my family, I am reasonably versed in political etiquette. I must say though, your president is a well-mannered leader who generously offered unqualified assistance to Beltigersk. It is the sort of assistance that binds nations together," Rebel said. "But no, there was no envoy."

"I don't follow," AJ said.

Sharg approached, joining the group. "It is not until this moment that I am fully convinced of your ignorance in this matter." While it was Sharg who spoke, the voice belonged to someone else, someone AJ had hoped never to talk to again.

"Um, Queen Beltigersk?" AJ asked, realizing he had no name to give her otherwise.

"A reasonable identification," she answered imperiously.

"What have you done to Sharg?" AJ asked, instantly angry.

"She is unharmed." Beverly whispered inside his head.

"Sharg is not harmed. I have transferred from my Fimil host and my residence is quite temporary. I do not answer to the likes of you," Queen Beltigersk said. "Your king requires that you return me and my daughters to Beltigersk and that you provide physical security as you do. I was not in favor of awaiting your arrival, but alas, I could not be sure which of my daughters could be trusted."

"There you are. Wasn't completely sure it was you, Queen. What a pompous windbag," AJ said, shaking his head. "For the record, he's my president, not my king and he can't tell me what to do."

"AJ, you're talking to a head of state," Baird warned.

"Oh, I've talked to this one a couple of times and she's a real piece of work. She tried to keep me locked up as a pet on Beltigersk. I'm sure you've heard the story."

"I have," Baird said. "Don't forget what's happening here, AJ. The United States, really the entirety of humanity has a chance to do something important. We can't get distracted by petty insults."

"I don't see the problem," AJ said. "You've got the queen. Take her back to Beltigersk. Let her do her thing. Done."

"That's just it, isn't it?" Jayne said. "She can't go back because she doesn't know who to trust. She thinks it could be Beverly trying to take the throne. She has no idea if it's Beverly or Alicia or one of the other sisters."

"There are few things Beltigersk can rely on," Queen Beltigersk said. "Even with family, we don't bond as easily as humans. Our alliances are tenuous, so we rely on agreements and laws. I do not wish to believe either of my daughters would place Beltigersk at such great risk. The one you call Beverly has always been erratic. She placed us all at great risk with her fight against Korgul. She knows I do not support her positions, so it would be logical for her to attack me so that her agenda continues."

"You thought she'd risk your whole world? That she'd try to drag a volcano on top of all her people?" AJ asked, unbelieving.

"It was not easy to believe, but the evidence is clear. One of my daughters is a traitor."

"Are you even listening to yourself? Beverly's agenda was to save Earth. Just look where humanity stands now. Without Beltigersk, Korgul is going to come after Earth, but this time they're gonna do it with guns and bombs," he said, becoming irate. "Do you really think that's what Beverly wants? She's trying to free us."

"AJ, you need to calm down," Baird said.

"I'm not gonna calm down." He jerked his arm away from Baird. "Alicia, who apparently gets a free pass on this, attacked Beverly – damn near killed her! Hurt her so bad, I don't know if she's going to be okay. You brought this problem to Earth. I can't even imagine what you were thinking. Are you really that short of friends?"

"Members of the Galactic Empire will not become involved in internal matters of state," she said.

"You're messed up, lady," AJ said. "Beverly almost died. She still could."

"So, you have said. You should understand, I am responsible first to Beltigersk. I could not risk myself while it was unknown which of my daughters betrayed our people, a matter, might I add, that remains unresolved. Explain how 49231125-0-B was attacked."

"Kakaren."

"She says, *Kakaren*," AJ said, still fuming.

"Prove this to me," Queen Beltigersk said. "Sharg will touch you. If you are lying, I will cause you immense pain. Do not play games with me, human."

AJ gritted his teeth. "I wish you were about five feet taller so I could punch you in the nose," AJ said, holding his arm out. "Do what you need to do."

"Mother?"

"*49231125-0-B, I am pleased that you still live. It is distressing to find that you suffer so. The human says your sister, 64838718-0-A, used Kakaren on you. Is this true? I did not know she was capable of this. Further, I do not understand how you live and also make this claim.*"

"*You underestimate the humans, Mother. I did not escape. I was rescued. My fight for life continues. My mind is a jumble and I float as a drop of water in a vast pool. Even now, without your strength, I would not be capable of response. 64838718-0-A has betrayed the Beltigersk people. Oh, how I wished that I had known of your survival. I may yet pass, but at least I know it will not be with heartbreak.*"

"*Daughter, I will judge your truth. If I find that you lie, I will destroy you. I will mourn your loss, but I do this for Beltigersk.*"

"I submit to your judgement, Mother," Beverly answered.

"Wait, BB don't. She can't be trusted," AJ said, subvocalizing, not sure he'd even be heard.

"It is too late, human," Queen Beltigersk answered. "I have sifted my daughter's mind with judgment. I despise her love for you humans, but find she has spoken truly. I will allow her to pass peacefully in the knowledge she has been faithful to her people."

"Go home, Mother. Lead our people and do not pander to Korgul or Cheell," Beverly said. "Tell me you will do this and I will gladly fade away with the knowledge that I have achieved what I set out to do."

"Do I have a say in this?" AJ asked.

"This human should not be heard," Queen Beltigersk said.

"His spirit is stronger than you are willing to credit," Beverly said, and AJ could hear the smile in her voice. "Albert Jenkins, I am richer for our time together. I will treasure this bond always."

"Wait. This is stupid! Alicia isn't going down that easy," AJ said, plowing forward. "I guarantee she isn't just going to let you waltz back home and take the throne. We're being chased by Cheell and I bet Korgul aren't that far behind."

"The Tok will not allow such a thing," Queen Beltigersk said. "Alicia will not successfully launch a Karaken upon me. I will be ready for her."

"Mother you must be careful. Alicia is very strong."

"Then I must be stronger."

"And you're willing to let die the one daughter who would go to the ends of the universe to save you? Don't be stupid!"

"AJ, we have incoming!" Darnell's voice ripped AJ from the semi-trance-like state in which Beverly and the Queen had been in conference. A moment later, Darnell plowed into him and Sharg, forcing them over a low stack of crates.

TWENTY-EIGHT
NINETY SECONDS

"What in the heck?" AJ asked, pushing at the broken crates.

His question was answered by the now familiar sizzle of Cheell weapons impacting objects close by.

"They're coming through the back," Darnell said. He took his weapon from its holster and returned fire.

"How many?"

Blue laser fire illuminated the interior of the warehouse and AJ traced its origin to one of Baird's special forces.

"Maybe ten," Darnell said.

AJ ducked his head out from around a crate, trying to get a better view. Cheell soldiers had taken cover and were firing on Baird's soldiers. It was clear the battle was going poorly for Team Baird so far. AJ grimaced with frustration as he saw Loveit's familiar figure crouched behind a steel post.

"Sure could use a reticle, BB," AJ said, aiming at Loveit's backside. There was no response and no reticle. He swallowed and tried not to think about her statement about fading away. He fired a pair of shots and was rewarded by a yelp as Loveit tucked further into cover.

"We must take the Queen from this danger," Sharg said quietly. "We must not allow this coup d'etat."

"I'd settle for not getting killed at this point," AJ grunted, ducking back in the face of blistering return fire. "Where's Jayne?"

"Over by Baird," Darnell said.

AJ pointed down the aisle that would take them parallel to Baird and her men. "We need to move."

"Just thinking that very thing," Darnell said.

"Oy, you kids need a hand?" Firing with abandon, Queenie leapt from cover and dove into the aisle next to them. Popping back up, he continued firing, covering Lefty as he crawled over to join them.

"I'm getting tired of this Loveit clown," Lefty growled. "What's he got to do with all this anyway?"

"I say we grab the bloke and beat out his teeth until he tells us," Queenie said.

"I'm not sure that works like you think." AJ popped out and fired at the concentrated Cheell force.

"Oy, I'm certain it does," Queenie said, dangerously.

"No reason for them to turtle up like that unless they have reinforcements coming," Lefty said. "We need to get scarce."

"Suppose we could talk that little elephant fella into getting us a ride outta here?" Queenie asked. "He seems like a right good little sailor to me."

"Only you would think he's good," AJ grumbled, lifting to see if Belisk was even still around. In fact, he was with Jayne and Baird, and had his own weapon out, returning fire.

"Baird, fall back to Belisk's van," AJ called out over the blaster fire. "We'll cover."

"Copy," Baird called back.

"Go!" Lefty yelled.

As a group, Darnell, Lefty, AJ, and Queenie stood and fired mercilessly on the Cheell positions. As they did, Baird's group raced for cover near the van.

"No! Don't let them get away!" Loveit's voice could be heard over the din of gunfire.

"Loveit, by the authority of the President of the United States, you are ordered to stand down and turn yourself in," Baird called, hearing the traitor's voice.

"Go screw yourself!" Loveit fired his weapon, which inspired his group to follow suit. There had been almost no casualties in this firefight, a fact that wasn't lost on AJ. He believed the Cheell were playing to just not lose, instead of taking risks to win. It supported Lefty's assertion that Loveit was awaiting reinforcements.

"We're good, Jenkins. Your turn," Baird called back. "Go!"

AJ grabbed Sharg by the arm and hoisted her along with him. Without help from Beverly, he was surprised at how heavy the reptilian woman was. "We gotta go, Sharg."

"I am terrified, Albert Jenkins. My feet will not move," she said.

"Gotta move, Luv," Queenie said, grabbing her other side. They raced into the open just as Baird and her team opened fire on Loveit's position. Fortunately, Sharg found the will to run. Helping quickly turned into a matter of controlling the powerful Vred's path and directing her into Belisk's van.

"And now we'll be taking a new ride," Belisk said, jumping in behind with Greybeard and Jayne right behind him.

"Let's go, Baird!" AJ called.

"Negative, Jenkins. We'll provide cover. Get out of here," she said.

"You can't hold them," AJ called back.

"We'll hold 'em long enough. Move out, soldier!"

AJ flashed back to another major who'd given her life to the cause at Area 51. Like Dittany, Baird was a true believer in the mission. While AJ couldn't fault her logic, he hated that she was so ready to put her life on the line.

"Dammit, just get in!"

"You're wasting time, Jenkins. Move it out!"

AJ slammed his fist into the back of Belisk's chair repeatedly. "Dammit. Dammit to hell! Move out, Belisk. Damn you, Loveit!"

He turned to fire out of the van's open door but before he could pull the trigger, they'd already disappeared into the vertical shaft. Imagining what might come next, he pulled at the broken door, sliding it shut as far as it would go.

"What are you doing, man?" Lefty asked, sitting on the bench next to the door.

"It doesn't close." AJ said.

"Were you not a door gunner back in 'Nam?"

"It's different. All I've got is this stupid ray gun."

Lefty pushed his rifle into AJ's hand and scooted over. "Nah, son. It's just a matter of perspective."

AJ accepted Lefty's hand and sat on the edge of the bench seat, allowing the sliding door to open. He located a belt on the chair and snapped himself in, hanging his legs over the side of the chair and scanning for trouble. For a moment, he was back in the jungle.

"Where are we going, boss?" Belisk called after they were sailing along in traffic, a thousand yards over the cityscape.

"Need to get back to Upper Marska," AJ said.

"What are we doing, AJ?" Jayne asked.

"We're going to end this thing. Baird's buying us time. We need to use that and get back to Beltigersk first so BB's mom can get back to business."

"But Alicia..."

"Her royal highness says she can take Alicia," AJ said. "Look, this isn't even my decision."

Belisk banked hard and bled elevation faster than a rock could fall, finally careening off the street below and bouncing upon impact.

"Is that freaking necessary, Belisk?" AJ asked angrily.

"Past that curb, weapons fire is strictly prohibited. Under no circumstance should you use your weapons," Belisk said and turned to Sharg. "To the Beltigersk people, I wish you great speed on your most important journey."

Piling out of the van, AJ looked back at the unusual Fimil.

"What's your part in all this?" he asked. "Why would you risk yourself?"

"A small action to save two nations. I am glad to have fulfilled my small part," he responded. "Go now and be quick. History awaits."

AJ realized he knew almost nothing about the Fimil man. But in that moment, he also realized he knew everything important.

"AJ, we've got to go," Jayne said, pulling on his arm.

"Be safe, Belisk," he said and raced after his friends, who had already crossed the unassuming curb.

Departure for Upper Marska in two minutes.

The voice seemed to resonate from the low buildings surrounding the square where the elevator rested.

"So, do we need tickets or not?" AJ asked.

"We needed them," Lefty said. "We had to borrow credits from Sharg."

"Yes," Sharg answered. "It is a standard fare."

AJ slowed as they approached a ticket vendor wearing familiar clothing. "Seven for Upper Marska."

"Thirty-five hundred." This time the vendor was female.

AJ touched the ticket acknowledgement. "When I was boarding to come down, I was told there were three classes of tickets but they'd run out of economy."

The Fimil smiled. "It is an old joke amongst my people. There was a time where the amount you paid for a trip was considered a status symbol. This was long ago rejected and I assure you, there is but one rate."

"Was the ticket person making fun of us?"

"AJ, we don't have time for this," Jayne said.

"Most certainly not. The joke told in full would have you purchase first class tickets at a standard rate. This communicates to you that we value all of our visitors."

"That is the..." AJ bit his tongue.

"AJ," Jayne interrupted, pulling him away.

"Be safe, traveler," the Fimil called after him.

"There's Loveit," Darnell growled, reaching for his holster.

AJ held his hand out. "Don't do it Big D, this is a no-fire zone."

"Like he'll respect that."

"Just get on the platform," AJ said.

Loveit picked them out of the crowd easily and with a cohort of Cheell following behind, he beelined for AJ's group.

"Keep steady, human," Sharg said, although AJ knew it was the Queen speaking.

"Sorry, I missed you back there," Loveit said, grinning at his double entendre.

"What are you doing, Loveit?" AJ asked, not giving way as Loveit crowded his personal space. "Get tired of selling out America? Now you're selling out other nations?"

"Don't try to make it sound like you're some sort of patriot," Loveit shot back. "You've been in this for yourself since the beginning. First you get yourself a new set of legs, then a new girlfriend. You think your crap don't smell."

"What are you getting out of it?"

"Why? Do you want in on it? I'll make you a special deal; turn over the nano worm and you'll never see me again. Better yet, I'll give you a billion credits. You can live in luxury on any planet in the whole damn empire. Take it," Loveit said, waggling a credit chit at AJ. "In case your bug isn't working so well, that's a ten million credit chit. You'll get the other nine-hundred ninety million when I've got the worm."

"Do you remember that kids' game ninety seconds in heaven?" AJ asked.

"You mean where kids stand in a closet and are scared to touch each other?" Loveit asked.

"Yeah," AJ said, grabbing the extended chit from Loveit. "That's what I'm hoping for. Ninety seconds with just you and me in the same room." AJ flicked the chit into a small crowd where it landed undetected on a young Fimil woman's clothing. "That's what I think of your deal."

A trio of Cheell advanced menacingly toward the group of Fimil where the chit had landed but slowed when a warning throb of red light illuminated their feet. Seeing the warning, the Fimil group scurried away to join another group, forcing the Cheell to abort their attempt to retrieve the still undiscovered chit.

"That was stupid, Jenkins," Loveit said. "That was ten million Galactic Credits. That's more money than you're worth in five lifetimes."

"Probably right. But I'd never take money that was earned by selling out my country. You're a disgrace, Loveit."

"Where are you going to go, Jenkins? I've got a warship. We'll follow you wherever you go. You're as good as dead."

"Fuck off, Loveit."

AJ moved away from Loveit and the Cheell, knowing if he stayed near he'd eventually give in to his strong desire to kick Loveit's ass.

"What are we going to do, AJ?" Jayne asked, quietly.

"We outrun them," he said. "Lefty, how exactly did you get here?"

"Experimental spaceship from Space Force," he said.

"Let me guess, *USSF Bluebird?*"

"Close. *USSF Golden Eagle*," he said.

"Well, that's something," AJ said. "She got any teeth to her?"

"A couple ray guns and some sort of experimental magnetic thingy," Lefty said. "We never got a chance to see 'em in action though."

"No shit?"

"Actually, pretty solid bathrooms."

"You remember where you parked?" AJ asked.

"Nope, but I bet my girl Rebel does."

"You looking to swipe another ship? You're such a bad man," Rebel said, appearing on Lefty's shoulder, leaning comfortably against his ear.

"Guilty. Maybe you could get word to Baird about the *USSF Cardinal*. I can't remember exactly where she's parked, but I'm sure Seamus does," AJ said.

"Can do."

"What about Tork and Chok?" Jayne asked.

"Might be best if they get left behind for this next ride," AJ said.

"DAMN!" AJ stopped, taking in the *USSF Golden Eagle*. While their general hull shape was similar, the *Golden Eagle* was considerably larger than *Cardinal*. It was also covered with armor plating. "She's all grown up."

"You think Baird is gonna be pissed about us swiping her ship?" Darnell asked.

"Seamus, buddy, can you get us onboard?" AJ said.

Greybeard barked once and stretched against the docking terminal.

AJ shrugged and pressed a thumb onto the terminal. He took it as a good sign that a semi-transparent walkway extended out to the waiting vessel. Without the hesitation he'd previously felt, he walked out onto the path and tried not to think about the fact that he could easily fall thousands of feet if he missed a step.

"I wish Tork was coming along," Darnell said, joining AJ next to the entry hatch.

AJ twisted the hatch lock open and pulled the door back. "Honey, we're home," he called, the automatic lights turning on as he entered. The layout was nearly identical to *Cardinal's,* albeit stretched out and capable of half again as many crew.

"You good to sail this?" Lefty asked.

Greybeard barked happily, joining Darnell in a cockpit configured for four instead of two. "She's loaded with Fantastium. Oh, that's new, I haven't seen a Blastorium gauge before. We're full on that too. Controls look similar. I think I'm good."

"We should get rolling," AJ said. "Do you know how to tell Marska we're leaving?"

"I've got it," Darnell said. "Marska space control, this is *USSF*

Golden Eagle requesting an exit lane from Barrel District, one oh four, over."

"You sure it works that way?" AJ asked.

"Seamus is doing translation," Darnell said, winking.

Within ten minutes, they were exiting the docking bay and speeding away from the massive spaceport.

"See about getting a jump lane out so we can get to jump-space as fast as possible," AJ said. "I'll sign for it."

"Just about to ask," Darnell said. "Come acknowledge this."

AJ answered a few questions and watched as another ten thousand credits fled from his account.

The process for entering the jump lane was identical to their trip in, although the surrounding shell was larger than the previous time. Another ten minutes later, they were in a queue for jump space, separated so they wouldn't end up going to the wrong destination by joining the jump space of the ship directly in front of them.

"Think we got out ahead of Loveit?" Lefty asked, watching nervously as they waited their turn.

"If we did, it wasn't by much," AJ said. "We've got a couple of jumps to make. Hope this girl can take a punch because I think we're going to find out."

"Sonnofabitch!" Darnell cried out in alarm and started swiping at controls. "Shit! Shit! Shit!"

Having flown with the man in numerous combat missions over enemy territory, AJ was probably more freaked out than anyone else aboard. Darnell, as most 'Nam pilots, was two parts crazy and three parts brass balls.

"Big D, what's going on?" he asked, noticing they'd slipped into jump-space. Did we go to the wrong place?"

"Negative," Darnell said, pointing through the windshield. Above and to their starboard, a slender silver ship hung. "They jumped in at the last second."

"I feel like Loveit might not have learned his lesson on Xandarj after all," AJ said, a wicked grin crossing his face.

"Nah, nope, you're not suggesting..." Darnell started.

"I remember that Cheell captain begging me not to spill the beans about us boarding their craft," AJ said. "I kind of put it out of my mind, but what do you suppose the odds are that he didn't share that info with Loveit?"

"You boarded a Cheell vessel while in flight?" Lefty asked.

"Major knackers, ya Mr. Albert," Queenie cackled.

"It's not that impressive," AJ said. "Jump-space makes most energy weapons useless. I was carrying a nine mil and a forty-five. Turns out the nine mil was just what I needed to boost my way between ships. Pretty hard to do without BB, though. Any chance you boys brought some pop guns along?"

"Never leave home without 'em," Queenie drawled. "Got a whole locker filled with goodies. What do we need? C-4? Semtex? How about an RPG?"

Rebel appeared, holding a couple pistols in the air. "Sorry, Queenie. None of those weapons will really work. A kinetic load that's accelerated by an initial burst is what does the trick in jump-space. I've taken a look at the information Seamus got from Beverly. I think it'd be a pretty easy task to take a sortie over."

"See why I love her?" Lefty asked, grinning excitedly.

While they'd been talking, Queenie had opened a cabinet and was pulling out a variety of handguns and rifles. "Feels like an M4 should be about right," he said, talking to himself.

"Would C4 work in jump-space?" AJ asked. "Just need it to blow a hatch in case they locked it."

"It is possible," Rebel said.

"This is a ridiculous idea," Queen Beltigersk said through Sharg. "You will not proceed with this foolish plan."

"I'm afraid this is where you get to learn about operational control," AJ said. "Big D, you and Jayne stay with the ship. If this turns into a shit show, do what you have to, but get Queen Belti back home."

"AJ, are you sure?" Jayne asked.

He nodded, pulling on a space suit from one of *Golden Eagle's* lockers. "Hate to press my luck doing this EVA twice, but if Loveit's aboard, I want ninety seconds with that asshole."

Ten minutes later, AJ, Lefty and Queenie were slipping through local space between the two ships. Without Beverly to guide him, he was nothing more than a package to be towed between Lefty and Queenie who, like he'd done before, took careful aim, adjusted their angles and fired bullets into space, pushing them unevenly toward their destination.

Finding handholds on the sleek ship was initially difficult, but Queenie found a spot to anchor to first and pulled Lefty and AJ into position, swinging them in a long arc back to the airlock hatch. Finding cover around the curves of the ship and as far away from the plastic explosive as they could, Queenie threw a simple manual switch. A shudder rippled across the skin of the ship, followed by a rapid expulsion of atmosphere.

The trio flowed through the opening and past the shattered airlock which was damaged more extensively than they had originally expected. AJ was first to see the closing emergency bulkhead and the only one to react quickly enough to slide beneath. He startled a pair of Cheell crew, whose first reaction was to flee. Tackling the first into the second, he took down both of the forty-kilogram aliens easily, slamming them into the wall, causing them to crumple to the floor.

AJ pulled back his spacesuit gloves and doffed the helmet, knowing that he'd need better maneuverability within the ship. That decision turned out to be his undoing.

"I wondered if we'd get this chance," Loveit's oily voice greeted him.

"Is it really just about the money for you, Loveit?" AJ asked, stepping out of the suit and turning. "Or do you just hate your home?"

"Give it a rest. You sound like a bad movie," Loveit said. "Of course, it's about the money. I deliver on this and I'm set for life. Sure, humanity is pretty much screwed, but what has anybody on Earth ever done for me? Big advantages for a rich man out here. Have you seen those Angelis chicks? I'm telling you, they put Victoria's Secret models to shame. I'm talking twenty on a ten-point scale."

AJ chuckled.

"What's so funny?" Loveit asked.

"You really are the king of assholes," AJ said. "I've never been around a jackass I couldn't compete with, but you take the cake. Even *I'm* embarrassed by the shit you say. I'm serious, that's really saying something. You're selling out five billion people because you can't get laid back home? That's seriously messed up."

"Pretty smart with the Semtex or was it C4?" Loveit said, waggling his pistol at AJ. "I knew you were coming. I've been waiting."

"Don't suppose you'd like to handle this like men, would you?" AJ asked.

"Actually, yeah," Loveit said. "I've been wanting a piece of you for quite a while. It's gonna feel good, you know, to finally put you down for good. And now, with your Belti rider all busted up, I don't have to worry about you cheating. Come and getcha some."

AJ launched himself forward, just as Loveit fired his pistol.

TWENTY-NINE
PIG IN A POKE

Pain tore at AJ's side. It wasn't the first time he'd been shot, nor the second, but the pain wasn't easily forgotten. He yowled in agony, but his focus remained on Loveit and he continued churning his feet against the deck. Momentum, as much as anything, propelled AJ into a surprised Loveit who tried a second shot. He missed AJ, managing to embed the nine-millimeter bullet into the adjacent wall.

"You're done, Jenkins," Loveit growled, bringing his gun down on AJ's back as AJ drove him into the wall. AJ's reward for his efforts was an audible *ooph* as Loveit's lungs were compressed.

The two men grappled and twisted until they both went to the deck, slipping on blood that had dripped beneath them. Surprisingly strong, Loveit managed to drag AJ forward, and tried to wrap his hands around AJ's neck. Sensing the move, AJ drew his head back and smashed his forehead onto the bridge of Loveit's nose, this time causing the traitor to scream and jerk back instinctively. Unfortunately, the move also momentarily stunned AJ.

Woodenly, AJ struggled to separate from Loveit, the back of his leg kicking against Loveit's weapon, sliding it along the floor. Loveit lunged. AJ's head cleared enough to react, lashing out brutally with an unbalanced strike. His blow elicited another cry from Loveit, but didn't knock him off course.

Focused on the gun, Loveit continued to struggle, pawing to get across AJ's legs. If Loveit got to the gun first, the fight would end as quickly as it had started. AJ grabbed at the spacesuit he'd dropped to the deck moments ago, wrapping the material around Loveit's face and pushing him back.

"Cheell will end you if I don't," Loveit mocked. "They're horrible fighters up close, but give 'em a couple of minutes, they'll find a long enough stick to poke you with."

AJ's back landed against the steel emergency door that had slammed shut, sealing in the ship's atmosphere. He could feel rhythmic tapping against the door: three short taps, two long taps, then three short – a familiar pattern. Too late now, but AJ wished he'd worked out some signals with Lefty and Queenie in case they got separated. Instantly, he realized that the signal could mean only one thing.

With reserve strength fueled by desperation, he lashed out, catching Loveit on the side of the face. He pushed Loveit away, turned and knocked quickly on the steel panel. He braced both hands against the cold metal and pushed off, sprinting away. Loveit, only slightly stunned, scrambled back up, quickly recognizing the opportunity afforded by AJ's flight.

"Where are you gonna run to?" Loveit asked mockingly, grabbing the gun off the floor. "What a damn coward!"

AJ zigzagged down the hallway. He avoided Loveit's first shot but was grazed by the second. He'd just cleared the corner when an explosion ripped through the space, pelting bits of plastic and steel into the wall behind him, the concussive force diminishing faster than ordinary physics would demand.

Atmosphere rushed out, pulling violently at everything in the ship. As quickly as it started, the brutal rush of air ceased. AJ placed a hand on the wound at his side. He wasn't bleeding anywhere near as much as he'd expected, but the bullet hadn't exited. A bad sign.

A pair of Cheell ducked their heads around the corner, looking to see if it was safe to come out. AJ stomped and growled at them, causing them to duck back for safety. Their cowardly actions made him chuckle, which in turn caused his side to hurt even more.

He turned back into the hallway and bit down on his tongue at the truly awful sight ahead. "Help me," Loveit begged.

Torn by shrapnel from the explosion, Loveit's body was a wreck. Worse yet, the violent decompression had sucked the man's broken body into the mangled hole made by Queenie's C4. Limbs had been twisted and deformed by pressure trying to drag him out into space. For a moment, he served as an imperfect seal.

"How?" AJ had recovered his spacesuit from the hallway. There were a few punctures, but they'd been sealed by green goo, some of which leaked out onto the surface. It might not be a perfect solution, but he set about donning the suit.

"You got to get me out of here," Loveit all but cried.

"Buddy, I'm not one for I told you so, but this shit is your own doing," AJ said, snapping his helmet into place.

"What are you going to do?"

AJ removed the gun from Loveit's mangled hand. As he leaned closer, he heard the sound of air escaping around Loveit's body. The noise was becoming louder as Loveit sank deeper into the hole.

"I think I'll go make a deal with the captain," AJ said. "Cheell have always seemed to be pretty easy to deal with."

"What about me?"

AJ turned and walked down the hallway. He hated that Loveit's mangled body would forever be part of the *horrible moments* movie reel which played in his head when he was feeling stressed. He would not add footage to that reel by actively participating in the man's final moments.

"I THOUGHT you said he wouldn't know you were coming," Jayne complained as she dug into AJ's side, searching for bullet fragments.

"You know what I really want to know?" AJ asked, his voice a little giddy and higher than normal.

"This should be good," Darnell chuckled.

"This super morphine you've got me on, why is it the first time I've had it?" AJ asked disjointedly. "I mean, I feel like cotton candy and pizza all wrapped up in a cheesy burrito."

"That is an unusual reaction," Sharg said, moving a suction tube into the open cavity as she assisted Jayne. "It is quite addictive and must be secured. I am surprised that it is so readily available in your ship's stores."

"What's the drug called?" AJ asked.

"No! Do not answer that," Jayne said. "It has no name, AJ. If you keep on, I will not allow you to be conscious for this surgery."

"Did I say cotton candy? It's like seeing a beautiful woman naked for the first time," AJ said. "Or the feel of Doc's waist where it starts to curve out."

"Bubba, you need to reel it in a bit," Darnell said, chuckling.

"But you know what I'm saying, right?"

"I've got my own list, but I'm feelin' you."

"I knew you would," AJ said with a sigh.

"Suture line," Jayne said, drawing an instrument along the wound opening, amazed as the skin pulled together, leaving a bright white line in its wake.

"Even better, we can flush that ... cotton candy out of his system," Sharg said, moving to do so.

"No," AJ complained, his eyes following the needleless syringe in Sharg's large hands. "Wow, is that a disappointment."

Jayne chuckled. "Not exactly the kind of thanks I'm used to after a successful surgery."

"You're right," AJ said, his head clearing. He accepted Sharg's help to sit up. "Honestly, you should try that stuff. Everything feels a little gray and dreary right now. Thank you, Doc, Sharg. I'm glad to have one less hole in me."

"I wouldn't have expected that reaction to the anesthesia," Jayne said.

"Good stuff," AJ said.

"I guess," she agreed. "Is the fighting over? Are Cheell going to let us get back to Beltigersk and deliver the queen?"

"I guess it depends on whether Alicia decides to put up a fight," he said. "I talked to the Cheell captain. They'll leave us alone when we make it to normal space."

"You can trust him?"

"He doesn't have much of a choice," Queenie said. "We might have rearranged his engine compartment just a little. If he doesn't jump back to Fimil, he'll be stuck in normal space and we'll get to try out our fancy new pew pews on an immobile ship. I bet the squints back home would like to see the data from that."

"If it's any consolation, we told him we'd stick around long enough to make sure he's able to get back into jump-space," AJ said.

THIRTY
ROYAL PAIN

"Are you ready for this?" AJ asked, looking at Sharg but talking to Beverly's mother, the Queen.

"I may have misjudged you," she said after a long pause.

"This should be good," he muttered under his breath.

"When I judged 49231125-0-B, I saw how much you cared for her. This is not unexpected, as hosts often become emotionally attached to their symbiotes. What is unexpected is how you have championed her last wishes, even though she fades," Queen Beltigersk said.

"So, she did pass?" he asked, tears forming at the corners of his eyes.

"Why have you continued?" she responded without answering his question.

"Beverly believed you were the best leader for Beltigersk," AJ said. "Don't think I'm completely unselfish, though. You don't hate humans, so you're better than Alicia."

"I don't love humans," she answered. "In truth, I find you weak and entirely unpredictable. I do not believe you have earned a place in the Galactic Empire. If not for my daughter's interaction, I would not be particularly concerned that Korgul and Cheell are fighting over such a poorly developed species."

"Don't hold back," AJ said flippantly. "Say what you think."

"I know you think I am evil. You no doubt share my daughter's belief that all sentients deserve the chance to develop to their potential without predatory actions of others," she answered. "In principle I don't even disagree with these rights. It is more that Beltigersk is not a powerful nation. What we have in power, we have gained only through careful cultivation. Simply put, we cannot afford to defend every species who needs a hand up. It is a matter of survival. You have seen evidence of this firsthand."

AJ nodded. "Humans use words like honor and integrity to define the reasons we choose to do the right thing, even if those actions might be difficult. I still believe in those virtues."

"Had I not had access to your memories, I might accuse you of empty words. As it is, I see that you have offered your life for these ideals on multiple occasions. I find that admirable." Sharg delivered the Queen's words with a toothy smile. "You see, the Fimil people share this same selflessness, as do Vred. Today, Sharg will accompany me, even though we will be attacked and potentially killed when I return home. The battle for Beltigersk is not over."

"I thought you had this," AJ said. "You were so confident you would stop Alicia."

"She is powerful," Queen Beltigersk said, unexpectedly reaching for and holding AJ's arm. "If I fail, she will destroy you if you do not leave. Under no circumstance should you follow me. If I fall, Alicia will prevail and you will be at risk. Do you understand?"

"I do."

Sharg gave a tight smile. "Let it be as it must be." She left the safety of the tunnel extending from the ship and walked through the door to a simple habitat.

A wail of pain passed through Sharg's lips after she'd walked only a few yards. Spinning around, she locked eyes with AJ. "Alicia is too much."

At first, AJ thought he was hallucinating, that perhaps he'd stepped into the room and was feeling the massive pain he'd experienced before. In front of him, Beverly had appeared, wearing her shiny silver space suit and suspended in the air as if by her rocket backpack.

"Hey, you," she said, grinning at AJ.

"What? How?" AJ asked.

"Mother used some of her energy to restore me," Beverly said. "She did it when Sharg reached for you."

"Why? She's getting killed in there." AJ watched Sharg writhe in agony on the floor.

"Because the Beltigersk people needed to see what Alicia's plan was. They needed to see her attack the Queen. It is up to us to end this, AJ," Beverly said. "I need to end this. I need to stop Alicia."

"And you're strong enough to take her?"

"I do not know, Albert Jenkins," Beverly said. "It is unfair that I ask it of you but in this moment, the future of Beltigersk and the future of humanity are locked together. Will you take me to battle?"

"Damn," he said, thinking about the high levels of pain from his last experience. "That's asking a lot."

"I know, AJ. You need to be brave. It is possible we'll both die," Beverly said. "Will you allow me to defend our people?"

"Damn, BB," he repeated with a sigh.

"Whenever you are ready, Albert Jenkins."

"Let's do this," AJ said, stepping forward into the room. As before, he was greeted with a wall of pain. Through gritted teeth he managed to say, "Get 'em, BB." And then he crumpled to the floor next to Sharg.

He blinked in confusion as some of the pain muted and his consciousness was transferred to a large, elegant hall with soaring columns, ornate marble floors and hanging tapestries. Beneath his feet was a wide path of purple carpeting that led to an elevated platform. Three figures occupied the platform. The first was an older woman in black dress robes lying crumpled on the floor. AJ recognized the woman as Beverly's mother, the queen. The second figure, standing over the queen, was Alicia. The third was Beverly, who was walking up the steps to the platform.

"Albert Jenkins. So good of you to join us, although it is not as if you were presented a choice. I thought it appropriate that humanity be given representation in this moment of judgment," Alicia said. As she spoke, a group of men and women, all dressed in formal black robes, appeared to the side of the carpeted walkway and perpendicular to the platform.

"Who are they?" he asked, struggling. No matter how hard he strained, he couldn't move.

"The Beltigersk Council, of course," Alicia said. "They will bear witness as I return Beltigersk to its rightful place. You see, there was once a time when Beltigersk was revered throughout the Galactic Empire. "With the intellectual prowess of my people and our domination of the Xandarj and many others, we ruled as we were meant to.

"Albert Jenkins, you have completely misunderstood my intentions – *our* intentions. You believe humanity to be beneath our notice, but that couldn't be further from the truth. You will become very necessary beasts of burden. Humanity makes it possible for Beltigersk to regain its position of dominance. You see, humanity is a great jewel in a barren desert and together we will rise in power.

"But first, we must cast out those leaders who would give up our power to forsake our rightful position in the Empire. And for what? Because leading the weak is cruel? I say not. The strong lead. Such is the way it has always been.

"Alicia, you're mad," Beverly said, interrupting her. "We've spread a vaccine to keep us and Korgul from Earth. We've even given it to Xandarj. There's no going back."

Alicia reached her hand out toward Beverly as if she was physically grabbing her by the neck. "No, dear sister, it is you who is mad. Do you think your *cure* is permanent? Do you genuinely believe that with the greatest Beltigersk minds working on the problem, your vaccine couldn't be defeated? Hasn't been defeated?"

Beverly gurgled as she struggled against the unseen force.

Glancing at the gallery, AJ noticed that three of the twelve Beltigersk had stepped forward and were chanting, their eyes closed. Thin threads of power coursed from their chests and streamed into Alicia. He growled as he realized she was getting help.

"What is that look on your face, human?" Alicia asked, letting up on her torture of Beverly for a moment. "Did you think I could become the new queen all on my own? Of course, I could not. Alone, I am no match for mother, but then, I am not on my own."

"Alicia, stop," Beverly pled. "Turn away from this. Beltigersk can't go back to the madness of the past."

"When I look at you sister, all I see is weakness," Alicia said, once again extending her arm and slowly clenching her fingers together.

Beverly cried out in agony and sank to her knees, even as she reached for Alicia. Seeing her in pain was almost more than AJ could take and he struggled against whatever held him still. At first, he couldn't budge at all, but as he strained, his feet moved slightly.

"What?" Alicia screamed, turning toward him. "That's impossible."

"Tricky word, *impossible*," he growled, placing one foot in front of the other.

"Stop, human," Alicia said. "I will give you life."

"Let Beverly go," AJ said. "Then we'll talk."

"You would give up your life for this one Beltigersk?" she asked.

"No. I was just thinking I wouldn't have to if I put my fist through your face."

Alicia moved one arm so her fingers pointed at AJ. Pain erupted. "You do not understand who has power here."

Even through the pain, however, he continued to move forward. "Stupid. Damn. Worm," he growled, tears running down his cheeks.

"You dare challenge?"

Alicia's eyes grew wide as she threw her head back and brought her other arm across so all her power was focused on him. AJ's feet were lifted from the carpet and his back arched as pain coruscated through him. He screamed in agony as pain like he'd never felt before wracked his body.

In desperation, he struggled to find Beverly. With vision blurred by tears, he found her on the platform crawling to her mother's body. He swallowed, realizing that these would be the last moments of his life.

"I'm sorry, BB," he mumbled.

A thin trail of wispy smoke carried across the chamber from the assembled council to the queen's still form, several strands splitting to merge with Beverly. AJ accepted death in these final moments of the battle and idly wondered if the council would end his life quickly or if the pain would continue for some time. His answer was slow in coming. While not outwardly religious, AJ had always believed in a Creator and desperately hoped his few noble actions outweighed a lifetime of self-styled living. Either way, he would accept what was coming.

Suddenly, blessed peacefulness descended, causing fresh tears of joy at his release. He was surprised when his knees touched down on the carpeted floor and with surprise, he looked up to find that he was still in the chamber where the battle had taken place.

"*I submit, Mother.*" Alicia announced, her voice weak.

The queen now stood on the platform with Alicia and Beverly kneeling in front of her. Glancing to the Beltigersk Council, AJ was surprised to see the whole group was also kneeling. Irritated, he shook his head in disgust, glad he wasn't bound by the same rules. It took him a moment to realized that he too was somehow kneeling.

"I also yield," Beverly added.

"Oh, hell no!" AJ said, coughing and pushing against the ground. The weight that held him down suddenly released and he was able to stand.

"Albert Jenkins," the queen said, looking directly at AJ from the platform. "I find your irascible nature quite pleasant for once."

"How's that?" he asked, rushing toward the platform. Before he could reach the steps, four new Beltigersk appeared in front of him and blocked his way. They grabbed his arms. "Let me go. I've gotta help her."

"Release him," the queen said, her voice conveying humor. "It is that dogged loyalty that has saved us all. We are indebted to you, Albert Jenkins."

AJ pulled Beverly into his arms and he felt like his heart might burst. A smile formed on her face. "Hey, you," she said.

"You're okay? What happened?" he asked.

"You distracted Alicia," Beverly said. "I needed to give strength back to mother. And then, those still loyal to us on the council joined in."

"How can I feel you. Am I dreaming? Is this real?"

"It is like that, AJ," she said. "But it is also quite real."

"I thought I'd lost you."

"It was because of your actions that you did not, Albert Jenkins," the queen said. "You are a hero and are to be named Friend of Beltigersk. A high honor. Do you accept this?"

"Sure," AJ said. "As long as you're not locking me up in a cage again."

"We wouldn't think of it," she said. "Your sacrifice and honor will be recounted by generations. Today and forevermore, let Albert Jenkins be known as Friend."

At the edges of the large room, hundreds of Beltigersk appeared and then thousands and then tens of thousands as the room expanded. A cheer washed over the masses like a great wave and for a moment, he felt the joy and adulation of the assembled.

In front of him, Beverly smile proudly.

"So, I take it we won," he said.

"Yes." she said, smiling broadly as the assembled crowd's laughter filled the room and then faded as he was transported back to the simple habitat they'd entered what seemed like hours before.

EPILOGUE

"You know what I don't get?" Darnell asked, sliding a folding chair up to the table in the middle of AJ's new kitchen. The structure had a roof and walls, but that was where construction had stopped.

AJ cut into the meatloaf and dropped a captured slice into the pile of brown gravy on his plate. Having survived mostly on MREs and alien food that was hit or miss – mostly miss – the smell was enticing. With gusto, he stuffed the thick square into his mouth. At the first bite, he knew something was horribly amiss. His eyes cut to Lisa, who returned an overly pleased look.

"What?" he managed, struggling to talk around the cardboard-tasting entre.

"Don't talk with your mouth full," she corrected, still smiling.

Meanwhile, Darnell had plucked his own piece of meatloaf and stuffed it into his mouth. "Oh! Aww, no! I thought we had this resolved, Lisa. Why are you doing this to me?"

Jayne, who'd wisely loaded her plate with salad, looked surprised. "What is wrong, Darnell?"

"The meatloaf. It's Lisa's old recipe," AJ said, washing down his mouthful with water. "The one where she was worried about Darnell's cholesterol."

"And yours too, Albert," Lisa said, perfectly pleased with herself.

"But I'm twenty again," Darnell complained.

"You no longer have a symbiote," Lisa said, raising her eyebrows. "And I'm not letting you do to your body what you did the last time. Learn your lesson, Darnell."

"That's cold," AJ said, but before Lisa could jump in, he changed subjects. "What is it you were wondering about, Big D?"

"Why was Loveit important?" he asked. "Why did Cheell vanish after we took out Loveit?"

"Politics?" AJ ventured. "BB?"

"Cheell weren't willing to invade Beltigersk directly," she said. "They also couldn't directly murder me or mother. Both actions would have opened them to litigation. Loveit was an independent actor whose actions could not directly be attributed to Cheell or Korgul. Had he managed to kill me and mother, Alicia would have been unhindered in her rule on Beltigersk."

"Why not just kill AJ on that cargo ship when Loveit had control of him?" Jayne asked. "It would have eliminated half of Alicia's issues."

"They didn't know where the Queen was," AJ said. "They needed us to bring her into the open."

"Will whoever screwed with that volcano be punished?" Darnell asked.

"The incident is under investigation," Beverly said. "It is unlikely action will be taken, though. Mother was returned to her seat and Cheell has disavowed the crews that were involved."

"I can't believe nothing happens," AJ said.

"Much happened, AJ," Beverly said. "Humans came to the aid of Beltigersk and stopped a coup. Rumors about this now abound. Rumors have also spread of men boarding ships in jump-space and threatening crews. Rumors will spread of gunfights through peaceful cities. Rumors of shiny space-faring vessels making their first trips through the galaxies will spread. Like it or not, humanity has gained much notoriety as a result of these last days."

"So, maybe *now* they know better than to screw with us."

"There are many who will come to this conclusion," Beverly said. "I believe humanity's position in the Galactic Empire will change more quickly now. There will be much interest. Not all of this fame will be good and I fear humanity will be faced with many hard decisions in the coming years."

"What about that threat to invade Earth by Cheell and Korgul?" he asked.

"With Mother back in power, that will be difficult," she said. "Beltigersk and humanity are now linked. By coming to Mother's aid in her time of need, you have linked our two societies. She will not like it, but she will work diligently to dissuade the Cheell and Korgul. She will be successful."

"How can you be so sure?" Lisa asked.

"How sure are you that Big D isn't getting the good meatloaf anymore?" AJ asked.

"Pretty sure," Lisa said.

"Beverly's Mother has a strong personality," Darnell said, chuckling. "I wouldn't bet against her."

"Yeah, that's my point with Lisa," AJ took another bite of meatloaf and decided to change the subject. "You've sure made a lot of progress on getting the house rebuilt, Lisa," he said. "Any trouble?"

"Insurance payout is a little light," Lisa said. "Costs have gone up. I was going to talk to you about that."

"Are we going to be able to finish?" AJ asked.

"No," Lisa said. "We'll get you dried in, but you're going to need another hundred thousand or so. I was figuring you could take out a loan or something."

"I wish we could translate Galactic Credits into dollars," AJ said. "We're sitting on some pretty good credits."

"Yeah," Darnell agreed.

"What about that?" Jayne asked. "Surely we could figure out some kind of exchange? Didn't Mads Bazer say she was interested in all the whiskey you could come up with?"

"We don't have a ship," AJ said.

"How's that different than last time?" Darnell asked, sitting forward in his chair.

Greybeard barked excitedly.

"No you don't," Lisa said. "I just got you back, you big sonnova-gun. You're not goin' anywhere."

"Don't be silly," AJ said. "Without Vred engines to start with, it'll take us months to get back into space."

But of course, that's another story entirely.

ABOUT THE AUTHOR

Jamie McFarlane is happily married, the father of three and lives in Lincoln, Nebraska. He spends his days engaged in a hi-tech career and his nights and weekends writing works of fiction.

Word-of-mouth is crucial for any author to succeed. If you enjoyed this book, please consider leaving a review, even if it's only a line or two; it would make all the difference and would be very much appreciated.

FREE DOWNLOAD

If you'd like to receive automatic email when Jamie's next book is available, please visit http://fickledragon.com. Your email address will never be shared and you can unsubscribe at any time.

For more information
www.fickledragon.com
jamie@fickledragon.com

ACKNOWLEDGMENTS

To Diane Greenwood Muir for excellence in editing and word-smithery. My wife, Janet, for polishing myriad rough passages so they are readable and kindly fixing my poor grammatical habits. I cannot imagine working through these projects without you both.

To my beta readers: Carol Greenwood, Barbara Simmons, Chuck Rivers, and Kelli Whyte for wonderful and thoughtful suggestions. It is a joy to work with this intelligent and considerate group of people. Also, to my advanced reading team, you're a zany, fun group who I look forward to bouncing ideas off.

Finally, to Elias Stern, cover artist extraordinaire.

ALSO BY JAMIE MCFARLANE

Junkyard Pirate Series
1. Junkyard Pirate
2. Old Dogs, Older Tricks
3. Junkyard Spaceship

Privateer Tales Series
1. Rookie Privateer
2. Fool Me Once
3. Parley
4. Big Pete
5. Smuggler's Dilemma
6. Cutpurse
7. Out of the Tank
8. Buccaneers
9. A Matter of Honor
10. Give No Quarter
11. Blockade Runner
12. Corsair Menace
13. Pursuit of the Bold
14. Fury of the Bold
15. Judgment of the Bold
16. Privateers in Exile
17. Incursion at Elea Station
18. Freebooter's Hold

19. Black Cutlass

Privateer Tales Universe

1. Pete, Popeye and Olive
2. Life of a Miner
3. Uncommon Bravery
4. On a Pale Ship

Henry Biggston Thrillers

1. When Justice Calls
2. Deputy in the Crosshairs
3. Manhunt at Sage Creek

Witchy World

1. Wizard in a Witchy World
2. Wicked Folk: An Urban Wizard's Tale
3. Wizard Unleashed

Guardians of Gaeland

1. Lesser Prince

Printed in Great Britain
by Amazon